ROSE
OF
JERICHO

NIGHTFIRE BOOKS BY
ALEX GRECIAN

Red Rabbit

Rose of Jericho

ROSE
OF
JERICHO

ALEX
GRECIAN

NIGHTFIRE

TOR PUBLISHING GROUP
NEW YORK

ROSE OF JERICHO

Copyright © 2025 by Alex Grecian

A Nightfire Book
Published by Tom Doherty Associates / Tor Publishing Group
120 Broadway
New York, NY 10271

www.torpublishinggroup.com

Nightfire™ is a trademark of Macmillan Publishing Group, LLC.

The Library of Congress Cataloging-in-Publication Data is available upon request.

ISBN 978-1-250-87471-9 (hardcover)
ISBN 978-1-250-87473-3 (ebook)

Our books may be purchased in bulk for promotional, educational, or business use. Please contact your local bookseller or the Macmillan Corporate and Premium Sales Department at 1-800-221-7945, extension 5442, or by email at MacmillanSpecialMarkets@macmillan.com.

First Edition: 2025

Printed in the United States of America

0 9 8 7 6 5 4 3 2 1

For Christy

She had the perpetual sense,
as she watched the taxi cabs,
of being out, out, far out to sea and alone;
she always had the feeling
that it was very, very, dangerous to live even one day.

—Virginia Woolf, *Mrs. Dalloway* (1925)

CAST OF CHARACTERS

THE JOURNEY

Moses Burke, a former Union soldier
Katie Burke, Moses's wife
Esmerelda Rosas, an abandoned child
Frank Smiley, a notorious cardsharp and horse thief
Poppy Buckland, believed to be a witch

THE VILLAGE

Rose Nettles, a former schoolteacher, widow, and heiress
Sadie Grace, Rose's partner
Rabbit Grace, Sadie's daughter
Clarissa Sinclair, Rose's estranged cousin
Benjamin Sinclair, Clarissa's son
Alice Anders, Clarissa's nurse
Lucy Knox, in love with Benjamin
Prosper Knox, Lucy's father and the village pharmacist
Charles Bowden, works at Prosper's drugstore and helps at the
train station
Dr Timothy Rumpole, the new village physician
Sergeant Newton Winter, the village constable, retired

Reverend Samuel Cotton, the village clergyman
Mr Mulacky, the village milkman
Jessica Hudson, the village innkeeper
James Doolittle, an itinerant handyman

BETHANY HALL

Housekeeper
Cook
Butler
Coachman
Gardener
Alexander, our narrator
Bell, his rival

ROSE
OF
JERICHO

1881

NICODEMUS, KANSAS

Moses Burke met Katie Foster at a Fourth of July potluck in a meadow beside the churchyard. It was a hot day, and Moses had taken off his shirt. A bandanna tied around his neck soaked up the sweat rolling off his scalp. He spotted Katie across the freshly mowed field of dandelion stalks, her hair clipped short, her dark face shiny as a river rock. She looked up and he looked away, embarrassed to be caught, and when he looked again she was making her way toward him, carrying two plates mounded high with beans and potato salad. Her shoulders were bare and her hips swayed, and Moses could almost smell the heat coming off her skin. She stopped three feet from him and held out one of the plates.

"I don't know about the beans," she said. "But I made the potato salad myself and you shouldn't eat it. I think the mayonnaise was off."

When he laughed, she frowned at him and shook her head. "I'm serious," she said.

"Then why bring it?"

"My Aunt Vida said I had to bring something."

He took a bite anyway, holding the fork up first so she would see he'd speared a big chunk of potato. The flavor was disagreeable, sour and tangy, and he swallowed without chewing, then scooped up another forkful. Katie grabbed the plate from him and tipped it, sliding its contents into the grass.

"Okay, then," she said. "If you don't die, come by Vida's home after church next Sunday and I'll walk with you, but I won't go farther than the mill."

Moses nodded and watched her walk away before he wiped his tongue on the sweaty bandanna. Then he found his mother and made her show him Aunt Vida's house.

Moses and Katie were married that autumn. They bought a small farmhouse down the road from his mother and they painted it blue. Moses—who could climb a tree like a squirrel but did not like being on ladders—painted the ground floor and watched from below as Katie painted the second story, climbing halfway up to hand her brushes and pails and rags, ready to catch her if she fell. In the evenings he filled the bathtub and scrubbed cornflower paint from her arms, from her face, from her hair.

He built furniture. A three-legged stool that wobbled unless it was placed on uneven ground, a sofa with one arm that came loose when they leaned on it. He built fires. Katie would lay with her head on his shoulder and they would talk about their lives before they found one another. Each of them had seen hardship and evil, in other places, in other times, but hardship and evil were distant memories now, miles away from their little blue home.

They made love on a thin green rug his mother had stitched from scraps of old dresses and skirts; they made love on bare wooden floors, and laughed as they plucked splinters from one another's backs. They made love standing up and sitting down and in fields covered with scratchy hay. They made love with a glance, with a smile, and with a whispered word.

A month after their anniversary, Katie got sick.

She wasted away over the winter. She was twenty-nine years

old, and her husband was a decade older. Moses had been to war
and had seen men die, but this was different, and he didn't know
how to help or what to say. He hid his sorrow from his wife,
and he hid his anger, and they spoke of a future they knew they
would never see.

Neighbors brought dishes covered with warm towels, and Katie accepted the food gracefully, though she no longer ate. Moses took the unasked-for casseroles to their tiny kitchen and left
them there. He let the dishes pile up. The food rotted and the
towels blossomed with mildew.

That Christmas he held Katie's arm as she stepped carefully
over muddy ditches caked with thin layers of ice. She stopped
and laid her head on his arm.

"We can go back home," he said.

"I'll be fine," she said, and took another small step forward.
"The morning sickness is making things worse today."

Moses stuck his foot in an icy puddle. Water filled his shoe.
He opened his mouth and closed it again.

"I wasn't sure at first," Katie said. "The doctor in Dodge City
confirmed it. He said I'll be showing soon. I'm going to get so
fat." She leaned in and whispered, "Huge."

Because she said it with a smile, it didn't occur to him that she
was delivering more bad news. When they arrived at his mother's
house, Katie leaned on the porch railing while she caught her
breath.

"I've been calling him Junior," she said. "Only until we think
of something better."

"I can already think of twelve names better than Junior," Moses
said.

When she was ready, he opened the door and they stood breathing in the scent of ham and potatoes until one of the littlest nephews

came and grabbed their hands and led them farther inside, where Cordelia Burke greeted them with kisses.

"Finally!" she said. "The children have been waiting to open their presents!"

Cordelia ushered Katie to a chair by the fire. Moses watched his wife from across the room as she greeted all the little nieces and nephews. He imagined her standing in a room filled with light, holding their child in her arms. He caught Katie's eye and winked, and she waggled the tips of her long fingers at him.

Walking home that night, she said: "You know why I married you, Moses Burke?"

He shook his head. He had no idea.

"You ate my bad potato salad. You accepted your fate without question." She grinned up at him. "I decided you wouldn't last much longer without me."

He nodded. It was true. He felt his throat close up and he wiped his eyes with the palm of his hand.

"Stop that," she said. "I won't be an excuse for you to mope around. This child's gonna need a father. I want you to promise me something. When I'm gone, you have to promise you'll be strong for this little one."

She patted her abdomen and Moses nodded. He couldn't speak. He wiped his eyes again and took her elbow and helped her home.

K atie died on a gray day in February, two minutes after the death of her premature child.

At the moment his wife drew her last shuddering breath, Moses heard the jangling of spurs and saw a dark figure from the corner of his eye. When he turned his head there was no one there.

That night he buried his wife and child behind the blue farm-house, breaking through the frozen soil with a hatchet, and fashioning markers for their graves from planks he pulled off his wagon. The following morning, before the sun rose, he set out after Death. The Grim Reaper had a head start on him, but Moses had a fast horse and a broken heart.

It had snowed for the better part of a week, and Death's mount had left a trail of deep hoofprints. Beside the hoofprints were the prints of a wolf or a large dog, and Moses had no trouble following them. For five days and five nights he rode, and he observed that Death had stopped many times ahead of him. Moses saw men digging fresh graves in distant fields, but he didn't slow. He pushed his horse onward, determined to catch the villain who had taken his wife.

He came upon Death on the morning of the sixth day. Fog had settled in a shallow valley between two limestone ridges, where the first rays of sunshine couldn't reach. Death was squatting beside a small campfire, rubbing his hands together and staring into the flames. A yellow dog sat beside him at the edge of the fire, and a pale horse stood nearby, tethered to the trunk of a bare elm.

Death looked up as Moses approached.

"Come, friend," Death said. "Warm yourself by my fire."

Moses drew his pistol and shot Death through the eye. The Grim Reaper fell without a sound and rolled into the campfire, stirring up a shower of sparks. Moses turned to shoot the yellow dog, but it was already running. He fired at it anyway, but the distance was great and his hand was shaking with the cold.

He pulled Death's body out of the fire, then sat and waited to see if the dog would come back. Having murdered the Angel of Death in cold blood, Moses thought he ought to feel something. Triumph or regret or fear. The fire warmed his face, and a cold breeze tickled the back of his neck, but all he felt was a hollowness in his chest. Katie was dead, and his promise to her had ended two minutes before she drew her last breath. There was no reason to go forward, and there was nothing to go back to except an empty farmhouse that had been painted cornflower blue in happier times.

He checked his pistol and saw that it still held four bullets. He set the muzzle against his forehead and pulled the trigger. He heard a click as the hammer struck, and the muzzle jerked against his skull, but there was no flash of light, no instant of pain, no sharp drop into oblivion.

Confused, he cracked the pistol open and checked the chamber again.

It held three bullets and a spent casing.

"Strange," he said to Death's corpse.

After a while, he stood and approached the pale horse. He untethered it and removed Death's saddle and bags, heaving them into the fire, where the old leather smoked and sputtered. He slapped the horse on its flank and watched it gallop away.

He fetched a short-handled shovel from his gear, and broke through the crust of ice, then dug a trench, and buried the body. It was hard work. Death was big-boned and heavy, and the snow was deep.

When he had finished, Moses scattered dirty snow over the campfire, and stowed his shovel, then he mounted his old Appaloosa and rode away.

I am sent to wait for Moses Burke at his eventual destination. It will take him more than seven days of travel, by your reckoning, to reach me. On a whim—I swear it is a whim—I decide to pass the time until he arrives by chronicling the end of Death and what will come after.

SEVEN DAYS
REMAINING

Benjamin Sinclair loitered outside the train station of Ascension, Massachusetts, waiting for the eight o'clock local. Beyond the tracks, at the top of Vinegar Hill, the big house also waited. Bethany Hall had sat vacant for a decade until a Philadelphia lawyer, acting on behalf of an unnamed client, purchased it from the village council. The house was the oldest structure in the county and had loomed high on the hill overlooking the village for more than a century, casting its long shadow down the wide avenue that stretched from the train station to the post office.

Grackles had built a nest in the porch lamp; the garden was overrun with tasseled weeds and volunteer trees. The stained glass window above Bethany Hall's front door had been broken, and roughly a quarter of the shingles had blown off the roof in a storm the previous winter. The village had voted against spending the money to replace them.

It was widely believed that the house was cursed, but the council declined to have it torn down for fear the curse might be passed to them.

Three days after the Philadelphia lawyer left Ascension, a crew of workmen had arrived and begun restoring the house. The temperature dipped below freezing at night, and a blanket of snow covered the path that led up to the house, but the sounds of sawing and hammering could be heard around the clock.

Early one morning in February the workers marched back down Vinegar Hill to the train station. The next day, five strangers arrived. They were tall and stooped; they wore identical black over-coats and wide-brimmed hats that obscured their features. They stood for a long moment on the station platform before trudging up the hill. The villagers saw lights in the windows that night as Bethany Hall's new servants went about preparing its rooms.

Benjamin Sinclair had decided to stake out the train station in hopes of meeting the house's new owners. There was little else to interest a teenage boy in Ascension. Anticipating a long wait, he had brought his telescope, but heavy black clouds hid the sky from view, and lightning flashed at the horizon. Thunder built and rolled, rumbling across the icy fields and shaking the platform under his feet. He took shelter beneath a wide green awning just as the heavens opened and rain hammered down on the station's roof.

A few minutes later a black carriage rolled up out of the gloom. The coachman pulled his dripping cloak around him and lowered his hat, hiding his face in shadows. Two of them waited in silence.

The eight o'clock train arrived on schedule, and three passengers debarked. The first was a thin woman dressed all in black, with graying hair pulled back tight against her scalp. When Benjamin leapt forward to offer his arm, she smiled and pressed a nickel into his hand. She was followed off the train by a girl with short brown hair tucked up under a waterproof cap. Benjamin thought at first she might be his own age, but something in her dark eyes made him decide she was much older than she appeared. She refused his arm and looked away down the tracks, frowning and tapping her foot.

The last passenger to step onto the platform wore high leather boots, tan trousers, and a thick bear fur coat that looked so heavy Benjamin wondered how she could stand upright. Her red hair hung loose around her narrow face, and she looked at Benjamin with an expression of amused curiosity. She took his arm and opened her umbrella, moving it to cover him.

"Who might you be?" she said.

"Benjamin Sinclair, ma'am. I was—"

"Benjamin?" The older woman interrupted. "Are you Clarissa Sinclair's boy?"

"Yes, ma'am."

"How wonderful! I haven't seen you since you were very small. I'm your cousin Rose."

Benjamin blinked in surprise. "My cousin bought that house?"

"Tell me," Rose said. "How is your mother? Has there been any improvement in her condition?"

Benjamin shook his head. He was still considering the novel idea that he was related to the owner of Bethany Hall, and it had begun to dawn on him that he might get a chance to finally see the inside of the house.

"I wish I could have come sooner," Rose said. "I was making arrangements for the house when I got a letter from your mother's nurse. I rushed things along as quickly as I could, but . . ." She raised a hand to her cheek. "Oh, I'm sorry. This is my . . . Well, this is my friend Sadie Grace and her daughter, Rabbit."

"Rabbit?"

The silent coachman climbed down from his high seat and lurched up the steps to the platform, his black cloak dripping. He took Sadie's umbrella and offered his elbow, but all three women ignored him.

"Please tell your mother we've arrived at last," Rose said to Benjamin.

"She sleeps most of the time," he said. "I never know if she can hear me."

"I'll visit her tomorrow. Whether she hears you or not, please tell her that. Tell her I've missed her dearly and I'll be staying here in the village now. I've taken a position as schoolteacher."

"Teacher?" The village had been without a schoolteacher for

many months, and Benjamin had not considered that someone new might assume the job.

"I imagine we'll be seeing quite a lot of each other now," Rose said. "I'm looking forward to catching up. I can't believe how tall you've grown."

"Can I help with your luggage?" Benjamin hoped he would be invited up the hill.

"Thank you, no," Rose said. "Coachman will see to the luggage."

"We'll see you soon, Benjamin," Sadie said.

She kissed him on the cheek, then rapped her knuckles against the faded green planks of the station wall. The pitter-patter of rain on the awning slowed, then stopped. The clouds above them parted, and sunlight slanted across the platform.

"You'd better run along before it starts up again."

Benjamin nodded and lifted his hat to them, then he turned and hopped down the platform steps to the icy road. His left foot slid out from under him, and his telescope banged against his leg, but he regained his balance and moved into the spiky grass, where there was better traction. He didn't look back to see if his cousin had watched him stumble.

Prosper Knox stood behind his new soda fountain scooping ice cream and cracking eggs into tall glasses for a crowd of young villagers. When Benjamin entered the drugstore, Prosper grabbed another glass from the counter behind him and spooned in a dollop of bright red syrup.

"What's the good news, Young Master Sinclair?"

Charles Bowden yelled, "Do tell, Benji!"

"Settle down, boy," Prosper said.

"There's three women moving in up there," Benjamin said.

Lucy Knox was sitting at the counter, and he reached past her to accept a cherry soda from her father.

"One of them is my mother's cousin," he said. "I guess she's going to be the new teacher. There's another lady with her, and a girl who might be about my age."

"Is she pretty?" Lucy said. She tried to sound as if it didn't matter to her, one way or another.

Benjamin shrugged. Outside, the clouds had rolled back in, and what he could see of the sky through Knox Drugs's big front window was dark and ugly. Lightning abruptly turned the air white, as thunder shook the rafters; rain lashed at the window and pounded on the roof, searching for a way in. Benjamin's eyes opened wide, remembering that Sadie Grace had rapped her knuckles against the wall of the station just as the rain had let up. The storm had subsided exactly long enough for him to return to the village and find shelter.

"The ladies are alone?" Daisy Merrick said. "Their husbands aren't with them?"

"No, ma'am, it's just the three of them. But they had a coachman who took them up to the house."

"Oh, I would hate to live in that house," Lucy said.

"Far as I could tell, they did a damn good job fixing the place up," Benjamin said.

"Watch your language, son," Prosper said.

The door opened again, and the new village doctor stepped inside, accompanied by a blast of cold air and a spray of rainwater. He had arrived in Ascension the previous week, and had not yet met many of the villagers. He stamped his boots on the threshold and removed his hat.

"Be with you in two shakes, Dr Rumpole," Prosper said. He waved his ice cream scoop. "And I mean that literally."

"You were saying the house looks different?" Lucy Knox said to Benjamin.

"They made it look good as new," he said. "Everything except that big window. They put in plain glass, and it's not as pretty as it was."

"Plain glass is more respectable, in my opinion," Prosper said. There was a smear of cherry syrup across the front of his apron.

"I always wondered about that window," Lucy said. "It seemed prideful to me. Too fancy for regular people."

"Like it was a church," Charles Bowden said.

"I bet it still looks evil, though," Lucy said. "Even without the stained glass. Sometimes when I look up at it . . . I mean at night, it looks like it's alive. Like it's staring back at me." She bit her lip, worried she might sound foolish, but Benjamin wasn't listening. He was leaning against the counter, talking to Charles.

"That place is no church," he said. "Even at the bottom of the hill my heart was beating so fast I worried it'd give out."

"Bottom of the hill might be close enough for it to grab you," Charles said. "I mean, if you died there at the station, the house could take your ghost and keep it with the others. Maybe, maybe not." He shrugged as if it were a widely held theory that had yet to be tested.

"Ghost?" The doctor blinked and ran a shaky hand through his hair.

"Oh, of all the haunted houses around here, sir, Bethany Hall is without a doubt the most haunted of them all," Charles said.

"Nonsense. Which house is this?"

"It's the one at the top of the hill," Benjamin said. "There's been nothing but ghosts up there as long as anyone can remember, but now my cousin's moving in."

"Well, it's true that place has been empty awhile," Prosper said. He produced a small package wrapped in brown paper and set it on the counter. "But I can remember a time when people lived in Bethany Hall, and I'm not as old as all that. Ichabod Bailey was the village doctor once upon a time, and he was the last to live in that house."

"Until now," Benjamin said.

"That house has always been grim business. Supposedly it was designed by the son of a railroad tycoon for his new bride, her name was Bethany, and she moved in there when it was still being built. The poor girl flung herself off the roof of the house after a bricklayer defiled her—my apologies, Lucy, but those are the facts as I know 'em. Two days later her husband walked into the village holding that bricklayer's severed head high, swinging it back and forth along the path as if to light his way."

Charles Bowden snatched the brown paper package off the counter and waved it about, squinting down at the floor. He failed to get a laugh, and Dr Rumpole quickly grabbed the package from him, stuffing it into a pocket of his overcoat.

"That poor child," he said.

"It's not just her," Benjamin said. "People have been disappearing from around here for years."

"Mostly women and girls," Lucy said.

"And people say their ghosts end up in that house," Charles said.

Lucy shuddered; her father shook his head and grunted, trying to open a jar of cherries. There was a fresh pair of ears for the village gossip, and sodas had become the secondary order of business.

"I don't know about all that," Prosper said. "But the story goes that whoever inherited Bethany Hall turned around and sold it to a Texas cattle rancher." The lid popped off the jar of cherries and rolled across the counter. Lucy stopped it and handed it back to him.

"Thank you," Prosper said. "That rancher, the new owner, got himself struck by lightning on the path up from the train station. He never even laid eyes on Bethany Hall."

"I heard that one," Charles said. "They laid his body out on the parlor floor, and the men who carried him inside said there were words burned into his flesh by the lightning."

"Never proven," Prosper said. He handed a cherry soda to the doctor and wagged a finger at Charles. "By the following morning the body had turned to a pile of ash, so no one else saw any such words, and those men who carried him off the path were illiterate and were known to be heavy drinkers."

Dr Rumpole said, "But what were the words? What did they think they saw?"

"The way I heard it, he had the words 'beef raised' burned on his chest," Charles said. "On account of he grew up on a ranch."

"Hogwash," Prosper said. "Like I say, not a one of those men could read."

"Tell him about the lights at night," Charles said. "Or those three women who all married the same man without knowing it."

"No, tell him about Dr Bailey," Lucy said. "That's the worst one."

"Well, that's not a story for the squeamish, but I suppose you've probably seen some things, Dr Rumpole. The village lacked a doctor then, as we so frequently do, and the council offered Bethany Hall as an incentive. Ichabod Bailey responded to an advertisement, and he brought along his fifteen-year-old cousin to help keep the place up. Pretty soon a rumor got around that the doctor paid more attention to his cousin than was seemly, and sure enough, within a year the girl gave birth to a malformed baby who would not stop screaming."

"She killed her baby," Lucy said quietly.

"Yes," Prosper said. "I'm afraid she did. She carried that child down to the Ipswich and held it underwater, then she went back to the house and killed Dr Bailey with a hatchet. Have you met Sergeant Winter yet?"

Dr Rumpole shook his head. He set his untouched soda on the counter and fumbled with the package in his coat pocket. He glanced at the door.

"You'll like the Sergeant," Prosper said. "He's a good man. His father was the constable here back then, and when Dr Bailey's bastard baby was discovered on the riverbank, old Constable Winter forced entry to the house. He found the doctor's remains in the first-floor den. The young housekeeper was upstairs on her bed, her nightgown caked with blood." Prosper ran his hands down the length of his apron, spreading the cherry stain. "Simply caked with it. There was no sign she'd been injured, but she died the following week without saying a word to anyone. I have that from the Sergeant himself."

"Good lord," Dr Rumpole said. "So this Bailey fellow was the doctor I've come to replace?"

"Oh, no, no," Prosper said. "This was many years ago."

"Well, it's awful, of course. It's an awful story, but it has nothing to do with hauntings. There's no such thing. It's likely the girl was disturbed long before she moved into the house."

"But don't you think—" Lucy began.

Dr Rumpole interrupted her. "I'm sorry, but I must be going," he said. "Thank you, Mr Knox."

"I'll put that on your account," Prosper said.

When the doctor had gone, Prosper came around the end of the counter and peered out at the street. "He's a strange one," he said. "I'm afraid we might have to hunt up another doctor before too long."

Lucy took off her apron and folded it. She leaned in close to Benjamin. "Will I ever get to meet your cousin?"

"I guess so," Benjamin said, and he put his arm around her shoulders. "If the ghosts don't get her first."

Benjamin's mother lay quiet and still. She listened to the patter of raindrops on the windowpane and she wondered what was to become of her.

Clarissa Sinclair liked to think of life as a strand of pearls, each memory a shiny bauble that led to the next one and the next, until the string ran out. Until she had reached her end. Here was a pearl: jumping into the Ipswich with her cousin Rose, who would have died of embarrassment if anyone saw them in their wet clothes. Another pearl: her coming-out party, her hair done up in ribbons, her glossy new patent leather shoes, her father beaming with pride. And here was her wedding day: her mother's dress, Richard's new suit—the one she'd ordered for him from the Sears Roebuck catalog. Helping Richard start his practice. Finding a garden-level apartment they could barely afford—drafty and cold in the winter, so humid in the summer that the walls sweated—and decorating it with thin rugs and flocked green wallpaper. The pearl of Benjamin's birth: how silent he had been and the terrible certainty that her baby was dead, then the swell of relief that accompanied his first cries.

The string was too short. There ought to be more pearls.

She thought it barely possible that when her body failed, her spirit would wander unseen about the world, but this idea didn't appeal to her. She had seen spirits before, glimpsed them from the corner of her eye at odd moments, pale and staring from the darkest corners of the house, from under bridges and from behind trees. What was the point of all that? Why linger if all you had planned was to bother people?

And what about an afterlife? Some new world beyond her comprehension? She had gone to church nearly every Sunday since she was a child, but the preachers' stories never made much sense to her. Anything that resembled a Heaven or a Hell would require such a drastic change that she felt certain her essence would be lost in the process.

But maybe everything else would disappear when she died; maybe she was the glue that held the world together, and all of it would end when she did. It was a strangely comforting thought, but she remembered too well her mother's funeral, followed closely by her father's. She hadn't vanished when her mother's heart stopped, or when her father fell down the cellar steps.

If she could remove those two pearls from her string of memories, she would.

At least, she thought, her body would feed the Earth. It would be the last good thing she did. She would travel through the roots of a tree, up to its highest branches, fly to the clouds, and return as rain. She would be swept through riverbeds and washed into distant seas. She felt the slightest bit of awe at the thought of it.

She quieted her mind and listened to the storm as it began to subside, raindrops smacking the windowpanes less urgently with each passing second. Lightning flashed, a spark of incandescence behind her eyelids, and she counted, waiting for the thunder to follow. Her mother had taught her that a second of time between the lightning and thunder equaled a mile of distance to the storm.

She counted to three and heard the rumble. Three seconds, three miles. The storm was leaving. She was leaving.

Benjamin had grown into a fine young man. Such a lovely pearl. He no longer needed her.

Richard was having an affair. Such an ugly, misshapen pearl.

He no longer wanted her.

When she was gone, there would be a period of mourning—an item in the newspapers, flowers sent to the house—but eventually the people who cared about her would resume their lives, and she would begin to vanish from their minds. Someday there would be no one left in the world who knew she had ever existed. It was a sobering thought, and yet it was just the slightest bit liberating, wasn't it?

Anyway, she was tired.

She labored to draw another breath, but her lungs were no longer up to the task.

She saw another flash of light behind her eyes, something brighter than lightning. She heard a sound that was louder than thunder, something like a gunshot. She braced herself for the first glimpse of whatever awaited.

But nothing happened.

She lay there for a long time before opening her eyes and looking around the room. She considered ringing for her nurse, Alice, but left the bell on the table. She sat up and moved to the edge of the bed. The floor was cool and smooth against her bare feet.

She felt better than she had in months.

She stretched and yawned, and she stood up.

Barefoot and smiling, she walked to the bedroom door and opened it wide.

The night the weird sisters moved to Ascension, that same night Moses Burke buried the Angel of Death under six feet of snow and dirt, Prosper Knox's hunting dogs burrowed under a fence at the west end of his estate and escaped. The five dogs—two springer spaniels, two Irish setters, and a Kerry Blue—ran through the wooded acre behind the Sinclair house and splashed across an icy creek. They climbed an embankment and circled back through the village, crossing the alley between Knox Drugs and Herman's Meats, then bounded up Shiloh Road and climbed the curving path up Vinegar Hill.

The gardens outside Bethany Hall were buried under a glittering blanket of snow; the stems of dormant flowers and neglected shrubbery were entombed in ice. The spaniels, the setters, and the blue jumped a low fence and joined the gathering throng of creatures there.

When the dogs arrived, a family of raccoons moved closer to the big house; there were possums nearby, too, and a handful of skunks. A pair of ducks waddled up the path behind the dogs, followed by a doe and three fawns. A stag stood sentinel behind them, sniffing the air, his head bowed beneath heavy antlers.

A knot of feral cats hissed at the hunting dogs, then returned to the solitude of their grooming ritual. Mr Mulacky's old draft horse left its stable and ambled up the hill, stopping here and there to root for hard brown grass under the snow.

Above them all, sparrows perched in the trees and on the gutters above the front door; bats hung from the eaves. On the rooftop, a murder of crows cawed into the wind. Squirrels chittered at each other, and rabbits huddled quietly against the snowbanks, tense and alert, their ears twitching, their skin crawling.

The animals settled in. They watched the dogs warily; they watched the house.

They waited.

Rose Nettles slept alone in her new bedroom at Bethany Hall. She woke every so often and stared up at the tin ceiling, with its embossed pattern of grapevines. In the moonlight through her open window the vines took on the appearance of twisted rope, and the bunches of grapes became a host of watching eyes. From the garden outside, she heard snow crunch under heavy paws; she heard owls hoot, and bats squeak. Cats hissed, and a dog howled.

Then she slept again and dreamed that a well-dressed man had entered her room. The man's dark hair floated around his head as if he were underwater. His white cuffs and collar gleamed in the moonlight. He stood at the foot of her bed and fixed her with a curious stare. After a long while he spoke.

"You are not what I expected," he said. "You are quite ordinary." He cocked his head to one side. "And yet you have the aspect of someone who has visited a faraway place and come back unexpectedly."

"I almost died once," Rose said.

"Yes, I thought so."

"Who are you?"

"I hardly matter," he said. "Merely a middleman. Mrs Nettles, you should be aware that this place swallows people when they perish. It latches onto whomever enters its doors, it seduces them, and it absorbs them. But there is one room here that is currently devoid of spirits, a room that waits. It wants a tenant and I could provide it one, if you wish."

"I don't understand."

"You recently lost someone."

"My mother?"

"You could see her again, if you like. You could be with her forever, just by opening a door."

The man frightened Rose. As he spoke, his eyes seemed to move like fish in a pond, drifting farther apart, then reversing direction toward his nose. Sometimes his lips didn't move when he spoke, as if he had forgotten they were supposed to.

"No, thank you," Rose said. She tried to wake up. She closed her eyes and opened them again, but nothing had changed. The room looked exactly as it did when she was awake: the crawling vines on the ceiling, the open closet door and the shadows behind it, the butler chair in the corner with her slip draped over it.

"Hmm," the man said. "Well, it was only a passing thought. Perhaps an easier way of accomplishing what must be done. I have come to tell you that you must leave this place. You may take your witches with you or you could leave them here for me, but you must go, Rose Nettles. You must go somewhere far from here and change your name. You have the means to do so, but I am prepared to offer you money, companionship, a new home anywhere you would like. Leave Ascension tomorrow and you will have earned my gratitude. If I may say so, that gratitude is worth a great deal indeed."

"Clarissa—"

"Your cousin no longer needs you."

"I'm going to be the village schoolteacher."

"They won't let you teach their children. These people are small and they have small minds. They will never accept someone such as you."

"I know you're only a dream," Rose said. "But I wish you would leave me alone, sir."

The man straightened his shoulders, and his mouth became a red slit. His nostrils flared and his hair grew longer and thicker, pulsing and drifting like tentacles toward Rose.

Then he sighed.

"Very well. There are other ways, though they be trickier. Enjoy what time you have, Rose Nettles."

When Rose woke again, the room was empty and she was alone. She got out of bed, struck a match and lit the lamp on the windowsill, then she burrowed under her blankets and stared at the bedroom door. Eventually she drifted back into a dreamless sleep.

The yellow dog had traveled north all day, and Moses Burke had followed. The dog's tracks were clear in the snowy hollows and along the tree line where the woods met the trail.

Moses had no purpose in following the dog. If its path were more difficult to follow he would have given up and ridden off in another direction. He had never been good at tracking, but the dog's prints were pressed deep into the landscape, pointing the way forward, leading him on. He had nowhere else to go, nothing else to do, and he thought he might as well chase after that damn dog and see where it led him. It was somehow connected to Death. Maybe Moses would kill the dog at the end of their journey; maybe it would kill him. It made no difference to Moses.

Occasionally, Moses would lose the trail, and his resolve would waver, but then the dog would show itself, and Moses would press on. Pie, the old Appaloosa, was nervous about the yellow dog, and shied away when she saw it, but Moses spurred her on.

At the end of the day he made a fire, flint struck on steel, and warmed his hands. He watched the flames dance and he thought about Katie. He thought about the way her fingers caught in the wool when she tried to knit something, the way her back arched when they made love, the way she laughed when he slipped on the ice, then came to help him up. He thought about their life together and how that life had been cut short.

He opened a tin of beans and dumped them into a skillet, set it on a big rock at the edge of the fire. In his saddlebag there was a stack of corn tortillas wrapped in cloth. They had gone a bit moldy, but he picked off the green parts and charred what was left of them on the same rock that held the pan of beans. Katie had made him sleep outside whenever he ate beans. He looked around and realized her rules still held. He would be sleeping outside. The realization made him feel something besides sorrow and rage for the first time in days, and he tried to hold on to that feeling, stirring the beans so they wouldn't burn at the bottom of the skillet.

He heard something rustle in the underbrush and he sat back, watching the darkness behind the trees. A moment later a rabbit bounded out of the woods and tumbled through the campfire in a flurry of sparks. Moses jumped up as the rabbit got its feet under it and scampered away, squealing, its fur smoldering.

Moses squinted at the space between the trees. He gripped the wooden spoon and looked to where his gun belt was draped over a low branch behind his horse, three paces away. The Appaloosa was stamping at the snow, nervous, her ears twitching.

"Is that you, pooch?" Moses said to the woods. "You in there scaring the critters?"

But the rabbit's behavior worried him. Rabbits weren't the smartest of animals, but they were good at surviving. If a big yellow dog had chased it through the woods, Moses thought it would have stuck to the cover of the underbrush. A rabbit was at home in briars and thistles; the dog's odds of catching it were greater on open ground.

Something moved a few yards past the tree line, a deeper black than the darkness. Whatever it was, it was large. Much bigger than the yellow dog. Moses heard the flutter of wings, like a flock of sparrows taking to the air, then a single yellow eye opened from nothing and stared out at him.

He gripped the spoon tighter and eased sideways, a step closer to his gun belt.

Another eye winked into view, then another. The shape moved toward the fire and slender branches quivered around it. He saw the wings now, dozens of them, hundreds, all massed around the shadowy thing in the woods. He counted eleven eyes, then twelve, then thirteen, and when they blinked in tandem he abandoned all thought of his pistol and backed away. Maybe, he thought, he could hide under the snow on the open fields behind him. Maybe a thing with so many eyes couldn't hear him, or smell him. Maybe a thing with so many wings couldn't move fast across land.

He wasn't watching where he put his feet, and nearly tripped over a log, then looked down and realized it wasn't a log. It was the yellow dog, crouched low, its gaze fixed on the strange thing in the woods.

The dog paid no attention to Moses. Its lips were pulled back from its teeth and the hair along its spine bristled. It growled at the creature and Moses felt a wave of kinship wash over him. He had thought he was ready to die, but the sound of so many wings, and the blinking of those bright yellow eyes, had caused all the ancient survival instincts to kick in.

As if by silent agreement, he and the dog moved at the same time. The dog leapt over the fire and disappeared in the shadows, while Moses ran to the horse and unstrapped his shotgun. He grabbed the gun belt and pulled his revolver from its holster.

The horse nickered, shifting her weight from leg to leg. Moses stroked her nose to settle her.

He heard a thump and felt the ground shake beneath him and the fire went out as he spun back toward it. Behind heavy clouds, the moon was a vague glow somewhere in the eastern sky. A series of shadows—gray and black against the blue of the nighttime snow—flickered over and around each other through an eddy of dying sparks. Looking at them made Moses's stomach turn. He

had once been hit in the head and when he regained conscious-
ness everything had looked blurry and out of focus. He was reminded of that moment as he tried, and failed, to look directly at
the monster in his camp.

He saw the dog—the slippery shape of it—bounding around
the periphery of the shadowy thing, darting in at it and falling
back. He heard the dog yelp. The monster rolled five of its eyes
in Moses's direction and he fired his Colt at those eyes until the
pistol clicked and clicked again, then he emptied both barrels of
his shotgun into the shimmering air above the dead campfire,
hoping he wasn't shooting at the dog.

The eyes suddenly disappeared, the flapping of wings went
silent, the shadows resolved into the harmless shapes of tree
trunks and snowbanks. The woods relaxed, and the fields around
Moses seemed to grow larger.

Moses cracked the shotgun, reloaded it, and slung it over his
shoulder. He strapped on his gun belt, and reloaded the revolver.
Then he stepped over the smoldering campfire and entered the
woods.

The air was unseasonably warm and sticky. There were no animal sounds, no rabbits running, no owls hooting, or deer crunching through the icy glades. The absence of sound and scent hit
Moses like a physical force, but he felt the presence of the dog
beside him and was oddly comforted.

"Didn't you know I was most likely going to kill you?" he said
to the dog, and the sound of his voice restored life to the forest.
He heard water running—some faraway creek pushing against
its banks—and leaves rustling. He felt a cool breeze on his scalp.

He took a deep breath and backed out of the woods. The yellow
dog followed.

"I don't know what that thing was," Moses said to the dog.
"And I don't know if you saved my life or I saved yours, but I

guess we're even now. I won't hunt you anymore. You can go your way and I'll go mine."

The dog sat and tilted its head.

"Of course, that poses a question," Moses said. "I don't know which way is my way. I only just now figured out I don't especially wanna die, but that doesn't change the facts of my life at the moment."

He looked again at the dark trees. "But I do know I want to be far away from these woods."

He returned the shotgun to its scabbard, but he didn't strap it in. He wanted it to be handy if the monster came back. He found his skillet, six yards away from the campsite, its handle bent, and used a handful of snow to clean out the remains of his uneaten beans. He un-hobbled the Appaloosa, then he packed up his few other belongings and swung himself into the saddle, more difficult to do with the gun belt, but he didn't think he would take that off again anytime soon.

He turned the old horse's nose east, toward where the sun would be rising in a few hours, and he set out across the fields.

The dog followed.

I can't believe it," Benjamin said. He tossed the book he wasn't still reading on the table, startling his mother's nurse. "I should cable my father to let him know she's recovered."

Alice frowned at him and continued to straighten the parlor, fluffing the pillows and stacking the magazines. She was bird-like and pale, with fair hair and eyes like faded denim. She left Benjamin's telescope where it was on the divan, afraid she might misalign a knob or leave a fingerprint on the glass.

"I think you should wait," she said at last. "Maybe a day or two."

"Why?"

"I don't know." She shrugged. "It might be better not to—"

"You think Mother will get sick again, don't you?"

"I hope not."

"She won't. I've decided it. She's finally healthy, and Father will let us go home now. Everything will go back to normal." With her feather duster, Alice poked at the rubbery leaves of a jade plant in the corner. She examined a brown spot and scraped at it with her fingernail.

"Alice, have you ever heard of a place called Positano? It's in Italy."

"I don't think so," she said, without turning around. "Is it close to Rome? I've heard of that."

"My father says Positano's the most beautiful town in the whole damn world, and he'll take me there someday. Now that Mother's better, maybe we can go. Say you'll come with us, Alice! You'd love it there, I know you would. And we ought to have a nurse along, just in case. One of us might fall off a cliff or get a lungful of seawater, and there you'd be to bandage us up and pat us on the back. I'll talk to Father about it."

Alice plucked the diseased leaf and crumpled it in her fist. "That sounds nice," she said.

Benjamin stood, and picked up his book, and carried it to the shelves. "You've already taken another position, haven't you? I should have guessed you would."

"No, I haven't," Alice said. "I wouldn't think of abandoning your mother when she was sick."

"But now that she doesn't need you?" He squinted at the book-case, looking for an empty space.

"I never gave it any thought," she said. "I've been too busy to think about the future."

"Then it's settled." Benjamin gave up and tossed the book back on the table. He clapped his hands together. "You'll come with us. I'll arrange it." He wagged a finger at her. "You'll have to lobby hard for Rome, though. Father says it's a woman's city, like Paris. He says London is the best and most masculine city. Clubs on every street where men gather to smoke and drink and talk about politics. Father's been everywhere, I suppose."

"He's an accomplished man."

"Between us, though, if you suggest Rome, I'll back you. I've always wanted to go."

Alice smiled, despite herself. "Me, too," she said. She smoothed the leaf out with her thumb.

Benjamin picked up his telescope. "I'm going up to the roof. Do you want to come? I'll show you how to find Orion."

"Another time," Alice said. "I should look in on your mother and go to bed."

"Suit yourself. I'll see you in the morning."

When he was gone, Alice took another look around the room and doused the lamps. She knew Benjamin meant well, but he was a child, and he always would be. His life was full of boundless possibilities, and he had no reason to question his good fortune. He was a Sinclair, and she was an Anders, and there was a world of difference.

She hoped he would get to see Rome someday, but she knew she never would.

In the village, two men worked quickly, burying a woman behind the church. One of them held the lid of her coffin down while the other pounded in nails. They wore dark cloaks and painted masks. As they worked, the woman screamed and battered the inside of the box with her fists. She used her knees to push up against the lid, but the man holding it down was strong.

One by one, their nails bit through the corners of the pine coffin, sealing her inside.

When they were done, the men used rope slings to lower the box into a hole they had prepared in the rocky soil near the tree line. One of the men paused with a shovelful of dirt. "Starting to snow again," he said. "But rain's softened the ground. Timing's everything, isn't it?"

"Hurry up and let's get home," the other man said.

The first man grunted and picked up the pace. When they had filled the hole, they tamped the fresh mound with the backs of their shovels.

They parted ways outside the church. One limped away up Shiloh Road, while the other took a shortcut home, through the back of the potter's lot.

When she could no longer hear the men laboring above her, the woman finally stopped screaming. She waited until she thought the night had ended and the sun might be rising before she began to scream again. Her timing was off. It was five o'clock in the morning, the moon still high on the western horizon, and no one heard her except the milkman Mr Mulacky, who thought the sound echoing across the churchyard was the wind in the tops of nearby trees.

Sadie Grace couldn't sleep. She dressed quietly in the dark and slipped out through the back door. She tromped down to the woods, cracking through a hard crust on the snowy slope behind Bethany Hall, relishing the cold air on her face and the comfort of her thick bear fur coat. At the bottom of the hill the forest stretched as far as Sadie could see in every direction, the trees bare and tangled and gray. She found an opening in the tree line and jumped over a snowbank, into the stillness. She peeled a strip of bark from the trunk of a tall oak and folded it into her mouth, chewing as she walked, softening the bark with her saliva. She could smell a sharp note of winter-green in her own misty breath.

She found a patch of dead moss on the side of a pitch pine and scraped some of it off with her thumbnail, adding the moss to her plug of oak bark. She coughed and a fat brown rabbit erupted from a thicket to her left, bounding away, zigzagging this way and that. Sadie smiled and changed course, following the rabbit through tangles and over deadfalls. She stopped and dug into the soil under a rotted, ice-covered log, and found a nest of hibernating beetles. She added one of them to the growing mass in her cheek.

The trees grew closer together the deeper she went, and she watched for a clearing, turning back and moving uphill whenever she felt she had drifted too far from the house. When she finally broke through a copse of white oak into a glade blanketed in glis-tening snow, she was disappointed to see that someone had found it first, and had spoiled its natural beauty.

A structure had been erected there in the middle of the woods, sturdy and well maintained, a single story with a stone founda-tion, solid walls, and a jerkinhead roof. Sadie approached it carefully, watching for signs of habitation. There was a chim-ney, but no smoke; there were windows, but no lights. The snow around the cabin was free of human tracks.

She swallowed the wad in her mouth, then jiggled the knob on the cabin door.

Locked.

She sighed and stepped back, studying the surrounding woods. There was no sign of movement anywhere, so she bent and breathed into the keyhole above the knob. She pictured the pins in the lock and thought about how they might fall into place if they were so inclined. She heard a click and jiggled the knob again, and the door swung inward on well-oiled hinges.

The sharp scent of vinegar wafted out at her, along with something older and mustier. Sadie backed away from the threshold and found a broken branch, whacked it against the trunk of a spruce to shake off the snow, then carried it into the cabin. She spoke a few words, pricked the tip of her finger on the splintered end of the branch, and the wood ignited.

In the flickering light of the torch she saw that the cabin was dominated by a low stone table, polished smooth by years of use. There were no chairs, only a small wooden platform behind the table. It looked to Sadie like an overturned crate reinforced with brackets. The floor was lined with flagstones, carefully fitted together around a rock-lined fire pit before the table.

She could see now why so little light penetrated the windows; the glass was smeared with soap and ashes from the pit.

She crouched low and swept her free hand over the floor. Whoever had scrubbed the flagstones had done a poor job of it. There was a dried black residue caked into the narrow grooves between the stones, and she scraped at it with her fingernail. She sniffed the gunk and tasted it at the back of her throat.

Blood.

Sadie sat back on her heels and looked around the cabin again, wondering who had built it, who had used it, and how long it had gone undiscovered within the clearing.

Eventually she stood and held the torch higher. The back wall seemed to ripple in the firelight. She moved around the table and raised her torch higher. Animal pelts were nailed in an evenly spaced row just above her eye level, and a second row had been started below the first. Sadie counted twenty skins in the top row, and seven in the lower row. She reached out and ran her fingers through the long brown hair of the nearest pelt.

When she realized she was touching a human scalp she didn't cry out or even pull her hand away, but a shudder ran through her body.

Sadie knew what she would find if she sifted through the ashes in the stone pit.

She closed her eyes and when she opened them again she was surrounded by women, huddled together in the small room, some hugging each other and some holding hands, but all watching Sadie with eyes that were wide and bright. One of them, a girl no older than thirteen, drew her lips back in a snarl that was both angry and fearful. An older woman put her arm around the girl's shoulders and bowed her head toward Sadie.

After a moment, the women faded back into the shadows, but Sadie could still hear their voices, low murmurs that might have been mistaken for the creaking of the rafters.

She blew frost across the tips of her fingers to strengthen them, then pulled a nail out of the wall, letting the scalp drop into her other hand. She turned it over, and touched the leathery skullcap, brought a handful of hair up to her face to inhale the dusty scent of a dead woman.

The next scalp was plastered to the wall with mildew, the husk of a dead spider tangled in its dirty yellow locks. Sadie laid the first scalp on the table and pulled the blond scalp free. She combed out the spider and brushed mold from the hair, then placed it on the table beside the first. She went down the line, taking down each scalp and acquainting herself with its texture and scent before setting it on the table with the others. When she had finished removing the top row, she worked her way back again, pulling the second row free.

After an hour the walls were bare and Sadie's fingers were bleeding.

At least twenty-seven women had been murdered in the cabin.

Twenty-seven people had gone missing and their stories had ended in that lonely place.

Atop a stone table.

In a fire pit.

On a nail.

People disappeared all the time, of course, especially where winters were harsh and prospects were scarce. Sadie knew this. *But surely someone looked for them,* she thought. *Surely someone cared.*

And yet the cabin stood still and silent in the middle of the deep woods. No one had looked hard enough or long enough to find it.

Dust and rot, time and trauma, had taken a toll on the women's remains, but Sadie had their scents now. She closed her eyes and imagined them standing with her again in that small space. She focused on each of them in turn and held their images in her mind. When she felt she knew them, she touched her torch to the pile of scalps and stepped back.

Hair smoldered and smoked, sparks fizzed and sputtered. The scalps blackened and curled. Sadie sang to the fire and it grew. She howled and threw her torch, and the stone table broke in half.

She left the cabin and did not turn back to watch it burn.

She marched in a straight line up the gentle slope toward Bethany Hall, her boots sinking into the pristine snow, and found a clearing she hadn't noticed on the way out. Trees formed a perfect halo around a circle of bright moonlight, where a stag stood nosing beneath the snow for green roots. One of his ears twitched and his head rose, his wide rack like the branches of a moving tree. Sadie stepped out of the shadows and its black eyes focused on her. She and the stag stood quiet and still for a long while before he turned and leapt away.

Sadie knelt in the center of the glade and retched. She brought up the wad of bark and moss and beetle shell, spitting it into her hand. It was smooth and hard, like a seed. She dug a shallow hole in the snow, dropped the seed in, and covered it over.

She closed her eyes and breathed the cold air of the forest. She smelled smoke in the distance, but knew the fire would not spread far from the cabin.

After a time, she stood and laid her palms against the cold trunk of a sycamore. She sapped its stillness, then left the glade and marked its place in her mind. She quieted her thoughts, and as the first rays of sunlight sparkled on the snow she walked out of the woods and up the hill to her new home.

SIX DAYS
REMAINING

My beloved brother,

Were I capable of envy, I might have strong feelings about the division of our labor. May I trust that you are enjoying the fresh air and sunshine where you are?

As for myself, I am in an unfortunate space, dark and dusty and cramped, but there is a large window that looks out on the village. Yes, I know, the window is unnecessary, but I think it is a quaint lens through which to view this realm. You must allow me my eccentricities.

The Other is here, too, but he has yet to interfere in the unfolding events. I suspect he is biding his time, a waiting an opportunity for mischief. No matter. Everything will happen as it must, regardless of The Other's intentions.

There is no possibility of posting this letter, of course, but it amuses me to write it. I have found a good supply of paper and ink, and I am setting down my observations about this place and these people as if someone, someday, will read it. The exercise is a welcome distraction.

Oh, Raphael, I do look forward to spreading my wings again, and lifting my face to bask in the glow of His light, but we must wait for this to end, one way or another.

I will see you soon, I know.

While you are out there, won't you please smell a flower for me?

Yours in faith and duty,
Alexander

Rabbit rose with the sun and climbed out of bed. Bethany Hall was massive, barren, and drafty, but workmen had scraped the walls and painted them so that they almost glowed in the light through the tall windows overlooking the woods.

The bulk of their possessions was not due to arrive until later in the week, and the house's empty rooms echoed with every footfall. Rabbit had spent the first decade of her life on the plains of the Midwest, roaming through fields and thickets, and she had spent her second decade in Philadelphia, prowling the quiet galleries of libraries and museums. She was comfortable with solitude, but Bethany Hall did not feel silent—it felt hungry.

She had decided to pass her first morning in the new house by taking inventory of its ghosts. Dr Ichabod Bailey had stocked an abundance of notebooks and ledgers, pencils and quill pens, in the expectation of a long and productive career in Ascension. From a shelf in her room, Rabbit picked out a small empty journal with the doctor's name stamped in gold on its brown leather cover. She opened the book and wrote *Who Has Stayed Behind* at the top of the first page.

Then she went looking.

There was a woman in an upstairs room with her back to the door, her nightgown oily with blood, and there was an old man sitting in the ground-floor study, pretending to read a book. Rabbit made note of each of them.

A man in a dark suit stood at a high table in the butler's pantry, endlessly polishing silverware. He looked up and nodded politely at her, then returned to his work.

Rabbit wrote *Butler?* in her notebook, and in parentheses she wrote *(He seems friendly).*

A man writhed and shivered on a rug in the parlor, his flesh charred and smoking, his lipless mouth opened in a silent scream. He rolled his eyes toward her as she entered and he reached out one skeletal hand. Rabbit backed out of the room.

Parlor, she wrote. Then crossed out the word and put an *X* next to it.

In the dining room, a phantom dinner party was in full swing, and a headless cat weaved its way across the top of the long table, padding softly around soup bowls and wineglasses. Across the hallway in the ballroom, a man in a blue uniform pirouetted across the floor with a pretty woman in his arms. Her swirling silk dress was trimmed in lace, and she danced lightly on the tips of her toes. Neither of them so much as glanced at Rabbit.

Happy spirits, Rabbit wrote. *(Do they hear music?)*

In the root cellar she sifted through a mound of loose soil and found the bones of a small child. Three women in white gowns watched her without expression.

Brides in the cellar, Rabbit wrote.

There was a small door on the cellar's south wall, dark wood with inlaid panels carved in an elaborate pattern of chains. Rabbit turned the knob this way and that, but the door was locked and didn't budge. She put her ear against one of the panels and heard a faraway heartbeat that might have been her own pulse. She frowned and licked the tip of her pencil.

I think someone is waiting down here.

She ascended to the third floor, opened the door to the attic and peered up the stairs, then shut the door and shook her head.

"No, thank you," she said aloud.

Avoid the attic, she wrote.

I am standing at the top of the attic steps and I breathe a sigh of relief when she turns away. Rabbit leaves the house, and I go to the attic window to watch her explore the grounds. There is a quality about her that bears watching.

O utside, the morning sun had warmed the snow, and rivulets ran through the crystalline gardens. Rabbit went out by the front gate and left it open behind her. Everywhere she looked there were animal tracks. She followed hoofprints to the edge of a copse, where an old woman stood in the shadows of the soft blue pines. Her white hair blew in a breeze that Rabbit couldn't feel. The old woman held out her cupped hands and opened them to reveal a golden locket on a chain. She unfastened its delicate clasp and spread the locket open across her palms to display a tiny watercolor portrait. Rabbit peered down at the hazy image of a man with a handlebar mustache—a ghost within a ghost—and the old woman seemed satisfied. She closed the locket, clutched it to her sunken chest, and backed into the trees, bowing as she went.

Sad, but proud of her jewelry, Rabbit wrote. *(Look for her necklace in the house?)*

Below that, she wrote: *Too many ghosts. Ask Sadie about dispelling them.*

When she had filled an entire page of her notebook with observations about the spirits of Bethany Hall, she closed it and went looking for her mother.

S adie was sitting beside the fire in the kitchen, pulling off a wet boot. She had left a snowy trail from the back door, and Housemaid was searching for a mop in the narrow closet beside the pantry.

"I'm bored," Rabbit said. "Can we go into town?"

Sadie smiled and pulled her boot back on.

"Let's," she said. "Where's Rose? She must be anxious to see her cousin."

Rose had overslept in the cool quiet room at the far end of the upstairs corridor. After half an hour of sorting through steamer trunks for the proper clothes, the three of them set out toward the village. Sadie and Rabbit had bags slung over their shoulders; Rose carried an umbrella and a flat box wrapped in brown paper.

The path curved downhill for half a mile around limestone outcroppings and through groves of sugar maples. The women walked single file in silence, their breath puffing out around their heads and drifting away.

"I was exploring this morning," Sadie said at last. "The other side of the hill's perfect for sledding. Let's check the attic. Somebody might have left one we could use."

"The attic?" Rabbit said.

"You'll smack your head into a tree and die," Rose said. "Besides, sleds are undignified."

Rabbit made a face behind Rose's back, then shuffled through the snow to catch up to her. She took Rose's elbow to steady her across a patch of black ice. "Everyone's going to die someday," she said. She tried to sound as matter-of-fact as possible, but Rose winced.

"You're probably right, though," Sadie said. "It would be undignified." But she smiled back at Rabbit and they bounded ahead through the snow. Rose smiled, too, and hurried to catch up, touching tree trunks alongside the trail to keep from slipping.

The path widened at the bottom of the hill, and the ground leveled out. They passed the train station, and Rabbit craned her neck to see through its high windows, in case their things had arrived early. She missed her art supplies and her books, and hoped to see stacks of heavy crates waiting to be hauled up the hill, but the station was empty.

They crossed the railroad tracks and stopped.

Space had long ago been cleared for buildings and roads, but it looked as if the trees were pushing back in, reclaiming their land. Here in a clearing was a dry goods store with a duck canvas awning, and in another clearing was a little schoolhouse of quarried stone with a high bell tower. Beyond the school they could see a graveyard and a church, then the road forked and the village was hidden from sight. Red-tiled roofs and white-painted pedimented porches were barely visible through the overhanging branches of sycamores, elms, and maples, and curlicues of smoke rose from unseen chimneys. Rabbit imagined how it would look in the spring and summer, leaves shrouding every curve in the road, and every building nestled away in its own woodsy niche.

"Hallooo!"

The voice came from behind a tree, so close that Rabbit jumped and slipped on the ice. Sadie steadied her as a boy popped into view, waving his arms and grinning.

"Remember me?" he said. "From yesterday!"

"Benjamin Sinclair," Sadie said.

"You do remember," Benjamin said. He stopped in front of them and lifted his arms, then dropped them to his sides, as if he had thought to hug them and decided against it. "Isn't it a glorious day?"

"You look like you're about to burst," Sadie said.

"I am going to burst," Benjamin said. "I was just looking for Lucy or Charles . . . I mean, I wanted to deliver the news, but she's . . . I mean, *they're* nowhere to be found, and my ears are already freezing. It's damn cold out here. You haven't seen them, have you?"

"We haven't seen them," Rose said.

"But we wouldn't know them if we did," Sadie said. "So far, you're the only person we've met."

"What's the news?" Rabbit said.

"My mother's out of bed! She woke up last night."

"That's wonderful," Rose said. "I was just on my way to see her."

"My father said she would never recover," Benjamin said. He took a deep breath. "He said she wouldn't see the spring."

"How awful," Sadie said. "Your father said that?"

"But he was wrong," Benjamin said. "She's up and about today, like nothing ever happened, and I'm on my way to cable him about it."

"Where is your father?" Rose said.

"He doesn't leave the city. He sent Mother here to the summer cottage to convalesce. There were friends and neighbors coming and going, day after day, asking questions and always looking sad. Father thought she ought to get some peace. I was supposed to be looking after her here, but there hasn't been anything to do." He shrugged. "I just . . . well, I can't tell you what a relief it is."

"It's such wonderful news," Rose said. "You should let your father know right away."

"If we see Lucy, we'll tell her you're looking for her," Sadie said. "And Charles, too."

"Thanks!" And, with that, the boy bolted up the road toward the train station.

"But we don't know Lucy," Rabbit said. "And we don't know Charles."

"Then we should tell everyone we see that Benjamin's mother is out of bed. We've only been here a day and we already have good news to share!"

Rabbit rolled her eyes, but when Rose turned and smiled at her, she smiled back.

———

Moses made camp again on a wide windswept plain where the snow was already melting away. There were no trees as far as the eye could see, and the rising sun sparkled in the bristly brown grass. He built a fire with a few fat sticks he had brought with him, and an armful of sun-dried weeds. The yellow dog stretched out on the other side of the fire and watched him. He watched it back. The weeds popped and sizzled; the sticks rolled against each other like living creatures. The stoniness that had settled in Moses's heart continued to shift. He was ashamed of himself for shooting the defenseless Angel of Death, and he was confused by what had happened in the aftermath. Killing Death had not brought Katie back to him; shooting himself had not transported him to her. There had been no consequences for any of the bad things he had done, and that seemed wrong on some scale of wrongness that frightened him. That wrongness was the only explanation he had for the monster he had seen in the woods. Moses wondered if there was something he could do to keep the monster from coming back, somewhere he could go or someone he could talk to. The only thing he knew for sure was that he was out of his depth.

The dog shut its eyes and breathed heavily, its paws twitching. Moses squinted all around him at the brightening plains. He didn't see glowing eyes; he didn't hear flapping wings. He moved to a more comfortable position on his side and watched the flames dance, and eventually he fell asleep.

When he woke again, the fire was out and the dog was pawing through one of his saddlebags. Moses jumped to his feet and threw his hat at the dog, who loped a few feet away, then sat on its haunches and cocked its head at him.

"Dammit, dog, you sure made a mess of things," Moses said.

"Who told you to follow me anyway? I didn't ask for your company."

Biscuits were scattered about, but Moses counted them and decided he still had as many as he ought to. The dog hadn't eaten any of them, and it hadn't clawed open his tin of jerky, either. Most of the eggs were still in the bottom of the saddlebag, but one had broken, and Moses picked out as many bits of shell as he could before using his handkerchief to sop up the yolk.

The dog watched him.

"My biscuits not good enough for you?" Moses said.

He brushed off the untouched biscuits and wrapped them in a piece of clean sailcloth before returning them to the bag, tucking them up against one side, as far as possible from the gummy residue of egg.

He circled the campsite, searching for anything that might have blown into the grass. At the foot of the big rock he had used for a pillow he found a thick book. It was bound in leather the same shade of brown as the grass, and had the word "Appointments" embossed on its cover. One corner of the book was charred and still smelled of smoke. Moses opened it and found a dried flower pressed between the cover and the first page, a black chrysanthemum. He turned the page, careful not to crumble the flower, and thumbed through the rest of the book, skimming page after page of names written in the same cramped hand. He found his wife's name, halfway down the second-to-last page: *Katie Burke.*

"You brought this," Moses said to the dog. "You went back and took this from Death's saddlebag and you brought it here, didn't you?" Moses ran his finger down the page beneath his wife's name.

He stopped on the name *Daniel Stauch.*

Moses had known Daniel well, had helped him dig a boulder

out of his back pasture the previous summer. He wondered if Daniel was dead, too, if he had died sometime after Katie. Sometime before Death left Nicodemus. There were more names after Daniel's, but Moses didn't know them: *Ronald Huff, Gerald Nagel, Anna Brosamer, Eben Lingard, Clarissa Sinclair, Sarah Farrell, Benjamin Sinclair* . . .

On and on went the list of names. It was clear to Moses that each of those names represented someone with an appointment to meet Death. He flipped to the last page and read the final name on the list: *Rose Nettles.*

It was another name he knew. He and Rose had traveled together many years ago, long before he had met Katie Foster.

The dog was still watching him. A scrap of paper trapped under its yellow paw fluttered in the morning breeze.

"What does this mean?" Moses said to the dog. "Is Rose Nettles already dead or did I shoot that bastard before he got to her?"

When he approached the dog it stood and trotted across the field. Moses picked up the piece of paper before it could blow away. It was thin, nearly translucent, and smelled faintly of a perfume Moses couldn't identify, but he recognized Rose Nettles's delicate handwriting marching across the page in neat straight lines. He had forgotten about the letter. It had come to him in the first days of his marriage to Katie and he had set it aside. He couldn't remember putting it in his saddlebag, but he supposed he must have done so.

He had written to Rose soon after proposing to Katie, had sent her his new address in Kansas. He hadn't heard back for weeks, but then the letter had come. She said she was living with her friends Sadie Grace and Rabbit in a big house in Philadelphia. Rose was delighted to hear about Moses's good fortune, but her mother had fallen gravely ill and they would not be able to attend his wedding.

Feeling guilty about his own happiness, Moses had never responded to her.

Thinking now about those early days with Katie, carrying her things into the house they had bought together, he was able to muster a small sad smile.

He refolded the letter and slid it into his bag alongside the tin of jerky.

He shook his head at the dog.

"I sure wish you could talk. I know you're up to something, and maybe it has to do with Rose Nettles, but I'm damned if I know what."

He saddled up and pointed the Appaloosa toward the distant hills. What lay beyond them, he didn't know. But the opposite of moving forward was dying. Only a day or two ago he had been ready and willing to die, but now he felt some sense of purpose stirring in him. He didn't know what it meant, but he felt it just the same.

Pie moved steadily across the plain, and Moses let her find her own way. He was deep in thought. He was thinking about the thing in the woods, and what would happen if it came back. He was thinking about what he might do if it did.

A fat brown rabbit bounded from the cover of a bayberry shrub, and the yellow dog chased after it. Moses watched them run, sprinting forward and doubling back, the rabbit always a hairsbreadth away from being caught. Eventually the dog gave up and came back.

"Rabbit," Moses said. He looked down at the dog, who was trotting easily alongside the horse, still panting from exertion.

Sadie Grace and her daughter, Rabbit, were witches, and he had seen them do impossible things. If anyone had heard of a creature with a thousand eyes and a thousand wings it was them.

"Philadelphia's as good a destination as any," he said to the dog. "But you don't have to come along. I don't need the company."

But the dog kept pace with the horse across the barren plain, and Moses was secretly glad.

A s the road curved, the three women passed tall trees that acted as a natural sound barrier between the train tracks and the village. The land flattened out and the forest gave way to a wide town square, surrounded on every side by shops and offices. A white picket fence bordered the village green and wrapped around the far side where storefronts and small businesses—including a drugstore, the village inn, a smithy, a printmaker, and a pottery shed—fanned out in a semicircle at the back of the square. Rabbit smelled horses, and she guessed the livery was located somewhere behind the inn. Wagons trundled down the icy side streets and pedestrians called out to each other across the wintery green, their frosty breath drifting across the plaza. The sky was clear, and sand had been scattered across the footpath to keep travelers from slipping.

Rose opened her umbrella. "For balance," she said.

She left them there and made her way up a wide path south of the square in the direction of her cousin's house at No. 17 Brynwood Lane. It had been decided that she would meet Clarissa alone first, before introducing her to the others.

Sadie and Rabbit went shopping.

In the general store Sadie purchased eggs, cornmeal, candle wax, and a salt lick, all to be delivered to Bethany Hall. She paid no attention to the furtive glances of the other customers.

Down the street from the general store, Sadie paced the narrow aisles of Knox Drugs, rubbing sachets between her fingers and opening jars of spice. A boy introduced himself as Charles and pulled out a ladder to get at some of the less popular salts and herbs that were kept on a high shelf, but the proprietor appeared and shooed Charles away before Sadie could tell the boy that Benjamin was looking for him.

"I'm Prosper Knox," the man said. "Like the sign says out front. Welcome to Ascension, Mrs . . ."

"Sadie. There's no need to call me Missus."

"Can I ask what brings you to our corner of the woods?"

"You can."

Prosper waited, his smile slowly fading. He grew more uncomfortable, folding and unfolding his arms across his chest. Finally, he took a step back and cleared his throat.

"So, what can I get for you today?"

Sadie produced a slip of paper from her front pocket. She handed it over, and Prosper produced a pair of reading spectacles. He studied the list and pursed his lips.

"I can get most of these for you today, but I'll have to order some of them from Boston. And, to be perfectly honest, there's some here I don't know what it is. Dittany? Never heard of it."

"Well, now you have. Will you be able to get it for me?"

He removed his spectacles and used them to point at her. "I can get just about anything you can name," he said. "If Boston don't have it, somebody will. I've got connections all over this country."

"As do I, Mr Knox," Sadie said. "But it's always good to have another. Tell me, is there a place nearby where my daughter and I might get a bite to eat? All this trudging through the snow makes a person hungry."

"Mrs Hudson at the inn makes a mean meat pie. Tell her I sent you and she'll take good care of you."

They said goodbye, and Mr Knox promised to have their order filled and delivered within the fortnight. The little bell over the door tinkled softly as they exited into the clean chilly air of the village.

"There's Benjamin again," Rabbit said. She pointed to a distant figure sliding along a path beside the main road, coming back down from the train station.

Benjamin stopped and turned, and when he saw them in front of the drugstore he waved, and hollered, but his words wafted away with his breath.

Rabbit shook her head to indicate she hadn't heard him, and he cupped his gloved hands around his mouth to shout again. "Do you want . . ." Again his words faded away, and again Rabbit shook her head.

Benjamin spread his arms out and shrugged his shoulders in exaggerated exasperation, then hopped over a snowbank toward them. An old swayback mare, pulling a dogcart that sagged under the weight of empty milk bottles, brushed against him, knocking him to the ground, and the wheels of the wagon rolled forward over his body. Crates of milk bottles toppled over the sides of the wagon and crashed into the street.

Benjamin's screams, and the meaty crack of his ribs, carried across the square over the sounds of breaking bottles and the squealing, frightened horse.

The low picket fence surrounding the town square was open at each side where gates might once have been. By the time the first set of wheels had thumped over Benjamin's body, Sadie was already running across the green, and Rabbit followed her mother, windmilling her arms to keep her feet from skidding out beneath her. Sadie's long legs carried her farther and faster than Rabbit could manage, and by the time Rabbit reached the scene of the accident, a small crowd of onlookers was gathering. Sadie helped Benjamin to his feet.

"I feel fine," he said. "Really, it surprised me, that's all."

But it was obvious that he wasn't fine.

His clothing was soaked with blood and there was a spreading pool of it beneath him. His left arm hung limp at his side, bent at an angle that made Rabbit's stomach turn. She could see pink flesh and white bone where his jacket had been torn open. And behind his ribs, a blue-gray organ pumped slowly, then still more slowly.

Then it stopped pumping altogether.

The milkman had jumped down from his cart and was pacing around in the road, wringing his hands and weeping.

"I never seen him there," he said. "I didn't mean it. I just never seen him till it was too late."

"It's all right, Mr Mulacky," Benjamin said. "You didn't mean anything by it, and neither did this old gal." He used his good arm to stroke the old horse's nose. "It was an accident, that's all."

"Your heart stopped beating," Rabbit whispered.

Benjamin looked down in surprise, and pulled the tattered remnants of his jacket across his chest. Sadie took off her heavy coat and draped it over his shoulders.

"Is there a doctor in the village?" she asked the milkman.

"I don't need a damn doctor," Benjamin said. "I feel fine. I really do."

"Aye, there's a doctor," Mr Mulacky said. "But the boy says he's fine." He had stopped crying and was suddenly defensive.

A girl standing at the edge of the crowd stepped forward. "Charles went to bring the doctor," she said. She raised her hand an inch, then dropped it back to her side, as if she wanted to touch Benjamin but thought better of it. Her eyes were wide and wet.

"What's your name, dear?" Sadie said.

"Lucy," the girl said. "Lucy Knox."

"How long will it take the doctor to get here?"

"His house is nearby, but I don't know."

"We'd better not wait," Sadie said. "Would you show us where to go?"

"Please just take me home, Lucy," Benjamin said. "I do feel a little shaken, after all, and I'd like to lie down."

"First things first," Sadie said, and she waved Lucy ahead of them, signaling that she should lead the way.

"The boy says he wants to go home," the milkman said. "He don't hardly seem hurt."

"Oh, be quiet," Rabbit said. "Count yourself lucky no one's blaming you."

Mr Mulacky blinked several times, then climbed back onto his cart and snapped the reins. The old hollow-backed mare lurched forward and plodded away up the road. Mr Mulacky looked back once, scowled at Rabbit, and continued around the bend out of sight.

Rabbit ran to catch up to Sadie, who was supporting Benjamin, and they followed Lucy Knox. The girl was moving swiftly and she glanced back every few steps to make sure they were still behind her. Benjamin dragged his feet, protesting that he felt fine, but he didn't sound altogether sure, and he looked pale.

Rabbit had no idea what he must be thinking or feeling.

She hadn't realized it was *possible* for someone to think and feel once their heart stopped beating.

Clarissa had briefly ventured out into the parlor that morning, and had spoken to her son and her nurse, before rushing back to the comfort and familiarity of her bedroom. She knew she ought to be tired of the room, of the yellow curtains, the ancient furnishings, and the tin ceiling. Instead she was hesitant to leave it, as if she belonged in that thirty-by-thirty-foot space and nowhere else. To calm her thoughts, she went through her wardrobe, taking each of her dresses from the closet and shaking it out before laying it on a growing pile atop the chest at the foot of her bed. When she looked up, Alice was standing in the doorway.

"Look at the state of these," Clarissa said. "Didn't anyone think to take care of my things?"

"I'm sorry, ma'am. It's just that you . . . well, everyone thought . . ."

Clarissa grimaced. Of course no one had presumed she would need her party gowns again. The doctor had been clear on the subject: Clarissa wouldn't live another month.

"We'll need to send some of these out for cleaning," she said. "They're positively caked with dust. They're brown with it, and I don't think any amount of airing-out will fix the situation."

"Yes, ma'am," Alice said. "I'll see to it, but there's a visitor downstairs."

Clarissa raised her eyebrows. No one had come to see her in ages. For the first two or three weeks after she arrived in Ascension there had been a steady stream of visitors, seemingly every villager she had ever met, all lingering for a few minutes with expressions of pity, or plastered-on smiles. They always left as quickly as they could without seeming rude, and none of them had visited twice. Clarissa didn't necessarily blame them. Few people were comfortable standing so close to death.

"Who is it, Alice?" She hoped it was Lillian Knox. She couldn't understand why Lillian had deserted her. They had been thick as thieves every summer for as long as Clarissa could remember.

"She gave her name as Rose Nettles, ma'am."

Clarissa's eyes went wide and she clapped her hands. Who

cared about fussy old Lillian Knox anyway? Rose Nettles had come all the way from Philadelphia to visit her ailing cousin. And wouldn't she be surprised to see Clarissa up and about!

"Tell her I'll be right down," she said.

Alice nodded and backed out of the room. Clarissa listened to the girl's light footsteps on the stairs, and wondered if Alice had inquired elsewhere for employment while Clarissa lay on her deathbed. Under the circumstances, it would be wise of her to have done so. Clarissa made a mental note to ask. She might need to increase the girl's pay in order to keep her.

Clarissa checked her hair in the mirror, and smoothed the front of her skirt. She glanced again at the pile of dresses and clicked her tongue, then left the room and closed the door behind her.

Downstairs, Alice had shown their visitor into the parlor. Rose stood in front of the taller of the two bookcases, running her fingers along the spines. She held a package under her arm.

"Richard reads everything," Clarissa said, and Rose turned around, a smile on her face. In their youth Rose had been mousy—her nose buried in a book or her knitting—and Clarissa had made a point of trying to draw her out, inviting her to social events and introducing Rose to her friends. She could still see that modest girl in the features of the woman before her, but Rose had changed in countless subtle ways. Her eyes flashed with confidence and satisfaction. Her hair, though streaked with gray, was styled well. Her clothing was understated, but expertly tailored, and her skin radiated health and satisfaction. The image Clarissa held of Rose had remained frozen in time, while the flesh and blood version had lived an entire lifetime.

"Honestly," Clarissa said. "If someone mentions a book, Richard sends out for it right away, but he rarely finishes them. They go on the shelf until he has to make room for a new one. Take what you want. Richard calls this his overflow library."

"Oh, Claire," Rose said. "I just heard the news that you're well again. Is it true?"

"I haven't felt so good in months." Clarissa crossed the room and pulled her cousin into an embrace. After a long moment, she pulled back and looked her cousin over again. "You look wonderful, Rose."

Rose hesitated. "I can scarcely believe you were sick," she said.

"Please, sit," Clarissa said, indicating the green brocade divan beneath Richard's hideous painting of wolves attacking a deer. The stag—or was it an elk?—stood on a rock situated slightly above the predators. Its antlers shone wickedly in the sunlight, and so did the wolves' teeth. Clarissa hated the painting and had taken it down three or four summers previously, but Richard had found it and quietly hung it back up. She noticed belatedly that Benjamin had left the *Inquirer* open, its pages scattered across the cushions, and she quickly gathered it up.

"I almost forgot," Rose said. "I brought you something."

She handed over the package, a flat gift-wrapped box. Inside was a red woolen blanket, barely large enough for a child.

"I knitted it myself."

"I love it," Clarissa said. "Are you hungry? I'll have Alice bring in some sandwiches."

"That would be nice. I came away without breakfast."

Clarissa picked up a bell from the end table and rang it. "Where are you staying?"

"The house on the hill."

"Not Bethany!"

"Yes, that's the one. Didn't Benjamin mention it?"

Alice entered and Clarissa ordered a quantity of sandwiches, then waved the girl out of the room, excited to return to the subject at hand. "I can't believe you've taken that old place. Is it awful?"

"We had it fixed up."

"I have so many questions."

Rose took a pipe from her bag and a pouch of tobacco. "Do you care if I smoke?"

"I suppose not," Clarissa said. "But I never knew you to smoke."

"It was Joe's." She tamped tobacco into the bowl of the pipe and struck a match.

"I was sorry to hear about Joe," Clarissa said. "But you hardly mentioned him in your letters."

Rose puffed until she drew smoke. "He loved me," she said. "That was good of him. And he stayed with me for a while after I buried him."

Clarissa blinked, unable to think of a response.

"Well, that's in the past," Rose said. "I have to be honest, I expected to find you at death's door."

"And yet I feel perfectly fine."

"Well, it must be true." Rose squinted at her. "You're not a spirit. You hugged me and I felt you do it."

It was a strange thing for anyone to say, but Rose had always been a bit queer. Clarissa laughed it off, but the remark stayed with her. She had been dying, had felt herself die, and yet it had never occurred to her that she might actually *be* dead.

She plucked at a corner of the red blanket in her lap and saw that it was already beginning to unravel.

Dr Timothy Rumpole wavered in his open doorway. His eyes were red-rimmed and bleary, and his dark hair stood on end.

"I was just on my way out," he said.

"Yes," Sadie said. "You were about to come take a look at this young man, but we've brought him to you instead."

"Good of you," Dr Rumpole said. "Very convenient."

He wore a moth-eaten smoking jacket, which he removed and hung behind the door, then gestured absently toward the rooms behind him and mumbled something incoherent. Sadie took it as an invitation to enter. She hung Rabbit's overcoat on the rack beside the smoking jacket, but left her own coat draped over young Benjamin's shoulders. Lucy Knox lingered for a moment, then burst into tears and rushed away down the porch steps. Sadie shut the door after her.

The doctor led them through a dark foyer into a parlor that held a dingy sofa upholstered in blue satin, stained and threadbare, and a scarred wooden table. The table held a long porcelain pipe on a tray, along with a variety of miniature pots and jars. The air in the room was hazy and smelled sour.

Sadie led Benjamin to the couch and made him sit, while the doctor picked up the tray of smoking paraphernalia and carried it out of the room. He came back a moment later with a black leather bag, and frowned down at Benjamin.

"What happened to him?" The doctor's voice was soft and he tended to look away into the corners of the room when he spoke.

"He was run over by a milk cart," Sadie said.

"He died," Rabbit said.

"I'm perfectly fine," Benjamin said. "I'm just a little cold."

"Well, let's take a look." Dr Rumpole sat carefully on the edge of his table and Sadie peeled her coat away from Benjamin's chest.

"Oh, my," the doctor said. He leaned in for a closer look, then sat back and put a hand to his mouth.

"Oh, my," he said again.

"It's bad," Sadie said.

"Oh, it's worse than that."

"I told you so," Rabbit said.

Sadie had thought Benjamin was already as pale as anyone could be, but upon seeing the doctor's reaction he blanched and seemed to shrink in on himself. His eyes flickered downward, but he didn't move his head to see the damage that had been done to his body.

"It doesn't hurt," he said. "If it's as bad as all that . . . well, I'd feel it, wouldn't I?"

"Possibly not," Dr Rumpole said. He ran a hand through his messy hair. "I have heard of people so traumatized that their brains refused to register pain. I've read that during the recent conflict between the states, there was a soldier who . . . well, anyway, it's fascinating, but I suppose this isn't the time."

He appeared to be energized by the strange case of Benjamin Sinclair. The doctor's lethargy had disappeared and he trembled with excitement.

"I'm afraid I must ask you ladies to leave the room now," he said. "I'll have to strip this lad of his shirt and vest. What remains of them."

"We'd prefer to stay," Rabbit said.

"I don't think a young lady—"

"The young lady has seen worse," Sadie said. "And we might be able to help. I know a thing or two about the healing arts myself."

Dr Rumpole opened his mouth to argue, then took a closer look at Sadie and raised his eyebrows. He shrugged. "Well, I can't make you leave, but I should warn you—"

He abruptly stood and staggered from the room through a low arch. Benjamin stared after him, his eyes wide with panic. Sadie took his hand and squeezed it.

"Benjamin," she whispered. She touched his cheek and turned

his face to look at her. "Benjamin, has anything like this happened before? Here in Ascension?"

Benjamin concentrated. He cocked his head to the side and his expression softened as he focused on something other than his injuries.

"My family only comes here in the summer," he said. "But we hear about things. Henry Lockyear got his arm caught in the saw at the mill, and he bled to death. I knew him a little from the summer before, and it was a damn shock to find out he was gone. And the April before that, there was a boy who fell in the river and was swept away. He got caught between some logs downriver, and they had a funeral for him the day after we arrived in the village that year."

He seemed to realize he was comparing his own situation to that of two dead people and his eyes widened again. He tried to stand up, but Sadie put a hand on his shoulder.

"That wasn't quite what I meant," she said. "There won't be a funeral for you just yet."

"Which is strange," Rabbit said. "Considering."

"Rabbit," Sadie said. "You hush. Now, Benjamin, this morning you told us your mother has recovered from her long illness. Do you think—"

She cut her question short as Dr Rumpole returned to the room with a pair of shears. Sadie gave Benjamin's hand another squeeze, then she stood and let the doctor take her place on the sofa. Dr Rumpole was so intent on the mystery before him, he seemed to forget he had an audience. He cut Benjamin's vest off and plucked at the bloody edges of the boy's shirt. Benjamin pushed ineffectually at the doctor's arms and weakly protested, but Dr Rumpole didn't seem to hear him. He cut the remaining buttons off the boy's shirt, letting them fall from their loops and clatter away across the floor. Rabbit scooped them up and held them, while Dr Rumpole pulled Benjamin's bloody shirt open to expose his mangled torso. A flap of flesh hung loose over Benjamin's belly, and three of his ribs were displaced. Blood had pooled above the boy's belt and was already congealing.

"This can't be," Dr Rumpole said.

He rolled up his sleeves and pushed one of Benjamin's ribs back into place.

"Please don't," Benjamin said.

"Does it hurt?"

"No, but I don't like it. It feels damn unnatural."

"It *is* damn unnatural," Dr Rumpole said. He stood and rubbed his bloody hands over the stubble on his cheeks. "I don't know what to do. I honestly don't know whether to send him to the hospital in Boston or deliver him to the graveyard."

"The graveyard?" Benjamin struggled to stand up, but his knees gave out and he fell back onto the sofa.

"I told you, you're not going to the graveyard yet," Sadie said.

Rabbit raised a skeptical eyebrow, but Sadie ignored her.

"Doctor, you're frightening your patient," she said. "Clearly you need to set his bones, stitch him up, and find something for him to wear home."

Dr Rumpole nodded. "Of course," he said. "I ought to have something around here he can wear."

"Good. But first he needs to be cleaned up."

"Right, right. I'll heat up some water and fetch a cloth. No, I'll need more than a cloth, won't I?"

The doctor rushed out of the room again, and Sadie patted Benjamin's hand. "What's happened to you is peculiar," she said. "But this is by no means the most peculiar thing I've seen. Why don't you close your eyes and try to relax? Rabbit and I will stay with you until the doctor's finished his business and then we'll take you home."

Benjamin nodded and closed his eyes. A moment later he was softly snoring.

"He's asleep," Rabbit said. "How can he be asleep?"

"He's had a strange day," her mother said.

"You know as well as I do that he's dead."

"Yes, I think he is."

"Then . . ." Rabbit gestured at the boy. "How?"

"I don't know," Sadie said. "But isn't it exciting?"

W hen the doctor had stitched up his wounds and set his broken arm, Benjamin led Sadie and Rabbit up Brynwood Lane to his home, a place he referred to as "the summer cottage." It was twice the size of any cottage Sadie or Rabbit had ever seen, and took up the entire length of the block, all brick and quarried stone, with sash windows and a gabled roof. It was surrounded by a picket fence that exactly matched the one around the village green. The hedges and vines along the fence had been cut back for the winter, but Sadie could imagine them in full summer bloom, when they would obscure the courtyard from passersby. They followed Benjamin up a cobblestone path to the front door, and he ushered them inside.

They found Rose Nettles reclining on a divan in the parlor, chatting with another woman. When she saw them, the other woman jumped up and rushed across the room. She was pale, and thin, with hollow cheeks and dark smudges under her eyes. Her movements were clumsy, as if she had just learned to walk or was long out of practice. She was clearly the sort of woman who fussed over things, and now she fussed over Benjamin.

"Benji, look at your clothes!" Her voice started low, but rose two octaves in the span of those five words.

"I'm all right," Benjamin said.

"He met with a slight accident in the road," Sadie said.

"Slight?" Rabbit said.

Sadie ignored her. "Dr Rumpole recommended he get some rest."

"The doctor?" Clarissa held her son at arm's length and squinted up at him. "Tell me what happened?"

"I said I'm fine, Mother. I was on my way back from the train station and Mr Mulacky's old horse ran into me. I hardly even felt it."

"I don't understand," Clarissa said. "The train station? The milkman's horse? And you've been to the doctor?"

"I went to cable Father that you're out of bed," Benjamin said. "I thought he ought to know." There was something defiant in the way he said it. Clarissa let go of him, and Sadie watched a parade of emotions pass across her face. Sadie wondered if, by communicating with his father, Benjamin had acted against his mother's wishes.

In the sudden silence, a girl entered the room, stern and petite, wearing a starched white uniform. Her fair hair was pulled back in a chignon under a nurse's cap. She stood silently in the corner of the room.

Rose had been watching from the divan. Now she stood and approached her cousin. She touched Clarissa's elbow and smiled.

"This is my friend Sadie," she said. "I mentioned her to you. And this is her daughter, Rabbit."

"Where are my manners?" Clarissa said. "Thank you for bringing my son home." Her body language shifted as she made the transformation from concerned mother to dutiful hostess. "Alice, would you take Benji up to his room? The doctor seems to think he needs rest."

Benjamin opened his mouth to protest, then shook his head

and hurried up the staircase, taking the steps two at a time. Alice followed him upstairs at a more sedate pace.

"Please, come and sit," Clarissa said to Sadie. "Alice has just brought a tray."

Indeed, a huge platter of tiny sandwiches—as well as cakes and cookies, toast points, and little pots of butter, jam, and cream—dominated the long table before the hearth.

"Thank you, no," Sadie said, then realized that Rabbit had somehow already taken two sandwiches and was pouring cider from an icy pitcher into a tumbler balanced precariously at the edge of the table.

"Rabbit," she said.

Startled, Rabbit looked up, her cheeks full, her eyes wide.

"That's quite all right," Clarissa said. There was genuine warmth in her laugh. "Alice always makes too much, and who will eat it if you don't?"

Rabbit peeled the bread from one of the sandwiches, and popped a slice of cucumber into her already-full mouth.

"Rabbit," Clarissa said. "What a curious name."

Rabbit shrugged and smeared a toast point with jam.

"Is it her given name?"

"We Graces choose our own names," Sadie said.

"That's an interesting idea," Clarissa said. She sat and gestured for Sadie to take the chair opposite. "Rose and I have just been catching up, but I still know so little about you all. How did you come to purchase Bethany Hall? I can't imagine! I've always been curious about the place."

"Then I suppose you should come visit," Sadie said. She sat on the edge of the indicated chair. She wanted a quiet moment to ponder Benjamin's accident in the road, she wanted to tell Rose about it, and she wanted to consult her books for any mention of dead boys who continued to walk and talk. But she reminded herself that most of her books were still in Philadelphia and wouldn't arrive for several more days. There was little for her to do at the moment but make polite conversation with Rose's conventional cousin.

"I have to see the inside of that house," Clarissa said. "Is it haunted? It is, isn't it?"

"I think it must be," Rose said. She glanced at Rabbit, who was gulping cider, her eyes closed.

Clarissa followed Rose's gaze, and leaned forward. She spoke in a loud whisper.

"How old is Rabbit?"

"We don't know," Rose said. "I don't think Rabbit even knows."

"Fascinating," Clarissa said. "What interesting friends you have, Rose!"

Sadie settled deeper into her chair, while Rose explained how she had met Rabbit first, then the girl's mother. Rabbit brought Sadie a plate of toast points, sloppy with jam and butter, and another tall glass of cider, and Sadie looked around the room. She tried to imagine what Clarissa's life must be like, and could not. It struck her, as it occasionally did, how odd her little family must look from the outside. The good Graces and their faded Rose.

Sadie licked strawberry jam from her lips and patiently waited for the moment they could leave Clarissa's house and return to their home on the hill.

C larissa said goodbye to her guests, then rushed upstairs and knocked on Benjamin's bedroom door. She heard him shuffle across the floor, and the door swung open. He was wearing a heavy oversized robe that Clarissa recognized as her husband's. Benjamin's eyes were sunken and bloodshot.

"Tell me what happened to you," she said.

Benjamin considered, then stepped aside and made room for his mother to enter the room. He turned his back to her and stared out the window.

"It's nothing to worry about," he said.

"But I do worry." Clarissa sat down on the edge of her son's bed and hung her head. "It's been a very important day for me, and if I'd lost you . . . Today, of all days? It would be such an unfair trade."

Benjamin turned from the window and sighed, then crossed the room and sat next to his mother.

"I'm sorry," he said.

He opened the top of the robe and showed his mother the ugly wound. Dr Rumpole's crude stitch-work was punched across his chest in an angry red arc, but the skin surrounding the sutures was pale and smooth, like parchment.

"I keep feeling for my heartbeat," he said. "I can't find it."

Clarissa pursed her lips and nodded. "I can't feel mine, either."

"This is the strangest day of my whole life," he said. "I don't understand a damn thing that's happened."

"Maybe there are things we're not meant to understand," Clarissa said. She took his hand. "I didn't say goodbye to you when you left the house today," Clarissa said. "I don't think I even knew you were gone."

"I was only going up the road a bit."

"The most frightening thing I can think of is the death of my child, and I was so preoccupied with myself I never gave you a thought."

"Don't be ridiculous," Benjamin said. "You had every right to be distracted. You died before I did."

"Well, that's how it's supposed to work. At least I got that part right." She stood and ruffled her son's hair. "I shouldn't be here with you today, but I am, and that makes me happy. Now get dressed for dinner. We ought to celebrate tonight. Do you want to eat at the inn?"

Benjamin shrugged, but he stood and went to the tall wardrobe against the far wall.

Clarissa closed his door and crossed the hallway to her own room. It smelled musty, and she could detect the mingled odors of rubbing alcohol and menthol and stale sweat.

She began sorting through the dresses she had piled on her cedar chest. When Alice appeared at the door, Clarissa tossed a blue gown at her.

"Clean this yourself, Alice. There's no time to send it out."

She was worried about the content of the telegram Benjamin had sent, worried that she would be summoned back to the city, now that she wasn't an embarrassment. If only she could have let Richard go on believing she was at death's door. If she returned to him she would have to attend his dull faculty parties, smile and nod like the dutiful wife he expected her to be. She would have to pretend she didn't know about his mistress.

Their friends in the city were Richard's friends, their things in the city were his things, but in the village Clarissa had her own life; she had her son, and her cousin. She simply wasn't ready to give it up and go back to being Mrs Richard Sinclair.

After all, she thought, *one doesn't often get a second chance at life.*

Dr Timothy Rumpole slipped into the drugstore, covering the little bell above the door with his hand to stop its tinkling. His head throbbed and he hoped to avoid attention. But Prosper Knox noticed him and motioned him over to the counter where he was leaning over a piece of paper that had been folded and smoothed back out. Several of the village's young people were gathered around him. Dr Rumpole didn't ask what they were looking at, but Knox told him anyway.

"The new women, the ones in the house, they want some things sent over."

The doctor nodded, and Knox seemed to take this as encouragement.

"The trouble is, I don't know what half of these are," he said. "I told them I did, but . . ." He shrugged. "Maybe you can help me, Doctor."

A young lady—Dr Rumpole recognized her as the girl who had run away after bringing Benjamin Sinclair to his house—picked up the list and handed it to him as if he had won a prize. Dr Rumpole found his spectacles in a shirt pocket and held the paper up to the light.

"Well," he said, "dittany is fairly common."

"Of course," Knox said.

"Frankincense, too."

"Certainly."

Dr Rumpole lowered the list and glared at the pharmacist. *Why ask me to look the thing over,* he thought, *if you're going to pretend you already know everything?*

His irritation was lost on Knox, though, so the doctor squinted at the list again. It was a fascinating catalog of herbs and spices, some of which the doctor had read about in old books, but had never actually seen.

"Garlic, wormwood, and so on," he said. "Most of these things are easy enough to procure. But this," he pointed, mildly excited. "This is unknown to me."

"Which one?" Knox tried to look over his shoulder, but the doctor was half a head taller.

"Rose of Jericho," Dr Rumpole said. "I wonder what that's for. Really, taken as a whole I wonder what any of this is for."

A mousy young woman standing at the periphery of the group cleared her throat.

"I've heard of it," she said. "Rose of Jericho, I mean."

"Do tell, Daisy," the first girl said.

"My mother knows a few small spells and tonics, and she taught me some things," Daisy said. She seemed to shrink under the combined gaze of the doctor and the pharmacist, and cleared her throat again. "She calls that plant by its other name, though."

They waited a long moment before Dr Rumpole prompted her. "And?"

"She calls it the resurrection flower, because you can't kill it."

"Nonsense," Knox said.

"It's true," Daisy said. "She says it won't die."

"What does she use it for?" Dr Rumpole said.

"Healing," Daisy said. "I think most of the things on that list are for healing potions."

"Potions," Knox said. It was halfway between a question and a cough. "Spells and tonics."

A low murmur ran through the crowd, and Daisy took a step backward. Knox snatched the list from the doctor's hand.

"Well," he said. "We wondered what kind of person would choose to live in that cursed house."

"Did we?" Dr Rumpole said.

"And now we know," Knox said. "Rose of Jericho, indeed!"

There was an undercurrent of menace in his voice. Dr Rumpole backed away and instinctively grabbed the bell again before opening the door. As it closed behind him, he saw Knox grab the elbow of one of the young men. They leaned in close to speak, and Dr Rumpole decided he didn't like the look on Knox's face.

————

They were halfway up the hill, headed back to Bethany Hall, when Sadie finally spoke. "I'm glad your cousin's feeling better," she said.

"To hear Claire tell it, she was at death's door," Rose said. "But I wish she would talk to the doctor. It would set my mind at ease."

Rose was panting, clinging to the trees on the icy slope above the train station.

It struck Rabbit with surprising force that her aunt was growing older, while she and Sadie were not. Or, at least, she and Sadie were aging at a much slower pace than Rose was. In that instant Rabbit understood that she would one day be alone. It was an obvious thought, but it had never occurred to her before. Distracted, she tripped over a rock hidden under the snow. Embarrassed, she stood and brushed snow off her trousers, then bounded up the trail.

Sadie and Rose spoke in low tones behind her, thinking she couldn't hear, but Rabbit's hearing was very good. She forged ahead and rounded a bend in the path. Up ahead she saw the spirit of the old woman standing in the shadows of the trees. The woman beckoned to her and held out her golden locket, but Rabbit ignored her this time. She passed Gardener, who sat on a stone bench against the wall of the house, waiting for spring to come, waiting for the snow to melt, so he could begin his work.

Inside, Housekeeper waited with clean towels. Rabbit sat on a chair in the foyer and Housekeeper pulled off her boots, rubbing her bare feet with a towel until they turned pink.

Rabbit felt they should name their servants, and had told Sadie as much.

"Says the girl who still calls herself Rabbit," Sadie said, and Rabbit had dropped the subject.

She heard footsteps on the path, and jumped up, padding

quickly across the kitchen floor. She heard the door open behind her, and she scampered up the stairs to her bedroom, pausing to check on the happy dancers in the ballroom. As far as she could tell, there were no spirits in her room. It was why she had chosen it. The headless cat slipped through the door behind her and leapt up onto the windowsill. It sat, its black coat glossy in the sunlight. Rabbit wondered if it could see without eyes; she wondered if it could hear without ears, and if it was able to groom its midnight fur without a tongue.

If Rose died in the house, would she become a spirit, forced to wander the halls forever? Rabbit couldn't bear the thought. And how long would Sadie live? Another century? Two? Rabbit couldn't imagine going on without them, but she suddenly knew she would have to.

She was startled by a knock at the door. When she opened it, Sadie was standing in the hallway, her cheeks flush, her feet bare.

"Let's look at the attic," she said.

Rabbit shook her head.

"Who knows what's up there?" Sadie said.

"You're just hoping there's a sled so we can scare Rose."

"Yes. But I've also got a general sort of curiosity about it. I'm afraid of it, and I don't like to be afraid of things. You've seen how many spirits we have around here, right?"

"Of course." Rabbit wondered whether her mother could see the headless cat on her windowsill. Rabbit was better at spotting ghosts than Sadie was, and Rose couldn't see them at all.

As if she had read Rabbit's mind, Sadie grinned. "I see your cat there. Come on, the attic awaits."

"I don't like the feel of it."

"You can sense something up there, too?"

"I just don't like it."

"You know, we'll have to explore it eventually. But I can't imagine there's anything up there we can't deal with. Can you?"

"Fine," Rabbit said.

They padded barefoot down the third-floor corridor to the attic door. Sadie opened it and they stood back, studying the dark stairs. The landing at the top was hidden in shadows.

"Wouldn't Rose like to come with us?" Rabbit said, thinking there might be safety in numbers. Thinking Sadie might change her mind if Rose were afraid.

"Not this time," Sadie said.

Rabbit sighed. She put a foot on the bottommost step and took a deep breath. Now she was committed. She plucked a hair from her head, wrapped it around her index finger, and held it aloft. It flared, then settled into a bright glow that illuminated the stairwell.

"You don't even need to draw blood," Sadie said. "Show me how you do that."

"I don't know how I do it," Rabbit said. "I just do it."

"That's not helpful."

Sadie brushed past her and climbed the stairs, moving slowly, her hand trailing along the wall beside her. Rabbit followed, her glowing finger held high to illuminate the steps ahead. She looked back at the rectangle of light below them. The cat came to the bottom of the stairs and sat. It seemed small and distant. Rabbit couldn't tell if it was watching them. The cat was one of the few spirits that moved freely about the house; it was surely familiar with every room, including the attic.

Come with us, she thought. But it didn't move from the base of the stairs.

There was a small landing at the top of the steps, and another door. They hesitated there. Sadie turned and searched Rabbit's eyes.

"There's something terrible behind this door."

"I feel it, too," Rabbit said.

"It's something different. Not like anything I've felt before."

"It's very strange."

"Is this a bad idea?"

"Yes," Rabbit said. "I told you it was, but we're here now."

"In for a penny, I suppose."

Sadie reached out and turned the knob. She pushed the door open.

The spirit of a girl named Naomi Clapper rushed past them and disappeared. Despite herself, Rabbit let out a short yelp, then she took another deep breath and followed Sadie across the threshold.

The room is dark and still, and at first they do not see me. I have tried to keep them from the attic, but here they are. As they step inside, I rise from my desk and spread my wings.

They see me now. An invisible chorus sings something lovely and soft as I greet them. I am beautiful and I am terrible, and I realize my appearance is causing them pain. I adopt the guise of a human, allowing them to gaze upon me without consequence or fear.

"Be not afraid," I say. It is what we always say. It is not a suggestion; it is a command. Otherwise your fragile hearts would stop at the sight of us. Your flimsy organs would liquefy.

"Hello, Sadie," I say. "Hello, Rabbit. I am Alexander."

"You're not a spirit," says Rabbit. "What are you?"

"You know what I am."

"Why are you in our attic?" Sadie says.

It breaks my heart to answer her, but I do so, and this is the gist of what I say.

The first thing you must understand is this. My kind is legion. We are notional, but we are also actual. We do not interact with time in precisely the way that you do. The same can be said for knowledge, for morality, even for physical matter. There is one thing, however, that you and I have in common, and that is energy. Energy moves around everything, and through everything. It is carried from one place to another, in one form or another.

And life is the most vital form of energy.

You must also understand that every so often a remarkable person is motivated to perform an impossible task.

Moses Burke is just such a remarkable person.

To feel such anger and grief that one might wish a cessation of death across the entire world is both touching and understandable. But to make that wish a reality? To carry out such a feat is unthinkable. Most people, nearly all people, would be unable to even perceive the Angel of Death, much less interact with that creature in any tangible way.

And yet Moses Burke's love for Katie Foster was so all-encompassing that he was unable to avoid finding Death. His bullet, which ordinarily would have gone unnoticed by that humble Reaper, could not have failed to miss its mark. In short, he was fated to end Death that day.

And so he did.

As I say, this has happened from time to time in the past, and it is a cause for concern on every plane of existence. Energy is suddenly unable to move, and the idea of purpose begins to erode. Hopelessness and frustration set in. Eventually, hatred becomes more commonplace than love. After the first time this happened, measures were put in place, and there is now a plan we must follow.

A short while before Moses found Death, a Host was sent to ensure that one of two things will happen: there will be a return to order, or there will be an entrenchment of chaos. One thing or the other. Structure or entropy. One will prevail, but which will it be? Which should it be? It is a subject of ongoing discussion amongst my kind.

It is now Moses's responsibility to deliver the mantle of Death to a new functionary, a new Death, but it is unclear whether he will succeed or fail.

He is carrying a symbolic artifact, which he must pass on to our chosen replacement or there will be no death in the world forevermore.

If he succeeds, this transfer will happen in Ascension, and so I am waiting in this small and stuffy attic to prepare for their arrival. My brother and I hope for a return to order, but our counterparts are inclined toward chaos. It is a rare occasion for us in which there is no clear outcome.

When I have explained these things to the Graces, and have told them what will happen if Moses Burke succeeds in his mission, they ask many questions. They utter angry proclamations, and they promise to thwart my plans. I tolerate their questions and their anger, but the moment they leave my attic room I pluck the memory of our meeting from their minds.

Then I return to my desk and pick up my pen.

FIVE DAYS
REMAINING

Excerpted from the diary of Mrs Richard Sinclair.

Dear Diary,

I am alive! Or, if this is not life, I scarcely know what to call it. What a strange thing to put to paper, and yet there it is.

I believe Benjamin is experiencing a similar condition, and I do so wish he had been spared, but I am perversely grateful for this extra time with him.

I am curious to know whether we Sinclairs are unique or if there is something restorative about Ascension. I have snooped about in the village, looking for useful tidbits of gossip. This place doesn't seem quite as idyllic as I had always thought it to be! I'm told that Geoffrey Dawson's roof collapsed under the weight of snow and he was crushed. Recently, a black bear sniffed out deer blood in Andrew Pungen's icehouse and the bear was still there when he went out for a block of ice. Sally West fell from a horse and dashed her brains out on the path, and Warren Longberd's heart gave out as he was changing a carriage wheel.

All of these people were properly buried (in the case of poor Andrew Pungen, the burial was largely a symbolic gesture), and none of them has been sighted out and about. Why me, and not them? Why Benjamin?

There were rumors about something happening to the schoolteacher and the local doctor, but with a little digging I have determined that they simply ran off together. Of course, this left the village in a state of disarray as the council struggled to find adequate replacements for them, but it has worked to my benefit in that my dear Cousin Rose plans to stay here and take over the school! My good luck compounds daily!

Rose has become somewhat unconventional since I saw her last, but it seems ideal for her. I am of the mind that conventionality should be thrown out the window if it impinges on one's happiness. Our lives are too short for this constant cycle of pleasing our peers simply for the sake of pleasing them, as if our own wishes do not matter.

If I am alive, and I do seem to be, I am determined to actually live. I know all too well that this too shall pass.

As Moses crossed the border out of Kansas, the wind died down and the Appaloosa splashed across tributaries of snowmelt. The path ahead became choked with weeds, trees grew taller and thicker, and sometimes the trail disappeared altogether. Pie trotted easily along, her breath streaming from her nostrils and dissipating in the frosty air. Moses felt he could almost forget about the creature he had seen in the woods. Almost. He told himself he had seen a flock of eagles, or a species of owl he didn't recognize. Only some frantic bird of prey caught in the underbrush. He didn't believe it, but the idea was comforting.

The path wound through outcroppings of limestone where thin saplings jutted out at improbable angles. A hand-painted sign gave notice that Moses had entered Grundy County, Missouri.

"Hallooo!"

Pie bucked at the unexpected sound of a human voice, and Moses pulled her reins tight to keep from being thrown. He looked ahead and saw nothing, then adjusted his line of sight and noticed a pair of boots dangling in the narrow divide between two crumbling rock formations. He nudged the horse out alongside the trail and leaned forward to see past the rocks.

A man hung by a rope from the highest branch of a bare elm,

his hands tied behind his back, his feet swaying gently in the breeze. His neck was bent at a sharp angle so that his cheek rested against his left shoulder, and his face was black with swarming flies.

"Hallo!" the man called again, flies crawling over his lips. "Do I hear a horse down there?"

Moses dismounted and tethered the Appaloosa to a straggly pine. He drew his revolver and stepped cautiously forward, watching his footing on the loose pebbles.

"Now I hear footstamps," the man said. "Be you friend or foe, friend?"

"Looks to me like you already crossed paths with a foe or two," Moses said.

The man chuckled, which caused his body to jitter at the end of the rope. Flies buzzed up in a cloud around his head, then settled back down over his face like a caul. The noose was buried deep in the purple flesh of his throat. Moses swept his gaze up and down the trail and through the trees, then clambered up the outcropping. A quick survey of the land below betrayed no sign of movement. He slid back down and got his fishing knife from Pie's saddlebag.

"I'm gonna climb up there and cut you down, mister," he said.

"Who is that talking? I can't see too good on account of a blackbird ate up both my eyes."

"My name's Moses Burke, and I'm not your friend nor your foe. Just a passerby who doesn't mind climbing a tree to help a fellow."

"I'll make it worth your while," the man said. "I got cash money in my bag."

"I don't see a bag."

"Oh, well, it could be them men went and took my bag. That's what I'd do in a saturation such as this."

"Well, I wasn't cutting you down for a reward," Moses said.

"That works out fine then."

Moses clamped the knife between his teeth and grabbed a low branch. He swung himself up and got his balance, then scurried up the tree, moving easily from one branch to the next. He passed the hanged man and sat above him for a minute, catching his breath before shimmying out and away from the trunk with his arms and legs wrapped around the thick branch.

"You okay up there, friend?"

Moses grunted. He steadied himself and took the knife from his mouth. "Not the first time I cut a man out of a tree. Now hold still."

He sawed at the thick rope, noting with irritation that his old fishing knife had gone dull.

"How long this gonna take?" the man said.

"Long as it takes," Moses said. "You got somewhere to be?"

"I was thinking I might like to ride into Trenton and pay back the sonsabitches who done this to me. I think I can surprise them men. They strung me up a couple days ago, so they gotta be pretty sure I'm dead by now."

"That's a long time to hang," Moses agreed.

"Name's Frank, by the way. Frank Smiley, at your service. That is, I could be at your service once I'm on the ground, instead of up here where I'm only of much use to the flies and crows."

Frank chuckled and the rope jerked out of Moses's hand. He almost dropped the knife.

"What'd they hang you for, if you don't mind me asking?"

"Well, I wish you hadn't asked," Frank said. "Because it puts me in a pickle. I could lie to you and say I was innocent, but you sound like an educated man and you might not believe me."

"I probably wouldn't, now you said you'd be lying to me about it."

"I only said that because I already decided not to lie to you. Seems like you're cutting me down, one way or the other, so there's no sense getting you mistrustful of me. The plain truth of it is they pegged me for a thief."

Moses grunted again. He was halfway through the rope, but his knife seemed to be getting duller, and his arm was getting tired.

"The funny thing is, my worser crime was murder," Frank said. "I caught Johnny Farmer with three queens up his sleeve and I shot him dead on the spot. But his brother George come after me, so I selected to get out of town right then and there, with George fast on my heels. There's probably seven or eight of them Farmer boys, and if I shot George, too, they'd never stop coming after me. So I grabbed the first horse I seed, but that turned out to be more bad luck for me because that particular horse belonged to the sheriff of Grundy County. I suppose you can guess what he done about it, him and his deputies."

"You sure are a talker," Moses said. He had switched the knife to his other hand, but the rope seemed like it was getting thicker the longer he sawed at it.

"I do like to talk, that's true enough. I kept my mouth shut tight when them birds come for my eyes, so they wouldn't get my tongue, too."

Gravity finally began to work on the frayed rope, Frank's weight snapping strand after strand without much more prompting from Moses or his knife.

"Brace yourself for—" Moses said.

The final strands of the rope pulled apart and Frank plummeted to the ground. He landed with a loud *plonk* that drowned out the end of Moses's warning. Moses tossed the knife well clear of Frank, and clung to the branch under him for a long moment before beginning the trip back to the trunk and down.

It took him longer to descend than it had taken to climb the tree in the first place, but at last he dropped from its lowest branch. He leaned against the trunk and spent a moment enjoying the feel of the earth under his feet, then went looking for his knife.

"I coulda done with a bit more warning than that," Frank said. "Coulda broke my dang legs, falling like that. Lucky I don't think I did."

The knife had stuck itself in the roots of a soft pine behind Frank, and Moses pulled it free. He rolled Frank over and cut the bindings on his wrists, trying hard not to slice into the bloated flesh surrounding the ropes. Frank talked and talked, but Moses ignored him. When he had sawed through the last of the rope, he helped Frank to his feet, wiped the blade of his knife on his trousers, and walked back to the Appaloosa.

"You ain't saying much," Frank said. "Hope you don't think I ain't grateful, 'cause I sure am."

"My mama raised me to be of help whenever I could. That's all this is."

"I wished my mama had done the same," Frank said. "In case you're wondering, she didn't raise me in that way, but it don't make me a bad man. For instance, I can tell from your voice that you are a negro, sir, but I ain't had a single prejudiced thought about you yet. Course, part of that might be on account of you cutting me down from a tree."

"Think nothing of it."

Frank snorted and spat a wriggling mound of maggots into the brown grass beside the trail. "I ain't never been one to judge a man by the coloration of his skin."

"I feel the same," Moses said. "Your skin is purple, going on rotten."

"Yeah," Frank said. He massaged his wrists and scooped gunk

out of an eye socket. "I had some time to consider on things up there and, friend, I think I might be a dead man."

"I'd agree."

"So I been meaning to ask you something, being as I died and that must make you either an angel or a demon. See, I thought I'd wake up in Hell, but I don't think I never went to sleep in the first place. But if I am in Hell and you are a damn black demon, did you only cut me loose for a trick? You gonna start pokin' at me with a fork now, or lead me blind into a pit full of fire or sharp spiky things?"

"I'm just a man," Moses said. "And I'm gonna ride on down the road now."

"Well, you can't leave me here like this, sir."

"Why not?"

"You saved my life," Frank said. "The Chinese laundryman in Trenton would say you're responsible for me."

"Doesn't seem like I did save your life. You said yourself you're a dead man."

"But I'm talking to you, and that makes me at least partly alive. Or else I am in Hell, and you really are a demon, which would make you responsible for me either which way."

Moses shook his head, knowing Frank couldn't see the gesture, and mounted the old Appaloosa.

"Wait," Frank said.

Moses sighed.

"You go on up this trail, and you're gonna reach Trenton within half a day." Frank was trying to pull the rope off his neck, but it was deeply embedded. His fingernails dug black furrows into his flesh. "You might get there in less than that, come to think of it."

"Good," Moses said. "I could use a bath and a shave, maybe a bed for the night."

"Well, I guess them things would be pretty resplendent, if you was a white man." Frank shot a sly smile at a spot three feet left of Moses. "Folks in Trenton don't take kindly to negroes, such as yourself. You're likely to end up decorating a tree like I done."

"Thanks for the advice."

Pie snorted, impatient to get going, and Frank sensed he was losing his audience.

"Thing is, if you had yourself a grateful white man to grease the wheels for you, it might go different. Folks might think they was stepping on my toes if they interfered with my negro. You and me traveling together? Nobody'd bother to mess with us, I don't think."

Moses looked down at Frank. The horse thief—not to mention gambler and murderer—was filthy and bedraggled, and a few stubborn flies still skittered about his eye sockets. Moses's stomach turned. He wasn't sure anyone in Trenton would recognize Frank as a white man. Or any kind of man at all. Moses felt an iota of pity for Frank Smiley, which he knew was more than Frank would have felt for him, were their positions reversed. Assuming Frank was right about the people in Trenton, Moses figured he could leave the trail, travel north for a while, and avoid the town ahead. He could follow creeks and tributaries upstream until he eventually reached a place with good people who might give him a bed and a bath.

But Frank?

Moses could well imagine what would happen to Frank, stumbling around blind, waiting to be discovered by the very people who had already hanged him. It was possible they'd have no more luck killing him if they drew and quartered him, or set him on fire, or gutted him and fed him to their pigs. But the experience would surely be unpleasant.

Moses sighed.

"Frank, would you like to travel with me a ways?"

Frank grinned at the spot in the air where he thought Moses was. "Yes, I would," he said. "I would indeed like that, Moses Burke. But for the sake of appearances, let's say you're the one traveling with me."

Easter Sunday was just a few weeks away and despite the cold weather, the churchgoing women of Ascension were already parading their spring finery. Their best Sunday dresses were unfolded from cedar chests—pink and yellow, grass green and robin egg blue—starched and pressed. Brilliant white bonnets, and straw hats adorned with dried flowers and gauze, emerged from boxes on top shelves. Gloves were mended, and corsets were laced. The sun had not made a full appearance in days, but glancing around the church Clarissa counted five parasols on display. Such unseasonal attire might have been deemed scandalous in the city, but in the tiny village it was merely a diversion.

Next to her, Benjamin was mouthing the words to "In the Sweet By and By," and Clarissa raised the volume of her own voice to cover for his silence, to make up for lost time.

We shall sing on that beautiful shore
The melodious songs of the blest;
And our spirits shall sorrow no more-
Not a sigh for the blessing of rest.

Reverend Cotton read from Corinthians, and Clarissa only half-listened. Three pews ahead of them, Lucy Knox turned and gave Benjamin the slightest wave of her white-gloved fingers.

Benjamin smiled back at her before Lillian Knox hissed something in her ear and Lucy turned back around.

". . . opened the fourth seal," Reverend Cotton was saying, "and I heard the voice of the fourth living creature say, 'Come!' And I looked, and behold, a pale horse! And its rider's name was . . ."

Clarissa tuned him out again. Even at the best of times, she could barely stand to listen to him. The preacher read in a monotone, and he whistled when he spoke the letter *s*. She daydreamed through the rest of the reading and then through Reverend Cotton's sermon, which—when she listened to a bit of it—sounded suspiciously similar to one he had given the summer before.

When the collection basket was passed, she dropped in a coin, and caught the eye of Daisy Merrick, who frowned at her. Clarissa quickly found a second coin in her purse and tossed it into the basket before it was pulled away.

When she knelt at the altar to take communion her stomach turned, and she felt suddenly and violently ill. She rose quickly, before Reverend Cotton reached her with the plate of bread, and scurried back to her spot in the back pew. Benjamin had not followed her up to the altar, and when she returned he slid over to make room for her.

She closed her eyes and waited for her stomach to settle, while the reverend read the second lesson. ". . . he was buried, that he was raised on the third day in accordance with the Scriptures, and that he appeared to Cephas . . ." The sound of his voice made her stomach churn harder. ". . . to all the apostles. Last of all, as to one untimely born, he appeared also to me."

To whom? She wondered. *Who wrote this?*

She kept her mouth shut tight during the final hymn, afraid she might suddenly vomit into the next pew, down the back of Sergeant Winter's blue Sunday suit.

When peace, like a river, attendeth my way,
When sorrows like sea billows roll;
Whatever my lot, Thou hast taught me to say,
It is well, it is well with my soul.

And then it was over, and she sighed with relief. Her stomach settled as quickly and unexpectedly as it had begun to heave. She gathered her purse and her bible and followed Benjamin to the aisle.

Reverend Cotton was already standing outside the open doors of the church, shaking hands and imparting words of wisdom as his flock dispersed for the week. Clarissa got in line behind Jessica Hudson; Benjamin left her there and raced ahead to catch up with Lucy. The reverend was talking to Lucy's mother, Lillian, who offered Clarissa a nervous smile and hurried away without waiting to talk to her. Lillian still hadn't stopped by the cottage, though she surely knew by now that Clarissa was out of bed. Clarissa felt her cheeks flush with humiliation and rage. Then Jessica Hudson was walking away, and the good Reverend turned his attention to Clarissa.

"Mrs Sinclair," he said. "I noticed you and your son didn't take the bread and wine this morning."

"I'm afraid I wasn't feeling well," Clarissa said.

"Oh, I hope—"

"No, I'm fine. I think it was all the people. I forgot how crowded the church gets this time of year."

"You're not usually here this time of year. What a miracle it is to see you."

Yes, Clarissa thought. *Just not miraculous enough to mention it during the service.*

But she said: "It was a lovely sermon."

"Thank you," Reverend Cotton said. "I'd hoped to see the new people here today. I thought I might pay a call on them, invite them to worship next week. Isn't one of them your cousin? Perhaps you would accompany me up the hill and make introductions?"

He reached out to take her hand and Clarissa recoiled. Her stomach turned again, and she swallowed hard to keep from retching. Reverend Cotton frowned at her.

"Are you sure you're all right, Mrs Sinclair? You don't look well."

"I think I need to lie down," she said.

"I'll get one of the boys to escort you home."

"No, please, Benji's right over there. Thank you, Reverend."

"Well, let's plan to visit Bethany Hall when you feel well enough."

"I'll keep it in mind."

In her hurry to get away, she slipped on a patch of ice, but caught her balance before she fell. She waved to Benjamin, and he broke away from Lucy. Clarissa took his elbow and they hastened away from the church.

"You know, Benji," she said. "I think the weather's changing. What if we had a picnic next Sunday? You could bring Lucy Knox."

"We could go directly from church," he said.

"Let's go even earlier. Who says we have to attend church every Sunday? It's not as if anything about it ever changes."

A t the back of Knox Drugs was a small workroom with a counter where Prosper Knox ground herbs and spices, funneling them into glass vials from a wooden rack on the back wall. Prosper stood when he worked because his chair no longer fit under the counter due to a profusion of boxes and crates crammed full of pig-bristle toothbrushes, peppermint sticks, toy tops, jacks, and yo-yos. There were baskets of dried plants, bins of chocolate candies, and canvas bags stuffed with coffee beans. Prosper had often thought about expanding the shop, building out from the back wall, but closing the shop long enough to make it bigger was unthinkable. So the toys and sweets, the tinctures and syrups, the pills and powders, had all been shoved under the counter and piled in the corners of the tiny workroom until there was barely enough space for Prosper to move.

The least busy day of the week for Knox Drugs was Sunday. Most of the villagers spent the morning at church, and the rest of the day cooking and eating and napping. After church, there was always a handful of customers shopping for sodas and pumice stones, but young Charles was able to handle this scant business by himself.

It was Prosper's day off.

While the rest of the village lined up for bread and wine, Prosper was on his hands and knees in the drugstore workroom, digging through the boxes, bins, and baskets, looking for the key to a battered mahogany trunk he had dragged out from under the counter. The trunk was always locked, and whenever Charles or Lucy asked him about it Prosper feigned ignorance.

"Darned if I can remember what's in there," he would say. "I lost the key to that old thing forever ago, but I don't guess there's anything important in it."

And when they asked him why he didn't get rid of the trunk to make space, Prosper would shrug again and say: "I ought to get around to that."

He would say, "Yes, one of these days I'll do that." And he would mix a soda and hand it over with a smile, and change the subject.

He had lied about losing the key to that trunk more times than he could count, but now it had actually happened and he was frantic. The stove in the corner was cold, but Prosper was sweating.

At last he gave up. He opened the back door and went to the woodpile, and returned with his dull and rusty axe. Splinters flew as he hacked at the old trunk, aiming for the lock, but missing two times out of three and ripping up long wedges of wood. At last the hasp separated and fell away and Prosper dropped the axe. He pushed the loose chunks of wood back into place and lifted the lid.

Inside the stained and battered mahogany trunk were four leather cloaks, four wide-brimmed hats, four knives with ten-inch serrated blades, and four masks. Prosper was the official keeper of these tools.

Prosper's grandfather had carved the identical masks, crude replicas of an illustration he had seen in an old book. They were painted red and black, with stylized yellow fire around the wide eyeholes, forked tongues snaking out between thin lips, and two curling horns at the top of each mask. Long strands of hair were braided through holes that had been punched along the edges.

Prosper thought of his mask, along with the cloak and the hat, as his glorious raiment. He thought of his knife as a mighty sword. In the three generations since the masks were carved, fewer than forty people had seen them. Twenty-seven of those people were women accused of witchcraft. He had begun to suspect there were more women in the village who deserved to see them.

When he was satisfied that his righteous implements were clean and sharp and ready for use, Prosper began the work of putting everything away. He had just shoved the trunk back under the counter when he heard the bell over the front door tinkle.

Church had let out, and Prosper's private hour had come to an end.

Charles Bowden stuck his head into the room. "I didn't know you were coming in this morning, Mr Knox."

"I was just leaving," Prosper said.

"Sorting through that clutter? I was thinking if things aren't too busy today, I might start clearing it out."

"No," Prosper said. "Leave it for me."

"I only thought—"

"There are family heirlooms stored in here. Sentimental things, you understand? Something that's precious to me might look like junk to you."

"Oh, sure," Charles said. "I'll leave it then."

The bell tinkled again and Charles hurried from the room. He was not an especially curious young man. It was one of the things Prosper liked best about him.

B enjamin turned the wrong way and started up the road toward Vinegar Hill. Still shaken by her experience in church, Clarissa called after him, "Benji, aren't we going home?"

"I'll meet you there," Benjamin said. "I want to see if Father responded to my cable yet."

Clarissa hesitated, then followed her son, stepping carefully over patches of ice. It wouldn't do to fall and break an ankle. More bed rest was not on her agenda for the season. They trudged up Shiloh in silence, and Clarissa found herself dwelling on the telegram that might be waiting for them at the train station. Had Richard dropped everything and cabled ahead to say he was coming to the village? Or had he sent for her, so he could examine her for himself? The possibilities were not good.

The station was unlocked and unmanned, and had been for

several months, since the ancient stationmaster had retired. As usual, the council was slow to fill an empty position, and it had been left to a loose coalition of village boys to monitor incoming communications and train schedules.

Benjamin helped his mother up the steps and entered the station first, throwing open the shutters to let in some light. Dust motes swirled and swooped at them, and Clarissa waved her hands in front of her face to dispel them. A single yellow slip of paper lay on the empty desk—left there by whatever boy had visited last—and Benjamin picked it up. He read it and handed it to his mother.

BUSY HERE STOP PLEASE INFORM OF
FURTHER CHANGES IN SITUATION STOP

She read the two short sentences and handed the telegram back to her son.

She was a "situation" and her husband could not be bothered to see her. She felt anger and relief, and these conflicting emotions commingled uncomfortably. She had been left to die in Ascension. In a real sense the village was meant to be her grave. And yet she had also been left to forge a life without Richard's disapproval and indifference. She wanted him to care, of course, but she never wanted to see him. She had been granted half her wish. He was not coming to the village.

Clarissa took a deep breath and watched the excited dust motes dance. If she could only have half a wish, this was the best half. She stared out the window and saw her cousin coming down the steep trail from the house. She imagined Rose, full of toast and jam, and eggs and ham, heading off to the village shops without a care in the world, and Clarissa felt a pang of envy.

Benjamin took her hand and she almost pulled away from

him, startled by the sudden contact, but then she squeezed his fingers, allowing relief to finally win out over anger.

She was free.

T he nurse at No. 17 told Rose that the Sinclairs had gone to church. She was welcome to wait in the parlor, but Rose politely declined.

She walked back down Brynwood Lane and across the green, but the Sunday service had ended. The church stood silent and empty. Rose squinted up the street behind her, wondering how she and Clarissa had failed to cross paths.

On an impulse, she pulled open the heavy church door. She walked up the aisle, breathing in the scents of cedar and myrrh, and chose a pew in the middle of the nave. The seats at the front were for people who wanted to be noticed, she thought, while the pews at the back were for those in a hurry to leave, or those who did not want to be noticed at all. The middle seemed to her like the best place to be. She sat, studying the altar and the oaken cross above it, and the high ceiling with its exposed rafters.

Silence settled over her like a layer of dust, and she closed her eyes. She had begun to think that the move to the village was a mistake. Her concern for Clarissa, and her nostalgia for their childhood together, had brought her to Ascension, but Clarissa clearly didn't need help. Rose had made an impulsive leap, and had dragged her family along, and now she doubted her decision. She didn't belong in a little village in the dead of winter, far from museums and libraries and theaters. Rose wondered if it was too late to sell Bethany Hall back to the village and escape. She would be happy to go anywhere else in the world, as long as the good Graces went with her.

She opened her eyes when she heard a door open behind the

altar. Reverend Cotton entered the chancel with a broom and dustpan. He had changed into a threadbare cardigan and a pair of woolen slippers. When he saw Rose, he propped his broom against the choir box and fastened the top button of his sweater.

"You must be one of the new ones from the house on the hill," he bellowed, trotting down the aisle, the soles of his slippers scuffing along the floor, the forgotten dustpan swinging at the end of his arm. "Welcome! Welcome to Ascension!"

He stopped in the aisle beside her pew and stood smiling. Rose got the impression he might like to slide in beside her.

"How do you like our village?" he said.

"It seems nice," Rose said. "I'm afraid we haven't seen much of it yet."

"Yes, the weather's been terrible this year, but I think the worst of it's past us." He noticed he was still holding the dustpan and looked around for somewhere to set it down, then gave up and hid it behind his back.

"I was just talking with Clarissa Sinclair about you newcomers. She promised she'd introduce me."

"Well, she's missed her chance. I'm her cousin Rose."

"Then you're the new teacher. The schoolhouse is just on the other side of the churchyard, so we'll be neighbors. I'm happy to help with anything you might need over there."

"I'll remember that."

"You're from Philadelphia? I've been there. Twice. Really, any big city is catnip for me. I lived in New York for a few years, and between you and me I miss the shops and restaurants."

"I was just thinking the same thing!"

"Not that there aren't nice little shops here in the village, but the food?" He shook his head.

Rose laughed, and the reverend finally sat down at the end of the pew. He set the dustpan on his lap and fiddled with it, and rubbed his nose with the back of his hand before speaking again.

"Clarissa's recovery is marvelous, isn't it?" he said. "The congregation prayed for her."

"You think that's why she's better?"

Reverend Cotton gazed up at the stained glass windows that bookended the front of the nave. One depicted the angel Gabriel visiting Mary and Joseph, the scene tinted pink and blue and green, the angel on its knees before Mary, who seemed to want nothing to do with her unearthly visitor. The reverend watched the kaleidoscopic play of sunlight through the window as he spoke.

"I try to imagine how she must have felt in that moment. How impossible it must have seemed, and yet she accepted it. I can't say why your cousin regained her health, but I think it's possible that prayer played a part."

"I suppose anything's possible."

He looked at her now, his brow furrowed. "I'd planned to invite you and your friends to Sunday service next week."

"I'm afraid we're not really churchgoers." She wasn't sure Sadie had ever attended a church service and she was certain Rabbit hadn't.

"A shame," Reverend Cotton said. "I hope you'll change your mind. I don't often get the chance to talk to new people."

"Feel free to visit us at the house."

The reverend chuckled. "Your house has a reputation. I told your cousin I'd like to see Bethany Hall, but between you and me I was secretly pleased when she seemed resistant to the idea." His eyes went wide and he reached out toward her, then drew his hand back. "Not that I won't come if you need me."

"Need you?"

"Work to do." He stood back up and lifted the dustpan. "'Tis the season for mud and slush."

"Do you mind if I ask why you left the city?" Rose said. "Why did you come to this village?"

"I was sent here, of course."

Bless his heart.

R ose stood at the churchyard fence for a moment, scanning the low gray rows of gravestones and, beyond them, the slate roof of the schoolhouse. Rather than backtrack to the road and around, she let herself in by the gate and walked among the tombstones, reading the names. Closest to the church were the oldest plots, the stones tumbled down or worn so smooth that she couldn't make out the names carved into them. The bodies beneath those stones were surely gone now, bone and rot, nothing left to identify.

The churchyard was peaceful; a low fog rolled across the manicured grass. The ground was wet and spongy, and her boots sank into it. The sky above was a uniform gray, and Rose felt as if she were floating in a void with only the dead for company.

"What a morbid mood I'm in today," she said to the grave at her feet. The name on the stone appeared to be Redford Knox. "I will try not to mope so much, Mr Knox."

As she walked farther from the walls of the church, the tombstones became gradually less weathered and more legible. There were statues and decorations. Some of the dead had fresh flowers in tiny vases at the ends of their graves, evidence of attentive loved ones. Infants and the indigent had been given plain wooden markers.

At the farthest edge of the yard, she found two neglected rows of graves, side by side, identifiable only by jagged rectangles of brown weeds, distinct from the carefully tended grass around them.

She counted twenty graves in the first row, seven in the second.

"Seven and twenty blackbirds," she said. But she knew that wasn't right.

She stepped across the weeds and crouched next to what appeared to be the most recent grave. She laid her hand on the cold mud and whispered.

"Who were you? Why weren't you loved?"

There was an answering *thump*, muffled and distant, but clearly originating from beneath the soil and slush. Rose fell backward, caught herself on the palms of her hands, and stood up quickly.

She heard another *thump*.

She looked back at the church and saw Reverend Cotton at a window, watching her. He pulled his head back and disappeared into the shadows of the nave.

"It's a graveyard," Rose said. "Of course it's haunted." Her voice sounded strange to her, caught by the fog and smothered.

She wiped her hands on her skirt and walked quickly away from the church, through the far gate, toward the schoolhouse and its promise of reason and order.

An air of neglect hung over the room. The floorboards sagged, and the chimney in the corner had crumbled, tumbling bricks onto the last row of chairs. The stove was charred and rusted, and Rose suspected the schoolhouse would fill with smoke if she lit a fire. A piano sat under a tarp beside the stove. All she could see of it were tarnished pedals and the splintery legs of a bench.

A sign hung beside the door.

GOOD CHILDREN OBEY

"DISCIPLINE YOUR CHILDREN, AND THEY SHALL GIVE YOU PEACE."—PROVERBS 29:17

Boys and Girls Shall Not Play Together. One Lashing for Fraternization.

Boys Shall Not Fight. Five Lashings for Fighting.

Girls Are Demure. Seven Lashes for Bringing Attention in Dress or Manner.

Trees Are Not for Climbing. Eight Lashes for Climbing.

Children Are Polite. "Please, Thank You, Yes Sir, No Sir." Ten Lashes for Failure.

Children Are Studious. Ten Lashes for Speaking Out of Turn.

Children Are Truthful. Ten Lashes for Lies.

Children Will Follow Instruction. Twenty Lashes for Disobedience.

Rose read the sign three times before tearing it down and wadding it into a ball. She tossed the crumpled parchment into the cold stove. It bounced back out and rolled under a desk, and she left it there. The place needed a good sweeping, and she'd get to it later.

A map of America pinned to the opposite wall showed only thirty-three states, and Rose made a mental note to ask the council for an updated map that included all thirty-eight.

There were many simple improvements that would make the cramped space more welcoming to her future students. The single window, for instance, was only a hole in the wall sealed with waxed paper. She added a proper glass window to her mental list. A bricklayer ought to be able to fix the chimney before classes began, and maybe the stove, too. She wondered if Butler or Gardener could be taught to do it.

She picked up a textbook from a stack on the floor, and opened it to a random page:

> *Although there is little need for a girl to learn mathematics beyond simple addition and subtraction, both species of children should learn to read, so that a boy may further his own instruction throughout life, and so that a girl may entertain her husband of an evening by reading aloud to him from the Scriptures. A woman need not necessarily know about writing, as lists may be made up by her husband in the morning, to be filled later in the day once her chores are complete. In this way, a girl's mind may remain untroubled, and peace may be kept within the household.*

Rose closed the book and tossed it on the stack. New textbooks went on her mental list.

She pulled the tarp away from the piano, holding her breath against the dust, and was surprised to find a child's sled propped against it. It was plain, but in good shape, and she almost clapped with delight.

She left the schoolhouse, but stopped and turned when she was halfway down the path to the main road. The building seemed expectant, small and alone in the snowy field, its nearest neighbor a graveyard. In her mind, Rose could see it with a new coat of white paint, its missing shingles replaced. She saw children running and laughing through the field on a warm spring day.

She heard songs and recitations echoing from its open window, its open door. She smiled and nodded and filled her chest with bright cold air.

It was a small thing, but it was vital: she had a purpose.

Benjamin slumped low in his father's favorite armchair. His coat was buttoned to his chin and his hands were jammed in his pockets. He watched Alice dust the bookcase.

"Why do you do that?" he said.

Alice was lost in thought and it took her a moment to realize he was speaking to her.

"Am I doing something wrong?" she said.

"You're not my mother's maid, or her housekeeper. So why are you dusting the damn books? Why do you cook our meals and clean up after us? You're a nurse, aren't you? Shouldn't you be . . . I don't know, doing nurse things?"

"I'm trying to be useful," she said. "Your family doesn't have anyone else."

"Then we should get someone else. Surely we can afford a housekeeper."

"Your mother hasn't had the time to interview."

This was true, but it was also true that Alice was afraid a new housekeeper would take her place. Alice hoped that as long as she kept looking after the cottage, it might never occur to Clarissa to employ someone else.

"She's taking advantage of you," Benjamin said. "Or you're taking advantage of her. I haven't figured out which."

He stood up, knocking the chair back on its legs, and stormed from the room as if they had been arguing.

Alice decided to spend the rest of the day out of sight. And hopefully out of mind.

Prosper's dogs were slower and heavier than they had been the previous summer, but he supposed that was the natural order of things. A few months in a dog's life made a big difference and it had been too long since they'd had a chance to run.

He watched them barrel through the underbrush and plunge into the shadows of the trees, their tails whipping. He turned back for a moment, and studied the windows of Bethany Hall on the hill above, then stepped over a snowbank and followed the dogs into the dark woods.

In theory, he had come there to hunt, but his rifle still hung over his mantel back in the village. As far as he was concerned, the dogs were free to corner and kill whatever they liked; Prosper was only looking for solitude. The woods were a safe haven from the grind of the drugstore, the demands of his family; they were a place to be at peace.

He ignored the braying of the pack and followed an invisible path beneath the blanket of snow. He took long deliberate strides, his boots kicking up a miniature blizzard. The snow was thin on the ground beneath the trees, and Prosper made good time, leaving a trail behind him that he could easily follow back out. He passed a familiar copse of white oak, and his pace quickened, but when he broke through a thick stand of spruce his breath caught in his throat.

The cabin was gone.

Where it had stood, there was a charred husk, gray and defeated looking against the brilliant white of the clearing.

The roof had collapsed, and all that remained of the walls was a low stone corral, the wooden frame burned away. He circled the ruined structure and stepped over the threshold, what there was of it. A fallen roof beam had split the altar in half; the pit was filled with singed timber, shingles, and window glass. Snow had blown in and over and through the ruins. A single plank was all that remained of the back wall, a nail driven into the top of it. He ran the tip of his finger around the blackened nailhead.

Three generations of work had been destroyed overnight.

He stepped over the pit and walked out into the cold clean air. He whistled for the dogs and waited. He thought about summer nights at the cabin: the fire, the flesh, and the blood.

After a few minutes he grew impatient and went looking for the dogs.

Prosper found one of the spaniels, the one named Butch, in a sunny glade. The dog's ribs were broken and one of his hind legs was crushed, the splintered bone thrust through his hide. The dog looked up, and bloody foam dripped from his muzzle. He growled and tried to lunge at Prosper, but his broken leg twisted, bone grinding on bone, and he fell. Prosper backed toward the safety of the trees.

He stumbled over a protruding root, then turned and ran deeper into the woods, away from the thrashing of the dying dog.

He had traveled perhaps a hundred yards when he found the other dogs. For a disorienting moment he thought he was at Richard Sinclair's summer cottage, looking up at the big painting that dominated their parlor: a deer in the moonlight surrounded by a pack of wolves, the image frozen in time an instant before the wolves attacked. The remainder of Prosper's pack had cornered a stag. He glanced at Prosper, then back at the dogs, his black eyes round and fearful. The stag's rack was nearly as wide as his body was long.

Prosper whistled again. The dogs were not trained to attack;

they were supposed to hold their prey until Prosper arrived with his rifle, but they ignored him. The stag did not. At the sound of his whistle the stag reared back on his hind legs and snorted, his velvety blue-black nose quivering, his muscles gliding smoothly under his thick winter pelt.

The dogs seized their opportunity and rushed forward as one, their teeth tearing at the exposed underbelly. The stag crashed back down onto his forelegs, his sharp hooves tearing a chunk out of the Kerry Blue's shoulder. The dog yelped and fell. Blood splashed from the stag's abdomen, steaming as it hit the cold earth. He tried to run, but one of the Irish setters clamped its jaw around the stag's left haunch and his legs buckled.

The stag started to go down, but caught his balance and bucked forward. The other setter and the remaining spaniel were suddenly there, working at his throat, gnashing and grinding. A gout of blood spurted onto the sugary snow. The deer stumbled again, righted himself, and leapt forward.

Dragging all three dogs, he charged at Prosper, who turned and ran.

The stag's heavy body shook the ground as he gave chase. Prosper heard another dog yelp. He heard something thump against the trunk of a tree behind him. He didn't turn to look. He kept running until he couldn't breathe, and still he ran.

He ran until he reached the line where the forest met the edge of civilization, and grabbed a low branch, bringing himself to an abrupt halt. He held the branch, knowing he would fall if he let go. He heard nothing now except the sound of blood pounding in his temples.

When he felt he could stand on his own, he turned and peered behind him into the darkness. He whistled for the dogs yet again, terrified the stag would hear and come running, but nothing responded to his call.

At last he gave up and staggered away from the trees toward the steep slope of Vinegar Hill. He stood at the bottom of the hill for a long time, staring up at the old house.

Prosper thought about the ruined cabin in the woods behind him. He thought about the new women who had moved into Bethany Hall.

He was not a great believer in coincidence.

W hy do you think it is?" Frank Smiley said.
        "What's that?" Moses said. His hat was low over his face. He had been dozing, enjoying the warmth of the fire and the rhythmic popping of sparks.

"Why do you think I didn't die when they strung me up back there?"

"Who says you didn't. You told me once already that you're dead. Maybe you are."

"Then how is it I'm talking to you? Unless maybe you're dead, too."

"Hell if I know," Moses said.

They lapsed into companionable silence and Moses began to drift off again. Frank had washed himself in a stream, whooping as he splashed himself with cold water. He had rinsed out his empty eye sockets, and Moses had found an old handkerchief, which he used to blindfold Frank, wrapping it around the top of his head and knotting it at the back. Afterward, it was easier to look at the talkative horse thief, and Moses found he could tolerate Frank's company a little more easily.

Not a lot, but a little.

"I guess nobody's had a funeral for me," Frank said, after a while. "I guess there ain't a lot of folks who'd miss me if I'm gone."

"Probably not," Moses said.

"How about you? You got anybody who'd stand up and say something at your funeral? Maybe sing a song or two?"

Moses shook his head, then remembered Frank couldn't see the gesture. He pushed his hat back and looked at the sky. The full moon cast a pearly glow on the clouds above him.

"No, I don't guess there's anyone I'd want to talk at my funeral."

"That don't seem right."

"I had a wife."

"Was she pretty?"

A log shifted in the fire and a shower of orange sparks fizzed across the wet brown grass.

"Yeah, she was pretty."

"Well, shit, I'm never gonna see a pretty girl again," Frank said. He was quiet for a moment. "A pretty girl used to be my favorite thing to see, besides from maybe a royal flush. It's a damn shame to be blind, that's all."

"Just means every girl you meet now's as pretty as any other. Everybody's the same amount of pretty."

"That's a good way of thinking about it," Frank said. "It sure is dark without my eyes."

"I imagine so."

"Moses?"

"Yeah."

"I'd like to touch your face."

"No, thanks."

"But imagine how you'd feel if you didn't know what I looked like."

"That'd be a blessing, Frank."

"I like to know what a man looks like if I'm riding with him. I'm a very visible type person."

"You mean to say you're a *visual* person."

"That's right," Frank said. "Least I used to be."

"Well, I'm still not gonna let you feel my face. Go to sleep, Frank."

Frank kept talking, but Moses let the blind man's voice wash over him without paying attention to the words, and he drifted off, thinking about Katie Burke. He saw her standing outside on a summer day, with the sun shining on her bare shoulders, her hair trimmed close to her head, revealing her slender neck. She turned and saw him and smiled, and his knees went weak.

He woke thinking spiders were crawling on his face. He sat up fast, batting at his cheeks, and Frank scrambled away from him, tumbling into the fire and crawling out on the other side.

"Jesus, Moses! Jesus, you scared me! I didn't mean nothing, Moses! I swear I wasn't doin' nothing wrong to you, nor harming you or whatnot!"

Moses snatched his Colt from its holster and took aim.

"I have to shoot you now, Frank."

"You got a gun on me, Moses? Jesus, don't scare me like this! I didn't do nothing to you!"

Moses blinked and swallowed hard. The pistol was shaking in his hand and his finger tightened on the trigger, but he reminded himself that shooting the dead man would accomplish nothing. He'd be wasting a bullet he might need if he encountered the creature from the woods.

He took a deep breath and holstered the revolver.

"I guess I won't shoot you."

"Thank you, Moses. You sure did scare me, jumping up so sudden and pulling a gun on me. It's irresponsible, is what it is, pulling a gun on your traveling companion."

"What were you doing this side of the fire?"

"I told you, I wanted to see what you look like, that's all,"

Frank said. "I was just lookin' you over, but in my own way." He held up his hands and wiggled his fingers in the air.

"Well, I hope you got a good feel, 'cause you won't get a second chance. Get going now."

"You can't turn me away like that, Moses. It's cold out there and there's animals. For Christ's sake, Moses, I'm a blind man. You wouldn't kick a blind man outta your camp."

"You probably won't die again."

"Something could eat me, though. Eat me up and crap me out, and what if I'm still alive after that? You gotta think things through, Moses. You can't send a blind man out into the night and not think he could get ate up and crapped out by a wild animal."

"Should've thought of that yourself, you dead ugly bastard."

"Look who's talking," Frank said. He smacked the dirt next to his thigh and let out an earsplitting guffaw. "Calling me dead, and all this time you been hiding the truth."

"Get out of my camp, Frank."

"I can go or I can stay, but either way, you got to admit that you're every inch as dead as me."

"I don't know what you're talking about."

"But can't you see we're in the same boat together, Moses? Didn't you notice you got a big old hole goes right through your head and out the other side? I done poked my fingers through both sides and they touched in the middle."

FOUR DAYS
REMAINING

They broke camp and rode out the next morning as if nothing had happened. Moses wouldn't let Frank Smiley on the horse; he tethered the blind man to the saddle with thirty feet of rope.

The yellow dog trotted alongside them for an hour, then ranged ahead, circling back every mile or two to keep tabs on the men. Moses noticed that if he let Pie pick her own way, she would follow the path of the dog.

Frank kept up a steady stream of chatter behind him, but Moses tuned him out. In a pique of anger the previous night he would have driven Frank from the campsite, but now that they were traveling again he felt the circumstances were different.

Moses wasn't particularly surprised to discover he was dead—he hadn't felt alive since Katie's death—but he was curious about the fact that he and Frank Smiley—who was even deader than Moses, if there could be degrees of death—were both still moving and talking, and he experienced a panicky few minutes when it occurred to him that his wife might be trapped in her grave. He quickly banished the thought. He had killed Death five days after burying Katie.

He concluded that he and Frank were riding across the Missouri landscape only because Death could no longer command them to lay down and leave their bodies. There was a turning point in the mechanism of death, a before and an after. If everyone who had ever died rose up when Death took a powder, Moses figured the Earth would now be overcrowded with people. Whatever was happening, it made sense that it had started the moment a bullet creased the Grim Reaper brain.

As strange as this seemed, Moses was even more curious about his indifferent reaction to it all. Frank seemed equally unfazed by their current state, even going so far as to treat it like a joke. Maybe, Moses thought, death was only difficult for the living to accept. For the dead themselves, it was simply the way things were.

He wondered if his soul had moved on to some afterlife, if that part of him had joined Katie somewhere else, or if it was trapped in his body, a caged and frantic bird, beating its wings against the bars.

The sun was directly above them, and Moses had begun looking for a good place to stop, to let Frank and the horse rest, when the yellow dog burst from the underbrush forty yards to their north. A minute later Moses heard a gunshot, and a divot of sod exploded from the muddy plain between them and the dog.

"You shooting at something, Moses?" Frank said.

"Somebody's shooting at the dog." Moses unholstered his revolver and tried to pinpoint where the shot had come from.

Another gunshot echoed past the horizon. A shell whizzed between Pie's legs, nearly creasing her belly, and tore into the ground behind them. A third bullet hit Frank Smiley in the right arm and spun him around. He fell on his face, then rolled onto his back and hollered.

"If they're shooting at the dog, they're a lousy shot!"

"I guess they're shooting at us."

"You or me?"

"I'm not exactly known around here."

"Must be me, then."

Another bullet plonked into the mud beside Frank, and he hollered again.

"Quit shooting!" Moses waved his arms, hoping the gunman

in the thorny brown bushes wouldn't perceive his movements as a likely target. "We're just passing through!"

An answering voice came from closer than Moses expected, given the man's inability to hit anything more vital than Frank's right arm. "Frank Smiley killed my brother!"

Moses scowled down at Frank, who was rolling back and forth, frantically trying to bury himself in the mud.

"You'd be brother to Johnny Farmer, then?" Moses said.

"I'm his big brother Billy. I got to avenge Johnny, even if he did cheat at cards more than necessary!"

"Well, I didn't have anything to do with shooting your brother," Moses said. "So quit shooting at me."

"I wasn't aiming at you!"

"Far as I can tell you weren't aiming at much of anything. Come on out here, so we can talk."

"If I come out, you'll shoot me."

"I'm putting my gun away, see?" Moses holstered his Colt and held up both hands, looping the reins around his wrist. The sound of gunshots had frightened the old Appaloosa; she was snorting and pawing at the ground. "I'm not gonna shoot at you. Come on out now."

A minute passed, then another. Pie turned in a slow circle, and Moses swiveled his head to watch the underbrush. Frank had covered his legs and part of his torso with mud. He hissed up at Moses.

"Get ready to shoot him soon as you can see him. Them Farmer boys ain't nothing to mess about with."

"You hush, Frank."

The bushes rustled and a tall skinny boy stepped into the sunlight. He was holding a rifle down at his side, and he reached up to pull his floppy hat low over his eyes.

"Where'd Frank go? I seen him a minute ago."

"He's around here somewhere," Moses said. "Keep that rifle aimed down. I'm a pretty fast draw."

"I ain't got a quarrel with you, sir. Unless you're a friend of Frank's. I seen you got him tied up behind your horse. You ain't Bass Reeves, are you?"

Billy Farmer didn't look a day over sixteen, which meant Johnny Farmer must have been a child. Moses glanced down at Frank and shook his head.

"No, son, I'm not Bass Reeves, but I'm no friend of Frank Smiley, either. I am sorry about what happened to your family."

"Dammit," Frank said. "Whose side you on?"

"I heard that," Billy said. "Wait, I can see him there in the mud!" He raised his rifle.

"Leave it," Moses said. "I can't let you keep shooting Frank. It scares my horse."

"I'm sorry for your horse, but I'm afraid I do need to shoot him. If you got to arrest me after, I won't fight you, sir."

"I'm trying to tell you . . . Oh, hell, Frank, stand up and speak for yourself."

"No," Frank said.

"Tell you what, Billy, I'll let you shoot Frank one more time, if you promise to take careful aim."

"Why?" Billy said.

Frank said, "Hey!"

"It's hard to explain." Moses took off his hat. "Whatever happens here you're not gonna kill Frank Smiley, so you're going to have to let it go."

"Hey, mister, what's wrong with your head?"

Moses leaned forward so the boy had a better view of the bullet hole.

Billy Farmer dropped his rifle. He took a quick step backward, tripped over his own feet, and sat down hard.

"Dang, mister, I can see clear blue sky through your skull."

"Yeah." Moses sighed. "I imagine it's unsightly, but I haven't been near a mirror lately. The fact is, I guess I'm a dead man, and Frank Smiley's dead, too. You can't kill a man who's already dead, so you might as well go on home and tell your mama the deed's done and Frank's a goner."

Frank stood up and swiped at his muddy clothes, while Billy sat and stared, his mouth hanging open. He was breathing hard, and Moses worried the boy might pass out. Moses had grown used to Frank's appearance, but he could readily see how horrifying the dead horse thief must look to young Billy Farmer. Frank's throat was still puffy and discolored, and the long scratches he had made with his fingernails had turned black. The fresh bullet hole in his right arm oozed as if he were running low on blood.

Billy closed his eyes and his breathing slowed, and Moses relaxed, thinking the boy was pulling himself together. But in a flash, Billy pushed himself forward onto his hands and knees and scrambled for the rifle. He grabbed it and lost his balance again, bringing the rifle up as he fell.

His old battlefield instincts kicked in before Moses could think to stop himself. In one smooth motion, he pulled his pistol and fired. The round hit Billy in the chest just as the boy pulled off a shot in Frank's direction. Frank slammed backward, his arms trailing like streamers, and in the same moment Billy Farmer slumped sideways and lay still.

Moses dismounted and stroked the Appaloosa's nose, settling her.

"Sorry about that, girl."

He ignored Frank, who was crawling around in circles, and approached Billy. Brilliant crimson spurted from the boy's chest in a steadily decreasing arc, spreading across the ground beneath him. His right hand twitched once, and relaxed.

"Well, dammit anyway," Moses said.

He squatted beside the body and waited.

Your name's Alice, is that right?" Dr Rumpole said. "Would you mind staying?" He glanced at Clarissa and smiled, his skin crinkling at the corners of his eyes. "I'm sure Mrs Sinclair would appreciate a woman's company."

Clarissa tried to smile back at him, but she wasn't sure it showed on her face. She felt perfectly fine. She was certain she didn't need a doctor, but Alice had insisted.

"I really don't care either way, Alice," she said. "You can stay or you can go."

"I'll stay if the doctor thinks it would help."

Alice blinked at Dr Rumpole in a way that struck Clarissa as coquettish. He was polite, and Clarissa supposed he was handsome in a disheveled sort of way. He gave off a mild sharp odor that wasn't entirely unpleasant, and there was something about his distracted but kindly air that made her feel at ease, despite her irritation with the whole process.

She and Alice and Dr Rumpole had gathered in the sewing room at No. 17 because Clarissa wouldn't allow the doctor in her bedroom, and there was no other space in the house where Benjamin might not walk in on them. The sewing room had been neglected of late. Clarissa hadn't straightened it up before leaving Ascension the previous summer. She hadn't felt well even then.

Dr Rumpole set his bag on the floor behind the closed door, and picked up a bolt of shimmering green satin from the single high stool. He looked around for a place to set it, and Alice rushed forward to take it from him. Not seeing any space for it on the long table against the wall, she stood holding the bolt of fabric across her forearms.

The doctor gestured toward the stool and Clarissa sat. She closed her eyes and unbuttoned her collar.

"Oh, no, Mrs Sinclair. There's no need to disrobe. Let's make this quick, shall we?"

She could have hugged him.

Dr Rumpole knelt and rummaged through his bag, pulling out instruments and stacking them on the floor, until he found his stethoscope. It was a stiff two-pronged fork that resembled forceps, but with earplugs where the handles would be. Clarissa had seen this new model that hooked into both ears at once, but her husband, Richard, still used the kind that looked like a tube and was held to one of the doctor's ears at a time. She was impressed that Rumpole had adopted modern technology.

"If you would sit up as straight as you possibly can, Mrs Sinclair, and take deep, even breaths? There you go. I'm going to touch you with this instrument, but it's nothing invasive or frightening, I promise." He shook his head. "I'm sorry, I forgot you're a doctor's wife. You know perfectly well what this is."

"Earmuffs?" Clarissa said.

It was a weak attempt at a joke, but Dr Rumpole chuckled and Alice smiled.

"Indeed," the doctor said. "I'm going to keep my ears warm while you sit and think about whatever makes you feel most comfortable. This will be over before you count twenty."

He fastened the prong end of the instrument into his ears and leaned forward to rest the stiff arm of the stethoscope against Clarissa's chest. She had braced herself for the contact, but she still jumped.

"Huh," the doctor said to himself.

Clarissa stared at the top of his head. He had attempted to get his cowlick to lay flat by plastering it down with pomade. The result was a clump of hair that bobbed up and down over one of the stethoscope's massive earpieces as he moved about. He slid the instrument around and dug the end of it into her skin, as if trying to pry a heartbeat from her chest. Annoyed, Clarissa plucked a sewing needle from the pincushion on the table and, without giving it a moment's thought, jabbed it into Dr Rumpole's neck.

The doctor grunted and the stethoscope popped off his head. Alice dropped the bolt of green satin, which hit the floor with an alarming *thunk*. Clarissa panicked and stuck the needle back in the pincushion, as Alice rushed forward with a handkerchief. She hesitated before pressing the cloth against his throat, where a bright drop of blood had appeared.

"Something stung me," Dr Rumpole said. "Do you normally get insects so early in the year?"

"It's been a strange season," Clarissa said.

Alice stared at Clarissa. "It certainly has."

Rumpole dropped the stethoscope into his bag. "Well, I think we're done here, Mrs Sinclair."

"I'll show you out, Doctor," Alice said.

"I can manage, thank you."

He opened the sewing room door to leave, then turned and glared at the pincushion.

"A very strange season indeed," he said.

Rose struggled up Vinegar Hill, using thin trees along the path to pull herself forward. She had the abandoned sled tied to a rope slung over her shoulders, and every time it bounced over a rut behind her the rope dug into her chest. She knew she would have a nasty bruise the next morning, but it would be worth it, she thought, to see the smile on Rabbit's face.

But when she got to the top of the hill and pulled the sled into the kitchen, where Sadie and Rabbit were playing checkers, it was Sadie who jumped up and hugged her.

"This is perfect," she said.

"It was under a tarp in the schoolhouse," Rose said. "I suppose I should have tried to find its owner, but you mentioned wanting a sled, and I thought . . ."

"Yes," Sadie said, grinning. She sat back down and started pulling on her boots. "Let's take it out right now."

Rabbit shook her head. "We'll smash our brains out against a tree."

Rose rolled her eyes and smiled. "I know I worry too much."

"Nothing will happen to our brains," Sadie said.

"Anyway, it's cold out there," Rabbit said. "I like it here by the fire."

"The fire will be here when we get back, and we'll appreciate it even more. You should learn how to have fun. Come on!"

Rose laughed out loud. She rubbed her sore collarbone and followed Sadie to the door.

Rabbit sighed. She sat on the floor and reached for her boots. "Checkers is fun," she muttered. But the others were already outside.

Sadie stomped around at the edge of the slope, packing the snow to create a low ridge. She set the front end of the sled against the ridge to keep it from sliding down the hill on its own, then stepped back and put her arm around Rose. The sled was a simple thing—three long ash planks on a steel framework—but it had been well cared for. The metal parts were painted red, the wood was rubbed and polished, the runners oiled. There wasn't a trace of rust or rot.

"I actually am a little worried," Rose said. "What if Rabbit does hit a tree?"

Sadie brushed a wisp of hair behind Rose's ear and kissed her on the forehead.

"You never need to worry as long as I'm with you," she said. She yanked a strand of hair from Rose's head, and Rose yelped.

Sadie looked around and picked up a sycamore twig as long as her forearm and as big around as her thumb. She snapped it in two across her knee and laid the halves beside each other on the ground. She dragged the toe of her boot between them, then picked the sticks back up and wrapped the length of Rose's hair around them.

"Here," she said. She held the delicate bundle of wood and hair out to Rose. "Throw it."

"Throw it?"

"That way," Sadie pointed down the hill, toward the woods.

"I don't do this kind of thing. You do it."

"You're the one who's worried. So throw it."

Rose's shoulders hurt. Her chest hurt, too, and her eyes stung from the cold, but she drew her arm back and tossed the bundle as far as she could. It sailed over the edge, landed on the slope a few feet below them, and sank into the snow, leaving a long rectangular indentation.

"I'm sorry," she said. "It didn't go very far."

"It went far enough," Sadie said. "And it's pointed the right way. Good job."

The sticks moved under the snow, then began to slide. The sticks came apart, but the single strand of hair remained attached to them both, pulling the powdery snow smooth. Rose watched as a narrow trail formed down the face of the hill. Wherever it met a bush or a tree, the plants moved subtly aside, bending and bowing and making space. At the bottom of the hill a thick elm split down the middle when Rose's buried arrow reached it.

"I killed it," Rose said. "I killed a tree."

Sadie laughed. "We don't kill trees," she said. "We talk to them. They decide what they want to do. That tree will be two trees now. Twins. They'll be stronger together. And look at that path you've made, Rose."

There was indeed a smooth plane down the hill. When it reached the bottom, the sled would naturally coast to a stop in a circle of pines that Rose wasn't sure had been there before. She reached for Sadie's hand.

"Okay." Rabbit appeared between them. "How does this work?"

The drugstore appeared empty when Daisy Merrick entered and pushed the door closed against the wind. The bell above her head tinkled twice, and Prosper Knox materialized behind the counter, wiping his hands on his clean white apron.

"Daisy," he said. "What can I do for you today?"

"My mother sent me for some things."

"For her potions?" His smile reminded Daisy of a tiger's snarl.

"Oh, nothing like that," she said. "Normal things."

She handed him a dirty slip of paper covered with her mother's nearly illegible scrawl, and Prosper looked it over.

"This will take me a few minutes," he said. "A shipment of costume jewelry came in this morning. Why don't you take a look?"

Daisy spent ten pleasurable minutes dangling cut glass earrings against her un-pierced lobes, and holding out her wrist to admire a variety of copper bangles. When Prosper finally called her name, she swept the trinkets off her arm and jumped away from the display as if he had caught her stealing.

He had wrapped her mother's things in butcher paper.

"Will there be anything else today?" he said. "Would you like to take one or two of those bracelets home? They look pretty on you. Why don't you wear them for a week or two, settle up later if you decide to keep them?"

"Oh, I couldn't." It seemed to Daisy as if the drugstore had grown warmer. Very warm, in fact, and very quickly. A bead of sweat rolled down her spine.

"Tell me, Daisy," Prosper said. "When you and your mother meet Satan in the woods, what does he make you do?"

"I don't know what you mean, Mr Knox." She heard the tremor in her voice and spoke carefully, trying to appear matter-of-fact. "We're not like that. What I said about the potions, that's just old-country recipes. Tonics and such."

She deeply regretted having said anything at all. She recalled rumors from three summers before about a pair of women traveling alone through the region, claiming to be able to ease common health complaints, improve sleep, and aid in childbirth. Those women had vanished from the inn overnight.

"Do you rut with him in the grass? Do you take his forked member inside you and bay at the moon like a dog?"

"Mr Knox!"

"You seem upset, my dear," he said. "Did I say something?"

"My mother's expecting me." She took a step backward as he came around the end of the counter.

"Wait," he said.

She felt another bead of sweat form under her collarbone and slide between her breasts. She darted a glance at the door. Five steps away, maybe six.

Prosper scooped her order off the counter and held the bundle out to her. "You're forgetting this."

When she took it from him his fingers brushed against the back of her hand. "Daisy, I think you misunderstood me. You're a good friend of Lucy's, and I'd never say anything to hurt your feelings. Let me make it up to you, would you?"

"Good day, Mr Knox."

"We could take a walk together. The woods are lovely in the—"

The door swung shut and cut off the end of his sentence. Daisy clutched her mother's parcel to her chest and sprinted down the road toward home.

When the knocker clacked against the door Rabbit jumped, then ran to look through the Judas hole. Rose set her knitting aside and stood, blocking the way of Housekeeper, who had hastened to answer the door.

"It's your cousin's nurse," Rabbit said. "There's a carriage out there." To Housekeeper she said: "Tell Cook to bring cucumber sandwiches and lemonade."

"We don't have cucumbers," Rose said. "Nor do we have lemons."

"Why not?"

"It's winter," Rose said.

"Then where did your cousin get them?"

"They're wealthy," Sadie said, unfolding herself from the divan and stretching her arms. "They can get things."

"We can get things," Rabbit said. She had thought they were wealthy. They had, after all, bought a house.

"Our methods are different," Sadie said. "And don't you think we should keep our staff out of sight?"

"They do a passable job of being people," Rabbit said.

"Your experience with people is limited," Rose said. "The villagers are already curious about us. If they meet our staff, they might become more than curious."

"Pitchforks and torches," Sadie said.

"Fine," Rabbit said. "But I think we ought to get cucumbers."

She took Housekeeper by the hand and led her to the kitchen where Cook was peeling potatoes. Butler followed them.

She told the three servants to wait in the kitchen, and ran back through the house to the foyer in time to see Rose invite Alice Anders inside. The nurse was carrying a heavy basket and Rose took one of the handles to ease the weight of it.

"The missus is waiting in the carriage with Benjamin," Alice said. "I'm to lay out a proper tea."

Rose scowled. "We're perfectly capable of laying out a tea service," she said.

"Of course, ma'am. It's only, we've arrived a bit unexpected this morning. We had only a vague invitation to your home, and Mrs Sinclair don't like to be a burden." She lowered her voice, as if Clarissa might hear her from the carriage. "She's been sick a long time, and nobody came around in most of that time. I think she'd like it if she could do things for herself, and for others, and to be appreciated for it."

Rose sighed and hefted her end of the basket higher. "Let's see what you've got in here," she said.

"The kitchen's very busy," Rabbit said.

"Ah," Rose said. "Of course. Then let's lay this out in the parlor, shall we?"

Alice followed Rose to the parlor, and Rabbit tagged along. They set the basket on a long low table that had come with the house—solid oak, inlaid with marble slabs, an invisible burning man writhing under it—and opened the top. Inside, there were wheels of cheese, and jars of olives, and pots of jam. There were carrots and turnips, a head of cauliflower, and a bunch of watercress. There was a tiny loaf of crusty bread, and there were two cucumbers, green and nubbly, already sweating in the warm room.

"Where do you get those?" Rabbit said, pointing.

"There's a lady in the village with a house of glass, where she grows things all year round," Alice said. She smiled at the girl. "The missus remembered you like these."

"It's kind of her to think of our Rabbit," Sadie said.

"I should peel and cut these, ma'am," Alice said. "And I should make tea for the missus, too, if you'd show me to the kitchen."

"Rabbit," Rose said. "Please have Butler take Housekeeper and Cook to the stables to visit with Coachman." To Alice she said, "They get so little time to socialize, but if you're here to take care of things . . . Goodness, my cousin must be freezing out there in the carriage. Let's bring her in, why don't we? The cucumbers can wait."

Alice raised her hands, as if she were about to object, but Rose marched out to the foyer, and motioned for the nurse to follow. Rabbit closed the door after them and ran to the kitchen.

I want to throw a party for you," Clarissa said. "It would be such a wonderful way to introduce you to the community."

Rabbit nibbled at a piece of cauliflower. "I don't know if I like parties," she said.

Benjamin was sitting by the hearth, far from the plates of food. He grinned at Rabbit. "I wouldn't expect much from an Ascension party."

Clarissa hushed him with a look. She was holding a cup of tea she hadn't touched.

"I perfectly understand," she said to Rabbit. "And I know this will sound selfish, but everyone gave me up for dead long ago, and I want to show them I'm still . . . Well, I need to *do* something. I haven't *done* anything in forever, and I want the villagers to see me again."

Rose crunched on a carrot. "What sort of party would this be?" she said.

"Something small," Clarissa said. "Something modest, something completely tasteful. It will be perfect, I promise."

"I understand why you need a party," Sadie said. "But why do we need a party?"

"Well, dear," Clarissa said. "Wouldn't it be good to have everyone turn out to meet you? Benji, you remember the party I threw for Lucy's coming out. Wasn't it fun?"

"Oh, please, Mother." Benjamin stood up too quickly and cracked his head against the mantel. It sounded like a gunshot and Sadie was on her feet immediately, ready to help. The boy appeared not to notice or care. "They don't want your silly party," he said. "This is embarrassing." He strode past Sadie without a glance, and went out through the foyer.

Clarissa got to her feet and looked around at Sadie, Rose, and Rabbit, her eyes darting and unfocused.

"I'm sorry," she said. "He doesn't mean to be . . . He misses his father and his friends, that's all."

"Sit," Sadie said. "He can wait in the carriage." She settled at one end of the sofa and patted the cushion beside her. Clarissa sat back down and Sadie took her hand. She slipped her index finger along Clarissa's wrist and raised an eyebrow as if she had just confirmed something for herself.

"Do you really think we need a party?"

Clarissa's eyes lit up. She pulled her hand free and patted Sadie's knee. "Yes," she said. "You do! I really think you do!"

"Well, if you say it's a good idea," Rose said.

"Rabbit?" Sadie said.

Rabbit was holding a jar of jam and a spoon. "Would there be cucumber sandwiches?" she said.

"All you can eat," Clarissa said.

"Then I guess a party would be all right."

————

The back room of the drugstore was a mess, and Lucy set to work tidying it. She could feel her father's eyes on her, could hear Prosper's boot tapping against the baseboard as he waited for her response.

"We need to clean up in here," Lucy said.

Prosper said, "Did you hear me?"

She picked up a rusty hatchet and ran her thumb lightly over its dull blade.

"We keep this by the woodpile," she said at last. "Did you bring it inside?"

"I'm serious about this," Prosper said, "You can't ignore me."

Lucy set the hatchet on a crate of lye soap and turned to face him.

"What do you expect me to say? I don't love Charles and I won't marry him."

"Be sensible," he said.

"I have a right to marry who I please."

"And I suppose you would choose Benjamin Sinclair."

"It doesn't matter who I would choose."

"Don't mistake this for a discussion," Prosper said. "Charles is an excellent worker, and he is respectful, which is more than I can say for you at this moment. I've decided the store will be his someday, and the best way to ensure that is to marry you to him."

Lucy absently picked up the hatchet again. She turned the handle and scraped the blade with her thumbnail.

"I am not a promise for you to make," she said. "Charles is stupid and boring."

"I find him interesting enough. He knows a lot of good jokes."

"Of course," Lucy said. "I want my husband to know all the best jokes. It's always been my dream."

"You have become willful."

"I'm not a child anymore," Lucy said. She laid the head of the hatchet in her hand, comforted by its cool weight. "I know what I want, and I want something more interesting than Charles."

Prosper raised a finger and wagged it. "You are not so old now that you've outgrown the strap," he said.

"You can use the strap if you want, but a beating won't change my mind."

Prosper threw his hands in the air. "He's not even a villager," he said. "Benjamin has filled your head with outside ideas and turned you against me!"

"Don't blame him," Lucy said.

"I've decided this. My father decided for me; your mother's father decided for her. It's the way things are done, and I'm sorry if you don't like it. I really am. I love you dearly, but I am more experienced than you are, and I have a family to consider. Over time you will grow to understand and appreciate my decision. You may even thank me. Now, go clean the soda fountain. Syrup's dried in the spigot."

Lucy stared at the floor, biting her bottom lip, her brow creased in thought.

"Go!" Prosper waved his arm as if throwing an invisible ball at her head, and Lucy flinched. The blade of the hatchet bit into her flesh. She gasped and thrust her bleeding hand into her apron pocket before sidling past her father and out of the room.

He waited a moment, collecting himself, and muttered a small prayer before following his daughter out of the workshop.

"Thank you, Lord, for testing me with a daughter."

———

The good Graces had not moved to Ascension to take the air or to socialize. They had no intention of hosting dinners at Bethany Hall, or throwing lavish parties. As a result, the servants had little to do from day to day, except attend to the immediate needs of their mistresses.

Since arriving, Gardener had sat on a stone bench at the side of the house, shielded by a hedgerow from casual observers, there to wait for spring. Coachman remained out of sight in the stable, caring for the horses. Only Housekeeper and Cook were kept busy in the house.

On a whim, Rabbit had decided Butler and Housekeeper were a married couple. As a consequence, Butler seemed to feel he was obliged to keep Housekeeper company as she went about her work, which often led to his being underfoot.

Rabbit found this amusing, but she noticed that the ghost butler they'd inherited with the house was restless. He cycled through the duties he had presumably performed in life, and seemed annoyed by his counterpart.

Rabbit had some experience with ghosts, and she knew they existed at different levels of perception. Many of them were unaware of their surroundings and unable to recognize anything outside their routines, while others were able to see and hear the living. Some spirits could even interact in limited ways with the people around them. The ghost butler had noticed her on the day of her arrival in Bethany Hall, which made him the kind of spirit she liked best. The kind she could talk to, even if he couldn't talk back.

This afternoon, she took Butler's elbow and walked him to the kitchen. He quietly objected to being separated from his wife, but the servants had little willpower of their own, and he quickly gave in, allowing himself to be steered toward the pantry where the ghost butler was making an inventory of the stewed vegetables.

"I don't know your name," she said to the ghost butler. "So I've decided to call you Joe, because I think that's a good name for a spirit."

The ghost butler paused in his count of the canned beets and turned to her with a scowl.

"Joe, this is our butler," Rabbit said. "We call him Butler. He doesn't have a better name because we haven't named them yet. Sadie says we'll probably leave them all in the woods to rot when we move away."

The ghost butler folded his arms and regarded Butler with renewed interest.

"I thought the two of you should to try to get along while we're here," Rabbit said. "Butler means well. As much as he can mean anything. He just wants to do a good job, and right now his only job is pestering Housekeeper, so that's what he's doing. He doesn't mean to bother you. He probably can't even see you. Anyway, please be patient with him, and with the rest of us, too. Rose's cousin is healthy again, and this place is pretty dull, Joe, so I imagine we'll be moving away soon."

A stray thought caused Rabbit to frown. Someone had told her they couldn't leave Bethany Hall yet, but she couldn't remember why. It had something to do with the attic, but she was sure she hadn't gone up to the attic. She was trying to pinpoint where this contradictory notion had come from when the ghost butler spoke.

"Please don't call me Joe," he said. "It's not my name."

Rabbit let go of Butler's elbow and backed out of the pantry. Spirits were usually trapped in a limbo state, slightly out of step with everyone else, as if they were stuck in time just moments ahead or behind the living. They were speechless; they flickered in and out of sight, and could not wander far from wherever their bodies were buried.

As soon as she lost her grip on him, Butler hurried away to find Housekeeper.

"Perhaps you could call me Bell," the ghost butler said.

"I'm sorry, Mr Bell," Rabbit said. "I've never heard a spirit talk before."

"Is that so? Have you ever tried to talk to one?"

"I can't remember."

"You should be aware you do not have enough stewed tomatoes on hand to last the rest of this winter. In late summer, provided you have not already left her to rot in the woods, you might think to have your kitchen creature jar twice as many tomatoes as did the previous tenant of this house."

"The previous tenants?" Rabbit said. "Did you work for them? Are they still here? Are they spirits, too?"

Bell smiled. He stared up at the ceiling for a moment, then back down at her. "No," he said. "No, I have never worked for anyone here."

"But you must have died here."

"Is that so?"

Rabbit decided to try a different approach. "Do you know any of the other spirits here?"

"I haven't bothered to interact with them," Bell said. "I imagine they're terribly dull."

Which meant he had never danced with the ghosts in the ballroom or joked with the guests at the endless dinner party. He counted jars of tomatoes and polished silverware with a cloth that could never disturb the dust.

"You must be lonely," Rabbit said.

Bell's smile didn't touch his eyes. "My dear, you have no idea."

The village flower shop was located beside the pottery shed on the north side of the green. Behind the shop was an enormous greenhouse, built in 1849 at great expense by the writer Nathaniel Fielding for his young wife Flora. Fielding had brought his bride to Ascension soon after the failure of the Brook Farm, hoping the quiet village would prove beneficial to his writing routine. Flora Fielding, eighteen at the time she arrived in Ascension, loved flowers above all else, and Nathaniel, forty-three years old and wildly in love with his wife, was determined to make her happy. He surprised Flora with plans for the greenhouse on the first anniversary of their marriage, and hired ironworkers and carpenters from the surrounding counties. He was stung by a bee the week after construction was completed, and died soon thereafter. Flora burned his final unfinished manuscript and turned the first floor of their home into a flower shop.

When Clarissa opened the door of Flora's Petals, she was nearly overwhelmed, as she always was, by the smell of the place. The air was thick and humid, despite the cold outside. Clarissa turned in a slow circle at the doorway and looked around. There were delphiniums, sweet peas, bunches of lilac, and carnations. Masses of carnations. Clarissa felt her foul mood lift, the stress of the day floating free.

She breathed deep and sighed.

Flora Fielding appeared above her on the staircase that led to her private rooms. George Herman, the butcher, peered over Flora's shoulder, waved to Clarissa, then retreated.

Flora, her eyesight poor, leaned far out over the top step, clinging to the banister with both hands, and shouted down: "Is that you, Lucy, dear?"

"It's Clarissa Sinclair."

"Oh!" Flora hurried down the stairs and flung her arms wide. She gathered Clarissa up in an embrace and held her for a long minute. She smelled like lavender and rose and potting soil.

Flora eventually let go and held Clarissa at arms length, examining her. Clarissa smiled, but she was certain she looked wan

and pale. Flora, on the other hand, looked like the human per-
sonification of a blueberry pie. She was dressed head to toe in
purple, but her misbuttoned blouse was streaked with mud, and
there were tiny green leaves stuck in her hair. She was older now
than her husband had been when he died, but she had never re-
married.

"I was so happy when I heard you were feeling better," Flora
said. "But you look as if you haven't eaten in years. Did you get
the vegetables I sent?"

"They were delicious, Flora." Clarissa hadn't even tasted them,
but the memory of Rabbit Grace munching on cucumber sandwiches brought a smile to her face. "Flora, I'm planning a party
and I need flowers. Lots of flowers, and I'm afraid I'm in a terrible
hurry."

Flora tapped her chin with a dirty fingernail and glanced toward the back of the house. "It's been a harsh winter, but a few
varietals have done well. I have the prettiest pink camellias; I
have rhododendrons and lilacs, and the calla lilies and daffodils
are thriving! Tell me what you need."

"Flora, I need it all. I need everything you have. I want this to
be the best party anyone in Ascension has ever seen!"

She had a sudden terrible feeling that this would be her last
party, but she shook it off and smiled. She had spent months
thinking there would be no more parties. To have even one was
a blessing.

Sadie was in the woods.

She found the sunlit glade, where a fresh dusting of
snow had filled her tracks. At the center of the clearing,
her seed had sprouted through the snowcover and become a sapling overnight. She circled it and looked all around her at the tall

trees. The sycamores had lost some of their bark and branches, as sycamores will do in a high wind. She gathered thin twigs and strips of bark, and wove a nest, which she placed on a high branch of her sapling.

She patted damp leaves into the bowl she had formed, then threw her head back and roared. She spat at the ground and stepped away.

She sat with her back against a thick old elm and waited. It was hard to wait, but she did it. She put a hand against the elm's rough bark, and she thought about the rings at the tree's center, that natural record of its seasons in the wood. Her new little tree, the oakling at the center of the glade, would never form rings. It would mature too quickly to keep an account of its growth. It would never be troubled by termites or grubs or woodpeckers. It belonged to Sadie, and the creatures of the wood would keep their distance unless she invited them.

She had grown similar trees before: another oak near her cottage in Burden County, a hawthorn tree in the courtyard of her Philadelphia home. Squirrels had nested in them, as well as sparrows, finches, and crows, too, because she preferred them to other birds. They had brought her gifts and knowledge, and in exchange she had given them shelter and food. She wondered what had happened to the hawthorn in her absence. She thought about the home she had shared with Rose and Rabbit in Philadelphia, and she hoped they would return to it someday soon, but lately she was troubled by the notion that someone was coming to Ascension. Someone was coming and she needed to stay at Bethany Hall until they arrived.

After some time, a crow approached from the north. She circled overhead, spotted Sadie in the glade below, and flew away. An hour later the same crow returned carrying something shiny in her beak. She circled again and landed on a branch of the elm above Sadie. Sadie watched her. The crow set her prize down, then hopped out to the end of the branch and cawed, but Sadie was quiet. It would be bad magic to compel the bird. She had made a nest, and that would have to suffice.

The crow took a moment to preen, picking at the glossy feathers under her wing, then hopped back toward the trunk, picked up the object she had brought, and dropped it at Sadie's feet. Sadie fished it out of the snow. It was a small key, with a distinctive curlicue design on its iron handle. She dried it on her scarf and put it in the pocket of her bearskin coat.

Satisfied that a fair trade had been made, the crow flew from the elm to the slender sapling and examined the nest Sadie had made. Sadie turned and walked away from the glade. She didn't look back to see whether the crow had accepted the nest. She had accepted the key.

Rabbit met her when she was halfway to the house, the steep slope becoming gradual, the snow thinner, but the walk harder. Rabbit's eyes darted around the hillside.

"I was thinking of going down to the village again," she said. "What are you doing in the woods?"

"Making new friends," Sadie said. "Come with me tomorrow and I'll show you."

Rabbit stared past Sadie at the tracks she had made in the snow. "Why are we here?" she said. "I mean why can't we go back home?"

Sadie glanced up at the attic windows of Bethany Hall, barely visible above the curve of the slope. "Something is going to happen and we needed to be here when it does."

"I have the same feeling, but I don't understand it," Rabbit said. "I'm worried."

"So am I," Sadie said. "But I think whatever's coming will follow us, no matter where we go. This is as good a place as any."

She put her hand on the back of Rabbit's head, and they walked up Vinegar Hill together.

The dead stag nosed under the snow until he found a clump of tender green grass. He sniffed, but didn't eat. Nearby, the springer spaniel named Butch dragged himself in a slow spiral, growling at the trees, his broken ribs grinding, his shattered leg plowing a shallow trench behind him.

At the edge of the clearing, two squirrels burst from the underbrush, one chasing the other in an erratic zigzag. The dog lunged at the squirrels and collapsed, slamming his cold dry nose against the ground. The squirrels chittered angrily at him and bounded up a tree trunk, scurrying round and round, watching the helpless dog struggle to catch them.

Almost casually, the stag raised his head and leapt forward, trailing a rope of intestines. With the jagged tip of one antler, he gored a squirrel, pinning it to the tree. The squirrel squealed and squirmed, her tiny black eyes bulging. Her playmate abandoned her and leapt away, disappearing into a thicket beyond the clearing.

The stag pulled his antler free and limped back to his clump of grass, while the dead squirrel flopped into the snow at the tree's base. A moment later she rolled over and chittered angrily at the sky.

Less than a quarter of a mile away, the spirits of twenty-six women stood in the ruins of a burned cabin. They waited.

Lucy Knox was sitting at the long low counter of Knox Drugs when Rabbit entered the shop. Lucy waved her over and ordered two sodas. Charles served them and stood ready to refill their glasses, but Lucy shooed him away.

"Have you tasted a soda before?" she asked Rabbit.

"Of course," Rabbit said. "I lived in Philadelphia for ten years, maybe longer. I'm not very good with clocks and calendars, but there was a soda fountain around the corner from our house."

"Oh," Lucy said, disappointed. She saw Charles angling back toward them, pretending to clean the counter with a dirty rag. She pointed a warning finger at him, and he veered off. "It's just that Benjamin told me you lived out west with Indians, and log cabins, and fields of corn."

Rabbit nodded, considering. She took a sip of her soda. Charles had used too much cherry syrup, but she liked it. It coated the back of her mouth when she swallowed, and the cloying sweetness lingered. She took another sip.

"That was when I was younger," she said. "I did live in a cabin, and there was corn."

"But then you moved away?" Lucy sighed. "I bet Philadelphia's twice as big as Ascension."

"Bigger than that," Rabbit said. "Much bigger."

"I knew it."

"You should go someday."

Lucy slid her glass along the counter, watching the trail of condensation that followed it.

"Did you know my father owns this place?" she said.

Rabbit took another sip of cherry-flavored sugar and wiped her lips with the back of her hand.

"He wants it to stay in the family," Lucy said.

"I'm practically family," Charles said. He had quietly drifted close to them again, leaving a red streak along the counter behind his rag.

"Charles, stop listening to our conversation," Lucy said. "It's none of your damn business."

"You ought to be nicer to me, Lucy Knox," Charles said. But

he slid his rag down to the other end of the counter and pretended he wasn't listening to them.

"I don't think this place is so bad," Rabbit said. "It might be nice to own it someday."

"It's all right, I suppose. If you want an anchor around your neck. If you want to stay in one place and never see anything else. At least, that's what Benji says. He's sure to leave Ascension now that his mother's better." Lucy glanced up as if Benjamin might choose that moment to walk through the door. Rabbit followed her gaze and caught her thought. So did Charles.

"There's other boys would be glad to marry you if you looked at 'em twice," he said. "He ain't the only boy in the world."

Lucy blushed and swirled her soda around the inside of the glass. Rabbit raised an eyebrow at Charles, and he stepped sideways through the curtain into the back room.

"My father should give the place to him, and leave me out of it," Lucy said.

"I think Benjamin will probably stay in the village now," Rabbit said.

She was thinking that people usually lingered in the place they had died. But Lucy shook her head.

"Anyway, who says I have to get married?" she said. "Your mother isn't married. Is she happy?"

Rabbit stared glumly at the bottom of her empty glass while she considered the question. She wondered if she could get away with working the soda fountain herself.

"There was a man who used to come to Philadelphia to see Sadie," she said. "His name was John Riddle. He stopped visiting about a year ago, maybe two, and Rose said he married another girl back in Burden County, where we came from. Sadie didn't seem sad about it at all. She said she was happy for Mr Riddle.

I guess she could marry just about anyone if she wanted to, but I don't think she cares about that."

"Maybe I'll be like her," Lucy said. She thought it was strange and sophisticated that Rabbit called her mother by her first name. She couldn't imagine calling her own mother "Lillian." "Maybe it's not so bad to be an old maid," she said. But judging by her melancholy tone of voice Rabbit wasn't convinced she meant it.

Rabbit had never thought of Sadie or Rose as old maids. It felt like an insult, but she couldn't figure out why. Irritated, she hopped off her stool and went around the end of the counter to the fountain. She took her glass with her.

Bethany Hall is haunted, isn't it?"

Rose stood in the doorway of the nursery, her hands folded in front of her, looking out the big picture window at the snowy woods beyond the house. Sadie looked up from a potted *angelica archangelica* and nodded.

"It is," she said. She laid down the knife she was using to prune the plant, and wiped her hands on her trousers. "Would you like me to show you?"

Rose slowly turned her head, as if a spell had been broken, and gazed at Sadie for a moment before responding. "Yes," she said. "Please do."

Sadie and Rabbit were adept at spotting phantoms—although Sadie would be the first to admit Rabbit was better at it than she was—but Rose was generally ignorant of the unseen things around her. She had once seen her dead husband, but she was dying at the time, and the barrier between worlds had been thin for her. When she recovered from that ordeal she lost the knack, except when Sadie helped her see.

Sadie took Rose's hand and led her out to the hallway. They sidestepped the parlor where the burned man lay screaming on the floor, and began their tour in the ballroom, where the elegant couple danced to an endless silent waltz.

"Oh, they're perfect," Rose said.

"You can tell they're in love," Sadie said.

Rose squeezed her hand. "Can they see us?"

"If they choose to," Sadie said. "But seeing us might break the moment for them. Time flows differently for spirits than it does for us. It's like a river, and we're always in the rapids, being swept along, just trying to keep our heads up. For them it's a gentle current, full of calm pools and eddies. They can pause and enjoy a single minute forever, if they want."

"So they've chosen to live in this moment together," Rose said. "I like that."

The man in the blue suit smiled as if he had heard her, and the woman twirled the hem of her silk dress.

"I can't hear them," Rose said. "I can't hear the music."

"Spirits can be seen, but they're never heard."

"You're sure? They don't make any sound at all?"

"Not in my experience," Sadie said.

They left the dancers there, and went across to the dining hall, where a party was in full swing, as it always was. A red-faced man with an enormous mustache ladled soup into a woman's bowl, and passed the tureen to the next man. A stout woman wearing a cook's cap and an apron bustled into the room carrying a platter of carved meat. A young man with his tie askew tried to pour wine into his glass, missed, and dumped the bottle in his lap. The guests next to him jumped up, and a woman seated at the head of the table wagged her finger at the boy. A moment later, the man with the mustache ladled more soup for his lady friend, and the drunken boy reached for the suddenly full wine bottle.

"We've sat here at this table to eat our supper," Rose said. "Were these people always here?"

"There was an old man at the foot of the table the day after we moved in, but he's gone now. I think he grew tired of the party and moved on."

"Where did he go?"

Sadie shrugged. "Maybe we'll find out someday."

A little boy stood facing a corner of the room, flickering in and out of sight, his back to the party.

"I wonder if he's being punished," Rose said.

"He might be from a different time than the others," Sadie said. "He might be playing hide-and-seek with his brothers and sisters in an empty field a hundred years before this house was built."

"Oh, I hope so."

A black cat circled them and scampered away down the hall.

"That cat is missing its head!"

"He is an otherwise unremarkable cat," Sadie said. "I'll show you the cellar next."

Rose shuddered when she saw the women in white.

"They're angry," she said. "I can feel how angry they are."

"They can't hurt you," Sadie said.

"I don't like it down here."

Rose started toward the stairs, but Sadie lingered. She squinted at the small door set into the far wall. She tried the knob and when she found it was locked, she knelt and breathed into the keyhole. She imagined the tumblers sliding into place and jiggled the knob again, but nothing happened. The door didn't budge.

"That's strange," she said, but when she turned around Rose was already gone.

Sadie traced her finger over the patterns in the wood. "I'll come back," she whispered, then she hurried to catch up to Rose.

Upstairs, in the room across from Rose's, a girl lay in bed. She was barefoot and uncovered, her legs and nightgown plastered with blood. Her long limp hair hung over the side of the bed, dripping water that disappeared before it touched the floor.

"What happened to her?"

"When the villagers talk about our house being haunted, this is probably the spirit they're thinking of. She was involved in a local scandal."

Sadie related the story of Ichabod Bailey and his poor cousin. Rose went and sat on the edge of the bed and reached out toward the girl, but drew her hand back.

"She wouldn't know it if I tried to comfort her, would she?"

"She drowned her baby in the river. Does she deserve comfort?"

"Everyone deserves comfort. Maybe especially her."

Rose leaned closer to the silent form on the bed and whispered, then stood and smoothed her skirts and took a deep breath.

"There are so many spirits here," she said. "This must be an unhappy place."

"Maybe not," Sadie said. "It's full of people who couldn't bring themselves to leave."

Rose held out her hand and Sadie took it again. They left the girl alone in her room and closed the door. Rose had a sudden thought and gasped.

"What about my bedroom? Is there a spirit in my room?"

"Do you really want to know?"

Rose's eyes widened and she shook her head. "Maybe not."

"Your room is all yours," Sadie laughed. "I haven't seen any spirits in there, and if Rabbit's seen any, she hasn't mentioned them to me."

"Oh, thank goodness!"

Rose pointed at the door to the attic and smiled impishly. "I would bet a hundred dollars there's a spirit up there," she said. "As a girl, I always imagined our attic was full of nightmares."

Sadie frowned. "Let's leave the attic for another day," she said.

Sadie leads Rose away, down the stairs and around the hall past the parlor, and I in my attic room turn away from the landing. I fold my wings, sit back down at the desk, and dip my pen once more into the inkwell.

The yellow dog circled Billy Farmer's body, then trotted away to explore the nearby woods.

Moses cleared his throat. "You gonna lie there all day, son?"

Billy opened his eyes. "Am I dead?"

"The way I see it, you are and you aren't."

"I don't know what that means." Billy propped himself up on one elbow. He hacked and spat a gob of black blood into the mud. He looked down at his ruined chest, then away at the horizon. "I guess I must be dead."

"You're about as dead as me, or Frank over there." Moses gestured vaguely in the direction of Frank and the horse, but didn't bother to look. Frank had gone silent, which Moses counted as a blessing. "I was trying to tell you, before you got all jumpy. Frank was hanged by the neck for three days, and he's still talking up a storm. Me, I got shot in the head, and didn't even feel it. Until pretty recently I thought it was a misfire."

"Who shot you?"

Moses had hoped the boy wouldn't ask.

"Well, I did it to myself," he said. "Point is, there's nothing you can do to Frank because somebody else got to him before you could. Like I said before, go home to your family and tell 'em Frank's done for, which is the truth. But you should probably change your shirt before anybody sees you."

"This is all pretty confusing."

Moses nodded. "It's a new situation. All I can think is—"

He was interrupted by Frank Smiley, who had found the short-handled shovel in Moses's saddlebag and was galloping across the field, screaming incoherently, the shovel held high over his head. Moses reached for his pistol, but the blind man tripped over his own bootlaces and fell face first at Billy's feet. The tip of the shovel sliced cleanly through Billy's left knee and buried itself in the earth beneath him.

Billy hollered and scrambled backward, leaving half his leg behind. Moses left his Colt in its holster. He stood and kicked Frank in the head, and the blind man crawled away, moaning.

"Who went and kicked me? It didn't hurt noways, but you shouldn't've done it."

"My leg's messed up now!" Billy said.

"Dammit, Frank," Moses said. "You chopped Billy's leg off. You didn't have to do that."

"He shot me, Moses. It's self-defense. I was in my rights. He shot me in my arm."

"So what? He didn't do you any harm. Dammit anyway."

Moses walked past Billy to where the bushes met a straggle of young trees. He turned and pointed at Frank. A useless gesture, since Frank couldn't see him do it.

"You stay put there, Frank. You, too, Billy. No more violence, you hear me?"

Neither of them responded, and Moses decided there wasn't much he could do if they decided to go at each other again. He scuffed the toe of his boot under the brown leaves until he found a stout branch, about four feet long. He broke off the stubby twigs, and left a fork at one end of the branch. He brought it back and held it out to Billy.

"Not as good as a leg, but it'll help you walk until you can find something better."

Billy held out his hand, and Moses helped him up. They got the forked end of the branch under his armpit and Billy took a practice turn around the field, hobbling clumsily along, jabbing the blunt end of the branch at the ground with so much force that Moses half-expected him to topple over. Billy stayed upright, though, and a few minutes later returned to Moses.

"It'll work okay," Billy said. "I got my horse back there in the woods. I guess I can get home all right."

"Good. It's up to you whether you want to mention to your family that you're dead."

"I don't guess I will. Seems like a lot to have to explain. I sure do wish I could've killed Frank Smiley, though. That's a real regret I have."

"I can hear you over there," Frank said. "And I don't appreciate what you're saying." He had sat back down and was running his hands over his face, poking and prodding the flesh. "I think I might have broke my nose when I fell down."

"Good," Billy said. "I guess I'll settle for that."

"At least this didn't turn into more of a shoot-out," Moses said. "That'd be an exercise in futility." He was quietly proud of himself for bringing the conflict to a diplomatic end, but he had noticed that death seemed to bring with it a measure of acceptance, and he knew he couldn't take all the credit for the ceasefire. The fact that he had killed Billy was already forgotten.

Billy stumped away toward the trees on his makeshift crutch, crunching through a thick carpet of wet leaves.

"You gonna need some help getting up on your horse?" Moses said.

"I'll manage," Billy said. He pointed at Frank. "Damn you anyway, Frank Smiley."

"Your brother had three queens up his sleeve," Frank said. "I was in my rights."

"Johnny was a kid. He didn't know no better. Damn you, anyway," Billy said again. Then he turned and limped away.

Moses watched him go, then swung himself up into the Appaloosa's saddle.

"Moses?" Frank said. "You better hitch me up again so I don't wander the wrong direction."

"You and I have reached a parting of the ways," Moses said. "You've worn out the last bit of my patience, and I'm no longer inclined toward your company."

"What'd I do to you, Moses?"

"That boy wasn't even armed anymore. You didn't have to chop off his foot."

"I wasn't trying to chop off his foot. I was trying to stove in his dang head."

"Well, you shouldn't do that, either."

"You can't leave me here, Moses. I'm bound to run into a tree or get ate by a coyote or some such."

"I wish you luck, Frank Smiley."

Moses turned Pie's nose northeast, and rode away. The yellow dog came running after him.

THREE DAYS REMAINING

Excerpted from the diary of Mrs Richard Sinclair.

Dear Diary,

It is hard to think of what to write. No it is hard to think of how to write. I find that my thougts are scattered and I hardly recognize them as my one. I must try to focus and I must put on a brave face when others are around.

I think Alice watches me when I sleep. I dreamt she entered my bedroom last night and whispered my name, but perhaps I wasn't dreaming. I woke with the stragest feeling someone had been in my room.

I ~~know~~ no longer care for the girl's company. She agitates me, and smells very strange to me, as if she's powdering herself with some spice I don't recognize. Something vile and ~~force~~ foreign. I have begun to think I cant trust her, but I dont know if that's right or if I should not trust myself. Besides if I dismis her, where will she go? The poor thing has no one. I must think of a mersifull solution to our situation. I think I will h

News of the outside world reached Ascension slowly, and was often of less interest than the local gossip. The village printer circulated a single sheet each Saturday morning that was simply an anthology of items clipped from other, bigger, newspapers, but a few subscribers supplemented their weekly copy of *The Ascension Record* with publications from nearby cities.

Jessica Hudson fanned a selection of papers out on a table in the foyer of the Ascension Inn. She only had three guests at the moment, but she prided herself on accommodating the tastes and requests of everyone under her roof. She subscribed to ten different newspapers, and gave a boy at the station a nickel to run them down to her as soon as they arrived. She set the Boston papers at the top of the stack in the foyer, but didn't so much as glance at the headlines. Nothing happening in Boston could compare with recent events in the village.

Already thinking about orders he needed to fill, Prosper Knox absently munched on a piece of toast and glanced over the front page of the *Catholic Herald* while his wife, Lillian, glared at the pile of crumbs collecting on his side of the table. The headline above the *Herald's* fold read POPE LEO BREAKS SILENCE ON MIRACLES. In smaller type below the headline: RIFT AMONGST CLERGY. Prosper set down the toast and lowered his spectacles to read the fine print.

Alone in the rectory, Reverend Cotton folded his own copy of the *Herald* and laid it on the credence table. He smoothed the newsprint again and again, contemplating what it all might mean for his parish. There was a steady *thump*ing that came from the graveyard outside, but the sound was too weak and the wind was too high for him to hear it.

Two streets over from the church, Dr Timothy Rumpole answered the front door in his smoking jacket. One of the boys who was always loitering at the train station had brought a cable addressed to the doctor. The telegram was succinct. The doctor's brother had been washed over the side of a fishing boat in the Atlantic. David Rumpole's body had not been recovered, and he was presumed dead. Dr Rumpole read the cable three times, then wadded it and threw it at the fireplace. He dropped onto the sofa and reached for his pipe.

Sergeant Newton Winter found an item buried on page seven of the *New York Tribune* about a coma patient who had awakened the previous day. The man had been vegetative for four years, but had suddenly left his hospital bed, killed a nurse, and eaten her liver before being shot six times by a policeman. The ghoul had survived his wounds, and had been transferred to Bellevue Hospital for observation. Sergeant Winter grabbed a pencil from the drawer in his bedside table and began to compose a query to an associate on the New York City police force.

Lucy Knox glanced at the headlines of her father's newspapers, but the words barely registered. She wolfed down an egg and raced back to her bedroom, where she cut a length of red ribbon from a spool on the vanity and wound it around a long white box. She brushed her hair and put on her best dress, yellow cotton with brown polka dots, then stood in front of the vanity mirror and turned this way and that, examining her reflection. She practiced smiling, pretending she and Benjamin were alone together and she had Benjamin's undivided attention. She had decided the time was finally right to make her intentions clear. Lucy would be Mrs Benjamin Sinclair or she would be an old maid. Either way, it would be good to know what the future held.

At the Sinclair cottage, Benjamin shuffled through the assortment of newspapers Alice had laid out the previous evening: *The Boston Daily Globe*, *The Boston Courant*, and *The New York Evening World*. He picked one up at random and the headline below the fold caught his eye.

PATIENTS AT BOSTON CITY HOSPITAL WALK OUT!

In smaller type beneath the headline: DOCTORS PUZZLED AS ENTIRE WARD DIAGNOSES THEMSELVES. "THERE'S NOTHING WRONG WITH US!" IS THE UNANIMOUS VERDICT!

"Benji?"

He dropped the paper.

"I'm sorry," Clarissa said. "Did I startle you?"

She was wearing a dress that seemed at least two sizes too large for her, and she had applied rouge and lipstick inexpertly in an attempt to conceal her cold cheeks and lifeless lips beneath splashes of bright red.

"I was just thinking," he said. "I was thinking about how wrong you are."

"What did I—"

"You said we must be special, but I don't think there's anything special about us at all."

He watched a cloud of doubt and confusion settle over her, and he felt a strange satisfaction.

On the slim chance he might encounter more of Johnny Farmer's brothers, Moses had ridden straight north all day, away from Trenton, Missouri, and away from the blind horse thief, Frank Smiley. He had made camp that night under the exposed roots of an old cypress.

The yellow dog disappeared into the woods for an hour and brought back a pheasant. Moses got a fire going. He cleaned and cooked the bird, but could only swallow a mouthful of the meat. He tossed the rest to the dog.

In the morning they crossed an icy creek, the Appaloosa slipping down its steep bank and crunching through a thin layer of ice to the cold water beneath. They turned east from there. Moses had done the math and believed it would take him another three weeks to reach Philadelphia by horseback. Three weeks was too long. His anxiety increased daily, and he knew he needed to find a town with a train station.

As they neared the Illinois border, the air grew colder again. Wisps of snow caught in the tassels of tall grass like cotton balls. Moses skirted the woods, sticking close to the trail and finding open fields wherever he could, always with an eye toward the trees where there might be strange creatures or hanged men.

The sun was in the western sky when he came across a cabin. It was sturdy and neat, with tight corners, a shingled roof, and a tall stone chimney. It stood in the middle of a broad plain, dotted with small groves of trees.

Rainclouds were forming to the east, and the air had grown heavy. Lightning forked across the sky, followed by a low rumble of thunder.

Moses dismounted and tied the horse's reins to a hitching post beneath a window hung with pale blue lace. He pulled his hat down over the bullet wound in his head and knocked on the front door. When there was no answer, he turned the knob and cracked the door open.

"Anybody home? I don't intend any mischief!"

There was no answer, so Moses scraped the mud off his boots and went inside. The cabin was a single room, dominated by a heavy table positioned diagonally away from the wall, pinning one corner of a heavy rug. Scratches in the floorboards indicated it had been dragged, and the edge of the rug was crusted with dried blood. Two wooden chairs rested on their sides at the far end of the room, as if they had been knocked over and kicked aside by whomever had moved the table. The only other furniture in the room, aside from a bucket of firewood, was a rocking chair near the hearth.

The cabin's back door stood ajar. Moses drew his revolver and yanked the door open. A well-tended path curved away from the house, drops of dark blood dotting its smooth stones. Moses contemplated the distant trees, and wondered whether the injured party was still lingering nearby. He closed the door and bolted it.

He found cooking supplies and household staples in an alcove beside the fireplace: sugar and salt, bags of corn and oats, a rasher of bacon, and a dozen biscuits wrapped in cheesecloth. He checked the biscuits for mold and was pleased to see only a few tiny green spots he could easily pick away. Better than what he had in his bag. He filled a copper kettle with oats and corn, and took it out to Pie. He brought his saddlebags inside and whistled for the dog, and it came racing across the pasture, just as the first drops of rain splashed down.

He used an empty oat bag to start a fire, and piled on wood from the bucket, then pulled the rocking chair around and sat with his rifle on his lap, contemplating the rug and the table.

The storm picked up and thunder shook the cabin. Moses stood and opened the curtains so he could see his horse. He tossed a piece of bacon to the dog, then sat back down. He listened to the patter of rain on the roof and the crackle of knotty wood in the fireplace, and he closed his eyes.

He dreamed that he was carrying a small wooden box across an endless prairie. Inside the box was his heart, and each time it beat, his fingertips vibrated. Hands clawed up through the mud around him, clutching at his boots, yanking at the hems of his trousers, trying to trip him, trying to make him drop the box. He kept walking, steady and sure, holding tight to his heart, aware that with a single misstep he would lose it forever.

He opened his eyes. The fire cast bizarre shadows on the ceiling. Asleep at his feet, the yellow dog whined and pawed at the air. Outside the window, the sky was black. The room seemed smaller to Moses, the walls closer.

At last he got up and set his rifle within easy reach across the arms of the rocking chair. He left the table alone, but lifted the edge of the rug. A seam in the floor made a sharp right angle, marking one corner of a square. A cellar door. Moses stomped on the inside of the square, and there was a soft answering thump from under the floor. He stepped back and considered. The yellow dog woke up and came to his side, brushing his leg with its shoulder. Moses was grateful for the reassurance. He stepped forward again and moved the table a few inches, scraping it loudly along the floor so the person in the cellar would hear. He pushed the rug farther back, bunching it against the table legs. Then he sat cross-legged and leaned forward.

"You hear me down there?"

There was another thump from the other side of the cellar door.

"Give me one thump for 'yes' and two thumps for 'no.' Understand?"

Thump.

"This your house?"

Thump.

"Somebody trap you down there?"

There was a long silence, then at last an answering knock. Knuckles, not a fist. A weaker *yes*. Less certain.

Moses looked at the dog. "Looks like we've got a decision to make. It's possible whoever's down there deserves to be down there. Also possible they're armed and dangerous. I don't want to get another bullet hole in me, or have my leg chopped off."

The dog sat and watched him. It glanced at the front door and whined, then looked back at Moses. Outside the cabin, Moses heard a low whirring sound like saw blades spinning, or a fast carriage on a rocky road. The sound was barely audible behind the pouring rain and thunder, and Moses judged the cause of the whirring was still half a mile away or more.

"It's just one thing after another these days." He addressed the dog. "If something's coming our way, I guess we'll deal with it, but I don't think we ought to leave this person in the cellar. Everybody should have a fighting chance, you agree?"

The dog watched the cabin's front door and growled.

Moses moved his rifle from the rocking chair to the table,

stood on the cellar door, and shoved the table up against the wall. He flipped the corner of the rug out of the way with his foot to reveal a ring handle set into the floorboards.

"You still down there?"

Thump.

"I'm gonna let you out, but I'll have a weapon pointed at you, so don't do anything I'm apt to dislike, okay?"

Thump.

"Go on down the ladder and wait."

Moses stepped across the seam in the floor. He squatted, grabbed the ring, and pulled. The door swung open on greased hinges, slowly at first, then—as gravity began to work with Moses, rather than against him—faster. A stout pole swung loose from its underside and Moses eased the weight of the door back down. The pole fit neatly into a groove beneath the floor, bracing the door at an angle.

Moses picked up the rifle. The dog hadn't budged from its place by the door.

"You can come up out of there," Moses said. "Take it slow."

He heard shuffling down in the dark. The light from the fireplace didn't reach far beyond the raised cellar door, and Moses could only see the top four rungs of a ladder. After a few minutes, a tiny pale hand appeared around a rung. Another hand grabbed the rung above, and a head broke the surface of the darkness, thin dark hair parted in the middle. The head tilted back, and Moses was surprised to find himself staring into the eyes of a little girl. He wasn't good at judging how old children were, but he thought she might be eight, or maybe ten years old. Her eyes were wide and brown; her lips were pulled back in a grimace of fear, showing an even row of teeth.

Moses held out his hand and, after hesitating, the girl took it. He pulled her up and she stood blinking in the firelight.

She was barefoot, and wore a tattered dress that might once have been white. The left side of her face was burned and scabbed over, her left ear missing, her left eye partially obscured by puckered folds of ruined skin. Her throat was caked with dried blood, and bits of melted flesh were caught in her dirty hair.

The girl regarded him silently, then looked around the room. When she saw the dog she smiled and ran to it, and the yellow dog wagged its tail. It licked her neck, and she giggled.

Moses set his rifle down.

Benjamin!"

Startled, he spun around so quickly that he almost knocked Lucy Knox into the street.

"What is it, Lucy?"

"I just wondered where you were going."

"Why do you care where I'm going?" He had felt agitated all morning. Now that he thought about it, his agitation had been building since the milk cart accident. It was like a finger plucking some string that ran the length of his body. Strumming it harder and harder, to a tune he couldn't hear.

Lucy was carrying a slim lacquered box tied with a red ribbon. Her auburn hair hung loose around her shoulders. Her dark coat was unbuttoned, and under it she wore a yellow dress decorated with tiny brown polka dots that matched the spray of freckles across the bridge of her nose. She was a year younger than Benjamin and his feelings toward her were complicated. When he was in the city he rarely thought about her at all, but when he was in the village he rarely thought about anything else.

"I've been worried about you," Lucy said. She kicked at a melting chunk of ice. "I think it's lucky you weren't killed. I mean, I'm glad it wasn't as bad as it looked."

"I keep telling everybody, I'm fine. But I think they ought to put that horse down anyway. The damn old thing's a menace."

While they're at it, he thought, *they should put Mr Mulacky down, too. He shouldn't be allowed to drive a milk cart when he can't see five feet in front of him.*

"Oh, Benjamin, it's not the horse's fault. You jumped right out in front of it." She saw the irritation in his eyes and quickly changed the subject. "You still didn't tell me where you're going this morning."

"I guess I didn't."

He continued up the street, and Lucy paused only a moment before following him.

"Are you going to the train station?"

Benjamin sighed. "Yes," he said. "I'm going to take a look at the newspapers before they get delivered."

"Because of the strange things happening in all the big cities?"

Benjamin felt a flush of excitement. He turned and kept walking backward up the gentle hill toward the station so he could face Lucy while he talked.

"You noticed that, too," he said. "I want to see more papers than the ones we take at the cottage."

"What do you think is causing it?" Lucy picked up her pace and skipped a little to catch up to him.

"Have you heard of Halley's Comet?"

"In the sky?"

"Of course in the sky, dummy. It's famous. It passes by the Earth every seventy-five years, like clockwork."

"And you think it's causing mysterious things to happen?"

Benjamin shook his head impatiently. "No," he said. "It won't pass by again for almost a decade. But that's just one comet. There are tons of them up there. And other things, too. Things we can't see. It's well known that the moon's orbit affects the tides. Maybe there's something passing by us right now, only our telescopes aren't strong enough, or maybe nobody's looked in the right damn place yet, and it's affecting people the way the moon affects water. We're mostly made of water, you know?"

"You're so clever, Benjamin. I never think about things like that." She poked his arm, and Benjamin felt a spark of irritation, but he was also pleased she found his theory plausible.

When they reached the station, he bounded ahead of her up the steps, then held the door for her. As she passed him, she turned and her breast brushed against his arm. He thought to push her away, and the impulse surprised him. Her breasts, after all, had long been a subject of great interest for him.

The station was quiet and empty. The morning papers were stacked beside the door, bundled with twine. Benjamin used his pocketknife to cut open one of the bundles, and selected a handful of newspapers from various New England townships, plus a sampling from London and San Francisco. He took them to the stationmaster's office, and Lucy followed.

There was a window that looked out on the small waiting room, and a hutch that held telegrams, notices, and other sundry papers. A potbelly stove dominated one corner of the room, along with an overflowing box of firewood. The desk was bare and dusty and the stationmaster's blue leather chair was pushed up against the far wall.

Benjamin pulled the chair up to the desk and spread out the newspapers. *American Horse Breeder* wasn't likely to contain anything useful, so he brushed it onto the floor. Lucy set down her package and picked the pages up, tapping the edges together before refolding them. Benjamin scowled at her.

"I would have picked it up," he said. "Later, I mean."

"Of course," Lucy said. "I was only helping."

He turned his attention back to the papers. One front-page

story detailed a failed exorcism. A six-year-old boy had fallen down a flight of stairs and broken his neck. When he continued to complain about his breakfast, his parents sent for a priest. When the boy stabbed him in the leg with a pencil, the priest gave up—"I have done everything I can for this unholy wretch," he was quoted as saying—and the family had shut the boy away in a closet.

In *The Watchman*, a Baptist paper out of Boston, Benjamin found a piece about a dead woman who had woken up during her funeral and cried to be let out of her coffin. Her frightened husband had ordered the coffin lowered anyway, and the graveyard crew had covered it with six feet of dirt. One of the crew admitted they "ought to have let the poor lass out."

"Has anyone been buried here in the last few days? In the village graveyard?"

"I don't think so," Lucy said.

The Limerick, Maine, *Morning Star* had run a story about an unusual bank robbery. Cornered by authorities, the thieves had opened fire. Three of the four bank robbers had sustained mortal wounds, but still refused to surrender.

"It's happening everywhere," Benjamin said.

"But what do you think it is?" Lucy was playing with a button on her coat, turning it this way and that, and Benjamin found the repetitive motion intensely irritating.

"How the hell would I know? I'm a scientist, not a damn philosopher."

"Oh, Benjamin, I nearly forgot!" Lucy grabbed the white lacquered box and thrust it at him. "Open it."

He took it from her and untied the ribbon, letting it flutter to the floor, a twist of red across the pale hardwood. He lifted the lid and frowned.

"It's a letter opener," Lucy said. She fiddled with the button on her coat again, looking out the window as she spoke. "That's a real pearl on the end of it. I ordered it from Boston, and I was going to give it to you the other day, but then . . ."

"Lucy, I can't—"

"I know the pearl isn't very big, and I'm sorry, but it's supposed to remind you of the moon. You're always talking about the moon and the stars . . . Oh, never mind. I had it all worked out, but now it seems silly."

"Here, stop playing with that damn button," he said. "It's about to come off your coat."

He grabbed her hand and squeezed, and Lucy whimpered. Benjamin experienced a split second of shame for having hurt her, but when he saw the fear and pain in her eyes, he squeezed harder. The bones in her fingers ground against each other.

"Benjamin, please don't hurt me."

He liked the way her pretty features contorted in pain, and the confusion in her voice was strangely satisfying. He had always known Lucy was in love with him. Or she thought she was. Lucy Knox, who had never been out of the village, who had never visited a theatre or a museum, or even seen the house in the city where he lived. They had almost nothing in common, and yet Lucy would probably do anything to be with him.

Anything at all.

"Give me a kiss, Lucy," he said. "I know you want to."

"Benjamin!"

She tried to pull away, but he yanked her closer. He grabbed her by the waist and wrestled her onto his lap. The blue leather chair creaked under their combined weight.

"Please, Benjamin!"

She began to cry. Disgusted, he shoved her off his lap, and she crawled away from him.

"What's wrong with you?" he screamed. "What do you want

from me? You've been pestering me for years, following me all summer long, interrupting every private minute I ever had! Well, here I am, you stupid bitch! I'm right here!"

He stood up abruptly and the chair shot across the room behind him, coming to rest once more against the far wall. A part of him realized how badly he was overreacting, but he was unable to stop himself. Angry and confused, he staggered toward Lucy, who was huddled against the door, trying to work the knob above her.

Benjamin tripped on a corner of the box of firewood. He reached down and grabbed a stout piece of wood that resembled an axe handle, roughly the size and length of his forearm. Lucy finally managed to turn the knob and pulled the door open, but he used the piece of wood to push it shut again.

"Benjamin, I don't understand." Tears streamed down Lucy's face, and snot ran from her nose. Her lips were gummy with saliva.

"You disgust me," he said.

He said it quietly, and with finality. Raising the firewood above his head, he felt powerful. He brought his makeshift weapon down as hard as he could, blood pounding in his ears. He raised the stick and brought it down again. And again.

After a time—he didn't know how long it was—he dropped the piece of firewood. Lucy Knox lay quiet and still on the floor at his feet.

"Lucy?"

Bewildered, he looked around at the stationmaster's bare and dusty office, at the papers on the desk, at the bloody piece of wood at his feet, at the body of the girl who had loved him. He had a fuzzy memory of Lucy crying, but he couldn't remember why or what had happened to her.

The sleeve of his coat was stained red with blood and he swiped at it, smearing Lucy's blood across the palm of his hand. With the toe of his boot he moved her out of the way, then opened the office door and shut it behind him.

He stood on the station platform for a moment, looking up the hillside to make sure no one was watching, then he jumped down to the snowy path and ran all the way back to No. 17 Brynwood Lane.

Sunlight broke through the branches above them and slanted across the snow in the forest glade. Overnight, Sadie's sapling had doubled in height, and the crow's nest had been carried upward as the tree grew. The crow peered down over the edge of her nest, looking from Sadie to Rabbit and back again.

"Hello, little friend," Sadie called. "Are you going to hatch something for us?"

"I don't understand," Rabbit said. "This is what you've been doing in the woods? Talking to birds?"

Sadie laughed. She patted the trunk of the little tree. "This looks like a tree, it smells like a tree, it grows like a tree. But two days ago this clearing was empty. Look."

She pointed at the tiny green bud of a new leaf.

"We'll have to keep an eye on it," she said. "It's sprouting early, so it's especially vulnerable right now."

"How can it sprout anything? There's snow all around."

"Once it's grown to its full height this tree will be green all year round. This will be where we center and focus our power."

Rabbit was alarmed by the notion that they might be in the village for another year, but she said: "How did you make it grow so fast?"

"I pulled the energy that flows under the forest to this spot and

I told it to be a tree. Or rather, I suggested it might like to be a tree, and it agreed with me."

"Can you show me how to do that?"

"I can try," Sadie said.

"Is that a real bird or did you grow it, too?"

"She's a real crow. Crows are very smart and they can sense magic when it happens."

The crow cawed and fluttered her wings.

"Yesterday she bought her nest from me, and in the next day or two, when her first egg is ready, I plan to buy it from her." Sadie gave the tree a last loving pat. "Come on," she said to Rabbit. "I want to show you something else."

They left the glade and Rabbit followed her mother, stepping in Sadie's footprints. The air was crisp, the sun was bright, and birds chirped overhead, but Rabbit felt uneasy. She watched her mother's back, Sadie's shoulders rolling gracefully under the bear fur as she pushed through the snow, her red hair fluttering in the breeze.

Eventually they stepped through a gap between the trees and entered a clearing. At the center of the clearing was a tumbledown cabin, its plank walls stunted and charred, like rows of black teeth embedded in gums of stone. The smell of burnt wood hung over it like a cloud.

Rabbit sneezed, and wiped her nose with the back of her hand. "You did this?" she said.

Sadie nodded.

"Why?"

Sadie motioned for Rabbit to follow, and they crunched through the snow to the front wall. Rabbit brushed her fingers against the blackened wood. It was cool, and crumbled at her touch. They crossed the threshold, and stood on the stone floor of the ruins, and dead women gathered around them like tattered moths at a campfire.

"So many," Rabbit whispered.

Sadie pointed to where the back wall had stood. "There were twenty-seven scalps nailed there. It was some kind of collection. This place . . ." She looked down and shook her head.

"How old were the scalps?" Rabbit said.

"Some were older, maybe sixty or seventy years. But a couple of them were only a year or two old. One of them was fresh."

"Then this wasn't some random woodsman or traveler."

"I don't think it was one person," Sadie said. "This took a long time and a lot of effort."

Rabbit stepped around her and stood before the wide stone table, its cracked and blackened surface split by the roof beam. She rested the palms of her hands against it and felt the same sort of shock she got when she touched metal on a dry winter's day. She gasped.

"Rabbit?"

Rabbit pulled her hands away from the stone and shook her head. Her vocabulary wasn't large enough to describe what she felt. She wanted to ask Sadie for the right words, but she knew there were no right words.

"Rabbit?" Sadie said again.

"I'm glad you burned this place," Rabbit said at last. "But burning it wasn't enough."

She narrowed her eyes and the earth trembled. The floor shifted and mortar crumbled. Dust and debris whirled around her. The ground rolled and rumbled, and a fissure opened in the center of the cabin floor, widened into a chasm, and swallowed the ruined stone table. Sadie lost her footing and went down on one knee. She pushed against the beam to keep from rolling forward into the sudden chasm.

"Stop it!" she yelled. "Rabbit, listen to me!"

Rabbit didn't respond, but the earthquake subsided, the ground settled, and Sadie stood and let out a long breath she hadn't realized she was holding.

"This place is already destroyed," she said. "Any more of this and you'll damage the woods. Let the living things have this place back. Give them time. Trees and vines will grow through all this and tear it down and absorb it back into the earth, but that won't happen if there's nothing left."

She put a hand on Rabbit's shoulder, and the girl turned, wrapping her arms around Sadie's waist, burying her face in the folds of the bearskin coat.

"I'm sorry," she said.

"I shouldn't have brought you here," Sadie said. "You and I, we don't think about things the same way."

"I'm sorry," Rabbit said again.

"It's not a bad thing, but I don't know if I can teach you what I did with the tree."

Rabbit let go and wiped her nose again. She seemed diminished.

"I can feel what happened here," she said. "It's still in the air."

They left the cabin and walked away from the clearing. Trees closed in on them and they heard small animals moving in the underbrush. The air was fresh and clean, but the smell of burnt wood lingered in their nostrils.

Sadie led the way back to the house, but when she turned at the bottom of the slope Rabbit was gone.

Rose approaches the attic stairs and I set down my pen. I had hoped to avoid this, but it will happen anyway, despite my hopes. It has already happened. I have already written it.

I stand and face the door as she mounts the steps. She hesitates with her hand on the knob, then turns it and pushes the door open. I unfurl my wings once again and allow her to gaze on

my majesty. As much of it as she is able to perceive. She must
understand what I am, and understand the importance of what
I will now tell her.

"Be not afraid," I say. "I have been waiting for you, Rose
Nettles."

Rose had seen many strange things, and she had read about even stranger things. But what she found in her attic was worse than anything she could have imagined.

She said, "I knew there would be something terrible up here."

"I am indeed terrible," the creature said. "My name is Alexander, and I have come here for you."

"For me?"

"No, I have not come to kill you," the creature said, and she knew that it had read her mind. She felt her knees buckle.

"Please sit, Rose," it said.

It gestured toward a tangle of wooden chairs in the corner, and Rose wrestled one out. She set the chair upright and sat down. It wobbled, and she rocked it back and forth. She smoothed the folds of her skirt.

"I am indeed here to end your life as you know it, but not in the way that you imagine. I have come with a proposition for you."

Rose sat up straighter and squared her shoulders. She clasped her hands in her lap, prepared to listen.

"A proposition?"

"You have seen your cousin Clarissa Sinclair. She walks among the living, though she is no longer one of them."

"You mean she died."

"I do. And her son, Benjamin, has likewise succumbed." The creature paused, as if listening. "Ah. And now Lucy Knox has succumbed, as well."

"Lucy?"

"Benjamin has murdered her. The fault lies not entirely with him. The natural order has been disrupted. It is why I was dispatched to see you."

"Me?"

"I understand. You believe yourself to be unimportant. And yet, like each of your species, you are a rarity. You are a singular point. A pearl on a string, as your cousin might say, and you are more special than most because Moses Burke has chosen to come here, to this house."

"I don't understand."

"Do you remember Moses Burke?"

Rose smiled. "How could I forget Moses?"

"He remembers you, as well. He remembers your partner, Sadie Grace, and her daughter, Rabbit. He believes he is coming here to ask for their help, though he does not understand why he is actually making this journey. He brings a talisman with him. He is the bearer of a sacred duty, which he will pass on to you."

"Duty?"

"Without knowing it, he has chosen you to take up a dreadful burden. You will become Death. It is a great honor."

Rose stood. She walked to the window and looked down the hill at the woods.

"What will happen to Sadie and Rabbit?"

"They will continue to be."

"Without me?"

"You, as you think of yourself, will cease to exist."

"Will I see them again?"

"You will see them again. They will live a very long time by your standards, but at some future point they will require your attendance. Eventually, everyone dies."

Rose watched a crow circle the treetops. It dipped and banked, and caught the wind.

"No," she said.

"No?"

"I won't do it. Find someone else."

Alexander sighed, but it seemed performative. Rose thought everything the creature did was a show. Every word, every move, seemed calculated.

"My species does not have free will, but your species labors under the illusion of choice. I suppose you may choose to reject this responsibility, but should you do so, you will doom the world to a state of undeath."

"What will happen?"

"There will be endings without beginnings. Everyone and everything will, in time, conclude their lives, but they will remain. Their souls will be trapped in their bodies. Their spirits will wither and decay. There will be great unrest, great unhappiness, and there will be no release from it. Neighbor will turn on neighbor, friend on friend, as their souls agitate for freedom. Chaos will reign on Earth."

"But I'll be with my family?"

"Yes."

"Then I stand by my choice."

"Rose Nettles, you were a daughter, and you lived with your mother until she sent you away. You were a wife, and you lived with your husband until he died. You have never chosen anything for yourself, but now you think only of yourself? You were a schoolteacher, but you abandoned your students. You were a farmer, but were unable to sustain the land. You have failed in your every endeavor. Now I offer you this singular distinction and you choose failure again?"

"I took care of my mother, and my students, and my husband. I buried him myself, and I buried my mother. I took care of Rabbit when she had no one else. I have spent my entire life caring for others, and neglecting myself. Don't I deserve happiness?"

"No one deserves anything, Rose Nettles. You have always been a servant. Be a good servant."

She shook her head. "There are spirits dancing in the room below us, because they want to be together as long as they possibly can. Why shouldn't I have as much as they do?"

"Because you will doom everyone."

"Find someone else."

Alexander almost smiled. The creature inclined its head a millimeter.

"I already have. I knew your choice before you opened the attic door. I knew it in the moment Moses Burke slew Death. You may leave now, Rose Nettles. I have events to record."

Rose stood and picked up her chair and carried it to the corner. She set it on the pile and watched it slide, its legs catching in the legs of the other chairs, coming to rest in a knot of curved and polished wood. She went to the door, but paused with her hand on the knob. She didn't look at Alexander when she spoke.

"I'm sorry. I hope you can forgive me."

"Of course," Alexander said. "It's what I do."

Rose closed the door behind her and immediately forgot about the thing she had met in the attic. She forgot about the strange conversation they'd had. She descended the staircase and went looking for Sadie.

She felt as if she had neglected some important chore, but she couldn't think what it could be.

———

In the stationmaster's office, Lucy Knox rolled over and got to her feet. Blood dripped from her nose and from her right eye. She gazed at the mess Benjamin had made, and clicked her tongue in disappointment.

She used the hem of her dress to dab at the blood on the floor, but quickly realized it was hopeless and gave up. She pushed the office chair back up to the desk, and put the bloody piece of firewood back in the box. She gathered the newspapers and carried them out of the office, to the stack beside the door, then left the station and staggered down Shiloh Road to her house.

She was glad she didn't have to help her father at the drugstore. It had already been such a stressful morning.

Rabbit ran beneath the low branches of blue pines, their bows heavy with snow, and hopped over white dunes, until she found the wide clearing at the center of the woods where the magical tree had grown. It was already several feet taller.

A man stood with his back to her and his head raised, gazing up at the oak. He wore a black suit, but no coat or hat. His dark hair did not move in the light breeze. His hands were clasped behind him, and the white cuffs of his shirtsleeves formed perfect bands around his slender wrists.

"Hello, little Rabbit," he said without turning around.

"Hello, Mr Bell. What are you doing out here?"

He turned and regarded her for a moment before replying. "I enjoy an occasional stroll in these woods," he said. "Bethany Hall can get a bit stuffy."

Rabbit tried to calculate the distance from the pantry to the clearing in the woods and decided the butler's body must be buried somewhere near the base of the hill.

"There is already an egg in that crow's nest," Bell said. He patted the trunk of the new oak. "It would seem your mother is creating a familiar."

"How do you know what she's doing?"

"I know a great deal," Bell said. "What I do not know is why Sadie Grace has chosen to consolidate her power here in Ascension."

Rabbit left the shadows at the edge of the clearing and circled the big tree so that it stood between her and Bell. She leaned to her left, then to her right, and stared at him around the trunk. He ignored her and watched the high branches where the crow hopped back and forth, cawing down at them, worried for her egg.

"If you were to climb this tree and look in her nest, you would see a black egg. Isn't that odd? An egg as black as midnight. An egg that was not there yesterday, in a nest that was not there, in a tree that has grown at the snap of your mother's fingers."

Rabbit looked up at the crow. She wanted to see if there really was a black egg. She wanted to climb up and look in the nest, but she didn't want to do it in front of Bell.

Bell stepped back from the tree and peered around the trunk at her. He searched out her eyes and held her gaze. When at last he spoke there was warmth in his voice.

"I haven't lied to you yet, have I?" He smiled.

He was an odd ghost, she thought. Able to communicate freely and move about, unlike the women at the cabin or the brides in the cellar.

She said, "Do you remember being alive?"

Bell paused before answering. A gust of wind swirled through the woods and whipped snow down on them from the branches above.

At last he shook his head. "I'm afraid I don't. At least, not the way in which you mean."

"Why do you all stay?" Rabbit pointed up the hill, to where the old woman stood in the shadows of the pines, holding her golden locket out for them to come and look. "Why did she stay here? Was she a bad person?"

Bell stroked his chin and took a deep breath, though he required breath as much as the old woman's spirit did, which is to say not at all.

"There is a . . . well, a position of some authority in this world. I suppose you might think of it as a sort of escort. It is often called the Angel of Death, but it is not an angel in the truest sense of that word. Rather, it is almost always a former human who has an understanding of death because they have lived under its shadow. They come at the final hour to ease one's passage, but sometimes a person can't see this escort, or they refuse to accept the guidance being offered. Sometimes the dying and the dead are simply too wrapped up in their own worries to pay proper attention to Death, or they are filled with such raw emotion that they are unable to think of anything else. For these reasons they get left behind."

"So it's bad to feel emotion when you die?"

"I should imagine it's unavoidable."

"Then it's not fair."

Bell chuckled. "You are still very young."

Rabbit turned and stared into the woods. "There's a place out there," she said. "There are women, a lot of them, and they were murdered."

Bell shifted his gaze to the trees, then back to Rabbit. "I see," he said.

"Do you know what happened to them?"

"Why should I care?"

"Could you tell me who killed them?"

"For a favor like that, I would normally exact a steep price,"

Bell said. "You would owe me something precious in return for such information, but for you, little Rabbit, I will make an exception. The truth is there is no single person responsible for those deaths. It is this village. It is the people who live here, the people who have lived here for generations."

"Generations? But there must be someone . . . Tell me who's most recently murdered a woman."

"Benjamin Sinclair."

Rabbit gasped. "Benjamin killed them?"

"Not at all. That wasn't what you asked."

"Then who?"

"Well, there is the local druggist, and I do suppose the retired constable qualifies. But there have been many others."

"That's enough for now," Rabbit said. "That gives me something to go on."

"Now you owe me a favor."

"No, I don't," Rabbit said. "You made an exception for me."

"But you asked more than one question."

"I didn't agree to anything and you can't hold me to it."

Bell chuckled again. He stroked his chin and studied her. "Tell me about your visit to the attic," he said.

She ran the palm of her hand over the tree's rough bark, and felt the cold of it sink into her skin.

"I haven't been to the attic," she said.

"Haven't you? Well, it's a stuffy old place for stuffy old things, but you may wish to venture up there sooner rather than later," Bell said. "In fact, you may wish to make a note of it before you go up. Write down your intentions and put the note somewhere you'll see it. You wouldn't want to forget."

The crow cawed, and Rabbit glanced up. When she looked for Bell again he was gone.

A lice found Dr Rumpole sitting on a bench in the village square. She paused at the fence and watched him for what seemed to her to be a long time, but he didn't move. Finally she stepped through the gate and walked across the green, her heart beating fast. A twig snapped under her boot and he finally noticed her, swiveling his head slowly in her direction, as if his neck needed oiling.

"Doctor," she said. "Are you all right?"

"Why wouldn't I be?"

"It's cold, and . . ."

She touched the sleeve of her coat, and he glanced down at his misbuttoned shirt.

"Hmm," he said, surprised. "I came out without my jacket."

"I'm sure you had important things on your mind," Alice said.

"I know you, don't I?"

"It's Alice. We've met."

"Yes, that woman you work for jabbed me with a pin."

"Oh, did she?"

"I think we both know she did." He smiled. "Can I help you with something?"

"Me? Oh, no, I was just being friendly."

"Well, Friendly Alice, I'm terrible with names, but I'll remember yours."

"If you're going home, I could walk with you a little ways. It's the same direction."

"Actually, Alice, I think I'll sit here a while longer. It makes me terribly sad to even think about that house they gave me."

"There are other places. The inn's very nice, and Jessica does up a good meal every evening."

"That, my dear, would require some ambition on my part. No, I'll just sit here until I feel like doing something else, then I'll either go home or I'll sleep on this bench. In my mind, they are equal."

She laughed, but he only stared at her stony-faced. There was an awkward silence that stretched out while she tried to find her way back into the conversation. Finally, she gave up.

"Well, good day, then," she said.

She walked carefully away across the icy grass, worried she might slip in front of him and embarrass herself. When she reached the street and looked back, he waved at her and she hurried away up the street, feeling too warm in her heavy jacket.

"That man needs looking after," she whispered to herself.

L ucy Knox snuck up the stairs, sliding along the wall to avoid a stretch of steps that creaked in the middle. She locked herself in the bathroom and removed her clothes. Her best yellow dress was ruined. She dropped it into the bathtub and ran water over it, thinking she would let it soak and scrub the blood out later, thinking she could rescue it.

Her mother called out from the landing. "Lucy? That you, dear?"

"Yes, Mother! I'm taking a bath!"

"Be quick. Your father will be home soon and I need your help with dinner."

Lucy closed her eyes and stood in front of the mirror. She set her palms on the vanity and leaned her head against the cool glass. She had grown up with Benjamin—one summer at a time—and she thought she knew him better than almost anyone. They had taken long walks in the woods, and brought picnic baskets. They had laid on blankets under the stars, and he had pointed out the ones he knew and named them for her. His father was pushing him to pursue medicine, but she knew Benjamin didn't want that. He wanted to find new and distant planets; he wanted to name asteroids and plot the distances between craters on the moon.

She had told him about her own dreams, how she would someday write a great novel, or a play and it would be the talk of the season. How maybe she would leave Ascension and tour the world, signing books and giving lectures. These were things she had never spoken aloud to anyone, and she'd held her breath, waiting for him to laugh.

But Benjamin hadn't laughed. He had only asked her what kind of stories she wanted to write.

He was all hers for three or four months every summer. For the rest of the year, she would dream that they could someday build a life together, he as a scientist, she as an author. They would meet at the end of each day, enjoy a cocktail on their terrace and watch their children play on the back lawn.

It *could* happen, so she never let herself think that it wouldn't.

She wondered where the pearl letter opener had gone. She hadn't seen it in the stationmaster's office when she'd tidied up. She made a mental note to go back and find it. It had cost her every penny she had, but it was a real pearl, and it was the moon. It was *them*, summed up in a piece of stationery, and she loved the idea of it. She had thought he would love it, too.

She turned from the vanity and wrung out her dress. She draped it over the edge of the tub, then pulled the plug and started the water for a bath. She had so far avoided looking at her reflection; she was worried her face might be bruised.

She stood in front of the mirror with her eyes closed, listening to the soothing rush of water behind her, then took a deep breath and opened her eyes.

Downstairs, Lillian Knox heard her daughter scream and dropped a pot of boiling water on the kitchen floor.

D aaaaisssyy . . ."
The voice echoed down the alley beside Knox Drugs. Daisy Merrick stopped and squinted into the darkness.
"Mr Knox, is that you back there?"
She turned at the sound of a second voice coming from the green across the road.

> There is a flower within my heart, Daisy, Daisy!
> Planted one day by a glancing dart . . .

"Sergeant Winter?" Daisy heard the panic in her voice and put a hand up to her mouth. "Are you all right, sir?"
The Sergeant leaned against the picket fence, holding his cane in both hands. Prosper Knox emerged from the alley, wearing a flat wooden mask that was painted to look like a monster's face. Its colors were faded and it was rimmed with a tangled mass of dirty hair.
"Mr Knox, what—"

> "Daisy, Daisy,
> Give me your answer, do!
> I'm half crazy,
> All for the love of you!"

He broke off singing and rested his shoulder on the drugstore wall. "We'd like to show you something," he said. "Daisy, would you come with us?"
"I don't think I—"

"You can trust us," the Sergeant said.

"My mother's expecting me." She held up a side of bacon wrapped in brown paper for them to see. "I was just fetching dinner. Mr Herman might still be . . ." She glanced at the butcher shop, but there was no sign of movement behind the window.

"This won't take long, girl," Sergeant Winter said. "We'd like to ask you some questions."

"What kind of questions?" She tried to sidle past Prosper Knox, but he stepped into the path ahead of her. In her peripheral vision she saw Sergeant Winter push away from the fence and start across the street toward them, swinging his cane, favoring his right leg.

"It's about the potions your mother makes," Prosper said. "I'm sure you help her with that, don't you?"

"Potions? No, I told you, I—"

"Those that practice witchcraft," Prosper Knox said, "are an abomination before the lord."

"Prosper," Sergeant Winter said, a note of irritation in his voice. "Keep your temper."

"With all due respect," Daisy said, "I think the lord has changed his rules lately."

"Watch your tongue, girl."

"How do you explain Benjamin Sinclair?"

Winter stopped and frowned and lowered his cane to his side. "Benjamin? What about him?"

"He died, and everyone knows it." She pointed toward the other side of the green. "I saw it happen. Mr Mulacky hit Benjamin with the milk cart and it rolled right over him. You could see his ribs. You could see everything. And there was so much blood."

"He's fine," Prosper said. His voice was muffled by the mask, but he sounded uncertain. "I've seen him in the shop."

"He died, but he got up and walked away," Daisy said. "And it's not just him. There are miracles happening everywhere, and nobody *really* dies anymore." Daisy took a shuddering breath and drew up her shoulders. "Anything you do to me. If . . . I mean, if you hurt me, I'll get back up like Benjamin did. I'll go home to my mother and we'll eat our dinner as if nothing happened here at all. I have nothing to fear from you."

"Nonsense," Prosper said. "A witch will say anything to save her own skin."

"Most people would," Winter said. "But I've heard the rumors, I've read the papers. There is something happening, and it's not just happening here."

"Witchcraft."

"Maybe so," Winter said. "Maybe not. Either way, this girl didn't cause it."

"I never did anything," Daisy said.

"Go home, Daisy."

"Newton?" Prosper said.

"You heard me," Sergeant Winter said. "This isn't the day. Go home, girl, and thank whatever deity you worship that this evening wasn't your last."

Daisy didn't wait to hear what Prosper Knox said next. She tucked the side of bacon under her arm, gathered her skirts, and ran.

T he girl's name was Esmerelda Rosas, and she had died on a Monday. She sat in the rocking chair by the fire, and although she told him she wasn't cold Moses found a horse blanket for her in the alcove.

Moses sat cross-legged on the hearth and they talked, but he was also listening to the sound of the whirring thing in the distance.

"Have you seen my cat?"

Moses shook his head.

"Her name is Iggy," Esmerelda said. "I suppose she will come back when she gets cold. She always does, but she might be afraid this time. She might blame herself for my death, even though it was an accident.

"I was carrying wood for the fire, and she got between my feet and tripped me. I fell into the fireplace and hit my head and burned. My father carried me to bed and put butter on my burns and sang to me, but I couldn't hear him because I was being loud. My face hurt, and my arm hurt, too. It felt like the fire had stuck to me and was digging inside me, digging all the way to my bones.

"But then everything stopped hurting. I told my father. I thought he would be happy, but he yelled that I was . . . I was muerta, and he cried and pulled his hair. He carried me to the cellar. He was going to leave me there in the dark. I was not very obedient. I fought against him and hit him with my fists."

She balled up her tiny fists to show Moses, and he thought it would break his heart if she hit him.

"My father was surprised that I would hit him. He grabbed my hands and let go of the cellar door, and it fell on his head. It made a big noise. The last thing he said was 'mi pequeña rosa.' It was what he always called me when I was alive, but he said it in a small voice. He laid there for a long time with his head sideways under the door. There was a little light that came from the gap, and I sat at the top of the ladder and kept him company until his eyes became cloudy and I knew he was dead. Then he woke up and left me down there and I heard the table moving on the floor. Then I didn't hear anything again until I heard you. It was a long time that I was down there by myself. Thank you for coming to let me out."

"I'm glad I did," Moses said. "What happened to you is probably my fault. At least the part after you fell in the fire."

"Don't be silly, Mr Moses. You weren't even here."

"Just the same," he said. "You stay here a minute. I have something I need to do."

Moses stood and took a lantern down from its hook. He slung his rifle over his shoulder.

"I'll be right back," he said.

Esmerelda said, "No!"

"I won't leave you on your own again. I just want to take a quick look around." To the yellow dog, Moses said, "You'll keep an eye on her for me?"

The dog turned in a circle and settled by the fire, and Esmerelda scooted to the ground and laid her cheek against its warm fur. Moses gave her what he hoped was a reassuring smile, then slipped out the door, closing it softly behind him.

The rain had stopped, and the clouds had rolled away, revealing the moon and stars. Moses could hear the familiar whirring sound as it grew closer.

"Get off my back, you terrible thing," he muttered.

He circled the house to the narrow stone path and followed the trail of blood down to the trees. The copse behind the cabin was small, smaller than the others that dotted the landscape: a few dozen saplings, sheltering the dead leaves and shaggy grass beneath them. Melting ice dripped from low branches, and Moses drew in a long breath, enjoying the dark loamy scent of wet vegetation.

A mouse the size of his thumb ran over the toe of his boot, and a shape pounced from the darkness, just missing the tiny creature. The mouse scampered back and forth, while a tortoise-shell cat scrambled after it, darting in and out of shadows, until the mouse finally scurried away beneath the leaves. Undaunted, the cat came to Moses and swam around his ankles, pushing her head against his shins.

"Iggy?"

He bent to pet her, and she offered her cheek, then hissed and scratched the back of his hand. Moses instinctively sucked at his dry skin as he watched the cat saunter away across the snow. "What I get," he said.

He pushed his way through the curtain of skinny trees, looking for footprints or more blood. He bent low and swung the lantern slowly back and forth, kicking leaves aside with the toe of his boot. He was staring at a lumpy patch of ground when a pair of eyes opened, and a face thrust itself up from the mud. The man spat leaves from his mouth and used his tongue to push dirt past his teeth and over his lips.

"Déjame," he said, his voice slurred with mud.

Moses fell back against a tree trunk, and breathed a sigh of relief when it held his weight. The swinging lantern illuminated the rough contours of the man's body, and the sludge around him, where he had evidently tried to bury himself in a shallow trench.

"I have to think you're Esmerelda's dad," Moses said.

"Déjame," the man said again.

"I don't speak Spanish. I know I should. I just don't have a knack for languages."

"Leave me," the man said. "I belong here."

"In case you were wondering, she's okay. Your daughter."

"She is no longer my daughter. There is a devil in her, and there is one in me. What have I done to bring this curse on us?"

"I doubt you did anything," Moses said. "It's a bad situation, is all."

"Déjame."

"That little girl would sure be glad to see you," Moses said. "Why don't you come back to the cabin, get a bath, warm up by the fire?"

Esmerelda's father closed his eyes, virtually disappearing in the darkness.

"I'll tell her you asked after her," Moses said.

The eyes didn't open again. Moses waited quietly and counted to a hundred before walking away from the shallow grave and out of the little grove.

The sounds of whirring and grinding were closer now, drowning out his footsteps as he crunched across the tundra to the cabin, watching for black ice and hidden trenches along the way.

When he opened the cabin door, the dog ran past him into the night. Another copse of silver maple stood fifty yards from the cabin, and the dog stopped ten feet short of it, running back and forth, barking at the trees. From the darkness behind the maples came an answering roar. The tops of the trees shivered, and a shower of leaves scattered to the ground.

An eye opened between the trees, its pupil slitted like a cat's, the iris a brilliant green in the light of the moon. Moses raised his rifle and took aim. Another eye appeared beside the first, then another. Moses counted, moving the muzzle of his weapon back and forth. Thirteen eyes, blinking at him in sequence. He heard wings beating in the shadows, and knew there was a blurry shape hovering there that would make no sense to him, even if he could see it. His empty stomach heaved.

He lowered the rifle and stepped forward.

"What do you want with me?" he said. "You can't kill me because I'm already dead. If you're planning to drag me down to Hell, then get it over with; just stop scaring my dog."

The eyes all blinked at once.

He felt something brush against his hand, and looked down to see Esmerelda standing beside him. Her tiny fingers curled around his wrist as she squinted at the thing in the trees. The eyes moved as one, staring back at her.

"Let me go on," Moses said to the thing in the trees. "I'll ride on from here first thing in the morning. I can't stop you from following me, but I wish you wouldn't."

The eyes moved again, to focus on him, then one of them winked and they all disappeared. The whirring noise faded, and the trees were still.

Moses knelt beside the girl. "Esmerelda, as soon as I can get to a station I plan to head up to Philadelphia by train. I don't know if that monster can move fast enough to keep up with a train, but I'm hoping it can't. I want you to come with me. I'd rather not leave you here."

"I will come with you, Mr Moses," the girl said. "I don't want to be alone anymore."

"Then it's settled." He glanced again at the empty copse, where the yellow dog still raced back and forth, growling at the trees. "I wish I knew what that thing wants from me."

"You should not be afraid of it."

"Why the hell not?"

"Mr Moses," Esmerelda said, "don't you know an angel when you see one?"

L ate that night, as most of Ascension slept, a great black bear loped down Vinegar Hill. She stopped at the train station and sniffed the air. She smelled blood and fear. She smelled death.

She continued down Shiloh Road, exploring each building she passed. She marked Knox Drugs with her scent, and did the same at the home of Sergeant Winter, and at the Sinclair's summer cottage.

Benjamin Sinclair was on the roof of the cottage with his telescope, watching the sky. Lucy Knox's blood was still crusted under his fingernails. He heard the distant caw of a crow; he heard leaves rustling in the wind. Benjamin looked down at the street and saw the bear's black shape separate from the shadows below, moonlight caught in her glossy coat.

The bear paused and looked up at him. They stared at each other, the bear and the dead boy, for a long moment. Then the bear turned and ambled away up Brynwood Lane toward the south edge of the woods.

When he could no longer see the bear, Benjamin bent over his telescope and resumed studying the face of the moon.

TWO DAYS
REMAINING

T he day began with a brief flurry of snow that melted as
the sun rose.

A host of small boys on bicycles braved the wet roads to
deliver invitations from Clarissa Sinclair. There was to be a grand
party at Bethany Hall to welcome the newcomers to Ascension,
and most of the village was invited. It was late notice, but the invitations were met with curiosity and excitement.

Naturally, Sadie, Rose, and Rabbit were sent invitations to
their own party, but the delivery boy did not know who lived in
the hall. When he saw four men standing on the covered porch,
he mistakenly thought the big house belonged to one of them. He
handed over his three envelopes without a word of explanation,
and rode back down the hill believing he had completed his task.

The men on the porch had arrived only moments before the
boy on the bicycle. They had worked together for many years,
traveling throughout New England and up and down the coast.
In spring they hauled lobster traps, and in summer they used
scythes to cut and bail hay; in autumn they picked apples at the
many orchards that dotted the countryside. In winter they hauled
firewood and scraped snow from roads and bridges. The smallest
of the men, James Doolittle, generally spoke for them all. He
took off his hat and held it against his chest when Housekeeper
answered the door.

"Ma'am," he said. There was the hint of a question in his voice.
"We've been sent by Mrs Sinclair to get your house ready for a
party."

Housekeeper looked past the men and saw a wagon heaped with lumber. She backed up clumsily and gestured for James to enter. He nodded and stepped over the threshold while the other three headed back to the wagon and began to untie ropes.

James followed Housekeeper to the ballroom and she lurched away. A moment later Rabbit appeared.

"Are you the lady of the house?" James said.

"I guess so," Rabbit said. "One of them."

"These must be for you." James handed over the three envelopes. "I'm . . . We're working for Mrs Sinclair."

"She doesn't live here."

"Yes, ma'am, she said she'd meet us here. Do you know exactly what she wants us to do?"

"Nobody tells me anything," Rabbit said.

"No, ma'am, they don't tell me much, either. All I know is we're supposed to do some work to the ballroom. Mrs Sinclair wants a stage built and some tables, and we've only got two days to do it, so I guess we better get to work."

Rabbit set the invitations on a table by the door and led James to the ballroom on the third floor. He stood in the doorway and surveyed the cavernous room, bigger than many entire homes he had worked in. Tall windows lined two of the walls, casting narrow bars of sunlight across the gleaming floor, and five chandeliers hung from the high ceiling. A piano stood in the far corner beneath two of the windows that looked out over the gardens at the front of the house.

"You know where she wants the stage?" James said.

Rabbit shrugged. "It's already pretty busy in here. You could put tables along the wall there." She pointed. "But don't get in the way of the dancing."

James felt the hair on the back of his neck stand up as he looked at the empty ballroom. He thought he could probably squeeze forty long tables into the room, and still have space between them to walk around. The girl seemed utterly serious, though, so he nodded as if he understood her concern.

"Then we'll start setting those up along the wall," he said.

He left her there, staring into the empty room, and went back outside to help the other men unload the wagon. He was glad they had such a short deadline. He didn't want to spend any more time in Bethany Hall than he had to.

Moses put Esmerelda on the old Appaloosa and led the horse away from the little cabin where the girl and her father had died.

"What is your horse's name?" Esmerelda said.

"Doesn't matter. She doesn't know her name."

"But she has one?"

"Pie," Moses said. "Her name is Pie."

"Pie?"

"I like pie." He looked up at her and raised the brim of his hat. The sun was behind her head, creating a bright halo; the burns on her face were momentarily invisible. "And I like my horse."

"I like her, too. I think Pie is a good name for a horse."

"Thank you."

Moses had decided to risk going in to the next town. Without Frank Smiley along, the Farmer brothers would have no reason to associate Moses with the murder of two of their own. And there might be a train station. If there was any help to be had in Philadelphia, he needed to get there faster than the horse could carry him. People were dying, people like Esmerelda, and while he was glad of the girl's company, he thought she ought to be able to lie down and rest. She deserved to be reunited with her family. He hoped to find Esmerelda's people in the nearby town. In his experience, folks with their own culture tended to band together and form communities outside white society, far enough to feel comfortable but near enough to get work. He thought she might be safer and happier living with a Mexican family close to where she had grown up.

"Do you have a wife, Mr Moses? Is there someone who is sad that you're dead?"

Moses guided the horse around an outcropping. He checked the sun and saw they were making decent time. He looked at the horizon and saw no rainclouds. After a long while he answered.

"I did have a wife," he said.

"Is your wife dead, too?"

"She died before I did. Back when people stayed dead."

"How did she die?"

"She took sick." He thought that was all he had to say on the matter, but he surprised himself by continuing. "She was thirty years old when she died. When I met her, she was twenty-seven, and her name was Katie Foster. Her father did not care for me, but she didn't mind too much about that." He studied the horizon again. "We had a baby."

"You had a baby?"

"Not for long."

"What do you think happened? Why do you think they stayed dead and we didn't?"

"I think somebody made a mistake," Moses said. "A bad mistake, and I think he'd better do anything he can to fix it."

They traveled in silence for six or seven miles, Moses leading the horse at a leisurely pace. Northeastern Missouri gave way to southern Illinois without much change in the landscape to mark the line between states. The ground rose along gentle slopes and fell away into shallow valleys. Trees grew more abundant, and they came across several small ponds where Pie drank while Moses and Esmerelda washed the dust from their necks and forearms.

The yellow dog ranged out from them for hours at a time, coming back to trot beside the horse for a while, then disappearing again.

"What's your dog's name?" Esmerelda asked when they were sitting beside a gully filled with green water.

"Not exactly my dog," Moses said. "Belonged to a fellow I met a few days ago, and stuck with me."

"Won't the other man miss his dog?"

"I don't think so."

"You should name it."

"I imagine it already has a name. I just don't know it. Why are you so set on knowing the names of things, anyway?"

"It's important."

"Well, if it's so important, you can name the dog."

"Naming a dog is harder than naming a horse," she said. "I'll have to think about it."

"Take all the time you want. That dog'll probably run off anyway."

But the dog found them again a mile north of the gully and stayed with them for the rest of the afternoon, keeping pace with Moses and the horse, running off occasionally to sniff at something, but never running far.

The sun was setting when they came to a pockmarked wooden sign that read WELCOME TO PROGRESS.

Moses stopped the horse and motioned for Esmerelda to lean down. He took a handkerchief from his vest pocket, doubled it over, and tied it around the lower half of her face, knotting it at the back of her head. He arranged her dark hair across her forehead.

"Less questions we get, the better," he said.

He pulled his hat down low and pulled on the reins, and Pie followed. He led the horse up the road and over a steep hill. Below was a flat scattering of buildings, and in the distance, where the houses thinned out, Moses was relieved to see train tracks. A crowd was gathered in the town square. Moses couldn't see what the commotion was about, but they'd have to pass through the square to get to the tracks. He took his revolver from its holster and handed it up to Esmerelda.

"You know how to use this?"

She nodded.

"Keep it under your shawl. Don't show it to anyone, but don't hesitate to use it if you have to. And if you do have to use it, try not to hit me. That's Colt's almost as big as you are."

He pulled his rifle from its scabbard on the saddle and held it loose at his side, then he walked on into town, leading the horse and the dead girl.

The yellow dog had disappeared again.

B enjamin was looking up at the squat weatherworn school-house when the waxed paper window was peeled away to reveal Rose Nettles's face. He was so startled that he stepped on a patch of ice without seeing it, slipped, and almost fell. He caught himself, his arms out at his sides, his legs bent at awkward angles, a high-wire act at ground level.

"Are you all right?" Rose called out through the hole in the wall.

"I'm all right," he hollered back. "What are you doing?"

"I'm getting the place ready for spring. It's in a terrible state. How long has it been since anyone taught here?"

Benjamin shook his head. The school was always closed when he visited Ascension in the summer. Curious, he trotted up the path, watching for patches of ice where the trees cast shadows.

Rose stood just inside the door, her cheeks red from the cold, her hair tied back with a kerchief. She opened her arms wide and said, "Voilà!"

Benjamin had only seen the inside of the schoolhouse once, during an afternoon walk with Lucy while his mother lay dying back in the cottage. He remembered a tumble of bricks and saw that Rose had stacked them neatly beside the fat old stove. The room was cold and smelled strongly of linseed oil. The desks and chairs, though worn with age, were clean and smooth and shiny.

"I've arranged for a man to come fix the shingles and glaze the window, but the odor was overpowering, and I needed a little fresh air."

"As long as it doesn't storm again."

Rose raised her eyebrows in faint alarm. "You don't think it will?"

"How would I know?"

"I see you watching the sky all the time."

"All I know about the weather is that sometimes it gets in the way of seeing the stars."

Rose laughed, and although she had a pleasant laugh, it made Benjamin feel sick to his stomach. He picked up a ball of paper from the floor, smoothed it out on a desk, and read the bold line of type at the top.

"'Good children obey'?"

"Oh," Rose said. "All the things here are from different times. Textbooks from one generation, maps from another, the desks and chairs are all mismatched. Whoever made that list was considerably stricter than I will be."

"I should damn well hope so!"

"Benjamin Sinclair! Language!"

She laughed again, and he smiled despite himself.

"That's ten lashes for me," he said.

"We can let it go this time," Rose said.

"I deserve them, though" Benjamin said. "Anyway, I'd better get going."

"You look pale. Are you all right, dear?"

"I don't know," Benjamin said. "There's a sort of sound in my head that gets louder. Like I'm getting closer and closer to a bee-hive. Only it's not really a sound. It's more of a feeling."

"That must be unpleasant."

"It makes me . . . I guess I feel anxious all the time, or maybe angry," Benjamin said. He pushed a chair up onto one leg and slowly twirled it. "What do you think happens to us when we die, Cousin Rose?"

She took a moment to consider. "I don't know," she said. "I was married once, and I was unhappy in my marriage. He wasn't a bad man, by any means, it just wasn't a good match and I could never bring myself to love him the way he wanted me to. Every morn-ing I would wake up and look at the ceiling and feel sad when I thought about the day ahead of me. I would think about all the ways I was going to disappoint my husband because I couldn't be the person he thought I was. But then, one day, out of the blue, my life changed completely, and now I get to spend every day with people I love, and I have realized that every change that happens in our lives brings an opportunity, if we look hard enough for it."

"What does that have to do with death?"

"It's a sort of analogy, dear. Perhaps when we leave some things behind, we get other things, and maybe they're better."

"Maybe they're worse."

"Poor Benjamin," she said. "Tell me what's bothering you."

He stopped twirling the chair and let it fall. "You're going to die, Cousin Rose. And when you do, you'll ruin everything, and you'll lose everything."

She sighed. "Well, you're in a mood. Yes, someday I will die, and probably sooner than I would like to think, but that's all the more reason to cherish what I have. And who knows? Maybe there's another big adventure ahead of me. I'd like to think so."

"I think death is something awful," he said. "I know it is."

"Listen, when we're very young, the world is nothing but possibility, such an abundance that it blinds us. As we get older, the possibilities grow fewer and smaller, until we see that we're moving fast toward a single point. And when we realize that, we begin to notice what's around us, and we're better able to appreciate it. That single point is death, and the fact of it lets us see what matters. Not that we should rush toward our deaths. Just the opposite. Gather up life and really look at it. Soak it in."

Benjamin shook his head, but Rose held up her hand to stop him.

"Hush now. It's cold, and there's nothing left to do here until that window has some glass in it. I'll walk you home. Things will look brighter with a warm fire and a little brandy."

Benjamin shook his head again. "I'm not fit company."

"Nonsense. You've had a lot to worry about, that's all. You're a good boy."

"You don't know anything," he said. "Not a damn thing."

He shoved a desk out of the way and stomped out of the schoolhouse, slamming the door behind him.

Through the empty window casing, Rose heard him shuffle away down the icy path. She grabbed the rules for children, and squeezed the ball of yellowed parchment until it was as small and tight as she could make it, then carefully placed it back in the stove.

D r Timothy Rumpole ran his fingers over the threadbare fabric beneath him. The couch, along with the rest of the furniture, had come with the little house on Twisdale Road. Nothing was his, except his clothes, his medical instruments, and the tray of drug paraphernalia that currently rested on the table in front of him.

He scowled at the tray, wondering if Prosper Knox had sold him weak opium. Rumpole's brother was dead, and the doctor had thought to numb his grief, to slip away in a beautiful haze, but here he was, awake and perfectly lucid on a ratty old couch that didn't belong to him.

He was startled out of his reverie by a knock at the door, and he stood quickly, grabbing his favorite red jacket from the coatrack. One of the village boys was on the porch. Charles Something. Dr Rumpole could never keep their names straight.

"Mr Rumpole?"

"Doctor."

"Sorry," Charles Bowden said. He was fidgeting, looking down at his feet. "Dr Rumpole, something's happened at the train station. I went up there, like I do, to sort the mail, and when I went in the office, I saw it. It was everywhere, and a lot of it, too!"

"A lot of what?"

"Blood, sir. At least, I think it's blood. It's everywhere."

"Whose blood is it?" Dr Rumpole looked around the room for his bag of medical equipment.

"Well, I don't know whose blood it was, Mr Rumpole."

"*Doctor* Rumpole, and what do you mean you don't know? Who else was at the station?"

"Nobody. There was nobody there."

Charles looked up and down the street, and it belatedly occurred to the doctor that he should invite the boy inside, but by now he was mildly annoyed, and anyway the moment for niceties had passed.

"I'm sure it's all right," Dr Rumpole said. "Someone's had a nosebleed and gone home to rest. This dry winter air causes—"

"Well, no, sir, if it was a nosebleed, somebody leaked every drop of blood out from their nose. I'm trying to tell you it was—"

"A lot of blood, yes."

"It really was." Charles finally looked up at the doctor and made a tiny noise deep in his throat. "Mr Rumpole, are you all right, sir?"

"I'm fine." He didn't bother to correct Charles this time. He thought there might be something wrong with the boy.

"You've got sick all over you, sir."

Rumpole looked down at himself. His jacket was open and the front of his cornflower blue shirt was splashed with vomit. He had worn the shirt especially for the occasion, so he would be found in his finest clothes after swallowing his entire supply of opium. He hadn't realized he'd thrown up on himself.

"Ah," he said.

"You look a little green, too, sir."

"Look—Charles, is it?"

The boy nodded.

"Charles, there's nothing I can do about an empty building. I need a body of some sort. I suggest you go get Sergeant Winter and take him up to the station. Let him do his job and if he needs my assistance he'll send for me."

"Okay, Mr Rumpole," Charles said. "Oh! I almost forgot. You got a telegram, sir. Down at the station. That was why I thought to come here in the first place."

"I have another cable?"

"Yes, sir." Charles fished in his coat pocket and dragged out a folded slip of yellow paper. "It's good news, sir. I hope you don't mind that I read it."

Dr Rumpole snatched the telegram from Charles's hand, and slammed the door in his face. He unfolded the paper and read.

DR TIMOTHY RUMPOLE

NUMBER 5 TWISDALE ROAD ASCENSION MA

  GOOD NEWS YOUR BROTHER DAVID FOUND

FLOATING IN PACIFIC AFTER TWO DAYS

BELIEVED LOST WAS WITH ANOTHER FISHER-

MAN BOTH MEN BLUE FROM EXPOSURE BUT

MAINTAIN THEY ARE HEALTHY DAVID

MISSING TWO FINGERS BUT OTHERWISE IN

GOOD SPIRITS AND FULL OF ENERGY STOP

                WILLIAM PETTIGREW

                    CHIEF PURSER

          ARTHUR STALL AND SONS

Dr Rumpole picked up his pipe and struck a match, then extinguished the flame and dropped the match on the tray. He stared at the pipe for a long moment before snapping it in half and flinging the pieces into the fireplace.

There were two eggs in the crow's nest. One was jet black, smooth and shiny and flawless; the other was splotchy and olive colored. Sadie sat on a high branch of her oak tree and stared at them. The crow perched on the branch above her, its head cocked to one side, regarding her silently.

The tree had more than tripled in size overnight, and now towered over the surrounding woods. She had been able to see the top of it from the windows of Bethany Hall when she woke up, an undulating cloud of green pinned against the brown latticework of winter boughs.

"Which of these is for me?" she said.

The crow watched her.

"We struck a bargain, you and I. I offered you security and

comfort, and in exchange you were to offer me your first egg." Sadie pointed at the nest. "I don't know which of these is your first egg."

The crow dropped from her branch, spread her wings, and circled the tree, spiraling down to its roots. She pecked in the mud and preened herself, then flew back up and settled at the edge of the nest.

Sadie touched the green egg and the crow hopped down into the nest. She used her beak to move straw around the green egg. Sadie smiled. She reached in and took the black egg.

"Thank you," she said. "Your chick will be safe with you here, and I will take care of this other one."

She popped the egg in her mouth so it wouldn't break, and clambered back down the tree. On the ground, she put the egg in her bag and slung the bag over her shoulder.

"Hello, new friend," she said to the egg. "I have plans for you."

Benjamin walked around the deserted green, his fists jammed deep in the pockets of his coat. He felt an inner fury that he chalked up to equal parts guilt and confusion.

The drugstore's windows were dark, and there was no sign of activity inside. Benjamin felt a prickle of dread along his scalp. He closed his eyes and stamped his feet against the cold.

Of course, he thought, *of course Lucy's body's been found by now. Sergeant Winter would already be questioning their friends. Prosper and Lillian would be making arrangements for their daughter's remains. The rest of the village would be gathered behind closed doors, speculating about what had happened to poor Lucy. Good, pretty, wonderful Lucy Knox.*

He silently cursed himself. He hadn't even bothered to clean up the mess at the station before leaving, and he was sure he had left clues to his identity. As he paced, trying to decide whether to go confess his crime or simply return home and wait for Sergeant Winter to arrest him, he noticed a girl watching him from the far side of the green. She started toward him, and he pretended to be looking at the ducks that were hung in the window of Herman's Meats. He could see the girl's reflection in the glass. She wore a veil, but she had on Lucy's new violet skirt and a black blouse he had seen her wearing the week before.

When she was too close for him to ignore, he raised his hand. "Lucy?"

"I wondered how I'd feel when I saw you, Benjamin, but I've surprised myself," she said. "I'm nowhere near as angry as I thought I'd be."

"Oh," Benjamin said. "That's good. How are you?"

"How do you think I am, Benjamin? I do love you, but I'm beginning to think you might not be the brightest star in the sky. Let me take your arm, and we'll walk."

She seemed more confident than he had ever known her to be. He held out his arm and she put her hand on his elbow. She led him up the street away from the drugstore. He tried to see around the edge of her veil, but she turned her head, blocking his view.

"Your face," he said. "Is it bad?"

"I had to pin some of it back in place," she said. "When I get up the nerve, I'll sew it properly. I'm sorry I'm not as pretty as I was."

They walked in silence for a while, until Lucy let go of his arm and turned to face him. She leaned against the church wall and regarded him through black lace.

"To be honest, I don't think I enjoyed life all that much anyway."

"I am really sorry."

"It's not all bad," she said. "At least we don't have to worry about dying or getting old. I don't know why this is happening, but it might turn out to be a good thing."

Benjamin thought about his conversation with Rose and shook his head. "I've had longer to think about it all," he said. "I've been dead for days. I think I'll have to go back to the city. Now that my mother's doing better, my father will want us to return. I'll finish my studies and find a position with a firm somewhere. Or maybe I'll go into practice with my father. But as time passes, my friends and colleagues will get older. I don't know what will happen to me. Maybe I'll decompose, or maybe I'll age naturally and die again someday. But what if I don't? What if I never age, while everybody around me gets old? People will notice, and I won't be able to stay in one place for very long without being accused of witchcraft or something. I'll never have anything normal again, nothing that lasts or matters. My life is over, Lucy. I mean, of course it is. And so is yours. I'm sorry."

"Then don't go back to the city. You don't have to do what your father says. Stay here in the village with me. I'll write books and send them to New York, and no one will ever know where I am or what you did to me."

"The same thing will happen here. How long before your parents notice there's something wrong with you?"

Lucy shrugged. "Then maybe it would be best to kill them, too. Maybe we ought to kill everyone in this whole silly village. Then this . . ." She touched her chest first, then his. "This wouldn't be unusual at all. We could be together forever and no one would blink an eye at us."

Benjamin's eyes widened. Lucy held out her hand and he could see the shadow of a smile behind her veil.

"Come," she said. "We'll start with my father."

Rabbit sat in a corner of the dining room; she watched the partiers and she listened to the men working in the ballroom upstairs. She had a tablet of paper on her lap, and she sketched each of the ghosts at the table. The drunken boy, the angry woman, the man with the magnificent mustache. She used a chunk of charcoal to rough out their broad outlines, then added details with a sharp pencil.

Bell appeared at the far end of the room and approached her, dodging the ever-present cook, who was forever bringing the same tainted meal to her doomed employers.

"They look like they're having fun," Rabbit said.

"They never look any other way," Bell said.

"Except that boy standing in the corner. And maybe the one who spills his wine."

"Imagine living your worst moment over and over again for all time," Bell said.

"No, thank you. What do you think of this?"

She tilted her tablet toward him, and he leaned forward to take a look.

"You have made the cook seem lively, and even enthusiastic while performing the same murderous task she always does," he said.

"Did she really kill them all?" Rabbit said. "If so, it seems like they enjoyed their last meal."

"They did. And it's now the only meal she will ever cook."

"I think I understand why the guests might be stuck here, but why would she want to spend forever serving the people she killed?"

"Oh, Rabbit," he said. "Little Rabbit."

"I'm not so little."

"Of course. And I'm sure you have nothing to feel guilty about."

"I don't know why I talk to you," she said.

He straightened and bowed. It was an exaggerated gesture, as if he had suddenly realized he was in a strange country and didn't speak the language.

"I have overstepped," he said.

He turned on his heel and circled around the end of the table.

Rabbit called out to him. "Mr Bell, why do you talk to *me*?"

He did not look back. He passed through the far wall, and the tail of his coat seemed to catch for a second in the plaster.

"None of the other spirits talk to me," she said.

But he was gone.

Rabbit watched the young man spill his wine again; she watched him leap up in exaggerated worry, and she wondered what it would be like if she never left Bethany Hall.

They were an odd sight for the townsfolk of Progress, Illinois—a black man leading an old horse, with a Mexican child in the saddle—and those gathered in the town square stopped what they were doing to watch them. The black man's hat was pulled low on his head, and the girl wore a bandanna around her face. Their shoulders were hunched, as if they intended to get through the center of town without being noticed or challenged.

The mayor of Progress was holding one end of a length of rope. He handed it to the man next to him and stepped forward.

"Hey there, boy," he said to Moses. "What brings you to Progress today?"

Moses pointed down the street behind the mayor. "Does the train stop here?"

The mayor turned around and shot a quizzical look at the gathered throng behind him. He wasn't sure whether to answer the stranger or upbraid him for not answering his own question. It suddenly occurred to him how odd the scene in the town square must look to an outsider. Two men each held a length of rope. The ropes were tied to the wrists of a young woman, whose hair and dress were dripping wet. Behind them was a large tub full of water. Another woman was on her hands and knees, tying more rope around the wet woman's ankles. A stout man stood nearby, ready with a team of four horses, and the rest of the town had crowded around the periphery. It seemed like an explanation might be in order. The mayor smiled at Moses.

"I imagine this looks a mite peculiar to you," he said. "You must be wondering what all's going on."

"It looks to me like you tried to drown that woman, and now you're about to pull her apart with a team of horses," Moses said. "That sound about right?"

The mayor was startled. "Actually, yes, that is correct. But you ought to understand, this woman is a witch."

"I guess that explains everything then," Moses said. "The train? Does it stop in your town?"

"Mister," the mayor said, "I'm trying to explain, in case this seems outrageous to you. In case you don't think we're such good folks here. We got us a town emergency on our hands. You see, Poppy Buckland over there, she put a bad curse on our town, so we had to drown her. But she wouldn't stay drownded, and when we fished her outten that tub, she got right back up and headed for home. So now we got to do something more drastic."

Poppy Buckland had not yet said a word. She glared at Moses and Esmerelda, and she even glared at Pie. Her skin was pale blue. Water flowed from her hair and her dress, trickled down her legs, and pooled around her feet.

Moses sighed. "I suppose you want me to ask what this woman cursed you with, but if I were to guess I'd say it was ignorance."

"No, sir," the mayor said. He was a born politician, and he

had begun to think of Moses as a constituent to win over to his side. "Poppy cursed us so nobody in Progress dies anymore. Well, naturally we thought it was a blessing at first, but before too long we figured out it was a curse. Virgil Blinken got both his arms crushed changing a wagon wheel, but he didn't die and his arms ain't growing back, so now he's got no way to make a living. Jenny Sperling's crazy old man shot her, and now she's missing half her head. I ask you, who's gonna marry a girl with half a head?"

There was a loud sob from the back of the square. A young woman broke away from the crowd and ran up the street away from them, holding her hands over her face.

"Anyhow, we got to kill this witch so the curse can lift from this town. Then Virgil and Jenny can lay down and die like they's supposed to, and we can get on with things like normal."

"Sounds pretty simple," Moses said. "But if nobody can die, how are you going to kill this woman?"

"Like you said, we're gonna pull her apart with the horses."

"What you're gonna do is pull off her arms and legs and leave her in the same sort of trouble as your other people. Virgil and Jenny."

The mayor stared at him and shook his head. He looked up at Esmerelda on the horse, and cleared his throat. He raised his shoulders, then dropped them in defeat.

"Well, hell," he said. "When you put it so blunt, I can see we didn't think it all the way through. It's possible we got a little carried away."

"We come this far already," said the man with the team of horses. "Can't hurt to try."

"Seems like a wasted effort," Moses said. "And then somebody'll have to take care of this woman, since she won't be able to do much of anything for herself, having no arms or legs. Who's going to do that?"

The mayor shook his head again. "Not me, no, sir."

"Well, somebody's got to."

The mayor glanced at the woman who had tied Poppy Buckland's ankles.

"Don't you look at me, Horace," she said. "I got five children of my own to take care of. Not to mention Virgil, now he's got no arms."

"Best let this woman go," Moses said.

"But the curse," Horace said.

"She didn't put any curse on you," Moses said. He took off his hat and lifted his head so the people standing behind the mayor could see the bullet hole in his skull. "It's not your town that's been cursed. What's happening to you is happening everywhere. It's happening to everybody. It wasn't Poppy Buckland that did it. Maybe let her go, Horace. Killing her again won't do you any good."

The mayor blinked rapidly and took three steps back. He bumped into Poppy Buckland, who kicked out at him, and he lost his balance. He sprawled face forward in the dirt, and Poppy spat a yellow gob at him that landed on his neck. He got slowly to his feet and took a dirty cloth from his pocket. He wiped his neck, and gestured ineffectually at Moses.

"Settle down now, Poppy. We don't even know this man. He could be a damn black liar."

Moses was still holding his hat in his hands; the bullet hole was visible to everyone in the square.

Esmerelda had not said a word since entering the town. Now she pulled Moses's handkerchief down under her chin and brushed the hair away from her eyes revealing the damage to her face.

"He's telling you the truth," she said. "You people are not even a little bit special."

There was a light breeze from the north, and Mayor Horace's wispy hair fluttered about his scalp. He tucked the rag back into his pocket and wiped his fingers on his vest. There was an air of dejection about him. The men dropped the ends of their ropes, and Poppy pulled away from them. She drew her foot back, aiming another kick at Horace's ample backside, but Moses raised his hand.

"Might not be a good idea, ma'am," he said. "You might not want to rile him back up."

She glared at him, but lowered her foot.

The crowd began to disperse, and Moses put his hat back on. He stroked Pie's nose to settle her, then caught Horace's eye and pointed again at the distant end of the street behind the mayor.

"About that train . . ." he said.

I told you something bad happened here," Charles said. "Something really bad happened."

"I'd say so," Dr Rumpole said. He set his medical bag on the floor of the train station and put a hand to his lips. He had brushed his teeth and changed his shirt, but there was still a whiff of vomit on his fingers.

"I appreciate your help here, Doctor," Sergeant Winter said. "I'm a bit out of practice and can use a fresh pair of eyes." He lit his pipe and examined a streak of blood on the wall beside him. "Did you touch anything, Charles?"

"I suppose I did," Charles said. "Let me think." He picked up an armful of firewood from the box by the door and added it to the hot stove, inadvertently scorching the log that had been used to murder Lucy Knox. "I didn't know it was blood right away, sir. The room was dark and I just thought somebody spilled something. Ink or maybe coffee."

"Coffee?"

"Well, I don't know what I thought."

"I see," Winter said. "And what did you touch?"

"Well, first I lit the lamp because it was dark."

"So you said."

"Yeah, I guess I touched the lamp over there."

"And then what did you do?"

"Then I checked to see were there any telegrams waiting on the desk, and there were. There were three of them, which I translated right away. They're in Morse code, you know, and someone has to turn that into plain English."

"I understand," Winter said. "So you decoded the telegrams on the desk."

"That's right. There was one for Dr Rumpole, and one for George Herman the butcher, and one for a lady up at Bethany Hall. The one for Dr Rumpole was good news about his brother. Congratulations again, sir."

"That's all right," Dr Rumpole said.

"The cable for Mr Herman was about a shortage of hamburger meat, and—"

Winter cut him off. "Perhaps you'll let me guess what happened after you did all that. You gathered your telegrams, ready to deliver them, and you finally turned to leave, facing the room from the desk there, and in the light from the lamp you were able to discern that the dark areas on the floor and on the wall were not, in fact, coffee. Does that sound right?"

"I guess that's why you're the policeman, sir."

"And you ran to get help?"

"Well, I thought maybe I could kill two birds. I mean I had the cables to deliver, but also I ought to tell somebody about the blood."

"So you went to the doctor."

"That's right. I told him about the blood, and he said to fetch you."

Winter pointed the stem of his pipe at the doctor. "You didn't want to take a look for yourself?"

"He said it was your job, sir," Charles said.

Both men glared at Charles, who used his fingernail to scratch a patch of dried blood off the desk.

"I don't see any bodies here," Dr Rumpole said. "Or anyone in need of medical attention. I stand by my initial assessment that this requires an investigator, not a doctor."

"Nevertheless, I think your scientifically trained mind may be of use. These are interesting times we find ourselves in." Winter puffed on his pipe. "Charles, you saw nothing else out of the ordinary?"

"Besides all this blood?"

"It's more than I would expect from a nosebleed," Dr Rumpole conceded. "This results from a severe injury of some sort. I don't think anything as bad as an arterial wound, but maybe a punctured liver, or a laceration of the scalp. It's hard to imagine anyone walking away from this. The body must have been moved."

"Given what I believe is happening," Winter said, "both within this village and in the outside world, I have little expectation that a body will be found."

Dr Rumpole raised an eyebrow.

"Revenants," Winter whispered. "Witchcraft," he said more loudly.

"Nonsense," Dr Rumpole said. "Yes, there are strange things happening, but—"

"Sure," Charles said. "Everybody knows Benjamin's dead, but he don't want to talk about it."

"How else do you explain that, Doctor?"

"I'm sure there's a scientific—"

"What was the good news about your brother?"

"Excuse me?"

"Charles brought you a telegram."

"It's just that . . . Well, David was swept overboard a few days ago, but now they've found him."

"You mean they've found his body? I suppose that's good news in the sense that you can properly bury him."

"He's not . . . um." Rumpole glanced down at his relatively clean white shirt. "He appears to be healthy."

"Is that so? After days at sea? I'm glad for you."

"I'm not ready to blame village superstitions," Dr Rumpole said.

"That's the keen scientific mind, but you know it's not only happening in the village. Your brother is only one example. The papers are full of this sort of thing if you know what to look for. No, I agree, this is not the work of a single witch, but I don't rule out witchcraft."

"That doesn't make sense to me."

"I can think of no other rationale." Winter pulled a small change purse from his pocket. "I'm done here," he said. He fished in the purse until he found a nickel, and set it with a stern click on the corner of the desk. "Charles, would you bring some of the other lads up here and get the place cleaned up?"

"Yessir," Charles said. He grabbed the nickel and stepped in a thick puddle of Lucy's blood, slipped, then regained his balance and pelted from the room, leaving a trail of bloody footprints.

"Well." Dr Rumpole picked up his medical bag and saluted Sergeant Winter. "I suppose I'll be off as well."

He stepped around the puddle, and avoided the smudges left by Charles's left shoe, paused at the door and turned as if he had thought of something else to say, then thought better of it and patted the doorframe. Winter listened for the sound of the outer door, and when he was satisfied he was alone he tapped his pipe out on the desk and put it in his pocket.

"You are a fool, Doctor," he said to the empty room.

He had hoped the doctor would offer an alternative explanation for the strange occurrences, something properly rooted in science, but instead Dr Rumpole had buried his head in the sand.

There was one person in the village he could talk to, one person who would understand his theory. Winter left the station and walked down Shiloh, past the drugstore, which was closed when it ought to have been open. He walked on, swinging his cane, increasingly disturbed by how empty the streets were, how quiet the village was, until he reached the doorstep of Prosper Knox.

He knocked, and after waiting a minute he knocked again, and heard footsteps approaching the other side of the door. It swung open and Prosper stood at the threshold. His clothes were wet with blood. The flesh hung from his face in ribbons, and a piece of his skull dangled behind his left ear, bouncing against his neck when he spoke.

"You're too late," he said.

Winter glanced past him into the front room where Lucy sat with an axe dangling forgotten between her knees. Her face was hidden behind a veil.

"Please come in, Sergeant," she said.

W hen Alice Anders entered the bedroom, Clarissa was standing naked in front of her wardrobe, frozen in place, clutching the edges of the open doors. She turned and silently regarded Alice.

Clarissa's muscles twitched and rolled as if something were scurrying up and down her bones. Her skin hung loose on her arms and around her waist. Her hip bones were bicycle handlebars, and Alice could count every rib.

"In this world," Clarissa said at last, "Alice, in this world you could not ask for more than I've been granted. I have known love. I have enjoyed security. I have material possessions. I have so many *things*, Alice, but I feel unhappy today. Why am I so unhappy?"

She began to cry, and Alice took a few tentative steps toward her. Clarissa fell into her nurse's arms and hid her face in the folds of Alice's white blouse. When she let go, she turned away and Alice felt a sudden impulse to run a finger down the protruding knobs of Clarissa's spine.

"I don't know why I thought I could throw a party at the last minute," Clarissa said. "Alice, why would I set myself up for such an enormous failure? And in front of the entire village!"

"It'll be a good party, Missus," Alice said. "After such a bleak winter, everyone'll be happy to go. They'll be happy to dance and eat and—"

"Don't condescend to me," Clarissa said. "Did you bring matches?"

Alice found the tiny box of matches in her apron pocket and held them out, but Clarissa was already standing at the window, looking down at the street.

"None of them fit me anymore," Clarissa said. "My gowns. I'm at sea in them. I want you to burn them."

"I . . . Ma'am, I cleaned the blue dress, like you wanted. I took the liberty of taking it in at the waist and shoulders. If it still don't fit properly, I'll make adjustments."

Clarissa turned from the window. There was hope in her eyes, but there was something else, too, something Alice couldn't identify. She remembered the woman Clarissa was as her illness had begun to wear her down; the look then was warm and inviting, but her eyes had dulled during her convalescence.

"Where did you learn to tailor a gown, Alice?"

"My mother taught me when I was a girl," Alice said. "I didn't always know I would be a nurse, and she thought the skill could be useful."

"You have so many useful skills, Alice. Where will you go now that I'm better?"

"I never gave it a thought."

"Don't be stupid. Of course you did. My husband wouldn't have kept you on after I died. For what? Do you think you're pretty enough to interest him?"

Alice stared at the box of matches in her hand. "My mother died three years ago," she said. "I don't have nobody else."

"You planned to replace me, is that it?" Clarissa's voice was a guttural whisper. "All you had to do was wait for me to die so you could seduce my husband and take my place in the household. You'd hardly be the first to think of it."

Alice dropped the matches and knelt to pick them up. "No, ma'am. I didn't like to think you'd pass, but I guess I would've found a place somewhere. Not with your husband, I mean. In a private practice."

"Perhaps with the handsome Dr Rumpole? I saw the way you looked at him."

Alice felt her face grow warm. Clarissa's lips were drawn back, her teeth bared, her gums black. Her sharp cheekbones caught the light from the window, illuminating shiny snail tracks of tears.

Spittle flew from Clarissa's lips when she spoke. "I'm sorry, Alice. I don't know why I say these things. I know you're a good girl. I really think you are, but oh, Alice, I hate you with every fiber of my being."

Alice could barely breathe. "But what did I—"

"Leave the matches and go," Clarissa said. "Get out of my room now. Hurry, Alice! For your own sake, hurry!"

Alice scrambled to her feet and ran. She turned and saw Clarissa crouched low as if preparing to leap. Alice slammed the door and ran down the hallway, through the parlor, and out the front door. She ran up the street, splashing through puddles of melted snow and ice. She ran until she couldn't breathe.

I know it's grotesque," Prosper said. "And I know it's asking a lot of you, but you must understand, it's not Lucy's fault. In a way, it was Benjamin Sinclair who killed me. He poisoned her mind against me."

"But your daughter wielded the axe," Winter said.

"She would never have done such a thing without Benjamin's malign influence. Help me, Newton. Help me take my revenge on him."

Winter sighed. "I don't entirely understand your reasoning."

Prosper slumped back in his chair and stared into the fire. "I had a good life, Newton. I was going to retire soon. I've taught Charles well, and the shop would have outlasted me, carried my name and legacy."

"It doesn't seem to me that much has changed." Winter averted his eyes and shuddered. "You could stand behind your counter for a century, serving up sodas and dispensing coke and opium, or you could go ahead and retire and manage your legacy long into the future. Death might be the best thing that's happened to you."

"I've been murdered, Newton, and that makes me very angry. Listen, I'll see justice done with or without you, but I honestly thought you, of all people, would understand. You and I have always acted to protect the integrity of this village."

"What's happened to you isn't witchcraft. It's happening all over the world. There simply aren't enough witches to have done all this."

"You think there should be more of them?"

"Don't be childish," Winter said. "This is all too much. It would take the combined effort of thousands of them, tens of thousands. This is something beyond our understanding."

"Revenge isn't hard to understand."

"What do you propose to do? A dozen people saw the milk cart run over that boy. If that wasn't enough, what is?"

"I've been thinking about that, Newton. Guns and knives and milk carts may not put him down, but we could burn him. It hardly matters whether he can die if we reduce him to a pile of ash. We'll leave no trace of him on this earth."

Sergeant Winter had done far worse than what Prosper was asking. He couldn't even pretend to be shocked. Besides, he was curious. He had read nothing about burn victims among the undead.

"Very well," he said, "Maybe you'll get some satisfaction from this, but don't pretend it's for the good of the village. It won't bring Lucy back. Or Lillian, or yourself."

"But you'll help me?"

Sergeant Winter nodded. "If I must," he said. "I suppose I will."

"Good man! That's the Newton Winter I know!"

Winter pinched the bridge of his nose and sighed. "I suppose we'll need to make some sort of a plan."

"I thought we'd invite him out to hunt with us," Prosper said.

"Benjamin isn't the hunting sort, but it occurs to me that we might be able to coaxe him into the woods. Some dark night when we're all on Vinegar Hill together anyway, if you catch my drift."

A slow smile creased Prosper's mangled face, and he chuckled. It was a deep wet expression, accompanied by black pus that dribbled from his chin and rolled down his heaving chest.

"We'll take him from the party," he said.

Sadie gently cracked the crow's black egg against the rim of a silver bowl and peeled back the shell. Inside was a pale hatchling, cramped and curled and damp. Sadie used a clean towel to dry the chick off, and laid him in a bed of straw at the bottom of the bowl. His tiny beak and his clutching, trembling feet were pink. His eyes, when they opened, were bright red.

Sadie dropped the bits of black eggshell in a stone mortar and ground them to a fine powder. She plucked three red hairs from her scalp and added them to the mortar, along with a drop of blood and an ounce of warm goat's milk, then she stirred the mixture, adding water until it seemed thin enough. She drew some of it into an eyedropper and fed the hatchling. He drank hungrily, and chirped for more, opening his beak wide and bobbing his fragile head at her.

She napped in a chair by the fire, the baby bird in his straw-filled bowl on her lap. Rose dozed on the couch beside her.

When they woke, the crow was the size of Sadie's fist and had begun to flutter his wings. His feathers had dried and they glowed white in the sunlight through the parlor window. He fixed his red eyes on Sadie and stood on his wobbly pink legs, cocking his head first one way, then the other.

After dinner, Sadie and Rabbit took the young crow to the bottom of the hill and set him in the wet brown grass at the edge of the woods. The air was warm, and the sound of melting snow swept through the trees like a spring shower.

"We need to get ready," Sadie said.

"Ready for what?" Rabbit said.

Sadie watched the baby bird wobble through the grass. He stopped and shook himself and was lost from sight in a flurry of white feathers. When the downy cloud settled, the crow had reached his full size. He spread his new wings and flapped them a few times, then took to the air. He circled Sadie, cawed once, and flew away to the treetops.

"I don't know," Sadie said. "But I don't think we have much time left."

As they walk back up the hill, I watch from the attic window. Rose has refused her duty, and the witches are making plans. I have begun to worry. I pray that my brother will hasten Moses Burke on his journey.

Poppy Buckland lived in a one-room shack a mile outside Progress. It was cozy, and cluttered with an abundance of potted plants—they filled the surface of every table and chair, lined the floor along the baseboards, and hung from the ceiling. Where there was space between plants, there were books, stacked and piled precariously. There was a narrow cot in one corner of the room, and a tall wardrobe from which Poppy picked out a dress for Esmerelda. It was too big for the girl, but it was clean and trimmed with bits of white lace. Esmerelda loved it.

Esmerelda slept next to Poppy on the cot; Moses slept outside on the porch, rolled up in a horse blanket. He would occasionally wake to the sound of an owl hooting in a nearby tree, or a small animal scurrying through the bushes beside the house.

He didn't know whether he was awake or asleep when he heard the familiar whirring in the distance: the wheels of an endless wagon train, a giant grain mill. The sound approached like a storm across the prairie. Lightning cracked, thunder rumbled, but there was no rain.

Moses opened his eyes.

The thing he had seen in the woods watched him from the narrow road that bordered Poppy Buckland's property. Its thousand wings beat at the air; its thousand eyes blinked.

Moses watched the creature, and it watched him, and he had no way of knowing how much time passed while he lay frozen in place, unable to look away. Sometimes the thing took on the appearance of an ox, sometimes it looked like a man with flowing hair and a hawk's sharp beak.

After a time, it spoke.

"Be not afraid," It said. *"Hear these words and remember. The rose must remain a rose. It must not change, blossom or wilt, for a new season shall be ushered in when the chrysanthemum is plucked from the garden."*

Moses had a sudden flash of understanding.

"Do not carry the book to the hilltop. Disobey the Word and you shall be lost to all living memory. We have spoken and it is so."

The moon disappeared and the stars winked out, plunging the landscape into darkness. The sound of wheels rolled away. When he could move again, Moses sat up and grabbed the porch railing to steady himself. The moon and the stars reappeared in the sky, and the landscape sprang into view around the cabin. The thing was gone, but Moses was startled to find Esmerelda standing beside him, staring out into the night.

"Did you see it, too?" Moses said.

"I heard you yell," she said. "What did you see?"

"I had a dream. That thing you said was an angel, it talked to me."

Esmerelda plunked down on the porch and crossed her legs in front of her. She took his hand and stared hard into his eyes.

"You were visited," she said. "What did it tell you?"

"I think it was talking about a friend of mine. As far as I know, she's still with the witches I'm going to see."

"What did it say about her?"

"I think it told me to stay away from her. I think it said I should give up."

Esmerelda let go of his hand and stood up. She smoothed her new white dress and leaned against the wall of the house, watching the road. "I wish I had seen it. I wish it had talked to me, then I would know what kind of angel it is." "There are different kinds?"

She nodded.

"I don't know what to do."

Esmerelda turned her head to look at him. "You have a hole in your head and I was killed by fire. The world is broken and you have to try to fix it. You might fail, but you cannot give up."

"I guess I've come this far," Moses said. "If I can find out where she is, I should try to warn Sadie Grace. Maybe she can figure out if I'm doing the right thing. If I'm not, maybe she can stop me."

ONE DAY
REMAINING

Dear Diary,

This morning, when Alisses back was turned, I took a knife from the kitchen and hid it under my matress. I think it will make me feel more sekure to know I have ~~takin a pricotion~~ done something, even something so crude and awful as keeping a knife beneath my bed. If she enters my room again tonight I will be ready.

The thought of it does not truble me much.

~~the bog for chosen gris me porridge~~

P oppy boiled water and made tea in the morning, serving it in three mismatched earthenware mugs. Moses sipped at his politely, though he wasn't thirsty. Esmerelda walked around the shack, leaning down every few steps to sniff the plants.

"What is this one called?" she said.

"Pokeweed," Poppy said. "It's used to soothe rashes."

"You're really a witch?" Moses said.

"Folks in town say I am," Poppy said.

"Could pokeweed heal my burns?" Esmerelda said.

"I don't know, but I'll give you some."

"You should leave this town," Moses said to Poppy.

"This is my home," she said. "I've lived here since I was a girl."

"Those people might've settled down for now, but they'll be back as soon as the next person meets with an accident."

"I doubt it. They're not bad people, they're just not very smart."

"They seem like bad people to me," Moses said.

"What's this one?" Esmerelda said, pointing to a pot of drooping white flowers.

"Lily of the Valley," Poppy said. "You're finding all the poisonous plants."

"They look like little bells," Esmerelda said, running a fingertip over one of the blossoms.

"It helps with gout and palsy."

"Look, I've got a house down in Kansas," Moses said. "It's not much, but it's bigger than this place."

"You've barely touched your tea," Poppy said. "Would you like something else? I have whiskey, and some milk."

Moses shook his head. "How about you? You want any of that?"

Poppy considered the question while watching the steam rise from her mug, then she set it aside and folded her hands in her lap.

"No," she said. "I don't feel thirsty or hungry. I don't feel tired, either."

"You won't want to eat or drink much anymore," Moses said. "You might sleep a little. I tend to get a few hours. I don't know if I need it, but dreaming seems like it helps keep me on an even keel."

"You're saying being drowned has freed me from my needs?"

"Some of them."

"Then why should I leave? Those people can't kill me twice, can they?"

"They were going to pull you apart. Death isn't necessarily the worst thing that could happen. I met a fellow who got his eyes pecked out by birds."

Poppy shuddered.

"There's another reason to go. You're probably going to start feeling more . . ." He looked to Esmerelda for help explaining.

"I have been having dark thoughts," Esmerelda said.

Moses nodded. "I think the longer you stay dead, the angrier you get."

"Not angry," Esmerelda said. "Scared."

"Yeah," Moses said. "It's panic. I have an idea that when we die there's some part of us that's supposed to leave our body and move on. Now it can't do that. It's trapped and it's not happy about that."

"We are a cage," Esmerelda said.

"And I think it's worse whenever we're around the living," Moses said. "You stay in this town, and your neighbors will start to grate on your nerves."

Poppy chuckled. "They always have." She picked up her mug, took a small sip of tea, and shuddered.

"There must be a cure," she said.

"There are women I used to know," Moses said. "I'm hoping they'll be able to help. They're like you."

"They're witches?"

"Yeah, but now that we've met you, I've been wondering . . ."

"You wonder if I know the sort of magic that could change the world back to the way it's supposed to be?"

"Well, do you?"

"Mr Burke, I know how to squeeze an aloe plant and dress a wound. I know how to help a baby turn in the womb when it's upside down. I know how to ease cramps and headaches, but this?" She waved her hand to indicate the shack and everything outside it. "Whatever's happening now is far beyond my knowledge or ability."

Moses nodded. "Too bad. You could've saved me a trip."

"These women you're going to see, I hope they know better magic than I do."

"It's been a few years since I saw them. Rabbit was a little girl, but even then she could conjure a tornado out of a clear blue sky. And I saw her mother pull a tree out of the ground, without even touching it. Then she threw it at a man."

"Sadie Grace," Poppy said.

Moses nodded. "You know her?"

"I've heard of her. You know where she is?"

"Last address I have for them is in Philadelphia, so that's where I've been headed. But I don't know if they're still there. I've got no idea if I'm on the right track."

"Oh," Poppy said. "Well, maybe I can do just a little more than cure headaches."

She jumped up and went to the wardrobe in the corner of the room. Along one side of it were dozens of shelves, each holding hundreds of narrow slots, filled with packets and papers, twigs from various trees, and folded bits of fabric. She thought for a moment, then reached up to the highest shelf and produced a parchment scroll, which she carried to the fireplace and unfurled across the mantel. Rolled out, the parchment was revealed to be a map, the largest and most detailed that Moses had ever seen. With the firelight dancing behind it, every mark on the map seemed to move. Jagged blue riverbeds flowed, and red smudges that represented townships appeared to grow and shrink, as if transforming over time.

"I have three of these," Poppy said. "Bought them from a Russian midwife who wouldn't say where she found them."

"It's pretty," Esmerelda said.

"It is," Moses said. "But I already know where Philadelphia is."

"Say her name," Poppy said. "Say who you're looking for. Say it out loud."

"Sadie Grace."

"Wait," Poppy said.

She tore the map in half, folded the two pieces over each other, and tore it again. Esmerelda gasped. Poppy winked at her, then balled the parchment up and tossed it in the flames.

"Say it again," she said.

"Sadie Grace," Moses said.

"Sadie Grace," Poppy repeated, staring into the fire. "If she's alive or if she's expired, please find Sadie Grace within this fire."

The ruined map flared at the edges and rolled over, turning faster and faster on the stone floor of the fireplace. It rose into the air and twirled first one way, then another, throwing off sparks in every direction. Moses stepped back and pulled Esmerelda with him. The fiery map smacked against the inner wall of the fireplace and bits of brown paper fluttered out onto the hearth where they curled and turned to ash. The map flew up and crunched into the opposite wall of the fireplace, skittering up and down the bricks, grinding itself down as it crawled across the stones.

"It's a scrying spell," Poppy said. "Useful for finding lost people and livestock."

Within minutes, the map was gone, all but a small tattered bit of translucent parchment, black around the edges, floating above the fire on an updraft. Poppy reached out and plucked it from the air.

There was a red smudge in the center of the paper, and the name scrawled above it was still clear. Esmerelda looked up at the others with a scowl.

"Ascension," she said. "Where is that?"

The eight o'clock train arrived in Ascension on schedule, with no passengers, but with a great many crates and trunks from Philadelphia. Porters unloaded it all and left it on the platform.

An hour later, a coach trundled down Vinegar Hill and parked at the station. Two hulking men, their faces obscured by scarves and hats, loaded up the heavy freight from Philadelphia under the watchful eye of Rose Nettles, then she and the two men clambered onto the coach and it rolled back up the hill, more slowly than it had come down, riding significantly lower on its axels.

A lice is gone," Clarissa said. "Benji, Alice is gone!"

She tossed a piece of notepaper at him, and Benjamin caught it. He squinted at the spidery scrawl, silently mouthing the words as he deciphered them.

> *Dear Mrs Sinclair,*
>
> *I feel I must tinder my resignation, effective today. I excepted this position with the understanding that it would be temporerie. I am extremely pleased that you have made a full recoverie, as you say, and I feel blessed to have known and cared for you these past months. I am sure you will agree that you no longer require a full-time nurse, and I do not feel I am qualifyed to run a household.*
>
> *I believe you feel the same way. I canot otherwise explain what has happened between us.*
>
> *I have made up my mind to go and I canot bear the idea that you would try to persuade me to stay on in Asencion, so I am leaving. I hope you will understand.*
>
> *Sincerelie,*
> *Alice Anders*

Benjamin sighed. "What does it matter? You don't need a nurse anymore, and there's a dozen girls in the village who could look after the house for us."

"I need Alice. I need to get ready for the party, and she knows my preferences. There's no time to find someone else. Benji, you must go fetch her back right now."

Benjamin said, "But if she's chosen to go, shouldn't we respect—"

"You will bring me my Alice or I will tear out your eyes, Benjamin." She snarled and crouched, and her tangled hair fell across her face. "I will gouge them out with my thumbs and I will eat them. You won't be able to see me eat them, but you'll hear it. You'll hear each of your eyeballs pop between my teeth, and you'll hear me chew them up. Go!"

Benjamin went.

Alice Anders sat in the train station at the bottom of Vinegar Hill. She sat in the center of a long bench under the window that looked out on the tracks, with her bag on her lap. She had missed the eight o'clock, and she didn't know when the next train was due to arrive, so she waited. She thought about Mrs Sinclair, who had been kind to her when she first started in service with the Sinclair family. She thought about sweet Dr Rumpole and wondered if he would notice she was gone.

After a while, she stood and stretched, and set her bag on the bench. She strolled around the waiting room and examined the calendar, and the shuttered ticket window, and the stacks of newspapers awaiting delivery. Some of the papers looked stained and rumpled, and Alice thought maybe they had been dropped on the tracks.

There was little else to see in the waiting room.

The door to the office was ajar, and she eyed it for a moment before pushing it open and poking her head inside. She drew back and took another look around the empty waiting room, then took a tentative step into the office. There was a desk, a blue chair, a hutch with cubbies that were filled with little bits of paper, and there was blood. Alice had worked in health care long enough to recognize blood when she saw it. The side of the desk was splashed with it, the door was spotted with it, and there were coagulated pools of it everywhere on the floor; one puddle had a shoe print in it, followed by tracks that led back to the door.

Alice took another step inside.

"Hello," she said. "Is someone here? Is someone hurt?"

But the room was silent; the entire station was silent. She already knew there was no one alive in the building. There was a stillness in the room that she had felt before when people died.

She looked behind the desk, then got down on her knees and peered beneath it. A white lacquered box top lay across a spatter of blood. Nearby was the other half of the box, and in casting about she discovered that one of the streaks of blood was actually a length of red ribbon. A flash of light from the window refracted off a wide seam between the floor and the baseboard, and she used her fingernails to pull out a letter opener that was decorated with a small pearl.

Alice backed out of the room and shut the door. She stood for a moment, surveying her environment. She opened her hand and examined the letter opener. The pearl was iridescent and its milky channels caught the light in strange ways. She didn't know how much pearls were worth, but she knew they were valuable.

She had no prospects; she was leaving her employment with no destination in mind. A pearl might buy her a room, some food, some time to think.

But she understood that something terrible had happened in the station office.

She sat back down on the bench and thought. She decided she had two choices: she could run back to the village—she could rouse Sergeant Winter and explain what she had found—or she could stay where she was and wait for the train. If she went back to the village, Sergeant Winter would question her. He might even be suspicious of her. And he would surely take the pearl from her.

Alice picked up her bag and set it on her lap. She looked at the letter opener again, to reassure herself that it was real, that she had indeed found a pearl.

Then she closed her fist around the handle, took a deep breath, and listened for the train.

M oses set his saddlebags on the platform of the Progress train station. They weighed significantly less than they had that morning. He had given Poppy Buckland his remaining biscuits, jerky, and eggs, to use in trade on her journey to Kansas. He had also gifted her his little farmhouse, his rifle, and his horse, Pie.

He had sent a telegram care of Sadie Grace or Rabbit Grace in Ascension, Massachusetts. No response requested.

There was only one more thing to do.

He knelt in the dirt beside the tracks and beckoned to Esmerelda. The low whistle of an approaching locomotive sounded in the distance.

"This is where you and I part ways, darling," Moses said. "I want you to go down to Kansas with Poppy. My mama's there, and she'll take care of you better than I can."

"But you said we would go together. I think I would like your friends."

"Well, I think they would like you, too. But I don't know what's waiting for me there, and I don't want you any more mixed up in things than you already are."

"Thank you for worrying about me, Mr Moses. But you're forgetting that I am beyond worry now. I am no longer the *pequeña rosa*. I am the *rosa muerta,* the dead flower. I don't need anyone to take care of me."

She lowered her voice and leaned in closer. "Miss Poppy is very nice, but I will miss you too much if you leave me."

Moses glanced at Poppy, who stood holding the Appaloosa's reins.

"I understand," he said to Esmerelda. "I'll miss you, too, kid. But I don't want to leave you on your own again if something bad happens to me. Besides, I need you to look after Pie. I don't know if Poppy can handle that big old horse by herself."

He slipped a half-eagle coin into the girl's hand, then turned her around and gently pushed her toward the witch. He was surprised by the wave of sadness that washed over him as he watched the skinny little girl walk away.

"Bye, Junior," he whispered.

When the train chugged into Progress Station, Moses was ready, his saddlebags draped over his shoulder, his ticket ready. Poppy had tied a cloth around his head to hide the bullet hole, but he pulled his hat low anyway.

He gave one last wave to the witch and the dead girl, then he boarded the train at the last car. The coloreds-only carriage had no porter, but Moses wasn't carrying much and the only inconvenience he suffered was a familiar prick of anger.

The car was only half full, people sitting singly and in twos under a faded green ceiling. Moses found an empty bench and settled in. He assumed most of his fellow passengers were headed for the big cities, Chicago or New York, to work, or to visit their families. He thought he must be on a stranger journey than any of them.

A young couple sat across from him, the woman holding a

newborn baby. The man looked a little like Moses's own father, who had been a stern and unforgiving man. Calvin Burke had worked under the hot sun all his life and his soul was as thick and calloused as his skin. When Moses had announced he was going to fight in the war, his father stopped talking to him. Calvin hadn't said goodbye when Moses left, or even bothered to look at him. He had died while Moses was crawling across a faraway field with a first aid kit.

His father would never know that Moses had learned medicine, or that he had come home alive from the war. Calvin had never met his daughter-in-law. All that was left of Calvin Burke were unhappy memories.

Moses wondered, as he often had over the previous days and weeks, whether he would have been a better father than Calvin. Katie had changed him from an aimless wanderer to a dedicated husband; he imagined their child might have changed him, too.

He nodded at the young father sitting across from him, who tipped his hat in return.

An old woman sat by herself two rows ahead of Moses, and two men played cards on the floor at the back of the car. Moses wondered if any of them were dead, too. Maybe they didn't even know it.

A whistle blew and the train eased away from the station. Moses pulled his hat down over his face, leaned against the window, and was almost instantly asleep.

He was standing on the path outside his house, the house he had bought for Katie. It wasn't much to look at—a big box, painted blue, with ivory trim and a tumbledown chimney—but it was theirs. It was home. The front door stood open, and Moses walked up the path and entered. The whole house was open, every window and every door, and a warm breeze swept through it. It smelled like fresh grass, and clean dirt and sunshine. Katie came to him and kissed his cheek, and then their children came running. A boy and a girl. The boy looked exactly like Moses, and the girl looked like Katie. Moses knelt and grabbed them both up in a hug, squishing them together so that none of the three of them could breathe. The children gasped and giggled. He pressed his ear against each of their chests in turn, but he couldn't hear a heartbeat, only the steady click of wheels on steel tracks.

He woke with a bad taste in his mouth. The man across from him was asleep, but the young woman cooed at her baby. She looked up at him and smiled.

"You were snoring," she whispered. "My husband snores, too."

Trees rolled past the window, and Moses saw a pale figure running alongside the train, flickering in and out of sight as it passed behind hillocks and shrubbery. The yellow dog kept pace with the train, and Moses watched it, thinking he had never seen a dog that could run so fast, thinking about the whirring thing with all the wings and eyes.

He caught the young mother's attention and pointed out the window.

"Does that look like a dog to you?"

The woman glanced at the window, then back at Moses. She nudged her sleeping husband with her elbow, but he only grunted and laid his head against her shoulder.

"My mistake," Moses said.

He left his saddlebags on the seat, and exited the coloreds-only car. He picked his way through the baggage car. It was lit by a single lantern; the dark shapes of suitcases and steamer trunks and carpet bags loomed up at him from every direction.

He walked through another car where men in white coats cooked medallions of pork and big pots of potatoes. Pans sizzled and steam rose from the pots. It smelled good, but of course Moses wasn't hungry. He couldn't remember the last time he had eaten.

The dining car was next, and it was mostly empty; the lunch service had ended, and it was still too early for dinner. A little girl stood between the tables talking to a man, who had leaned down to listen to her. The man wore a pinstripe purple suit with a matching hat, and round spectacles with dark lenses. The girl wore a big white dress trimmed with lace. When she turned toward him, smiling, Moses saw the mangled flesh covering the one side of her face, the puckered skin around her eye.

"Esmerelda?" he said.

The man in the suit straightened and tipped his hat up.

He said, "Is that Moses Burke I hear?"

It was Frank Smiley, the horse thief and murderer whom Moses had abandoned in a field more than a hundred miles away.

Moses decided he was still dreaming.

Benjamin's head felt like a swarm of gnats whenever he was near anyone else, and he was glad to see that the village green was empty of people.

Only a week before, his future had seemed unappealing, but reasonable. He would presumably become a doctor and someday inherit his father's practice. He would marry a girl his parents thought appropriate and buy a house in the city. One day he would die in that house, and his own son would inherit the family practice, and marry someone predictable.

Death had disrupted all his plans and expectations. And yet, dying hadn't altogether ended his short-term prospects. Nor had murder. He wasn't in a coffin or a prison cell. He was running a mundane errand for his mother, and contemplating Lucy's plan to kill the villagers.

Somehow, her plan didn't seem entirely unreasonable to Benjamin, and yet murdering his summer friends and their families didn't sit right with him. He had been raised, as most people were, to believe that murder was the greatest sin a person could commit. He was dead, true, but certain beliefs were ingrained. It was, he thought, the principle of the thing.

"What am I supposed to do?" he said aloud.

The sound of his voice startled him, and he stopped walking. The sun behind Vinegar Hill formed a halo around the attic of Bethany Hall, and Benjamin saw a shadow flutter across the room behind the window.

Rose had claimed that death gave purpose to life, but what was the purpose of anything if you were already dead? Lucy's murderous plan made as much sense as anything else. He decided he would do what she wanted. Everyone, he thought, could do what they wanted. There were no longer any consequences.

"Damn it all, anyway," he said.

The sun rose a fraction of an inch higher, and the house disappeared in a blaze of light. Benjamin rubbed his eyes and kept walking.

He passed a stand of spruce and saw the train station ahead. He hoped Alice was already on a train, headed somewhere far from Ascension. He trudged up the steps to the platform and stamped his feet on the hard planks. He opened the door and took a deep breath and stepped inside.

Alice Anders looked up at him from the bench under the window, and the gnats in Benjamin's head began to buzz.

She said, "Benjamin?"

"Didn't the eight o'clock come through?" he said. "I thought you'd be gone."

"I missed the eight o'clock," Alice said. "Did you come to take me back?"

She was sitting in the middle of the twenty-foot-long bench. Her shoulders were hunched, and her hands were covered by the bag on her lap. Benjamin thought she looked anxious, and for some reason this made him angry.

"Mother sent me, yes."

"I can't go back, Benjamin. I thought I made that clear in my letter."

"I didn't read it," he lied. "Alice—"

"Something terrible happened here."

"What?"

"In the office," she said. "Go look for yourself."

He kept his eyes on her as he crossed the room. She had sharp cheekbones, and a slim throat that would collapse under the pressure of a man's thumbs. All she had to do was get on the train and leave, Benjamin thought. Why hadn't she gone? The buzzing in his head grew louder, and he felt a rising sense of panic, as if he were underwater and struggling for air.

The office door was ajar. Benjamin pushed it open and stepped into the room. The buzzing in his head quieted. He smelled iron in the air before he saw the blood splashed along the baseboards, across the back of the desk and the door. He didn't remember leaving the place in such a mess, but it was clear someone—Lucy?—had made a vain attempt to tidy up after him. The chair was pushed against the desk and the firewood was stacked neatly in its box. The red-speckled lid of Lucy's gift box was half hidden under the desk, and the length of ribbon lay at Benjamin's feet. He picked it up and wrapped it around his finger. Then he left the office and closed the door softly behind him.

"What do you think happened?" Alice said.

She had moved to the far end of the bench. He sat at the other end and played with the length of ribbon, twisting it around his fingers.

"I think it's pretty obvious. Somebody died here."

He watched the play of emotions on her face, but he thought most of it was an act. She had already guessed the truth. There was far too much blood for any other explanation to make sense.

"Did you kill someone, Alice?"

"Benjamin!"

"Don't worry, I'll help you hide the body. We can bury it in the woods, then come back here and take the next train away from this damn village. We'll run away together."

"Please don't say things like that."

"I'm only teasing, Alice."

"Well, I don't like it."

"I thought we were friends." He smiled. "I thought we'd grown close. We spent all that time together at the cottage with nothing to do but wait for my mother to die."

"Nothing to do?" Her nostrils flared and her upper lip curled. "You mean all that time I spent bathing your mother with a damp cloth and emptying her bedpan. Cooking your meals, and dusting your bookshelves, and sweeping your floor?"

He thought her sudden anger was probably meant for someone else; now that she had voiced it her expression softened, her cheeks turned pink.

"Why don't you move a little closer to me?" Benjamin said. "It's hard to talk to you when you're so far away."

Alice stared at the bag in her lap.

"I can hear you just fine," she said.

Benjamin unwound the ribbon and wrapped it around his fingers again, tighter this time. "Come here, won't you, Alice?"

She edged toward the center of the bench.

"Closer," he said. He stretched the ribbon between his hands, pulling it taut.

She slid another few inches.

He smiled and let the ribbon go slack in his hands.

"It's too bad about the train," he said. "I wonder when the next one is due."

"Whose blood do you think it is in there?"

Benjamin slithered along the bench until their shoulders touched.

"People get hurt all the time. It's when you're hurt that you know you're alive, even if it's the last thing you ever feel."

Alice looked up at him, and he saw no fear in her eyes.

"I always thought you were a nice boy, Benjamin," she said. "I'm sorry."

She raised her hands from her lap, knocking her bag to the floor, and Benjamin saw she was holding his own pearl-handled letter opener. She swung it at him, aiming for his throat, and he grabbed for her arm an instant too late.

I wish you'd gone with Poppy Buckland like I told you to," Moses said to Esmerelda Rosas. "My mama would have taken care of you."

"I wanted to go with you," she said.

He had taken Esmerelda and Frank Smiley back to the coloreds-only car of the Buffalo Express. After a quick glance at Frank, the young couple had gathered their belongings and carried their infant to the farthest bench.

"Before you accuse me," Frank said, "I had no idea you were even on this train, Mr Burke."

Moses eyed Frank Smiley's purple suit, the hat, the dark spectacles. A fur stole was wrapped around his throat. Moses knew the flesh beneath the stole was a close match for the purple of Frank's suit.

"Seems like your fortunes have changed since the last time I saw you," Moses said.

"You mean when you left me to rot in a field?"

"Looks like you did okay for yourself."

"A kindly couple chanced upon me and took pity. They offered me a ride to the next town, but sadly they succeeded to illness along the way. When they died, they left me their worldly goods."

"They died and left you everything, after riding with you a day or two?"

"Wouldn't they still need their things?" Esmerelda said. "Even if they were dead?"

Frank realized his mistake and grimaced.

"Nobody dies," Moses said. "Or at least they don't stay down anymore."

"Pshaw," Frank said. "You ain't as smart as you think you are, Moses Burke. And anyhow, it don't matter how I got what I got. It's none of your dang beeswax."

"What did you do to them before you stole their wagon?"

"I swear, Moses, the things you say . . . there's times I wonder if you even like me."

An uncomfortable silence ensued. Esmerelda brushed her hair with her fingers and swished it across her face like a curtain. Frank rearranged his fur stole and cleaned his dark spectacles with a woman's handkerchief. Moses pretended to be asleep. He let his chin fall to his chest and his hands drop to his sides. Esmerelda watched him curiously, then she smiled. She stretched and yawned and slumped against the wall.

F rank sat quietly for a time. He fiddled with his new pocket watch, opening it and snapping it closed, wondering what time it was and how far it was to the next stop. At last he grew bored and stood up. He walked out through the baggage car, the kitchen car, and the dining car, until he found a carriage that seemed to be empty. He could feel no presence, could smell no body odor or perfume. He heard nothing. He patted around him until he found an empty bench.

Frank settled in and sank back against the cushions, happy to find a moment free of guile and deception. It was bad luck to have ended up on the same train as Moses Burke. He had thought to reinvent himself on the journey to New York. He had hoped to be taken for a different sort of man when he arrived in the city, someone respectable, but Moses knew him. Moses would ruin everything.

Frank was trying to decide if he ought to leave the train at its next stop, rather than risk traveling any farther with Moses, when he heard the door slide open at the end of the car. Heavy footsteps marched up the aisle and stopped beside him.

A man said, "Ticket, please."

Frank patted the breast pocket of his purple overcoat.

"Got it right here, mister conductor, sir." He had a sudden idea, and in a rush of excitement he dropped the ticket. "Say, mister, I just heard tell there's a convict on this train, and he's waving a gun around, threatening women and children and such. It's got me aquiver with fright. You know, a blind man can't take no chances with his safety."

"I haven't heard anything of the sort, sir."

"You didn't hear that poor young lady crying about it a couple cars back? Yes, sir, it was pitiful. She said this dangerous man is in the negro car, and he calls hisself . . . Well, I think she said his name was Moses Burke."

I s there a Moses Burke back here?"

The conductor stood in the open doorway of the car. An older man was positioned behind him, holding a shotgun high across his chest. Moses heard squealing brakes, and felt the train shuddering to a stop.

"What's this about?" he said.

"Son, I'm gonna need to see your firearm."

The conductor was pink-faced and young. Moses's head buzzed. His face flushed. He kept his voice calm and measured.

"I'm no trouble for you," he said. "I'd rather keep my pistol. It's holstered and I promise it'll stay that way."

"Stand up please, son," the conductor said. "You need to come with me."

"What's happening?" Esmerelda said.

Moses leaned in close to her and whispered. "I'm about to get thrown off this train."

"Why?"

"Son," the conductor said, and Moses held up a finger, asking him to wait.

"I don't know why," he said. "But I'd bet money Frank Smiley's involved. Of all the things I regret, cutting that sonofabitch out of a tree is right up there."

"I'll go with you," Esmerelda said.

"No," Moses said. Watching the officials at the door, he reached into his saddlebag and slowly pulled out the appointment book he'd been carrying since the day after Death's end. The man with the shotgun twitched, but the conductor put a hand on his arm. Moses showed them the book to reassure them it wasn't dangerous, then pressed it into Esmerelda's hands.

"You take this to Ascension," he said. "You get it to Sadie Grace."

"But how will I find her."

"I'm pretty sure she'll know you're coming. She'll find you."

"Don't leave me again."

"I'll find you as soon as I can get away from these folks."

He patted her hand and stood, slung the saddlebags over his shoulder, and held his arms out at his sides.

"Let's get this over with," he said, and he allowed the conductor to lead him out of the car and off the train.

Alice ran through the woods behind the train station. She kicked off her shoes and pulled the hem of her skirt up off the ground. She heard Benjamin crashing through the underbrush behind her, choking and gurgling. He spat and growled and called her name, but she ran until his voice faded in the distance.

She didn't stop until she reached the high banks of a rushing creek. Snowmelt from Vinegar Hill flowed down through the woods, and eventually out to the Ipswich. A stag stood on the opposite bank of the creek, his antlers tangled in the shadows of the trees behind him. His hide appeared blue in the dim morning light, and when he moved toward the water his intestines dragged along the ground and snagged in the serrated brown shrubbery along the verge. When he noticed Alice, he snorted and swiped his tongue over his black nose.

At the faraway sound of baying dogs, the stag bellowed and reared up; his hooves came back down with a crash that shook dirt and debris down the creek bank. His hind legs bunched, muscles sliding across each other, and he leapt across the chasm, trailing guts and gore through the air behind him. The stag fell short and smacked into the side of the wet bank below her, his hooves tearing into spidery roots, his back legs scrambling.

Alice ran again. Brambles ripped at her clothing; whip-thin branches lashed at her face. The pulse in her temples sounded like hoofbeats. She expected at any moment to be knocked down and trampled into the forest floor, and she braced for the inevitable impact.

Then she broke through a tangle of brittle sycamore branches and found herself in a sunlit glade. At the center of the clearing was a mighty oak, wreathed in unseasonably green leaves, an impossible summer oasis in those winter woods.

She ran to the oak, grabbed hold of a low branch, and began to climb.

She woke in a fork high up in the oak, with no idea how long she had slept. She clung tight to the trunk and cautiously peered down, expecting to see the stag. She was so startled to see Sadie Grace looking up at her that she nearly lost her grip.

"Hello!" Sadie shouted. "What are you doing up there?"

"There's a deer," Alice said. "Be careful."

"I'm not worried about deer," Sadie said. She was wearing a black fur coat, and with her bright red hair and fox's face, she looked to Alice like some fairy-tale creature.

"It was an angry deer," Alice said. "With big antlers."

Sadie took a casual look around the glade and shrugged.

"You seem a little unsteady. Why don't you come down from there?"

"What if the deer comes back?"

"If a deer has antlers it's called a stag. Or a buck, depending on where you live."

"There are dogs, too, and Benjamin is out there somewhere."

"Benjamin?"

"He hasn't been acting like himself. I was scared."

"I promise you'll be fine, unless you fall."

Alice took another look around, though it was hard to see

much through the tree's thick green canopy. She clung tight to the tree trunk and moved her left foot out and down, squatting and feeling for the branch beneath her. When she found it, she nearly lost her balance, but managed to work her way far enough around the trunk to move to the lower branch, still clutching the one above. She moved slowly, descending one branch at a time, thinking of nothing but the next step, then the next.

When she ran out of branches she was still four feet above the ground.

"Jump," Sadie said. "It's not far."

"I've never climbed a tree in my life."

"You could've fooled me."

Alice sat on the branch, took a deep breath, closed her eyes, and swung out. She hit the ground and stumbled forward and Sadie caught her.

"See," Sadie said. "I knew you could do it."

"Oh," Alice said. The events of the day crashed in on her and she held her fists to her chest, drawing herself in, making herself smaller. "I got turned around and I couldn't find my way back to the station and then the deer was chasing me."

"It's okay," Sadie said. She put her arms around the young nurse and drew her in, enfolding her in thick black fur. "You'll be okay now. This is a safe place."

"I stabbed Benjamin Sinclair."

And once she had started, Alice found she couldn't stop talking. She told Sadie the whole story, including her resignation letter to Clarissa, and Benjamin finding her at the train station. How he had frightened her, and how she had stabbed him in the throat.

"I didn't mean to hurt him," she finished. "Not really. I just panicked, but he couldn't have meant me no harm, could he? He's usually a sweet boy. He looks at the stars, and he talks about the moon, and he's been kind to me, and I killed him."

Sadie stepped back. She removed the bearskin coat and draped it over the nurse's shoulders. Alice's knees nearly buckled under the weight of it.

"Don't you worry," Sadie said. "I'm certain you didn't kill Benjamin Sinclair. You couldn't have."

Alice sniffed and looked down at her hands. Her nails were broken, her knuckles were scratched. Her palms had been scraped raw, and she couldn't tell Benjamin's blood from her own.

"He was already dead," she said. "I knew he was. It happened to his mother, too. Mrs Sinclair died in her bed, but she wouldn't stay dead. Do you think this is the end of the world?"

Sadie contemplated the question. "I don't know, Alice. Maybe it is."

"The end of the world ought to be a long way off."

"That seems like a reasonable assumption," Sadie said. "Alice, I can't leave you out here in the woods."

"I'll go back to the train station. Benjamin must have gone home by now."

"There won't be another train until tomorrow morning," Sadie said. "You'll need a warm bath and a proper bed. I think you'd better come with me."

Moses came across Esmerelda as the sun was sinking toward the horizon behind him and the moon was rising in the pale sky ahead. The girl was sitting in a ditch, examining her left knee, and the yellow dog was nearby, watching up the tracks. It saw Moses and came running to greet him, then trotted the last few yards alongside him.

"I scraped my knee," Esmerelda said. She was cupping a handful of dried purple berries. "I thought I could use Miss Poppy's pokeweed on it, but I don't know how."

"Witches have a particular way of using things," Moses said. "Doesn't always work for us regular folk."

Esmerelda frowned and tossed the berries onto the train tracks. Moses knelt and scooped up a handful of snow. He rubbed the thick black blood off her knee.

"Least you didn't break your leg," he said. "You jumped off the train?"

"I couldn't leave you behind. You would be lost without me."

"I wanted you to take that book to Sadie Grace."

Esmerelda stood and swirled the hem of her dress so that it fell into place around her feet. There was a long wet swath of grime down the side of the gown. Moses sighed.

"I guess we're in this together," he said.

She smiled up at him, her hair parting to reveal her burned face.

"Yes," she said. She pointed down the tracks. "We know where we're going and we know where it is."

"At this rate, it should only take us a year to get there," he said. "Come on, then. We'd better get a move on."

T he village council drew matchsticks to determine who would address the matter of their children's education. Sergeant Newton Winter had drawn the short stick, and now he found himself seated in the front room of Bethany Hall across from Rose Nettles.

"I'm sorry to call on you so late in the day, Mrs Nettles."

"Please call me Rose. I'm not married."

She looked too old to him to be unmarried, so he took a chance. "I'm sorry about your husband," he said.

"Thank you," Rose said. "Is there a Mrs Winter?"

He grunted. "She passed some time ago."

"Then I'm the one who's sorry. I'm curious. Everyone refers to you as a sergeant, but I haven't seen any other policemen in the village."

"There's a sheriff in the county seat, about thirty miles from here. I haven't officially been a sergeant since I retired and moved to Ascension. This place doesn't require much policing, and I'm happy to help when I'm called upon."

"How kind of you."

"I'm afraid this isn't a social visit, Mrs Nettles. I should get to the reason I'm here." He shifted his weight to ease the pain in his hip. It always hurt most when he leaned forward, but he wanted to project confidence and finality. "The council has decided to look elsewhere for a schoolteacher," he said. "You are no longer being considered for the position."

"I don't understand."

"We thank you for your interest." He stood, careful to put his weight on his left leg. "Well, I think that's all of it. Good day to you, ma'am."

"Wait," Rose said. "Tell me why."

Winter sighed. "There are rumors in the village. Rumors that you and your . . . There is some suspicion that you and Mrs Grace are not . . . Ascension material."

"What does that mean?"

"Mrs Nettles, you are suspected of witchcraft, among other things."

Rose was silent for a moment, blinking in disbelief, then her shoulders shook and she began to laugh. When she had recovered, Rose stood and looked Winter in the eye. "Sergeant, I promise you I'm not a witch. Sometimes I wish I were, but I'm simply not."

"Beg pardon, ma'am, but that is what a witch would say. Witches are liars by nature, and it takes a great deal of persuasion to get them to admit their true nature. As I say, good day to you."

He limped out through the foyer and shut the door behind him. Rose went to the mantel and filled her pipe. She struck a match and frowned at the empty room.

"Persuasion?" she said.

The headless black cat jumped up on the mantel and nuzzled her hand with its shoulder, but Rose neither saw nor felt it.

S adie had filled the tub with hot water and was laying out clean towels when she heard a knock at the front door. She left Alice in the bathroom and descended to the ground floor, where Butler and Housekeeper were busy doing House-keeper's work.

"Aren't you supposed to answer the door?" she said to Butler.

The boy from the drugstore was on the porch. He was out of breath, and he shoved a slip of yellow paper at her.

"This came for you earlier," he said. "I'm sorry I'm late with it. I had to clean up blood. There was a lot of it!"

With that, he turned and hopped down the porch steps. Half-way across the front garden he turned and waved, and shouted, "I hope you can help your friend!"

When he was through the gate and gone, Sadie read the tele-gram he had brought her. It was from a man she had not seen in years, a man she had nearly forgotten.

SADIE GRACE OR RABBIT
CARE OF ASCENSION MA
   LONG TIME NO SEE STOP ON MY WAY TO YOU
STOP I HAVE DONE AN EVIL THING AND HOPE
TO FIX IT BUT AFRAID WHAT WILL HAPPEN

WHEN I ARRIVE STOP IF I HAVE MISJUDGED
PLEASE KEEP ROSE SAFE STOP I HOPE I AM
NOT WRONG AND THAT YOU WILL BE ABLE TO
HELP ME FIGURE OUT WHAT TO DO STOP
                    YOUR FRIEND MOSES BURKE

"Keep Rose safe?"

And in that instant, she remembered entering the attic of Bethany Hall with Rabbit, and she remembered what they had seen there.

She remembers that I am here to take Rose away.

I am sitting in the attic of Bethany Hall with my pen poised over my ancient ledger. I am in the parlor below, where the burned man rises and goes looking for his hat. In the basement, the brides are on their knees digging through the mound of dust and bones, shoving handfuls of dirt into their mouths. The old lady leaves her post beneath the blue spruce and carries her golden locket through the garden toward the house. The spirits are restless. They sense what is coming.

I am standing in the alley beside Herman's Meats, watching Clarissa Sinclair vomit. There is very little in her stomach, almost nothing to bring up, but still she heaves, one hand resting against the cold brick wall, the other clutching her abdomen.

I am at the village printshop, where Sadie Grace is purchasing a map of the area from Jaspar Upshaw. The printshop itself is on the map, represented by a small empty square. All the homes and buildings of Ascension are on the map, including Bethany Hall. Tiny train tracks march like stitches around Vinegar Hill, on through the woods and finally end at a white border, a quarter inch of blank paper. There is nothing beyond the woods.

Here there be dragons.

Benjamin Sinclair is taking apart his telescope. The stars no longer hold any interest for him. The sky is a blank canvas that he cannot prime or paint. Blood has soaked the front of Benjamin's favorite shirt. He stares at the wall and wonders what is happening—to him and to everyone he knows.

I am at the drugstore, where Charles Bowden, still out of breath from his errands, attempts a conversation with Rabbit. She is ignoring him, but he is not the type to notice.

Dr Timothy Rumpole has hung dark shrouds over the windows of his house, and now he goes from room to room, setting all the clocks to the minute of his death. When they are set to the proper time, he stops them.

At the Ascension Inn, Jessica Hudson frets over the supplies in her pantry. Two of her three guests have abruptly stopped eating, and her produce has begun to rot; her eggs are spoiling, her meat has turned. She has asked Mr Mulacky to suspend delivery of milk and cream.

I am in the graveyard, where a woman pounds fruitlessly against the lid of her coffin. There is no one here but me, and I am disinclined to help.

Everywhere I am, Bell is there, too. We do not speak. We are doing the same thing. We are marking Ascension in our minds, preparing for what is to come. For Bell it is a game; for me it is a duty. But however we choose to frame the events of the coming day, we are both aware that the village represents something much larger than the people in it. The destiny of the human race is at stake.

Of Bell and I, only one is truly concerned.

FINAL DAY

On the last day of Ascension, the villagers rose early to prepare for the party. Mr Mulacky was, as always, the first person out on the road. His old swayback horse had become testy of late, and had stopped eating. She had tried to bite him when he got his hand close to her nose. He wondered if her newfound contrariness could be chalked up to one last spurt of energy in her old age, but this morning she had allowed him to harness her to the milk cart without kicking or nipping at him.

He left three bottles of cream outside the back door of the drugstore. There was a wedge of light visible at the bottom of the door, and Mr Mulacky nodded in approval. He liked it when others were up and about when he was. The predawn hours were, in his opinion, the best time to go about one's work.

In the drugstore, Prosper Knox and his daughter, Lucy, heard the bottles clink against the stoop. They stood at the worktable in the back room, making plans.

"They're witches," Prosper said, for perhaps the tenth time. "Everything that's happened is their fault."

Lucy didn't care whose fault it was. She and her family were dead, and as far as she knew there was no coming back from that. There was nothing to be done except move forward and plan for the future, as strange as that might seem.

Prosper saw the faraway look in Lucy's eye and frowned, guessing the reason for it.

"What do you see in that boy anyway?"

Lucy could see her father's teeth through the gash in his left cheek. She watched his tongue move as his jaw worked. It reminded her of a slug. His left eye had gone white and cloudy, and it sat low in its broken socket, beneath its drooping eyelid. In retrospect, she thought she could have taken more care and made better aesthetic decisions when she took the hatchet to him, but she had been in a hurry at the time.

"Benjamin is the opposite of you," she said. "And that's what I love about him."

She saw her father wince, but it had been said and she couldn't take it back. In that way, hurting her father was a bit like dying.

"You will not see him again."

"Oh, Father, stop."

"I have something for you," he said.

He stooped and dragged a heavy trunk from beneath the worktable. It was battered and smashed, with deep gashes that reminded Lucy of her father's face. He drew back the lid and Lucy peered inside.

"I don't—" she started, but her father stopped her.

"Under the cloaks and hats," he said. "Hold on a minute."

He knelt and rummaged through the garments. Before she could ask why he kept a box of junk in the back of the drugstore, where space was at a premium, Prosper stood back up and set two curved wooden trays on the table. At least they looked like trays until he turned them over and Lucy saw that they were exotic masks with curly horns, fiery yellow eyes, and fuzzy braids around their edges.

"There were originally four of us in my generation," Prosper said. "But our numbers dwindled, and now there's just two of us left here, and one of the summer people when he comes."

He slid one of the masks toward his daughter.

"What you're planning," he said. "I think you deserve to wear this."

"What is it?"

"It's a holy relic. They can't curse us when we wear these because they can't see who we are."

"Who? Who can't curse you?"

"The witches. They consort with evil, and it corrupts them. It's our sacred responsibility to drive that corruption out of them. It's a difficult thing we do, but we know in our hearts that they've earned the punishment we mete out."

"Punishment?" Lucy was surprised she could still feel horror.

"I know what you're thinking, but these women have to be winnowed from our midst in order to preserve the village. My father did this job before me, and his father before him." There was a note of pride in his voice. "The work we do is good and pure, Lucy. It's for the benefit of the community. You need to understand that."

Lucy picked up the mask in front of her. She ran a finger over the brittle yellowing braids.

"This isn't fur, is it?"

"We keep their hair as a reminder and a talisman."

Lucy shuddered. "This is disgusting."

"You might change your mind," he said.

She dropped the mask on the table, but he picked up his own mask and put it on, tying it behind his head with thick leather cords. The limp braids of his victims' hair hung to his shoulders. It was hideous, she thought, but at least it covered his ruined face.

"You wouldn't catch me dead in that," she said. "Now what about my party favors? You said you had an idea."

He turned and studied the cluttered table, his movements stiff, the mask expressionless. The effect was disturbing, as if a statue from some country she had only read about had come to life and decided to visit the back room of Knox Drugs.

"This might have the effect you want," Prosper said. He produced a small bag of powder from the hutch above the worktable. "It's a special order for Dr Rumpole, but I always get twice as much as he asks for in case a shipment's delayed. I know he'll always need it."

"What is it?"

"Opium. Use enough of it, and it can knock out an elephant."

Lucy shook her head. "I don't want to knock out an elephant," she said. "Do you have something stronger?"

Prosper tapped a finger against the chin of his ugly mask, thinking. He nodded to himself and left the room, returning a moment later with an open box of rat poison.

"This will work as well on a person as it does a rat," he said.

She took the box from him and sniffed at the contents. "What's in it?"

"Potassium cyanide," he said. "I've heard it has a bitter taste, but of course I've never sampled it."

She licked her finger and plunged it into the box, then stuck the finger in her mouth.

"Lucy!"

"This stuff tastes awful. We'll have to mix it with something."

"Coffee?"

"I think lemon would work," Lucy said. "A little tartness and sugar to balance the bitterness. We'll make lemon cakes."

"They'll know what you're doing," Prosper said. "Those witches up the hill will know and they won't eat them."

Lucy shrugged. "Daddy, by tomorrow morning, the dead will outnumber the living. It doesn't really matter whether those women eat the poison."

"It matters to me," Prosper said. "Their evil will spread like a cancer if it's not checked."

Lucy didn't care about the women in Bethany Hall. They weren't even from the village. All she wanted was for her friends and family to stay together forever. All she wanted was to have Benjamin by her side until the stars winked out and the moon stopped shining.

C larissa stood in front of her mirror wearing a white slip. She noted with displeasure that her shoulders looked like horse's knees. Her collarbones strained at the skin above her meager breasts, her cheekbones were alarmingly sharp, and her eyes had sunken into her skull.

"I am a shadow," she whispered. "I am nothing, and no one loves me."

She vaguely regretted her argument with Alice, but she barely remembered what she had said, and had rung for the nurse three times before recalling that Alice had taken a train away from Ascension, bound for some far-off place where Clarissa and her worries could be safely forgotten.

This is what Benjamin had told her when he returned from the station, though not in so many words.

"I missed the morning train," he said.

Clarissa said, "What happened to you?"

His handkerchief was tied around his throat and his shirt was covered with blood. It was already turning black and pulling away from his chest like a stiff breastplate after a long day of jousting.

"I fell on the platform," he said.

Clarissa, who had begun suffering dizzy spells, had no reason to doubt him.

Grover Smalls had hit a deer the previous week in southwestern Nebraska—had seen it scooped up and impaled on the locomotive's cowcatcher—and he was still upset about it. He was already reaching for the brake as he rounded a tight bend with limited visibility. Otherwise, he might have hit the dead tree on the tracks.

He suspected it had been placed there because the nearest trees were roughly five-hundred yards away down a steep incline. In Grover's experience, logs didn't roll uphill.

He pulled back hard on the brake, and prayed, and the train squealed to a stop ten feet shy of the obstruction. He swung out of the cab and hopped down beside the tracks, felt the heat coming off his engine, and stomped around the side of the cowcatcher to take a look.

The tree trunk was three feet around, burned and partially split. There were stumpy remnants of branches at one end, and long tangled roots at the other, which made it look disturbingly like a headless man. Grover guessed it had been hit by lightning. Behind it he could see footprints in the snow and signs that the tree trunk had been dragged up the slope.

Grover shook his head. "Who on earth would do a thing like that?"

He saw movement in the periphery of his vision and turned in time to see a black man and a little girl in a white dress stepping up out of the ditch.

"Hey, you!"

The man smiled and held up his hands to show he wasn't armed.

"I have a schedule to keep," Grover said. "There is no money on this train, and whatever you might get outta my pocket ain't worth the trouble it took to stop me."

"Not after your money, friend," the man said. "Name's Moses, and this is my daughter, Esmerelda. I'd be happy to help you move that thing off the tracks in exchange for a ride."

"Sir, this is not a passenger train," Grover said. "And this is not a scheduled stop."

Moses wore his hat very low on his head; it nearly covered his eyes. The girl smiled sideways at Grover, but kept her head tilted away from him; her hair fell forward over her eyes.

"We've got people waiting for us, and we're in a hurry to get there," Moses said.

"I can't let you on this train," Grover said.

"We're quiet and we don't take up much room."

"We're going to Ascension," Esmerelda said.

"That's up by Boston," Grover said. "This route does go past Ascension and on to points north, but that place is not a scheduled stop."

"We'd pay you, of course," Moses said. He reached into his coat pocket and produced a half-eagle.

"Sir, this is not the passenger train. I'm carrying beeves, not people. The passenger train'll come through here day after tomorrow, first thing in the morning. It doesn't stop here, but you might be able to flag it down." He glanced at the dead tree on the tracks. "But please do it a more regular way. An obstruction like this could have caused some real trouble."

"We can't wait for the day after tomorrow," Esmerelda said.

"Well, I do wish I could help you folks, but this—"

"It's not a passenger train," Moses said. He took Grover's hand and pressed the coin into his palm. "Please," he said.

"I really shouldn't, but—"

"Oh, thank you," Esmerelda said. "You are a nice man."

Grover smiled at her. She didn't look a whole lot like her father. He rubbed the side of his nose and looked away up the tracks.

"Thing is," he said. "Thing is, I don't know whether I can even slow down for Ascension. It's not a scheduled stop and now I'm running behind."

Moses reached into his pocket again. He produced a second half-eagle and Grover Smalls blinked.

B ethany Hall was a bustle of vendors, deliverymen, carpenters, painters, and cleaners. The three women living in the house tried to be patient.

Rose asked two of James Doolittle's men to put the newly arrived crates from Philadelphia in the library. Butler attempted to help, but accidentally knocked one of the men down and dropped a box on his head. Rose told him to go find Housekeeper, and he dutifully lumbered away. When Alice Anders came downstairs, Rose took her arm and led her back up, away from the tumult.

"We'll let them sort it out," Rose said. "I hope the noise didn't wake you."

"I don't think I'll ever get a good night's sleep again," Alice said. "I close my eyes and I see myself stabbing that poor boy in the neck."

Rose gave her a reassuring pat on the arm. With all that had happened in Ascension, she didn't think any of them would sleep well for quite some time.

"Your clothes are in tatters, dear," she said. "You and Rabbit are nearly the same size."

She went to Rabbit's closet and came back with a blue cotton dress, finished with satin at the waist and cuffs.

"Oh, I couldn't," Alice said.

"Rabbit will never wear this," Rose said. "It was sheer optimism that prompted me to buy it for her. Besides, it matches your eyes."

Next, Rose went to her own room and selected a sunbonnet with a spray of sky blue flowers across the brim. She scooped up her hairbrush and a jar of hairpins. By the time she returned, Alice had changed into the dress and was admiring herself in the vanity mirror.

"It looks like it was tailored for you," Rose said.

"I feel like I'm putting on airs."

"Nonsense."

Rose made Alice sit, and pinned the girl's pale blond hair into a chignon.

"You've been so nice to me," Alice said. "You and Mrs Grace, but I can't stay here forever. I don't know what to do with myself."

"Here, turn around," Rose said.

Alice swiveled on the chair and Rose set the hat on her head. She tilted it and nodded to herself before pinning it into place.

"I'm going through something similar," Rose said. "In my experience, we feel most lost when we are being of no use to others. We must try to be of service, in whatever way our skills and temperament allow."

"I'm a nurse," Alice said. "That's all the skills I have. I don't suppose you want a nurse."

Rose stepped back and admired her handiwork. "No, dear." She fluffed the shoulders of the dress and nodded, satisfied. "But I think I know of someone who might."

———

After a quick breakfast of toast with strawberry jam, Rabbit took inventory of their newly arrived belongings.

"This is going to take forever to unpack," Rabbit said to the black cat.

She picked up a small box of Sadie's things—parchments and powders and dried brown herbs—and carried it to the nursery. Sadie had brought a small selection of plants with her from Philadelphia, and her collection was already growing, supplemented by cuttings she had gathered in the woods, and by three separate visits to Flora Fielding's greenhouse.

The nursery was long and narrow, and smelled like a forest. Three saplings stood in pots on the floor along one of the short walls, and every spare bit of space was filled with slatted tables and benches, all of which sagged under the weight of heavy clay pots. There was barely room to move without knocking over a plant.

Rabbit didn't know how to use most of the herbs that Sadie had collected. She wanted to learn Sadie's ways, but her abilities didn't work in quite the same way her mother's did. Sadie used things she found in nature to communicate with it and urge things into being, while Rabbit pushed her thoughts into the earth and sky and bent them to her will. She didn't understand why she and her mother were so different, and it frustrated her.

"You only know half your heritage."

Rabbit whirled and saw Bell standing on the other side of a long table. His face was partially obscured by the fronds of a potted lady fern.

"What do you want, you imposter?" Rabbit said.

Bell raised his eyebrows.

"I'll admit it took me too long to figure it out," Rabbit said. "But you're no spirit."

"I never said I was a spirit."

"You knew I thought you were."

"An omission on my part, perhaps," Bell said. "But I have never lied to you, little Rabbit."

"Tell me what you are."

"Oh, I'm a lot of things, but we can talk about that later, if you wish. I have something important to tell you, and time is of the essence."

Rabbit realized she was still holding the box of parchments and powders. She set it on the floor under a bench and crossed her arms. "I don't care what you have to say."

"Yes, you do. Now listen closely. There is a key under this potted plant."

"It's a lady fern. Sadie boils it for tea to ease Rose's aches and pains."

"Just so," Bell said. "As I say, there is a key hidden beneath this potted plant ."

"How do you know that?"

"Because I gave this key to a bird, and the bird gave it to your mother. In this way the key traveled in a brief circle, from this house to the wild wood behind us, and back to the house, all in the span of an hour or two."

"So it unlocks something that was already here before we came?"

"Very good," Bell said. "It unlocks a door in the cellar."

"I saw that door. The day after we got here, when I explored the house. What's behind it?"

Bell caressed a frond of the lady fern, and a brief smile flickered across his face. "Only someone's hopes and dreams."

"Whose hopes and dreams?"

"You are full of questions, but hardly ever the right ones. Now take the key and put it in your pocket. Someone is coming. When he arrives, you must persuade him to exchange this key for a book he is carrying."

"Who's coming?"

"You will know him. When he gives you the book, direct him to the cellar and bring the book to me. Or you may burn it, whichever you prefer, but you must not allow anyone else to take control of it."

"Why should I do anything for you?"

Bell chuckled. "I merely make suggestions. In all matters you are free to do as you wish. Only remember, whether you trust me or not, you and I are united in our concern for Rose Nettles."

Rabbit blinked and Bell was gone. She tipped the fern back and picked up a small iron key with a curlicue design on its handle.

"What's to stop me from looking in that room myself?" she said, but there was no answer, and after turning the key over in her hand she slipped it into her pocket and began to unpack Sadie's things.

Reverend Cotton tapped the pages of his sermon against the pulpit, and cleared his throat. He looked out over the ranks of empty pews and felt a pang of dismay. Friday morning was never the most well-attended service of the week, but he was usually able to fill the first three rows near the altar.

Today only two members of his congregation had shown up. Ginny Upshaw sat expectantly in the first pew, as she always did, and Jessica Hudson sat behind her. Jessica had not even bothered to wear a hat.

It was not hard for him to understand why attendance was shrinking. Word of what had happened to Clarissa Sinclair and her boy had spread. There were other rumors, too: a mysterious death at the train station, but no body to be found; Prosper Knox parading about the village in some sort of pagan mask; fires in the woods; and animals roaming the streets at night. Every day, there was more fresh gossip than the good reverend could keep up with. It seemed the women of Bethany Hall were at the center of much of the talk.

Then there were the tabloids bringing news of peculiar happenings all over the country, and everywhere in the world. Reverend Cotton struggled to make sense of it all.

If no one was dying anymore, then the promises he made to his flock rang hollow. There could be no eternal life in the hereafter if eternal life began in the here and now. What did the promise of Heaven mean to someone who would never see it? What did the threat of hellfire mean to someone with no fear of death?

Samuel Cotton felt sorely tested. He hurried through his sermon and sent his meager congregation home.

S adie spat on the dining room table and wiped her palm through the splash of saliva. She spread her new map out over the damp streak. The ghost of the clumsy young man scowled at her, then dropped the bottle of wine in his lap and leapt up in surprise. The red-faced man at the head of the table made a rude gesture. He immediately felt bad about it and turned his back to the room, stroking one end of his enormous mustache. The cook brought in her tray of poisonous meat and nearly set it atop the map, then changed course and set the tray in a new place at the other end of the table.

Sadie reached past the ghost sitting next to her and picked up his steak knife, which did not technically exist at that point in time. Like everything else in the room, aside from the table and chairs, the knife was a phantom. The china and silverware had long ago been sold at auction. The knife Sadie held had been melted down three years before she was born and had been used to make several pieces of fine jewelry.

I do not understand how she is able to hold this knife—this knife that isn't there—and I do not know how she can possibly use it to slice open her hand, but that is what she is doing.

Sadie's blood spattered onto the map, and she moved her hand in a slow circle over the crude illustrations. Blood dripped and dribbled across the paper folds. Blood fell along the outskirts of the woods that grew wild beyond the base of Vinegar Hill. It trickled in a thin line behind Flora Fielding's greenhouse and down around Knox Drugs. It cut through the inky crosshatching of the train tracks.

After a moment, Sadie picked up a linen napkin that had long since rotted away, and wrapped it around her wound. She looked down at her handiwork and nodded with satisfaction. A ring had been drawn around the village and its outskirts, a ring of witch's blood. There was not a hairsbreadth of space between the individual droplets. The village, as depicted on the map, was entirely cut off from the outside world.

The long-ago dinner party recommenced around her. The red-faced man turned around and ladled soup for the woman next to him, the cook brought another platter of carved beef, the boy once again fumbled with his bottle of wine.

Sadie snatched the bottle away from him before he could drop it, and took a long swig.

Dr Timothy Rumpole owned three dinner jackets and he had tried each of them on several times that morning, trying to decide if he could actually wear any of them to the party at Bethany Hall. He had on the one that was missing a button and had gone blue at the elbows when he answered the door.

Alice Anders stood on the stoop. She wore a festive bonnet, but there were scratches on her hands and wrists, and her wide eyes were bloodshot. For a moment Dr Rumpole thought she might be one of the dead, but then he felt bees buzzing in his head.

"Doctor," the girl said.

"Alice, has something happened?"

She nodded and her eyes welled up with tears.

"Give me a minute to fetch my bag."

"It's not that, Doctor. Could I come in?"

Dr Rumpole stepped aside and swept his arm out in an exaggerated welcome. Alice stepped inside and the doctor hurried past her into the front room, grabbed a jacket off a chair, and tossed it over his tray of smoking paraphernalia.

"Can I get you something to drink?"

"I'm sorry," Alice said. "I don't mean to impose."

"Not at all. What's troubling you?"

"I gave Mrs Sinclair my quitting letter yesterday." She drew her shoulders up and presented Dr Rumpole with a brave smile. "Well, I didn't exactly give it to her. I left it on the dining room table, but it amounts to the same thing."

"Ah, you're sure you won't have something to drink? No? Please sit. Um, yes, I suppose you'll be leaving the village?"

Alice glanced around the room and chose the threadbare divan.

She sat and arranged her dress skirt over her knees. The buzzing in Dr Rumpole's head grew louder, and his scalp began to burn.

"My mother passed away before I was hired by Mrs Sinclair. I got no other family and nowhere to go."

"And no one who would miss you," the doctor said, tapping a finger against his chin.

"I suppose not."

He had a sudden urge to leap across the table and choke the life out of poor lonely Alice. Instead, he stuffed his hands in his jacket pockets and took a seat at the other end of the divan.

"Will you be looking for another position then?"

"I thought . . ." Alice gave the room another glance and this time he saw her jaw clench. He followed her gaze and was reminded of how utterly shabby his house was. Her momentary grimace was quickly replaced by a hopeful smile. "Well, I thought you might need somebody. I'm a good nurse and I'm not picky about what needs doing."

"Oh, Alice, I'm afraid the village hasn't given me the budget for a nurse. I'm expected to soldier on here by myself."

"But I don't need much," she said. "You'll see, I'm very self-sufficient."

"Alice, I—"

"It's just that I thought . . . Well, and Mrs Nettles said you might . . ."

She stood suddenly and headed toward the door, but the hem of her dress caught on the corner of the table and stopped her short, causing her to fall back onto the divan. Dr Rumpole jumped to his feet.

"Are you all right?"

"Maybe I'll take that drink, after all," she said. "If you don't mind."

"Of course," Dr Rumpole said. "I'll be right back, and when I return let's discuss your future, shall we?"

"Yes, Doctor."

The untrustworthy Mr Bell had been foolish to think Rabbit would keep an important secret from her mother. It is a common flaw to imagine that everyone else is, deep down, flawed in the same ways we are, and despite his devilish nature Bell is all too common.

Rabbit found Sadie in the ballroom. James Doolittle and his men had finished their work, and they had done it without disturbing the phantom dancers. The beautiful couple continued to pirouette across the center of the dance floor, but they were now framed by a massive stage and a long side table. Three new kerosene chandeliers twinkled overhead, and a fresh coat of lavender paint had rejuvenated the neglected hall.

Rabbit held the iron key in the palm of her outstretched hand, and Sadie frowned at it.

"It was a gift from a crow," she said. "I don't know what it fits."

"I think I do," Rabbit said.

She led Sadie from the room and down two flights of stairs, across the front hall and through the kitchen, where they descended the ladder to the root cellar. Once again, Rabbit held up her index finger and a tiny flame sprouted from its tip. It flared into a bright torch, but generated no heat.

One of the brides stood in a dark corner, watching them. Her white gown was now torn and stained, and mud dribbled from her chin. She held a baby in the crook of her elbow, and stroked its fine ghostly hair. She snarled at Rabbit, who briefly wondered what had happened to the other two brides.

"There," she said. She pointed to the undersized door in the far wall. "I think the key fits that lock."

"What makes you think so?" Sadie said. She narrowed her eyes at her daughter.

Rabbit shrugged. She slid the key into the keyhole and turned it clockwise. There was an audible click, and the knob rotated with the key. The door swung silently open.

The darkness beyond the door was somehow more complete than the darkness of the cellar. Rabbit stepped ahead of Sadie into the room, and swept her glowing hand around, casting light into every corner.

"It's empty," she said. "He said there were hopes and dreams in here."

"Who said that?"

"I'm not exactly sure who he is," Rabbit said. "You've seen the ghost butler?"

"No," Sadie said.

"Well, there's a man in a suit. He's not really there, but he's not really a ghost. He talks to me sometimes, and he said we have to exchange this key for a book. He said it's got something to do with Rose."

"He mentioned Rose specifically?"

Rabbit nodded.

Sadie said, "Do you remember the thing we found in the attic?"

"I haven't gone up there," Rabbit said. "The attic scares me."

"We went up there together, but then we forgot about it."

Rabbit's eyes widened. Her mouth opened. She nodded slightly. "I do remember something," she said. "It's like a dream, though, or like a word I'm trying to think of, but can't quite come up with."

"Whatever that is up there, it wants Rose. And I think Moses Burke might be on his way here to help it. I don't know what he wants."

"Moses is coming? I love Moses. He'd never do anything to hurt Rose."

"We haven't seen him in a long time," Sadie said. "Maybe he's changed."

"Or maybe you're wrong."

"Right or wrong, I'm not taking any chances. I've drawn a ring around the village to keep him out."

Their breath was visible in the light Rabbit cast. Cold seeped in through the dirt walls and up through the dirt floor.

"We should never have come here," Rabbit said.

"We should leave first thing tomorrow," Sadie said. "The eight o'clock train."

"Rose might not want to go."

"I can be persuasive. I'll talk to her after the party."

"Moses Burke." Rabbit stared at the key. "I can't believe it."

"Don't worry," Sadie said. "She'll be okay."

"If we're leaving in the morning, I have something I have to do."

Sadie searched her daughter's eyes in the flickering light.

"Rabbit?"

"Don't worry, I'll be quick."

As they left the room Rabbit saw movement in her peripheral vision. She turned in time to see Bell's smiling face melt back into the shadows.

Grover Smalls could find nothing wrong with his engine. He got down from the cab and walked up the tracks, searching for obstructions. He traveled ten paces from the front of his train, then he stopped and returned to the cab. He frowned and shook his head, glanced up and down the length of the train, then walked back up the tracks. Two minutes later he was standing beside the engine again.

Moses Burke hopped off the car behind him and turned to lift Esmerelda Rosas down. On both sides, the land sloped away from the rails into thick winter woods.

"Something wrong?" Moses said to Grover.

"I can't figure it out," Grover said.

"Why did we stop?" Esmerelda said.

"That's what I can't figure out. Never happened before. This old girl just stopped cold on the tracks."

"Did the train hit something?" Esmerelda said.

"You see anything looks like it got hit by a train?" Grover shook his head. "Sorry to snap at you, child; I'm just puzzled. No, we didn't hit nothing, so far as I can tell."

"Something broke then," Moses said.

"Can't find anything wrong. Fire's stoked and we still got a head of steam built up. For some damn reason, she just coasted to a stop and sits here, when as far as I can tell she ought to be chugging on along."

"That's odd," Moses said.

"You wanna know another odd thing? I just tried to walk up the tracks a bit. Thought maybe we *did* hit something and it got thrown. But I didn't get no more than a few feet. One second I'm walking along, next I'm right back where I started."

Moses squinted at him, then stepped away from the engine and walked forward up the tracks. A moment later he was standing once again beside Grover.

"We watched you walk up there a little bit, then you turned around and walked back," Grover said. "You mean to do that?"

"I did not."

"You remember doing it?"

"I do not."

"Same for me."

"La brujería," Esmerelda said.

"Yup," Moses said. "I guess Sadie got the cable I sent."

The sun had moved from a position directly overhead and was beginning its descent into the western sky. Grover saw a white bird wheeling overhead and mistook it for a dove. As it banked, its eye reflected sunlight at him.

"Red," Grover said.

"What?"

"Bird up there has red eyes," Grover said. "That mean anything to you?"

"Not especially," Moses said.

"It doesn't mean anything to me, either," Esmerelda said.

When Grover looked again, the bird was already a white speck above the distant treetops.

"How far are we from Ascension?" Moses said.

"No more than five miles," Grover said.

"Anything else around here besides that town?"

"Well, I don't stop in Ascension, but I don't believe there's much of anything out this way besides a whole bunch of trees and grass, and some beeves like I'm supposed to be delivering today. But if I can't get my train moving, I'm gonna miss my delivery."

The sudden thought that he might fail at his job frightened Grover Smalls to his core.

"This is just not a scheduled stop for me," he said again.

Moses took off his hat and ran his hand over his head, careful to avoid the bullet hole. He contemplated the woods. After a minute he put his hat back on and cleared his throat.

"I guess she doesn't want us here," Moses said.

"What should we do?" Esmerelda said.

"I think I ought to finish what I started."

"But if this person is as powerful as you say, how can we go on?"

"I'm gonna have to back this train down the tracks," Grover

said to himself. "How far am I gonna have to back this train down the tracks?"

"I have an appointment to keep," Moses said. "I came all this way; I gave up my rifle and the best horse I ever rode. I didn't do everything I've done just to go back down the tracks with Mr Smalls. No offense, sir."

"None taken, sir," Grover said.

"I don't want to turn back," Moses said. "And I guess we can't go forward, but I wonder if we can maybe cut sideways through those trees."

"Look," Esmerelda said. She pointed up the rails behind the train. "The yellow dog caught up with us again!"

Esmerelda kneels down in the cold wet grass, and my brother runs to her. He has nearly completed his task. He has shepherded Moses Burke and Esmerelda Rosas, mi pequeña rosa, to the threshold of Ascension. It will be time for me to take a direct hand in these proceedings.

I would have explored the attic right away," Clarissa said, brushing at invisible cobwebs. "If I were you."

"I haven't had time," Rose said.

"Who knows what treasures are up here?"

"Well, there are chairs." Rose pointed to the tangle of ladder-back chairs jammed under the rafters.

But Clarissa was already wandering through the cramped space, touching each dusty tin trunk and yellowed paper parcel, as if they could convey their contents to her by osmosis. When she came to the desk under the window she opened the top drawer and closed it again, disappointed to find it was empty. She bent to examine a book that lay open on the desktop.

Rose cleared her throat. "How many chairs do you think we need?"

"Chairs?"

"You said we need more seating."

"Well, how many can you carry, dear?"

Rose glanced at the pile. "One."

"It would take us all day to bring those downstairs," Clarissa said. "Someone spent a lot of time up here. They were writing a children's story. Listen to this: 'Esmerelda will find her father sitting under a tree at a switchyard. He will weep and apologize, and she will forgive him, and they will return to their little home beside the silver maples, where they will never grow older and never die.'" Clarissa closed the book and ran a finger over the name embossed on the front cover. "Dr Ichabod Bailey? I heard he was a disgusting old man. Why would he write something like this?"

"I'll have Butler bring the chairs down," Rose said. "Let's go. I don't like this room."

Clarissa came around the desk and leaned against it. "I heard the council let you go."

Rose paused with her hand on the doorknob. "You're well informed."

"Of course. So what will you do now?"

"You didn't bring me up here for chairs, did you?"

"I suppose you'll go back to Philadelphia," Clarissa said.

"I haven't decided yet. I haven't even told Sadie."

"You have to stay, or I'll start missing you all over again."

"Won't you go back to your husband now?"

"Benjamin sent his father a telegram. Richard wrote back and said . . ." Clarissa put a hand to her mouth. "Oh, Rose, I'm so alone."

Rose went and took her cousin into her arms. Clarissa's skin was cold; she sniffed and kissed Rose on the cheek, and pulled away.

"I'm emotional these days," Clarissa said. "And my head's all buzzy. Stay here with me, Rose. We Nettles girls could turn this village on its ear, couldn't we?"

"Let's get through this party and we'll talk," Rose said.

"Yes, the party's the thing, isn't it. We'll have a grand time, and show these rubes how it's done, then tomorrow I'm going to corner you on the subject. You and Sadie and I will hash it out."

"Tomorrow," Rose said.

"And to think," Clarissa said, "a week ago I thought my life was over."

She wiped her eyes with the back of her hand and led the way back through the maze of forgotten junk. Rose followed. She paused in the doorway and looked back at the desk and a shudder ran through her. She hopped over the threshold and slammed the attic door behind her.

George Herman arrived at Bethany Hall at half past noon. He rolled a wagon up to the kitchen door, and he and his son unloaded a dozen chickens, a side of beef, three pork shoulders, and two crates of oysters, along with sausages and potatoes, bacon with corn muffins, tiny quail eggs, and two wheels of cheese.

At two o'clock five girls from the village showed up at the back door, having been hired by Clarissa to help Cook in the kitchen. They were initially startled by Cook's size; she was easily half again as tall as the tallest girl, and twice as wide as the stoutest of the five. None of them could understand a word she said— they decided she must be from a faraway country of mumbling giants—but her speed and enthusiasm won them over, and soon they were chopping, stirring, mixing, and folding as if they had worked for her all their lives.

At four thirty Flora Fielding arrived with a wagonload of fresh cut flowers—lilacs and daffodils, and vases bursting with camellias of every color—and vegetables—watercress for sandwiches, carrots, cucumbers, and green onions. The vegetables were taken directly to the kitchen. The flowers were dispersed throughout the house; the majority of them were arranged in the foyer—to make an immediate impression on Clarissa's guests—and in the ballroom upstairs.

A seven-piece band straggled up the hill half an hour later and began to practice on the new stage in the ballroom, while all around them candles were lit and flowers were stuffed into vases.

When the clock struck six, the wide front door was thrown open and Clarissa Sinclair planted herself at the top of the stairs, ready to welcome the village. It was a fine night for a party. The sky was cloudless, the moon was bright, and the air was crisp. The sound of the band's instruments drifted from the third-floor windows, inviting one and all to come listen.

Three or four couples arrived by carriage, but most Ascensioners chose to walk up the hill. Almost no one had passed up the invitation to visit the notorious murder house. Prosper and Lillian Knox were first to arrive, and after being greeted by Clarissa on the porch they were bustled inside where a hulking man in an ill-fitting suit took Prosper's coat and Lillian's wrap. The giant man said not a word, and wore a white plaster mask, which made Lillian uneasy but filled Prosper with a feeling of warmth and companionship. He, too, had chosen to hide his face, and wore his demon mask, adorned with the hair of his victims.

Daisy Merrick and her mother arrived next. When she saw Prosper in the drawing room, Daisy steered her mother along the hallway to the morning room, where they nearly bumped into a silent colossus in a housekeeper's uniform, carrying a tray of hors d'oeuvres. The woman wore a thick veil, but Daisy thought she could see vague indications of features behind it: eyes that didn't quite line up, an off-center nose, a gaping maw of a mouth. Daisy took a canapé and thanked the woman, who lurched away without responding.

George Herman returned to the house at the same time as Flora Fielding, and there was a moment of awkwardness wherein each of them offered to let the other enter first. Then the florist stuck out her arm, the butcher took her elbow, and, chuckling, they stepped over the threshold together.

Clarissa followed them inside and went to check on the girls in the kitchen. Cook was struggling with the beef, which had got a bit more done than intended, but there were trays of miniature sandwiches on the countertops, along with fried oysters and chicken pies, all ready to be taken out. Clarissa advised the girls to grind the beef and make a spread.

Dr Rumpole entered in the company of a striking young woman with white-blond hair, and several of the partygoers in the sitting room struggled to place her until Lillian Knox shouted, "Aha, it's the nurse!"

Ethel Merrick hushed her and Lillian blushed, then whispered, "It's Clarissa's girl, I'm sure of it."

"Well, isn't she moving up in the world," Daisy said. There was a note of envy in her voice that did not go unnoticed by the other women.

Benjamin Sinclair escorted Lucy Knox up the hill. He carried a silver tray covered with a checkered cloth. Clarissa gathered her son up in a breathless embrace. She motioned for Lucy to join the hug, but the girl shook her head politely, causing the edges of her veil to swish back and forth, exposing deep black wounds along her jawline.

"We brought a housewarming gift," Lucy said, grabbing the

tray of lemon cakes from Benjamin before it could tip. "I'd better get these to the kitchen."

She hurried into the house, and Clarissa relaxed her grip enough for Benjamin to extract himself.

"I've always liked Lucy. Are you two seeing each other now?"

"I don't know, Mother."

"It seems like half the people here are wearing veils."

Benjamin grimaced and his mother patted his arm.

"She was always so pretty," she said.

Benjamin's grimace deepened. "I should go see if she needs help," he said.

Benjamin hurried away as his mother turned to greet Jessica Hudson, the innkeeper.

Reverend Cotton was next to arrive, but seemed reluctant to enter the house. He lingered on the porch, shaking hands with each new arrival as if Bethany Hall were his church. After he spent five minutes nattering at Jaspar and Ginny Upshaw about their perfectly uninteresting printshop, while Clarissa fruitlessly tried to usher them inside, she finally lost patience with him.

"You might as well go in and join the party, Reverend. You can suck the joy from everyone just as easily in there."

The Upshaws fell silent, and after an uncomfortable pause, Jaspar carefully guided his wife around Clarissa and into the hall. Reverend Cotton descended the porch steps, and with a sheepish wave he turned and made his way back down the hill.

"I don't remember inviting him," Clarissa said under her breath.

Clarissa paid close attention to each new person, couple, and family who came trudging up Vinegar Hill for lemonade and gin and finger sandwiches, and as night fell and she had pushed the last new arrival through the doors—a clearly intoxicated Mr Mulacky—she took a deep breath and gazed happily around her at the gathered villagers. She was both pleased and mildly astonished by the turnout. If she had once been neglected by the village, she felt that she was surely seen again.

The seven members of the village band were eager to take a break. The oldest of them was sixty-two and the youngest was fourteen, and they had been playing for more than three hours.

Lucy had brought enough lemon cakes for each of them to take two. She and Benjamin left the musicians sitting at the edge of the stage with their snacks, and went downstairs.

"I could use a breath of fresh air," Benjamin said.

Lucy followed him outside, the empty tray swinging at her side, spilling crumbs along the path. The garden was still blanketed with a layer of sparkling snow where the shadow of the house had sheltered it from the sun.

"Have you heard of a place called Positano?" Benjamin said.

"Is it nearby?"

"It's in Italy," he said. "I'd like to go there someday."

"Have you been before?"

"No. My father has."

He stood with his hands in his pockets, staring at the sky. The scarf he wore to cover his most recent wound fluttered around his shoulders. Lucy liked the way he planted himself firmly on the ground with his feet apart, as if he were guarding against the pull of the moon.

"I can't stay here," he said.

"Oh, Benjamin, we've talked about—"

"It's not the same for you. You were born here. This is all you've ever known."

He glanced at her, but couldn't see her features behind the veil. He knew it wasn't his fault they wanted different things, but he felt guilty about it all the same.

"I think I'm like my father," he said.

"That's not true," Lucy said.

"He doesn't care about anybody. Not me or my mother. Not even when she was dying."

Benjamin rocked back on his heels, then forward on his toes.

"Do you hear bees in your head all the time?"

"Not when I'm around you," Lucy said. She picked a crumb of lemon cake from the tray, then turned the platter over and pretended to read the manufacturer's mark on its underside.

"I'd go with you," she said. "I mean, if you asked."

"I know," he said.

"I would never want to hold you back. What kind of wife would do that?" When he didn't respond, she said, "Everything will be different tomorrow. You'll see. I'm going to get more cakes to pass out. It's a good thing we brought so many. Everybody seems to love them."

She turned and drifted slowly through the garden. She lingered for a moment when she reached the gate, hoping he would call her back, but he didn't. Reluctantly, she rounded the corner of the house and hurried to the kitchen door, blinking back tears.

Benjamin laid down beside the path and watched the stars twinkle overhead. A white bird circled and banked above him. In the moonlight its eyes glowed red. A childhood memory made Benjamin smile, and he moved his arms and legs to form a snow angel until, feeling foolish, he tucked his arms in at his sides and lay as still as he could, imagining that the earth might fall away beneath him. Imagining he could float away.

"Benjamin's gone," Sergeant Winter said. "I saw him leave with Lucy."

"No," Prosper said, "I forbade her—"

Winter grabbed his friend's elbow and pulled him to a secluded corner of the parlor.

"For god's sake, Prosper, she murdered you. Your daughter is willful, and you are dead." Winter raised a finger. "You have lost control of your family."

Winter turned and stomped out through the foyer of Bethany Hall, his cane thumping hard against the floor. Prosper hurried after him, and nearly ran into a creature he mistook for a waiter.

"Refreshment?" Bell said.

"Out of my way," Prosper said.

He pushed past Bell, out the door, and down the porch steps, but paused at the garden gate and pushed up his heavy mask. Winter was ahead of him, limping down the trail toward the village. Prosper stood for a moment, enjoying the feel of the breeze on his face.

In that moment of cool clarity, he recalled the silver tray offered by the man in the dark suit. He turned and looked up at the house. Lights blazed in the windows, and the sounds of gossip and laughter floated down to him.

The tray had been piled high with scalps. Women's hair, blond, brown, gray, and black; curls and ringlets and braids, scraps of flesh still clinging to the bloody caps.

Prosper pulled his mask back over his face and raced after Sergeant Winter. In his haste, he failed to see Benjamin Sinclair, who had fallen asleep in a bed of frozen chrysanthemums.

Rabbit watched the white crow glide down the hill above Prosper Knox and Newton Winter, marking their location for her. She hoped Sadie would condone the use of her familiar, but Rabbit decided she could apologize later if need be. For now, the crow was useful. She set the old sled at the top of the slope and jumped on, sliding down into the woods, her cloak billowing behind her in the breeze. She left the sled at the bottom of the hill, and crunched through the snow. Ice melted under her feet, and trees glowed around her, lighting the way forward. With each footfall, the earth trembled.

Rabbit was angry.

A dead squirrel chittered at her from a branch. She ignored it. A bobcat followed her at a safe distance, its swollen face full of porcupine quills. A pair of starved and mangy foxes kept pace with the bobcat, their skin stretched taut against their bones. They were no longer prey, and the cat was beyond hunger.

Rabbit was aware of the creatures around her, but she was entirely focused on the path ahead. Snowbanks scattered ahead of her, deadfalls collapsed. The forest made room for her to pass.

At last she emerged in the clearing at the center of the woods. The skeleton of the cabin stood stark and black against the purity of the snowy glade. Rabbit's nose twitched and her hair fluttered, and she wished she had thought to bring her mother's warm fur coat.

A woman shimmered into view among the ruins. An idea of a woman, a memory, a spirit. Rabbit took a step forward. Another spirit appeared, then another. They formed a wide semicircle around her, and linked their hands, forming a chain.

Rabbit bowed her head, and cleared her throat. She reached

into the pocket of her cloak and brought out a handful of dry brown dittany leaves.

"I brought you something," she said.

Esmerelda had never been good at telling time. She knew it was early afternoon when she and Moses had walked away from the train tracks and into the woods. The sky was bright, birds chirped, and insects called; night had not yet entered her thoughts. But they had been walking a long time now, and the sun had set. Different insects were calling and different birds were hooting.

When she looked behind her, she could still see the break in the trees where they had entered the woods. She could see moonlight glinting on the train tracks. Grover Smalls had backed up his locomotive and moved on to his next scheduled stop. Esmerelda was no better with distances than she was with time, but she was sure they had not traveled more than fifty yards.

She reached for Moses's hand in the dark.

"This is taking too long," she said. "It's like we're walking through mud."

"Like we're swimming upstream," Moses agreed. "This is my fault. I told them to protect Rose from me if they had to, and I'm pretty sure that's what they're doing. I was a fool to think they wouldn't notice us sneaking through the forest to ruin their lives."

"We are not ruining anybody's life," Esmerelda said.

"I sure don't intend to, kiddo. It just feels like I ought to keep going."

The yellow dog ranged ahead, bounding easily through the underbrush and circling back to see what scant progress the others had made.

"It's funny that dog isn't having the same trouble we are."

From somewhere ahead came the sound of an animal crashing through the bushes, and the yellow dog leapt away again, disappearing into the shadows.

"At this rate it'll take us days to get anywhere," Moses said.

"We need magic," Esmerelda said.

"Did Poppy give you anything besides poison blueberries?"

"Those were not blueberries. They were pokeberries."

"Well?"

"No."

"Then we better keep walking," Moses said.

"What will we do when we get there?"

"If we get there . . ."

"What will we do?"

"I don't exactly know," Moses said. "I don't understand much about prophesies, and visions. I've herded cattle and I've learned a little medicine and I've gambled quite a bit, but not one of those things prepared me for this. What I think is that whoever gets Death's book is supposed to do his job, keep his appointments. I never thought about giving it to Rose until that angel told me not to."

"The book you gave me? The one in my bag?"

"I meant to get that back from you."

Esmerelda reached for the clasp on her bag, but stopped. She tugged on Moses's hand and cupped a hand behind her ear.

"Listen," she said.

They had heard it for several minutes without noticing: a low whirring sound, like wheels turning within wheels, growing louder as it came. It had started far away, but it was picking up speed as it moved through the trees. Branches cracked and snapped. Somewhere a dog yelped.

"The angel," Esmerelda said. "The angel is coming."

Bell finds the bloodstained map of Ascension under a folded blanket at the foot of Sadie's bed. He flings the blanket aside and contemplates the ring of witch's blood that encircles the village and the tangled woods.

"You interfere with them too much," I say.

Bell smirks. I have failed to surprise him.

"I liked our game better when you played as hard as I do," he says.

"I am older now," I say. "I have lost interest in your games."

"Then why not suggest one of your own? We have a long night ahead of us, waiting for your man to get here. I'm bored."

He has not spent a week in the attic. He has no idea what boredom is.

"I have faith in Moses Burke," I say. "The night won't be as long as you think."

Bell points at the map. Sadie's blood has soaked into the thin paper and has formed hairline tributaries throughout the pulp. It reminds me of briars, of prickly thorns and vines.

"The witch has done half my work for me," Bell says.

It is true that Sadie Grace is inadvertently helping him. But when she cast her spell over Ascension, her own rules had required her to be specific about that which could not pass through her barrier. It was a negative spell in that sense, outlining those things that would now be foreign and must therefore be resisted. Otherwise, deliveries would be suspended, and the villagers would not get needed supplies. Birds and squirrels, foxes and rabbits, butterflies and beetles, would be prevented from entering the circle, and without new life to fill them the woods would eventually die.

So she excluded Moses Burke, and only Moses Burke, from the village because he was coming to take Rose away from her.

Her spell had stopped a train in its tracks because Moses was on it, but witchcraft could not stand against the yellow dog that had arrived with Moses. My brother's presence had allowed Moses to enter the woods. That, and the man's indomitable character and willfulness.

I do have faith in Moses Burke, but I also know something that Bell does not: Moses is not alone.

"Moses Burke will never make it through the woods," Bell is saying. "You have your brother and I have mine, but I also have the good Graces in my corner, and you are outnumbered. If you concede now, we can all go home."

I find myself growing impatient with him. In my defense, it has been a long week.

"Perhaps you are right," I say. "Let us liven things up."

A tiny flame sparks to life in the center of the map, where the peak of Vinegar Hill is represented, then grows and spreads toward the woods on one side, and toward the village on the other. Curling blue worms of fire eat the train station, the drugstore, the churchyard. The village green blackens; flames march away up Brynwood Lane and down Twisdale Road. At the outer edge of the village, and at the railroad tracks beyond the trees, the ring of witch's blood erupts into shivery violet fire.

A curl of smoke drifts away toward the ceiling, and a gentle breeze sweeps through the room, taking with it a small pile of ash from the otherwise unmarked bed.

No trace remains of the map. Sadie's spell is broken.

Bell claps his hands. "Well played, old friend. It's good to see you have fun for a change."

Then he is gone and I feel a pang of regret for my childish display. Yes, I am older than I was when last we squared off, but I think it possible I am no wiser.

I sure wish that angel would leave me alone," Moses said.

He pushed Esmerelda under the roots of a sycamore and scooped leaves over her.

"Be as quiet as you can," he whispered as he covered her legs with dead black leaves. "It might be mad at me 'cause I ignored its warning."

"Don't leave me here."

"I promise, I'm just gonna lead it away and circle right back around. I don't know why we can suddenly move again, but I can't argue with the timing. I'll go as fast as I can and I'll see you in just a few minutes. Unless that thing eats me."

"Angels don't eat people."

"Good to know. Hush now, Junior."

Esmerelda never saw Moses again.

She heard him scramble away. He yelled to get the creature's attention, and banged a stick against the trunk of a tree. She heard the awful whirring of the angel's many wings, and heard it hesitate when it drew near her. Then it moved on into the woods, following the sound of Moses's voice. Trees fell behind it, crashing into each other, and splinters drifted down into Esmerelda's hair.

She waited under the maple for a long while, snowmelt seeping into her dress, dripping down her face, running between her shoulder blades. She thought about her father, and she wondered if he was still lying in a trench behind their little cabin. She wondered if he was thinking about her at the same moment she was thinking about him.

At last she brushed away the wet leaves and stood up. The yellow dog sat ten feet away, patiently waiting. For the third time in as many days, it had found her.

Number 17 Brynwood Lane was dark and empty.

"Benjamin clearly didn't come back here," Winter said. He turned away from the house and looked up the road in both directions.

"Where could he have gone?" Prosper said. "Could we have passed him on the green?"

"I'll be damned if I'm climbing that hill again," Winter said.

"We'll wait for him here. We'll ambush him when he comes home."

Winter was no longer paying attention. "What was that?" he said, pointing far down the street to where Brynwood met Shiloh Road.

Proper pushed up his mask and squinted into the darkness. "I don't see anything," he said. "It must have been—"

An inky shape loped into the intersection and stopped.

"Is that a dog?"

"Her name's Beauty," Prosper said. "I lost her in the woods the other day."

The Irish setter stood and watched them. After a moment another dog limped into view and joined her.

"My Kerry Blue," Prosper said. "Here, York. You're a good boy, York."

Beauty began to growl. York started toward them, moving slowly on his damaged leg, and the Irish setter followed. Behind the dogs, a great stag appeared in the street, its mighty rack framed against the moon. It sniffed the air, and snorted, and pawed at the icy dirt. The dogs began to bark.

"Retreat," Winter said. "Through the churchyard. Cotton will open up for us."

"Wasn't he at the party?"

"Run, man!" Winter hobbled away, moving faster than Prosper

had seen him move before, the tip of his cane clicking over the stones.

Prosper pulled his mask down and ran.

His breath whistled through the wet wound in his face. He kept his head down, watching his feet, trying not to trip. Behind them, he heard the injured dogs bay, growing closer with every passing second.

Prosper stumbled and fell, and smacked his forehead against a fencepost. The impact knocked him to his knees. Winter passed him and didn't look back.

"Don't leave me, Newton!"

He rolled over and looked up the road. A hedgerow rustled, leaves swirled gently to the ground, and York, the Kerry Blue, burst into view, followed closely by the male Irish setter, Beauty's littermate. Prosper covered his head with his arms, but the dogs jumped over him and kept going.

He sat up and ran his fingers through his hair. He closed his eyes and let out a long shaky breath. When he opened his eyes again the spaniel named Butch was staring at him. One of the dog's legs hung limp and Prosper could see cracked ribs poking through Butch's skin. He snarled at Prosper, then turned and crawled after the other dogs.

Prosper heard a scream. He got to his feet and stumbled across the churchyard. He found Newton Winter sitting against a tombstone. The Sergeant's legs were outstretched, and in his lap he cradled a steaming mound of gray intestines. The dogs circled a barren area behind him, sniffing at piles of dead leaves. Having torn Winter apart, they had lost interest in him. They didn't seem to notice Prosper at all.

Winter looked up at his friend, his eyes hooded, his cheeks spattered with blood.

"I'm killed," he said.

Prosper nodded.

"Help me put these back inside," Winter said.

Prosper removed his mask and laid it down. Winter scooped his guts onto its curved inner surface and Prosper helped him to his feet. They edged past the dogs and back to the road.

"I should sew these back in where they belong."

"Lillian's a good seamstress," Prosper said. "Or I could fetch the new doctor for you."

Winter's voice rose an octave. "Good god, man, I'm dead! You're dead! Half the damn village is dead! What's going to happen to us?" His scream echoed back at them from the empty street. "This isn't natural. This isn't real."

He fell against the fence and sank back to the ground. He dug in his pockets until he found a folded hunting knife, opened it, and began carving at a length of his intestines, folding them over on themselves and sawing until the two ends were held together by a thread of flesh. Prosper stood frozen in horror, unable to speak or move to stop him. Winter dropped the knife and bit into the gray meat, gnawing until it came apart and his entrails fell away. He spat and stood, leaning heavily on his cane, and kicked at the demon's mask with its grisly burden. His hollow abdomen steamed in the cool air.

"Now I'm free," Winter said.

"No," came a voice from the darkness behind them.

Rabbit Grace stalked toward them down Shiloh Road. Her trousers were caked with mud, and her eyes flashed in the moonlight. She stepped onto the green and the snow melted. The grass grew thick and tall, radiating out from her in a spreading circle that rippled in the night breeze.

Twenty-six women marched down the road behind her, holding hands, rank on rank. Prosper recognized some of them. Others had been killed in the little cabin long before he was born, killed by his father and his father's father. Their dried scalps had decorated the cabin walls for three generations. The women looked now as they must have looked in life, their eyes clear of pain, their hair restored to them: yellow, brown, dark, and fair. The women looked at each of the men in turn, and together they took a step forward.

"You are most definitely not free," Rabbit said.

Prosper Knox began to cry.

B ell wandered through Bethany Hall, from room to room and floor to floor, carrying a silver tray with nothing on it. Each hair on his head moved independently and according to its whim. The edges of his body blurred and jumped, causing the room behind him to shift.

When he entered the library, Ginny Upshaw glanced up at him and smiled politely before fainting. Jaspar Upshaw dropped a first-edition Dickens he was admiring and caught his wife before she hit the floor. He grinned at Bell, embarrassed, and dragged Ginny to a convenient armchair.

"She's been light-headed all day," he said. "Starved herself to fit into her favorite gown."

"I see," Bell said. "How can I help?"

"Oh, no," Jaspar said. "She'll be fine, really."

He had not yet looked directly at Bell, but he reached out absent-mindedly when the tray was offered and accepted a glass of wine.

"Thanks," he said. He arranged his wife's ball gown to cover an exposed ankle, and perched on an arm of the chair where she would see him when she woke up. He took a sip of the wine and smacked his lips.

"Can't place this vintage," he said, but Bell had already moved on.

He was carrying his tray of wishes along the front hall when Clarissa bustled in through the foyer and snapped her fingers at him.

"You," she said. "You're with the kitchen staff?"

Amused, Bell raised an eyebrow. "Ma'am?"

"We need food out here," Clarissa said. "Quick as you can. I'm going up to see if the ballroom's ready."

She twirled in a slow circle, taking in the clusters of people spilling out into the hallway. She looked for Rose and Sadie Grace and Rabbit, but they were nowhere to be seen.

"This was all supposed to be for them," she muttered. "Ungrateful."

"Always the way, isn't it?" Bell said.

"And it's always the same people talking to each other," Clarissa said. "This might as well be a church social. I need the new people out here to liven things up."

"New people?" Bell said. "Or perhaps some very old people? What a splendid idea. I believe I will arrange something for you."

Clarissa hurried away toward the kitchen. She felt vaguely nauseated.

"What a strange little man," she said. "Rose must have hired him."

D aisy Merrick was the first to see a ghost—*That cat's lost its head!*—but it was soon obvious to everyone that the partygoers were not alone in the house.

In the kitchen, Lucy Knox offered the remaining five lemon cakes to the village girls who were helping Cook. None of them noticed a woman wearing a torn wedding gown emerge from the root cellar and walk out through the door to the butler's pantry. This was Bethany, and she bore the distinction of being the first spirit to inhabit the house.

Rose was in the parlor when a burly cattle rancher in a ridge-top hat stumbled through, his blackened flesh sizzling. Blue flames shot out from him in every direction, scorching the wallpaper and the furniture. Rose backed into the table behind her, knocking over an arrangement of daffodils. The rancher tipped his hat to her, picked up the vase, and set it back on the table. Rose averted her eyes, but not before she saw the words *be not afraid* burned into his chest.

Clarissa entered the pantry where Bethany stood with her back to the door, rummaging through a drawer of kitchen implements. Bethany was panting, her shoulders heaving. She growled and hurled a spoon to the floor.

"Excuse me," Clarissa said. "Do I know you?"

Bethany turned and stabbed Clarissa in the eye with a silver cake knife.

"Give me the baby," she said, her white gown now stained with Clarissa's blood as well as her own.

An old woman knocked at the front door, and when Butler opened it she held out her hands and showed him a golden locket. Butler motioned for her to come in.

The little girl who had surprised Sadie and Rabbit on the attic stairs—her name was Naomi Clapper and she was six years old when she died—ran down to the third-floor landing and was surprised to find she could keep running. So she did.

Upon their deaths that evening from cyanide poisoning, the band members had lost interest in playing their instruments and had wandered away from the stage. The ballroom was deserted except for the village butcher and the florist, who had come in looking for a quiet spot away from the party. George Herman gathered Flora Fielding in his arms, and they swayed in silence, until Flora looked up at him and said, "We have company." George opened his eyes and saw a man in a blue suit and a woman in a shimmering gown dance past. The couple smiled at George and Flora, who smiled back at them and joined the waltz.

At the doorway, Naomi Clapper watched them for a moment, then ran down another floor to the dining hall where Dr Timothy Rumpole and Alice Anders had gone to escape the chaos. They were making awkward small talk when a sudden dinner party sprang up around them. Dr Rumpole had the presence of mind to catch a bottle of wine dropped by the young man sitting next to him.

The flickering boy in the corner of the room turned and began to cry. Naomi Clapper wagged a finger at him.

"Stop it," she said. "Come out of that corner."

The boy wiped his eyes with his knuckles.

"I'm Fred," he said.

"Hello, Fred. I'm Naomi."

Fred Elliott was a year older than Naomi Clapper when he died. His parents had taken him to the top of Vinegar Hill and told him to stay until they returned for him. He stood there for half a day, watching the woods below, before finally sitting down in the grass. He waited another day before easing onto his back so he could see the clouds. Thirty years later workmen arrived to begin construction on Bethany Hall, and Fred stood back up. Walls were built around him and he could no longer see the woods. A roof was put up between him and the clouds. Still he waited for his parents to come. He waited and he waited, until finally he turned around and realized there was a party going on and he hadn't been invited.

"Things seem different today," he said.

"I think we can go where we want. We don't have to stay with our bodies no more."

"How come?"

"There's an angel," Naomi said. "He lives in the attic, and sometimes he talks to me."

"What does he say?"

Naomi shrugged. "Who cares? Let's go."

She took Fred's hand and together they descended to the ground floor, just as Dr Ichabod Bailey left his study and lurched out into the passage. He was alarmed to find his home filled with strangers. He felt as if he had woken up after a long fever.

His cousin had done a great deal of damage with her axe, and Ichabod still wore the wounds. His left arm was missing below the elbow, and the corresponding foot was tethered to his ankle by a tendon. Half his throat was carved out, causing his head to bob and tilt at an alarming angle.

He held out a hand to stop Naomi and Fred, and patted his sweater pockets, looking for his spectacles. "Children," he said. "Where is your mother?"

At this, Fred began to cry again, and Naomi yanked him away down the hall. Dr Bailey watched them go, puzzled, feeling he ought to know them since they were in his house.

A woman in a white dress ran at him from the direction of the butler's pantry, waving a silver cake knife.

She said, "Where's the baby?"

"Ah," Dr Bailey said. "Boy or girl? I saw one of each just now. They went that way." He pointed, and Bethany handed him the cake knife.

"Thank you," she said.

"No, thank you," he said.

He mounted the stairs with some difficulty and stumbled down the hallway to the bedroom he had once shared with his cousin. She lay on the bed with her back to him, her bloody nightgown clinging to the high curve of her hip. He stood and watched her for a long while, and at last she moved. Only an inch or two, but he took it as an invitation. Ichabod sat on the edge of the bed and showed her the cake knife.

"You murdered me," he said.

She said nothing.

He said, "Did I do something to deserve that?"

She was quiet.

"I'm sorry," he whispered. "And I forgive you." He let the knife slip from his hand and clatter to the floor.

The house had been remodeled extensively during the many years Naomi and Fred had spent walled within it, and they got lost. The children wandered through the parlor and the morning room, and back to the passage outside the study. They peeked in and saw Mr Mulacky swaying back and forth, examining the doctor's bookshelves, then they scampered through the empty butler's pantry and passed through to the kitchen, where a girl was vomiting bits of lemon cake into a mixing bowl. Three other girls laid on the kitchen floor, one of them knocking the back of her head against a table leg, again and again. A fifth girl stared openmouthed at Naomi.

"Something's wrong with the cakes," the girl said. "But I don't feel sick anymore."

"I want cake," Naomi said to the girl.

She hadn't eaten in more than sixty years. Naomi's last meal had been a bowl of cold porridge her uncle gave her before locking her in the attic and leaving the village with a young man who had come to tend the horses.

"I want to go home," the village girl said. "I only came to help with the party."

Two of the other girls got up from the floor and watched the girl who was vomiting.

"I'm dead," one of them said in a matter-of-fact tone. "I feel certain of it."

"I want to go home," the first girl said again.

"Are we allowed?"

"Why not?" said the third girl.

The remaining girl on the kitchen floor stopped spasming. After a moment, she rolled onto her side and groaned.

"Tell Cora to stop sicking in that bowl," she said. "It smells disgusting."

The first girl picked up a rolling pin and smacked Cora, the vomiting girl, in the side of her head. There was a resounding crunch and the bowl fell to the floor. It spun in a circle, splashing the baseboards with half-eaten lemon cake.

"That's done it!"

Fred looked as if he might start crying again, so Naomi pulled him out through the kitchen door to the back stoop. They stood perfectly still for a minute. Naomi sniffed at the crisp air. Fred wiped his nose on his sleeve.

"I can see the trees again," he said. "I can see the sky."

"Where should we go?" Naomi said.

"I don't know," Fred said. "I can't remember any places except my corner."

"Let's find new places," Naomi said.

"Yes," Fred said. "Let's."

The two ghost children walked down Vinegar Hill, hand in hand.

The children are my small mercies.

For good or ill, this awful week in Ascension will end. Has ended. And yet the two of them remain at large in the world. Bell has inadvertently done something wonderful for young Naomi Clapper and Fred Elliott, and although I have not spoken to him about it, I imagine it vexes him that this good deed was not undone.

S adie stood at the top of the hill and watched Rabbit climb the path from the train station. She heard screams from the village below, and she smelled smoke. Rabbit's head was down, her shoulders slumped, and as soon as the girl was close enough, Sadie drew her into an embrace.

"I couldn't leave them there," Rabbit said.

"I know," Sadie said.

A white shape caught her eye, and she looked up to see the albino crow circling the house. She let go of Rabbit and held out her arm, and the crow landed. It hopped up to her shoulder and whispered in her ear, then flapped its wings and flew away.

"Moses is here," Sadie said.

"How?"

"My map is gone. The ring I made has disappeared."

"He can't come here."

"He already did."

Rabbit sighed. "I don't want to hurt Moses."

"Neither do I," Sadie said.

"What should we do?"

"I think we're going to give him his heart. And we're going to try to keep our own."

She spread her arms and dried the grass for six feet around them, then they sat and waited. They watched birds fly across the face of the moon, and they listened to winter creatures rustling in the weeds. Sadie was aware of things Rabbit was not, but she was quiet about the questing roots of the trees and the trickle flowing through the aquifer beneath them. She knew her daughter could do things she could not, and she took pride in that.

Presently, Moses staggered out of the woods and saw them sitting on the slope. He made his slow way up to them and when he arrived Sadie offered her hands. Moses took them and helped her up, and she brushed off her trousers.

"Ma'am," Moses said. And to Rabbit, "I guess it's been a while, young lady. You sure sprouted up."

"You look just the same to me," Rabbit said.

"That's kind of you to say, even if it's not true."

Rabbit wrapped her arms around him, and Moses smiled.

"I missed you, too," he said. "I guess I should've visited sooner."

Rabbit let go of him and stepped back, and Moses squinted at Sadie. He was still breathing hard from the climb. "I suppose you got my cable."

"I did."

"Then you know why I'm here."

"I have an idea," Sadie said.

"Can you help me or is this an antagonistic sort of meeting?"

"I wish I knew." She took a folded piece of parchment from her pocket. "Hold out your hand," she said. She opened the little envelope and shook a dozen tiny reddish-brown leaves onto Moses's palm. "Chew on those for a minute, then stick 'em in your cheek against your gums."

"What are they for?"

Sadie didn't answer. She refolded the piece of paper and put it back in her pocket. Moses hesitated, then did as he had been instructed.

"This tastes like shit," he said. "They gonna get a better flavor sometime soon?"

"Give it another minute," Sadie said. "Come on. We'll go in the back so we don't interrupt the party."

She led the way up the hill, and Moses followed. Rabbit fell into step with him and they walked together. Behind them, a thing with a thousand wings and a thousand eyes stopped at the bottom of the hill and watched them go. It had failed to keep Moses from reaching Ascension, and it had no further reason to be there. With a shiver of relief, it closed its many eyes, it stilled its many wings, and it winked out of existence.

The yellow dog followed Esmerelda through a glade where a verdant oak tree grew. She reached out and touched the oak's rough bark, imagining she could feel the life vibrating within it.

She knelt and beckoned the dog to her. She scratched its neck and whispered, "Find Moses for me."

She patted the yellow dog's nose and stood. Esmerelda's gown was wet and dirty, and her bare feet were numb from the cold, but she hardly noticed. What a blessing it was to be dead!

She followed the dog across the glade and into the woods beyond. They moved quickly, the dog and the little girl.

They entered the kitchen through the back door. The dead girls were gone, but they had left trays of wilting vegetables and plates of withering canapés on the counter. The icebox stood open and water was pooled on the floor beneath it. The cabinets were stained with vomit, and Rabbit pulled the collar of her blouse over her nose to mask the stench. Sadie closed the icebox and opened a window before leaving the room, while Rabbit grabbed a rag and mopped up the melted ice, then used the wet cloth to wipe down the cabinet doors. Sadie returned with a lit candle. She set it in the middle of a small round table in the corner, and the vomit odor was replaced with something minty.

Sadie took another look around the room and seemed satisfied with their hasty cleanup job. She grabbed an iron ring in the floor and pulled open the door that led to the root cellar.

"After you," she said to Moses.

He peered down into the dark, then pointed to the round table. "Can we sit first?" Moses said. "Can we talk?"

"Of course," Sadie said.

"Let's go to another room," Rabbit said. "That candle needs another few minutes to do its job."

"This is fine," Sadie said.

One at a time they sat. First Rabbit, watching the others, then Moses. Sadie sat last. She folded her arms across her chest and narrowed her eyes at Moses.

"I was wrong," Rabbit said to him. "There's a lot more gray in your hair."

"I imagine so," Moses said. He spat the mouthful of foul-tasting leaves into his handkerchief. "I've had enough of that stuff. What was it?"

"Something to make you more suggestible," Sadie said. "It's harmless."

"It didn't taste harmless," he said. He folded his handkerchief and laid it on the table. "You two must wish I'd stayed away."

Sadie said nothing. Rabbit clasped her hands and stared down at them.

"But you knew I was coming," Moses said. "So I figure you must have a plan."

"In your cable, you said we should keep Rose safe," Sadie said. "What did you mean by that?"

Moses hesitated. "There's a . . . a creature that's been following me. You probably saw it when I came out of the woods. Anyway, it's not like anything I ever saw before, and it told me . . . I don't remember the exact words. It told me not to be afraid, but I was. It said something about a rose and a garden, and I knew it was talking about Rose Nettles."

"How did you know?"

"I just did. It was talking, but it didn't have a mouth. It was sort of putting notions in my head."

"Did it say anything else?"

"It said I shouldn't come here. It said not to let Death back in the world or everyone would forget about me."

"But you came anyway."

"Seems like death being gone is a bad thing. People aren't any happier without it. They seem pretty miserable, in fact. And if that creature wants things to be like this forever, I shouldn't take its advice. Anyway, I don't especially need people to remember me. There was someone. I would've wanted her to think about me from time to time, but . . ."

He waved a hand through the air and shook his head. His eyes glistened in the candlelight.

Sadie and Rabbit exchanged a look and Sadie nodded. Rabbit produced the iron key with the filigreed handle. She set it on the table and pushed it toward him. Moses let it lay there between them.

"What's that for?" he said.

"Rabbit was told it's the key to someone's deepest desire."

"Whose desire?"

"Maybe yours," Rabbit said.

"Who told you that?"

"I'm not sure, but I think it might be the same sort of thing that followed you here."

Moses glanced at the open cellar door. "And what's down there?"

"A locked door."

Moses sat back and contemplated the key. He looked at Rabbit, then he looked at Sadie. She stared back at him.

"I don't know if I believe you. And even if I do believe you, I don't know if I deserve what you're offering. I did a bad thing, so I'm not here looking for magic trinkets or a pat on the back. All I want is to undo that bad thing I did. Look, I knew I was bringing trouble to your doorstep, but I hoped it wasn't more than you could handle. I hoped I wasn't making you my enemy by coming here."

Sadie watched him as the clock ticked on the wall behind her. "You're not our enemy," she said at last. "But like you say, you brought the enemy to us."

"We have to protect Rose," Rabbit said.

"Shouldn't she be here to speak for herself?" Moses asked.

"She doesn't know," Sadie said. "And she doesn't need to know."

"That key is yours," Rabbit said. "But you have to give me a book in exchange for it."

"A book?" But Moses glanced up at the clock, and Rabbit knew he understood.

"You have a book and we need it if we're going to help Rose. Moses, please give it to me."

Moses sighed. "The thing is, I probably would give that book to you. Maybe it's those leaves you made me eat, but I'd give it to you. I killed the fellow who had it. My wife's name was in that book."

"You killed him?" Sadie said.

"Yeah," Moses said. "I killed the Grim Reaper for what he did." Sadie said, "And you took his book of appointments?"

"And you were bringing it to Rose," Rabbit said.

"Like I said, I'd give it to you if I had it, but my traveling companion's got it right now."

"Your traveling companion?" Sadie said.

"She reminds me a little of you, Rabbit," Moses said. He smiled sadly. "I mean from the old days."

"Where is she?"

"I left her in the woods, but she's not too good at staying put. Right now, I imagine she's on her way up to this house."

Sadie sat up straight and the legs of her chair scraped against the kitchen floor. She and Rabbit exchanged a look, and Rabbit put a hand on her mother's arm.

"Mother, where's Rose?"

Sadie glared at Moses. "You shouldn't have come here."

"You should have tried harder to stop me," he whispered.

Sadie stood up so quickly that the candle flame sputtered and died. She and Rabbit raced from the room as the stench of vomit began to assert itself again. Moses sat back and watched the clock's pendulum as it swept back and forth.

After a moment he noticed the key on the table. He glanced at the open cellar door, then reached out and picked up the key.

Time has grown short. Death has been gone from the world longer than it ever was before, and my brother's efforts to hurry things along have not been entirely successful. Raphael is frustrated.

They emerged from the woods at the base of Vinegar Hill, and the little girl looked up the slope at the bright light that spilled through the windows of Bethany Hall above. To her, it was like a dream. She had never imagined a house so large, so foolish and wasteful and marvelous. She loved the crooked brick chimneys, the steep gabled roof that shone copper in the moonlight, and the nursery's wide bay window that overlooked the dense trees below.

She hitched her bag higher on her shoulder and followed the dog up the hill. The yellow dog chose the surest path, zigzagging back and forth, and circling around hidden impediments. At last Esmerelda unlatched the garden gate and walked up the path, took the four steps up onto the porch, and paused before the open front door.

There is a moment in which I think Esmerelda might turn and run away, back across the garden, back down the hill, through the trees to the railroad tracks. She might follow the tracks south, and perhaps Grover Smalls will have made an unscheduled stop. Perhaps he will be waiting for her, and together they will travel away from Ascension, back to the places she knows. Esmerelda will find her father sitting under a tree at a switchyard. He will weep and apologize, and she will forgive him, and they will return to their little home beside the silver maples, where they will never grow older and never die.

It might have happened, but this is the story of how Death returned to the world, not the story of a happy little girl.

Esmerelda takes a deep breath and steps over the threshold into the foyer of Bethany Hall.

At this same moment, I record the final sentence of this account and blot the page. This is what I write:

"When the dead were finally buried, the village council breathed a collective sigh of relief and began the hard work of rebuilding Ascension."

It is done. I close the ledger and set down my pen. I am anxious to go home, but I will miss my time in Ascension, and I will miss the people here.

Poor Bethany West, for whom this house was built, and poor Agatha Lamb, who bore her cousin a sickly child that didn't last the day. Observe Hamilton Tuckett, in his fabulous blue suit, who is, as always, dancing with Danielle Swann. Their last waltz was the finest moment of their lives, and they have savored it for all the years since. Here is Benjamin Sinclair, who loved the heavens but never got to see the world, and Lucy Knox, who loved a boy but was not loved in return. Spare a thought for Samuel Cotton, who doubts himself, and Timothy Rumpole, who loathes himself. Here, too, is Alice Anders, who will one day have a better life far from this place, and here is Clarissa Sinclair, who got to throw one last party. Let us not forget brave Daisy Merrick, who is watching her mother die of cyanide poisoning. Daisy and her poor mother have not assumed a large role in this narrative, but I love them all the same.

Bell is waiting for me at the bottom of the stairs.

"Lemon cake?" he says. He offers a silver tray and a sly smile. Oh, Bell!

I have arrived at the precise moment in which Esmerelda Rosas exits the foyer and stops in the front hall, unsure of what she should do next. Butler attempts to take her bag, but she pulls it away from him.

I have chosen this moment to reveal myself. I step forward and open my arms.

"Be not afraid," I say to her. "I have been waiting for you, mi pequeña rosa."

My brother wags his yellow tail, pleased to see me after this eternity on Earth.

"I hope you have enjoyed yourself," I say to him. "Next time, Raphael, I will shepherd the messenger, and you will keep the record."

It is a petty thing for me to say, but my brother knows it is my way of making a joke.

Esmerelda smiles at the yellow dog. "Raphael is a good name," she says.

Clarissa Sinclair stands nearby, holding a bloody rag over her eye. Jaspar and Ginny Upshaw have entered the morning room and are struck dumb by the sight of me. Now that I have made my presence known in the house, it is impossible to ignore me. I am felt in every corner of every room. George Herman and Flora Fielding, Timothy Rumpole and Alice Anders, Jessica Hudson and all the other villagers who have gathered this night in Bethany Hall understand that something extraordinary is happening, and they understand that they are a part of it, however peripherally.

Bell and Raphael silently acknowledge each other, and Bell raises an eyebrow.

"Moses Burke doesn't have the book, does he?" Bell says.

"No," I say. "Young Esmerelda is carrying it for him and she has brought it to me."

"You mean she's brought it to me," Bell says. With a grand flourish, he offers the silver tray to Esmerelda. "What is your heart's desire, my dear? You may take whatever you like from my tray, and all it will cost you is that nasty old book."

Esmerelda frowns at him. "But there's nothing on your tray."

Bell is confused by this, but I am amused. I don't bother to explain Esmerelda to him. Innocence is beyond his purview.

"Esmerelda," I say. "As you can see, the book you carry is in high demand. I am afraid you must now make a choice."

"Yes," she says. "I thought so."

I kneel before her and hold out my hand. "It does not belong to you," I say, and as I say it I think about what arrogant creatures we are, Bell and I. If only we could change who we are, even for this moment when so much hangs in the balance. But of course

I do not change, and Bell does not change. Esmerelda does not change, either.

She smiles. But it is a sad smile, and nervous. She pats the bag hanging at her waist where I know Death's appointment book rests alongside a comb, a small piece of cheese, an old button, and a half-eagle.

"This thing you want does not belong to you, either," she says. "Does it?"

"Child—"

"I am not a child. I am a body that hasn't laid down to die."

Esmerelda reaches into her bag and produces the appointment book. She clutches it to her chest and addresses Bell. "You said I could have anything? I would like to know that my mother is in a good place, and I would like my father to know I forgive him for leaving me."

"Will you give me the book?"

There is a stirring at the door to the foyer, and Butler shows a couple into the hall. The gathered partygoers silently part to let them through. Esmerelda's breath catches in her throat at the sight of her parents. Bell has conjured the mother from her proper place and the father from his hollow.

This, I feel, is a bridge too far.

"Enough," I say. "We have reached the end of the story. The book has been delivered, and order is restored. Girl, you will give the book to me so that I may pass it along to its proper heir or you can give it to her yourself. It makes no difference to me."

"Don't try to intimidate the poor thing," Bell says.

"Its proper heir?" Esmerelda looks down at the book. Her knuckles are white and she is shivering. "The rose?"

"That is correct."

"The rose will blossom? Is that what the other angel said?"

"Not precisely, but it is close enough," I say.

"*Does that mean the rose can make things right again?*"

"*You know,*" Bell says, "*you don't have to give the book to any-one. You can throw it in the fireplace. You can do whatever you want, girl.*"

"*What I want,*" Esmerelda says. "*I think this book will hurt Moses's friend Rose if I give it to her. He was afraid. But I think there is someone else. I think maybe I am the rose, and I think I will keep this book.*"

"*Oh,*" Bell says. He is confused again. For all his talk of chaos, his mind is quite ordered.

"*Yes, mi pequeña rosa,*" I say. "*My little rose, you may indeed take this burden if you wish. But it is a great and terrible duty, and I fear you do not fully understand what you ask.*"

"*If I can do this,*" she says, "*then that is what I want. May I say goodbye to my mother and father?*"

"*I will allow it.*"

The girl walks to the foyer, and Bell salutes me.

"*I already have a few ideas,*" he says. "*For next time, I mean.*"

I sigh, but he is already gone. At least he has had the decorum to surrender with dignity. I look for my brother, but he, too, is gone. It is my sole responsibility to promote Esmerelda to her station.

She receives a kiss on the cheek from her mother and a hug from her father, and with a final look back she leaves them at the door. She comes to me and holds out the thick book, bound in charred leather.

"*I am ready now,*" she says.

"*Very well,*" I say. I reveal my true face to her. I spread my wings and open my many eyes. There is the sound of whirring and grinding, and the guests at Bethany Hall come to their senses. Someone screams.

"*No,*" says a soft voice behind me. "*No, this isn't right.*"

It is Rose Nettles.

Moses paused at the bottom of the ladder and waited until he was able to pick out shapes in the dark cellar. The closest wall, to Moses's left as he faced away from the ladder, was brick and stone, the mortar rotted away, loose bricks piled like miniature pyramids on the dirt floor. Moses picked his way forward, skirting a mound of soil and a scattering of tiny bones, toward a dark rectangle on the wall.

Rats skittered away from him, squeaking complaints, their claws scrabbling against stone as they raced to their burrows in the wall.

Moses's head felt like a charcoal smudge rendered by an idiot's thumb. He wondered how much control he had over his actions, whether the foul-tasting juice from the leaves he'd chewed had influenced him to enter the witches' cellar.

Or maybe, he thought, *it's that I don't have anywhere else to go.*

The door was not large. The top of it barely reached Moses's nose. It was thick and sturdy, but dark from decades of dirt and moisture. Moses tried twisting the knob, but it didn't move. He held up the key as if presenting it to the door, then fitted it to the lock and turned it.

A sliver of light appeared at the bottom of the door, as if someone had awoken in the room on the other side, had sat up and lit a lamp. There was an audible click and the door swung smoothly out.

Moses took a step back.

His eyes had grown accustomed to the darkness, and he blinked rapidly as they adjusted again. He squinted into the light and blinked again and saw a shape. The shape moved toward him, and he recognized the sway of her hips. Her dark skin glowed in a light that seemed to have no fixed source, but filled the chamber beyond the cellar. Her hair was shaved up off her slender neck. Her eyes were wide, and filled with a mixture of joy and confusion, as if she were just as surprised to see Moses as he was to see her.

She held a baby in her arms. Their baby.

Moses said. "Are you real?"

Katie Burke nodded.

"I don't understand," Moses said.

She stepped forward and pushed his hat back. She touched the bullet hole in his forehead and trailed her warm fingertips down his cheek. He grabbed her hand and held it there, afraid to let go, afraid she would disappear.

She said, "What did you do?"

"I messed up, Katie."

"I always said you were doomed," she said, but she smiled.

She pressed herself gently against him, the baby between them in the crook of her arm, and he broke down. His knees buckled, and his nose ran, and he couldn't catch his breath. She held him until he was able to speak again.

"I missed you," he said. "Oh, I missed you so much."

"Then what took you so long to get here?"

"Oh, Katie, you have no idea."

She stepped back and beckoned to him, and Moses entered the room under Bethany Hall. The door swung shut behind him. After a moment, the light winked out and the cellar was dark again.

S adie and Rabbit had searched the house for Rose, and by the time they reached the morning room, the partygoers had formed a rough circle around three figures: Rose Nettles, Esmerelda Rosas, and Alexander of the First Rank.

I am an instrument of change, but I am unaffected by the change I bring. What happens in this room will have—has had, is having—a profound effect on every person in this house and in the world outside, but it matters little to me beyond the investment I have in these people. I have always been curious, which is unique among my kind, and now I find myself anxious, despite my knowledge of what the future holds. Rose is speaking. She kneels and puts a hand on Esmerelda's shoulder.

She asked, "What's your name, dear?" And the girl told her.

"Esmerelda, I overheard your conversation and I'm sure you're overwhelmed right now, everyone telling you what to do, but I really think you should give me that book."

"Mr Moses didn't want it to be you," Esmerelda said.

"Moses Burke?"

Esmerelda nodded.

"You know Moses? I have a million questions." Rose looked up at the winged creature and back at Esmerelda. "But there's no time to waste. I'm sure Moses had good intentions, but I'm very sure that he wouldn't want you to do this. I think *somebody's* got to do it, though, don't they? Someone's got to bring Death back."

Bell would disagree.

Rose, don't," Rabbit said.

Rose turned and smiled at her. "Rabbit," she said. "Do you remember when you were little and you would run away? I always came to find you, didn't I? Whatever this is, whatever happens, you must know I'll always look for you."

"Rose, please don't do this," Sadie said. Her voice broke. "I love you."

"I love you, too," Rose said. "But I was always going to leave you. You haven't aged a single day since we met. I think you'll always be as young and beautiful as you are now, and you would have had to watch me wither away." She sighed. "Look at this girl. Look how brave she is. How could I stand back and let her do this?"

"Ma'am," Esmerelda said. "Please don't worry about me. I already died."

Rose smiled and wagged a finger at her. "Young lady, if you don't give me that book right now, I'm going to lose my nerve."

Rose held out her hands. Esmerelda lifted the book toward her.

Two things happened then.

The first was this: Rabbit closed her eyes and the sound of fifty freight trains filled the air. The walls of Bethany Hall rumbled and shook. Plaster sifted from the ceiling, and floorboards warped. Windows broke and the foundation cracked. The west wall broke free from the house and slid down the hill. The roof sagged and crumbled. Portions of the ground floor fell into the cellar.

A fissure opened beneath the gardens, swallowing Benjamin Sinclair, and covering his body over with dead flowers. The crack in the earth ran down the hill like stitches popping free from a wound, toppling trees and diverting a tributary of the Ipswich, before burying the remains of the evil cabin in the woods.

Tremors were felt as far away as Boston, Springfield, and Providence.

Here is why the second thing happened: the house had sat atop Vinegar Hill for decades, and countless people had walked its halls and stood in its rooms. Many of those people had tracked silt and small seeds into the house, and some of that debris still stuck between the floorboards in the morning room. No broom was sufficient to dislodge all the dirt, though Housekeeper had done her best.

Sadie muttered something under her breath. She made a gesture with her left hand, and all the dormant seeds in the cracks of the floor began to grow. Weeds and saplings pushed up and out, and broke through the hardwood. Vines stretched from beneath the windowsills, twisting, seeking, and as all the other people in the room struggled to keep their footing, Esmerelda found herself bound and helpless in a living cage, the appointment book lashed to her arms.

These same questing vines curl in my direction, but as powerful as Sadie Grace is—and she may be the most powerful human I have encountered—I cannot be bothered. I have been too patient with these people. The vines grow new flowers, but the blossoms shrivel and die before they reach me.

"Rose Nettles," I say. "Is it your wish to assume the burden of Death?"

"It is," she says.

"Then it is yours."

In this moment, she is the most beautiful she has ever been. She positively glows. She smiles at her family, at Sadie Grace and at Rabbit, and then she is gone. The book is gone, too.

And Death has returned to the world.

When Rose took up the mantle of the Angel of Death, the dead stopped moving. They laid down or fell, and none of them got up again.

The outlaw Frank Smiley was sitting in a jail cell forty miles away, and had almost convinced the local sheriff that he was not the man on the wanted poster, and that the purple suit he wore had been bought secondhand, not stolen from a confused corpse. He suddenly snapped forward, cracking his skull on the iron bars of his cell, and at that same moment the sheriff finally noticed a bullet hole in the chest of his own suit.

In Ascension, Reverend Samuel Cotton witnessed five village girls fall at the end of Shiloh Road. He rushed to help them.

Behind him, a steady thumping sound from the graveyard went silent.

In the stable behind Mr Mulacky's home the old horse dropped in her stall.

In the village green, Prosper Knox and Sergeant Newton Winter abruptly stopped screaming.

The legs of a nine-year-old stag buckled under him and he dove headfirst into a stream, his rack digging ruts along the bank. A Kerry Blue, an Irish setter, and two springer spaniels settled down in brown leaves. Birds fell from the sky and squirrels fell from their branches.

At the top of Vinegar Hill, Esmerelda Rosas closed her eyes and slumped against her cage of vines. Clarissa Sinclair, Lucy Knox, and Lucy's mother, Lillian, collapsed onto the broken floor of the morning room.

Alice Anders reached out to Timothy Rumpole as he fell, and caught him in her arms. She lowered the young doctor to the dining room floor and sat beside him. She brushed a wild lock of hair from his forehead, and she sighed.

She said, "What now?"

All around the world, people lost their loved ones for the second time in a week.

Rabbit found Mr Bell smoking a cigarette and leaning against the chunky table in the butler's pantry. His tie was loose and he had unbuttoned the collar of his shirt.

"It's been a long week," he said. "And things didn't go my way."

Rabbit glared at him, and the foundation shuddered again. The silverware sparkled in its drawer. Bell blew a ring of smoke at her.

"Oh, stop that," he said. "You must learn to control yourself."

He stubbed his cigarette out on the tabletop. The polished oak sizzled, and maggots bubbled up from the wood, hundreds of them writhing and swarming toward the edges where they dropped to the floor and were lost in the cracks.

"I'm afraid my time here has come to an end," Bell said. "At least for the moment. This contest has reached an end and I must take my leave, but you could come with me, if you like. You are more powerful than your mother. She has nothing to teach you, but I could offer you a great deal. I could offer you the world."

Rabbit said nothing. She stared at him with her wide brown eyes, and Bell's suit shimmered with heat. Orange tendrils of flame snaked across the dark fabric; his wild hair sparked and smoked.

Bell laughed.

"Until next time," he said.

And with that he was gone.

1881

NEW ASCENSION, MASSACHUSETTS

The following morning, five enormous creatures staggered down Vinegar Hill carrying boxes and trunks and heavy crates. The creatures were made of dirt and spit, straw and wax. The boxes and crates were full of dishes that had been carefully packed, and clothing that had been carelessly folded.

An hour later, Sadie Grace and her daughter, Rabbit, accompanied by Alice Anders, left the ruins of Bethany Hall and boarded the eight o'clock train bound for the coast. They were never seen in the village of Ascension again.

At the exact moment the train pulled out of the station with the good Graces aboard, Charles Bowden found James Doolittle and his men camped under a bridge two miles outside Ascension. The men had already eaten their breakfast of biscuits and eggs, and had washed up in the creek.

"Reverend Cotton sent me," Charles said. "We need help in the village. There's a lot . . . A lot of people need burying. A lot of buildings need repairs."

James and the others were on their way to an orchard fifteen miles northeast of Ascension where they had hoped to get work pruning and planting in preparation for spring, but they reversed course and followed Charles back to the village.

In the following week, they cleared half an acre of trees behind the church, using the wood to make coffins. They dug thirty-six fresh graves and lowered the dead into them, then scooped in cold dirt. Reverend Cotton followed them, speaking a short prayer over each gravesite. To his credit, he was able to say something unique about each of the thirty-six, including a little girl who had been found holding a fistful of short yellow fur.

In sifting through the remains of Bethany Hall, James discovered a root cellar, filled with stones and timber, and overgrown with weeds and volunteer trees. In one corner of the cellar, in an area that might once have been a separate room, he uncovered the body of a man with a bullet hole in his skull.

No one in the town below could identify the body, and the dead man was buried in an unmarked grave.

A week after the event on the hill, one of James's men, a former whaler named Archie, felt a tightness in his chest and sat down hard on a mound of loose earth. James held Archie's hand for the three minutes it took the man to die. He later swore he saw a woman standing beside them at the moment of Archie's death. She smoked a pipe, and seemed vaguely familiar, and when she smiled at James he felt at peace.

The following day a new coffin was built for Archie, and a thirty-seventh grave was dug.

Reverend Cotton outdid himself with a homily about the raging sea and its bottomless depths.

When the dead were finally buried, the village council breathed a collective sigh of relief and began the hard work of rebuilding Ascension.

ACKNOWLEDGMENTS

I'm always amazed and humbled by the number of people it takes to bring a book into the world, and I'm profoundly grateful to everyone who works to make my stories better, as well as everyone who designs the pages, wraps them in eye-catching art, and pushes them out onto booksellers' shelves and into the hands of readers.

Thank you to both my agent Seth Fishman and my editor Kelly Lonesome for your expertise, patience, and enthusiasm.

Every single person I've interacted with at Nightfire has been positive, helpful, and wonderful to work with. You have kept me informed, got me to bookstores on time, and created the most eye-catching graphics. Thank you especially to Kristin Temple, Will Hinton, Claire Eddy, Alexis Saarela, Sarah Weeks, Michael Dudding, Valeria Castorena, Christine Foltzer, Jim Kapp, Jeff LaSala, and Rafal Gibek. And to Hannah Smoot, who has stepped in at the last minute.

Thank you to all the booksellers and librarians who help readers find their next favorite book, and to the readers who support us all.

And finally, thank you to my wife, my first reader. I would totally eat some bad potato salad if I thought it would impress you.

TURN THE PAGE FOR
THE FIRST ADVENTURE OF

Rabbit, Rose, Sadie Grace, and Moses

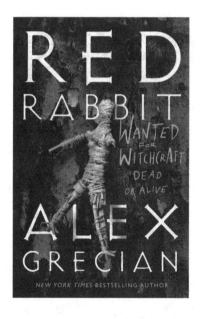

Available now from Nightfire

CHAPTER 1

Word of the bounty on Sadie Grace spread quickly: one thousand dollars to any man who could kill the notorious witch of Burden County, Kansas. Ned Hemingway eventually heard about it all the way down in Oklahoma, below the Cherokee Strip.

Skeins of honking geese were returning north, and the black oaks and river birches had begun to turn green by the time Ned crossed the border into Kansas. He was riding with Moses Burke out of Texas and they were taking their time, not especially interested in finding fresh employment until their funds ran out. Moses was vaguely interested in visiting a cousin of his in Nicodemus, and Ned thought he might go along to satisfy his curiosity about the place. After that, they'd discussed the possibility of circling back south to Dodge City, but it was an idle thought and susceptible to change, depending on their whim.

They stopped over in Monmouth, to give their mounts a rest and to play a hand or two of poker. It was late in the day, and Moses was holding two aces and an eight when the saloon door opened and an old man limped into the makeshift saloon. He had a shock of white hair that stuck out in all directions from under his hat, and he was carrying a child's body over his shoulder.

He dumped the child on a table, then stepped back and addressed the room. By that time, everyone in the place had set down their drinks and their cards to gawk at the new arrival. The women stood up and moved toward the staircase in case the old man meant to stir up trouble.

"She got my boy," the man said. "The witch got my boy."

Moses stood and pushed his chair back, abandoning the excellent hand he'd been dealt. He brushed past the old man and bent low, putting his ear to the child's chest.

"Get away from him," the old man said. "You ain't fit to touch him."

"This child isn't dead," Moses said. "But his arm's out of the socket, and if he won't wake up there could be something wrong with his head, too."

"What do you know about it?" the old man said.

Moses grabbed the child's arm with both hands, braced his foot against the table, and pulled. There was a loud pop and the table shook beneath the tiny body. The old man started forward, but Ned put a hand on his shoulder and spun him around.

"My name's Hemingway, friend," Ned said. He let the old man go and rested a hand on his holster. "My partner here is Moses Burke. He learned some medicine in the war."

"Not on my side, he didn't," the man said. He glanced down at Ned's hand on the butt of his gun and up at Ned's eyes under the brim of his yellow cattleman, trying to size up his odds.

"I don't doubt that, sir," Ned said. "Moses is particular about the company he keeps."

In fact, Moses had served under Dr John DeGrasse in the 54th Regiment out of Massachusetts. Dr DeGrasse, the only black surgeon to have treated Union troops, had chosen Moses and four other volunteers to help him in the field. In the following months, Moses had learned enough medicine that Ned sometimes thought his friend should have stuck with it, if there were a hospital that would take him on.

"I think this child will be all right," Moses said. "That arm will hurt for a bit, but it should heal fine. I'm more worried about the head wound. And there's something else that doesn't sit right with me, but . . ."

Moses broke off and shook his head as if arguing with himself. He caught Ned's eye and motioned him over to the far end of the bar. Ned followed, but kept an eye on the stranger, who was now hovering over the small body on the table.

"Regardless of what this man claims," Moses said in a low voice, "that child is not a boy."

"You sure?"

"As sure as I can be."

"You think this fella's lying to us," Ned said.

"I can think of a few reasons for that," Moses said. "Not all of 'em sinister."

"Or it could be he's not lying." Ned liked to look at things from all angles.

"In which case he doesn't know that's a little girl he's slinging around like a bag of beans."

"Might be worthwhile to ask him some questions," Ned said.

One of the women had fetched a damp cloth from behind the bar. She folded it in half and laid it on the child's forehead, while another woman pushed the old man toward the bar where the saloonkeeper set out a shot of whiskey. The old man accepted the drink and swallowed it in one gulp.

"Next round's on me," Ned said. "What's your name, old-timer?"

"Tom Goggins," the old man said. "Of the Omaha Gogginses, if you're familiar."

"Well, I've never been there," Ned said. "But why don't you join us, Tom of the Omaha Gogginses, and tell us what this is all about."

"What it's about," Tom said. "is a witch."

ABOUT THE AUTHOR

Emily Fitzgerald

ALEX GRECIAN is the national bestselling author of *Red Rabbit*, *The Yard*, *The Black Country*, *The Devil's Workshop*, *The Harvest Man*, *Lost and Gone Forever*, and *The Saint of Wolves and Butchers*, as well as the critically acclaimed graphic novels *Proof* and *Rasputin*, and the novellas *The Blue Girl* and *One Eye Open*. He lives in the Midwest with his wife, his son, their dog, and a tarantula named Rosie.